D0334498

of **COLEY BURNS**

The CONVICTION *of* CORA BURNS

CAROLYN KIRBY

NO EXIT PRESS

First published in 2019 by No Exit Press,
an imprint of Oldcastle Books Ltd,
Harpenden, UK
noexit.co.uk

Editor: Katherine Sunderland/Clare Quinlivan

A CIP catalogue record for this book is available from the British Library.

ISBN
978-0-85730-294-6 (print)
978-0-85730-295-3 (epub)

2 4 6 8 10 9 7 5 3 1

Typeset in 11.25pt Garamond MT
by Avocet Typeset, Somerton, Somerset, TA11 6RT

Printed and bound in Great Britain by TJ International, Padstow, Cornwall

Contents

CONTENTS

CONTENTS

The
CONVICTION
of CORA BURNS

NOUGHT
April 1865

born

Here you come. I put down my hand and feel your little head between my legs. Your skull, cupped in my palm, swivels. Bone grinds against bone and I cry out, Lord help me! Although I am forbidden to speak, even now. They push me down on to all fours, hands and knees pressed on to the slimy newspaper that is spread over the boards. Black letters swirl into red as I strain and bellow through clamped teeth. My shift is pulled up so that it hangs around my neck like a dripping cheese muslin. Something inside me gives and your whole head pops through. Then the rest of you slides out of me in a hot, squirty rush. There's rot and rust in the stone-damp air.

I collapse on to my side and reach out for you, warm and slippery with Lord knows what. Your face, swathed in lardy grease, glows white in the gaslight. Blood smears your tiny limbs. They start to wrap you in an old flannel rag and wipe the muck from your nostrils. They are too rough and I hear your voice. Good lungs on her, they say and smile. Not a thing I've seen them do before. They call me Mary and I wonder who that is.

I try to sit up but there is a mound of something under me that's in the way. One of them gets the knife with its dull rusty blade. Someone should have cleaned it with brick dust. Their eyes are wary when they see me looking but how could I try anything in this state? They ask me what your name will be. I touch your cheek and smell the sweetest spot on your milky newborn head. Cora, I say. It seems right for you who came from the heart of me. Then they pull you away. The ugly one grabs at my belly, squeezing the doughy softness, feeling for something. Hold still, she says with a hard hand on my shoulder and a terrifying gleam in her eye, you aren't quite finished yet.

ONE

October 1885

prison stays

'**H**old still.' The photographer looked up from his device but avoided Cora's eye. 'No. Stiller than that. For a count of four. And please do not blink.'

Did he think her made of metal? Glowering, she pressed her ribs against the prison stays. The camera gave off a gin-sharp whiff of ether.

'Ready now?' He twirled a scrap of grey hair around his middle finger then lifted the lens-flap. 'One... Two...'

His fidgetiness was vexing. And it was a liberty to take her likeness just before release as if she was a habitual criminal. Meaning it to look like a mishap, Cora blinked.

The photographer's stone-grey eyes locked on to hers, and then something in his countenance shifted. His face, less comical than Cora had supposed, seemed to whiten. It was as if he had seen, through his lens, the hidden awfulness of her crimes. Her stomach pitched.

'Beg pardon, sir.'

'Once more, then.' His attention slid to the floor. 'Stay on your mark.'

Cora's clogs shuffled inside the chalk-drawn feet on the boards and again the photographer looked into the lens. It was a dry-plate camera; dark shiny wood and black leather bellows. Expensive. And he didn't look much like a prison photographer; his coat was too clean.

He lifted the lens-flap and started to count but his voice this time was twitchy.

'One...Two...'

In the corner, the stout wardress folded her arms into a threat. Window bars threw a black grid on to the glossy brown wall.

'...Three... Four...'

The lens-flap squeaked shut and the photographer's mouth formed a shape he must have intended to be a smile. As he bent to the equipment at his feet, he slipped a sideways glance at Cora.

'And now I have some questions for you.'

'What sort of questions?'

The wardress lunged, keys beating against skirts, and a finger jabbed between Cora's shoulder blades, making her stumble forward. The photographer continued to rummage in his bag then placed a sheet of printed paper on the lid of the wooden travelling box. He took out a silver pencil, holding it up to the light to push an exact amount of lead from the point as he slid another look at Cora.

'So, your name is Cora Burns?'

She shrugged and the wardress poked her in the arm. 'Yes, sir.'

'How old are you?'

'Twenty, sir.'

Something in his stance stiffened. 'Do you know on which day you were born?'

'July the twenty-ninth.'

'I see, very good. Few know it so well.'

Of course she knew the date of her birth, but that wasn't it.

'Do you have a trade?'

'Oakum picker.'

'I meant before you were committed to this place.'

Cora knew perfectly well what he'd meant but the keenness of his curiosity seemed improper, even for a likeness-taker.

'Laundry maid, sir.'

'In a private house?'

'No, sir. In the Borough Lunatic Asylum.'

There was no jerk of distaste, only a raised eyebrow. He bent forward to write, backside stuck up in the air and breeches ballooning over his felt gaiters. If her release hadn't been so near, she'd have laughed out loud.

'What, pray, has been the length of your sentence?'

'Nine... nineteen months.'

'And your crime?'

She'd guessed this was coming but the question still brought a flutter to her belly. A sudden vision of a bootlace in her hands choked the words in her throat.

The wardress glared. 'Tell the gentleman!'

But the photographer waved a hand. 'No matter, madam. I can find out soon enough. The girl's reticence does her credit.'

Cora fought a tug of dizziness as she pictured him writing her offence on to his sheet of bond.

'And your parents, what sort of people are they?'

'I don't know, sir. I never knew them.'

'They are dead?'

'I suppose.'

His fingers tapped a complicated rhythm on the travelling box and his high forehead creased. 'So what else can you tell me of yourself?'

'I was brought up under the Board of Guardians. In the Union workhouse.'

'You were a foundling?'

'Not exactly.'

'How so?'

The silver pencil fluttered between his thumb and forefinger. Cora wondered, briefly, whether to lie but she'd a fancy to see his reaction to the truth.

'My mother abandoned me here when I was not three months old.'

'Here? At the gaol?'

'Yes, sir.'

'At the gatehouse, do you mean?'

'No, sir. She gave birth to me in her cell and when she departed from here left me behind.'

He stood straight now and unmoving. 'So, your mother was a convict too?'

'Yes.'

'And her crime?'

'I know only her name, sir. Mary.'

The photographer sprang forward to write.

Cora breathed out and pressed tight fists into the coarse apron across her stomach. She was glad that she would never know the answer to his last question for it was not impossible that the cause of her mother's conviction had been the same as her own.

seams

Her liberty clothes, as Cora put them on, smelled like day-old wash-water and everything was too big. Inside her Melton jacket, pale thread dotted the dark seams where she had let them out, month by month, to the final weft in the cloth. Now, the jacket hung loose in the wrong places and seemed to point to the part of her that was missing.

'Burns!' The squinty-eyed wardress shouted from the discharge desk on the other side of the folding screen. 'Out. Now!'

Now? Not likely. The wall-eyed bitch could wait. Cora wrapped her plaid shawl cross-wise over her stomach and tied a knot behind her back to pull the loose jacket tight. But the thought of how constricting the jacket had seemed last time she wore it brought a pang of emptiness. In the asylum laundry, she'd had to leave her shawl dangling over her belly to cover the gap between eyelets and hooks. They'd all looked sideways along the soaping-trough and must have guessed the truth. The shawl still had a whiff of asylum soap.

Cora turned to the dirty window. Her reflection was vague but she licked two fingers and rubbed quick circles along her hairline. A few stray wisps bounced into curls and a shiver went through her. No one could tell her not to do it any more. Through the shadow of her head on the glass, the red-brick gables of the asylum poked above the prison wall. And in the smoky distance, a gleam of wet slate marked the workhouse roof from the grey sky. Her whole life had been spent in these three buildings. Each, in its different way, had been worse than the last. But the thought of spending even one night anywhere else made her mind freeze over like the wash-house tap on a January morning.

'Out, I say. Now.'

Cora smirked to her reflection and felt bolder. 'Even if I'm not decent?'

'You? You'll never be decent.'

The wardress's good eye followed Cora across the room and watched her drop the striped prison garb into a jumbled heap on to the counter. Others might have given her a slap for that but the wardress was old and lazy, like her eye.

'Watch it, F.2.10. You're not out yet.'

'Going to lock me up again, are you?'

'I could. And then you wouldn't get this.'

The wardress tapped the corner of a brown envelope on the

counter. It was addressed in a flowing hand: *F.2.10.*

'What is it?'

'You want it then?'

Cora shrugged.

The wardress placed the envelope between them and ran her finger down a column in the leather-bound book. Then she reached below the counter and held up a small sack sewn into the shape of a pocket. A long string threaded in and out of the hemmed opening. *Preserving Sugar* was still stamped in faint ink across the canvas.

'Yours?'

The wardress emptied Cora's belongings across the counter; sewing scissors and a bobbin of white thread, a grey handkerchief, a lump of grimy soap and, on its loop of greasy twine, the half-medal. Then the wardress thrust her hand inside the pocket and pulled out a sheet of paper, furred along the folds. Cora held her breath as she read from it out loud.

'**Where Born:** *Birmingham Gaol, Female Quarters*... **Name and Maiden Surname of Mother:** *Mary Burns*...' Her good eye seemed to stay on Cora as she read.

'Yes. It's you all right.'

Cora wouldn't give her the satisfaction of asking what she meant.

'What about my money? I had more than a sovereign when I came in here.'

'Patience, girl.'

The wardress opened a drawer and counted sixpences and coppers into a pile.

'One, two, three... four shillings and sixpence.'

'And the rest?'

'The rest has been expropriated. Which means...'

'I know what it means. But what about my last month's wages from the asylum? Another pound.'

'Also expropriated. Paid from the Asylum Committee of Visitors direct to the gaol in order to fund your board and keep during your sentence. The governor has kindly made you this discharge allowance for food and lodging until you find work.'

'I'm much obliged. I shall book a room at the Grand Hotel.'

'Think yourself lucky to get anything.' The wardress pushed the pile of coins across the counter and dipped a pen in the inkwell. 'You'll have to sign for it.'

Cora scratched a spidery signature. She tried to remember the last time she'd written anything but couldn't. The wardress turned the ledger around and her face set into a toothless sneer.

'That's right. Cora Burns. Born to crime.'

Cora held out the pen with a smile as bright as she could fake. 'Like you were born always looking the wrong way?'

'Think you're clever, don't you? But I'd wipe the smile off your mouth if I was to tell you about your ma. Hardly the full shilling, that one.'

Cora flinched. 'My mother? What do you know of her?'

'I know that her and you are two halves of the same bad penny.'

The sneer dissolved into a cackle and bile rose in Cora's throat. An oyster of spit on that misshapen eyelid might be worth an extra night or two in the cell. But a starchy prison bonnet would flatten her already flimsy curls, and she'd not yet found out what was in that letter.

Cora bundled the birth certificate and her other belongings back into the pocket. She grabbed the brown envelope and stuffed that in too, then pulled up her skirt to thread the pocket strings around her waist, not caring who saw the stains on her petticoats.

'Can I go now?'

The wardress winked her good eye. 'Make the most of it. Won't be long till you're back.'

the towing path

Piles of sawn wood chequered the narrow wharf below the prison wall. Each stack seated a gang of porters, all sucking at clay pipes. Cora threaded between them, head down, until one of the men coughed and she looked up. The man gave her a toothless grin then puckered his blackened lips for a kiss.

Cora stared at him blankly for a moment before sticking out her tongue as far as it would go. Then, without waiting to hear the taunts, she ran. And, as she careered past the lock and on to the towing path, she heard herself break into a laugh as loud and mirthless as a lunatic's.

Her lungs heaved and her old boots pinched in new places. Cora stopped, panting, to let a towering barge-horse go by and realised how unused to movement she'd become. The lad poked a stick at the animal's shaggy fetlocks and a big eye rolled white behind the blinker. From the horse's flanks, rope sliced through dull filmy water to a longboat loaded with coal. At the rudder, a dirty-faced woman shouted a greeting but Cora's stare was fixed on the grey buildings across the cut.

Her hand slipped then through the familiar slit in her skirt seam and into the pocket. She felt for the small semi-circle of metal and let it lie like a bruise on her palm. The bronze was dull and brown as a Coronation penny. She ran a fingertip over the bumps of the raised image and the jumble of engraved letters.

... MDCCCLXI *IMAGINEM SALT*...

A tiny bronze hand pointing gracefully to the word *SALT* was the only part of the picture that anyone could put a name to. The other lumps and lines formed a cameo of indistinct drapery.

Cora now had no doubt that the missing half of the medal would reveal not only a meaning to the muddle of letters but also the slight frame and winsome face of Alice Salt. Who else but Alice could have given Cora the half-medal with its misspelt instruction to *"imagine Salt"*, and kept hold of the portion that showed her own face? As the solitary hours in her cell had ticked by, Cora's childhood companion and the cold inkling of what they might have done together, had come to occupy all of her waking thoughts. For only Alice knew what had really happened.

Cora's palm closed over the sharp corners. *Two halves of the same bad penny.* Maybe that old witch of a wardress had thought up her nonsense about Cora's mother when she'd seen the half-medal on the discharge-counter. As if Cora cared anything about Mary Burns. The name was nothing more to her than faded letters on crumbling paper.

A whiff of boiled bones from the soap factory blew across the canal. Suddenly feeble, Cora sank between two scraggy bushes on to mud hardened by coal dust. She looped the twine over her head and, unhooking the eyes at the top of her too-loose jacket, shoved the half-medal inside. Then she reached into the sugar-sack pocket for the envelope. Paper crackled as it opened.

To: Prisoner F.2.10
This is to direct you to a situation as Between Maid in a gentleman's residence. Although you have no character to present, Mr Thomas Jerwood makes this kind offer as the means to a prisoner's moral restoration and upon the understanding that should any concern about your conduct arise, you will leave forthwith. You will join a staff of four indoor servants. Your terms will be £8 per annum. Kindly make your way to The Larches, Spark Hill, Warks and report to Mrs Dix (Housekeeper) upon your arrival.
Capt GN McCall, Governor

The governor, like his nasty wardress, must be having a jest at her expense. Eight pounds a year was an insult. Half what she'd got as a laundress. And how could she be fitted to domestic service? She'd never been in a house. Cora stared at an oily rainbow on the canal as she tore the letter into a scatter of white paper across the black earth.

She heaved herself up and saw the poke of brick gables through nearby trees. The Borough Lunatic Asylum was the nearest she'd ever got to a home. Sometimes, when they'd all been at dinner in the servants' hall and the outdoor men had come in with gossip and jokes, she'd thought that they might almost be a family. She could still smell the asylum air steeped with mutton fat and floor polish, and imagine her own silly face grinning at the gasmen and the stokers.

With a horrible belch, Cora leaned over a thin bush and retched up a mess of runny oatmeal on to the sooty leaves. The skilly looked and smelt about the same as it did when she'd eaten it that morning. She spat the last of it on to the ground then wiped the back of her hand across her mouth.

It was time to make haste, however sickly she felt, towards the wide smoky blur of the town. On the way, she couldn't avoid passing alongside the workhouse but she'd keep her eyes fixed on the tottering cranes at the goods yard and a distant gleam of roof-glass from New Street Station. As she walked though, a shrill clang from the belfry caused Cora to turn. She could not then help seeing

the rows of dirty windows and close-packed chimneys. The sight of
the Union house brought a sudden ache to her throat and a picture
to her mind, clear as a photographic likeness, of the first time she
had seen Alice.

TWO
1874

the Union

She slipped in without Cora noticing. Only when Mr Bowyer rapped his cane on his desk did Cora look around from the blackboard, a nub of chalk between her fingers, and see a new face on the last row. The girl's bonnet was tied loosely and had slipped back to reveal the just-shaved bristles on her scalp. Her cheeks had the red flush of skin unused to warm water.

Mr Bowyer's cane whacked again, nearer this time. Cora felt a sigh of air on her neck before the slap of birch against the blackboard.

'Where is the date, Cora Burns?'

Cora stiffened. But she did not flinch, especially as the new girl was watching. Her hand wrote *Friday 3rd April* and stayed steady through the chalk loops.

'Now Cora,' Mr Bowyer said, 'continue with your problem.'

Cora was always called to the front for problems. She had come to realise, quite recently, that Mr Bowyer, although he seemed like a man, was not very old, probably not much older than the biggest girls in the upper dormitories. And he was not very good at problems. Sums, he could more or less manage. But when it came to working out the number of threepenny herrings to be purchased for eight shillings and sixpence, or the weight of each fancy bun in a two-pound dozen, he had to call Cora up to the front. He never let on to her that he couldn't work it out for himself and she kept his secret. There was unspoken payment for her silence. Once, he had given her a shop-bought biscuit. But she had never seen a fancy bun, or a herring.

When the bell rang and they went to the yard, Cora pushed herself to the front of the crush and laid hands on the girl as she came out of the school room door. That was what she always did with new ones; she'd pull them by the ear and give their wrists a Chinese twist, just so they knew that Cora was the toughest, the cleverest, the one who'd been here the longest. But this girl was different. There was a strange familiarity about her that made Cora entwine her arm in a friendly link and walk her slowly around the tall metal pole of the giant stride. For once, Cora didn't mind that Lottie Bolger had grabbed one of the chain swings before her.

Chilly spring air made the new girl shiver in her workhouse calico. Cora pulled her closer.

'Have you been in here before?'

The girl looked at Cora then slowly shook her head.

'What's your name?'

The new girl blinked. 'Alice Salt.'

Cora's laugh had a cruel edge. 'That's a funny name. Alice Salt; all is salt.'

Alice flushed. Despite the blotched skin, her face was a pretty oval with tiny cupid lips and almond-shaped eyes under thick brows. They seemed like the same shaped eyes, in fact, as Cora's own. And Cora's might also be the same shade of violety-grey but she had never looked in a glass clear enough to know.

All of the Bolger girls were rattling the chains on the giant stride and staring at Cora. Normally, she'd have taken this as a challenge, called them pikeys and threatened to spit in their beds, but today she turned her back. She tightened her arm on Alice's elbow.

'I'm Cora Burns. I'll look after you but you must do as I say. How old are you?'

Alice licked her cracking lips. 'Nine.'

Cora's eyes narrowed. Skinny little runt if she was nine.

Tears began to pool at Alice's eyelids. 'Today's my birthday.'

Birthday? Cora had never heard such a lot of stuck-up swill. She put both hands on Alice's wrist and forced the skin in opposite directions. A teardrop slipped through Alice's dark eyelashes and spilled down her cheek. But she didn't make a sound and her hand stayed on Cora's sleeve. Perhaps she did have guts after all. Cora wiped the drip from Alice's cheek and felt a twinge of remorse. She almost confessed that she was angry only because the date of her own birth was a blank. She might be nine as well, but couldn't be sure.

Then Cora looked down at Alice's wrist and jerked back in panic. A wheal of red skin puckered up Alice's arm into her sleeve. Alice saw Cora's expression and smiled through her tears.

'Don't worry, you didn't do that. It was from japanning.'

'What's that?'

'Don't you know?'

Cora grabbed hold of the scarred wrist, twisting it again to show that she was the one who'd ask the questions round here.

Later that night, when all the hoo-ha had died down and there was only spluttering and coughing in the dormitory, Cora made herself stay awake until the snuffling started. It would always get going as soon as the new girl thought no one could hear. Cora pulled back her covers, about to slip along the facing rows of iron beds, but a shivering figure in a too-big nightdress was already there at her bedside. Alice's face was washed in grey moonlight. She seemed almost to float on the cold air that slid through gaps in the floorboards.

'Will you budge up for me, Cora? I can't get to sleep on my own.'

She stole between the sheets and Cora pulled the lumpy blanket over their heads pressing herself around Alice's bird-like limbs. Alice wiped a hand across the burbling from her nose and whispered.

'I don't like that bed. Who was in it before?'

'Betty Hines.'

'What happened to her?'

'Her mother came for her, but it won't be long till she's back, I'd say. The mother's a widow and sickly so Betty's in and out of here like a rat in a drain.'

Alice turned in the bed and Cora could make out her eyes shining in the darkness.

'I hope your mother doesn't come for you, Cora.'

An odd tightness gripped at Cora's chest. She knew that she must have had one once but *mother* was just a word. She had never before imagined her own to be a living, breathing woman. Cora swallowed the tightness away and cut a hard note into her voice.

'It's best not to have a mother. Everyone who does can't stop blubbing.'

Alice put her hand on Cora's. 'I don't have a mother either.'

'Is she dead?'

Alice shook her head. 'I thought Ma was my mother until she told me that I was boarded out to her from the Parish. And now I'm nine, the Guardians expect me to get the same to eat as a grown-up. So Ma can't keep me any more.'

It took Cora a minute to comprehend what Alice was telling her. 'If she's not your real Ma, who is?'

But Alice could only shrug, her eyes glistening with tears.

In the next bed, Hetty Skelling coughed in a way that made Cora suspect she was wide awake and listening. Cora rubbed her big toe on Alice's icy foot and put her lips almost inside Alice's ear. Her voice was quiet as breath.

'We're the same then, you and me. And that's why, from now on, we're going to be sisters.'

THREE

October 1885

a likeness

By the time Cora got to Corporation Street the lights were coming on. An eggy whiff followed the lamp-lighter as he sparked each post into a fizzing yellow glow. Above the traffic, windows began to gleam, one on top of another, five sandstone storeys high. Shopfront mirrors glinted on to packed rows of tobacco pipes and toffee tins.

Cora stepped aside for a butcher's lad carrying half a pig on his shoulder. The coldness of the beast's waxy skin breathed across her face. She shrank away from it into the dazzle of a window and winced. Nothing had shone that bright for a long time.

It was a photographer's shop with a display of framed portraits. The sitters were placed in artificial scenes; a tennis party in a blurry woodland glade, a father trying not to laugh as he rowed his daughter in a pretend boat across a painted lake. All of them stared into the same void just beyond Cora's left shoulder.

She found herself scanning the black-and-white faces for anyone who might be a grown-up version of Alice. It was far-fetched, she knew. But if Cora held her breath for long enough she could still feel the beat of Alice's heart inside her own. So somewhere in the town's teeming streets and courts and terraces, Alice must live. Perhaps at this very moment she could be on Corporation Street, scouring these same unsmiling faces for one that looked like her Union house sister.

Curling gold letters spelt out *HJ Thripp & Son* on the shop's glass door. Cora pushed it open and a bell rang. Shelves and cabinets groaned with boxes of gelatine plates, fancy frames and viewing devices. The air reeked of camphor.

'Yes?'

The man's elbows rested on a glass-topped counter, his long beard almost sweeping the top of it. He gave Cora a smile that wasn't entirely pleasant and she tried not to look at him as she spoke.

'I'm after a likeness.'

'Very good. My son can do it presently.'

'I want it done now.'

'Do you indeed?'

'I've no need for a print. I just want you to take the likeness.'

'Well, I'm busy. I've no time to change the scenery or lend out fancy attire.'

'That doesn't matter.'

The man, Mr Thripp she supposed, looked her up and down. 'A tradeswoman's portrait is it? In your working clothes, with some tools of your trade?'

'No. A plain likeness, done as I am. How much?'

He raised his eyebrows. 'Two shillings.'

'How much if you keep it, to go in your window?'

'In the display? I hardly think…'

'I'll pay two and six.'

Mr Thripp straightened and came around the counter putting both thumbs into the little pockets of his discoloured waistcoat. He was a big man and seemed to fill the shop.

'Let's see how well you take before I decide.'

He pulled back a curtain and beckoned Cora through, pointing her to a padded chair beside a small table. Thin twilight fell from a wide glass panel in the ceiling. Mr Thripp went to the battered wooden camera already set up on its tripod and he slotted a flat box into the top.

'Now then, put your elbow on the table, lean your cheek upon your palm and look up at my birdie in yon corner.'

He pointed at a stuffed bird fixed above the doorway, its red and blue plumage deadened by dust.

She turned to face him, putting her hands in her lap. 'No. I'll look straight.'

He shrugged. 'That will not flatter. But it's your half-crown.'

After unscrewing the camera's lens cap, he flicked a switch on a tall lamp topped by a shiny disc. Light exploded. Cora told herself not to blink as black spots floated across her vision. The light faded slowly and Mr Thripp replaced the camera's cap. Then he took the plate-holder out of the camera box and disappeared into what seemed to be a cupboard. A line of orange light glowed along the bottom of the door. Glass clinked.

Cora looked up at the skylight and tried to blink away the silvery blotches swimming across her eyes. The chances of finding Alice like this must be slight. Perhaps she should run off now and save her shillings. She couldn't imagine how she'd get any more.

But then the cupboard door opened and Mr Thripp was back in the room. He was holding a sheet of white blotting paper behind a dripping glass plate. Vinegary fumes needled through the shreds of smoke.

'Not bad, as a matter of fact. Quite a singular face. Fetching in a way. It might make some stop and look.'

'So will you put it in the window?'

'Well…'

'And should anyone ask for me, you'll make a note of their name and directions?'

'Now, now. I'm not some kind of registry. I'll display the portrait for a period but that's all. Of course, if you want them, prints may be had. At sixpence each.'

Cora turned away from him to reach into her sugar-sack pocket. As she pulled her hand out of her skirt, she felt his eyes on her.

His voice thickened. 'And when the throngs begin to clamour for you, to where should I direct them?'

She shrugged and swallowed an urge to smash a nearby jar of purple liquid into his beard.

'I'm seeking a situation. So I'll return here to enquire.'

'What's your trade?'

'Laundress.'

His gaze slid over her, a smirk on his lips. 'You could try Mrs Small's on Bordesley Street. A common lodging house. She usually has something for young laundresses.'

'Are you having me on?'

'Why?'

'Am I to wash her "smalls"?'

His face jolted as he grasped the joke. Then he smiled. 'Sharp one, aren't you?'

He slipped the glass plate into a china tray of liquid on the shelf. Cora watched her own unsmiling monochrome eyes ripple under the water. Mr Thripp wiped his hand on a rag and stretched an upturned palm towards her.

'Let's call it two shillings then.'

Cora took care, as she dropped the coins, not to touch his skin. 'You'll put the likeness in the window tonight?'

He gave a mocking incline of his head. 'Anything else, miss?'

'Yes. Which way to Bordesley Street?'

common lodging

'Mrs Small's lodging house. Is it down here?'

The man grinned orange in the light from a tobacco-stained window. 'Why you going there, love?'

'For work.'

He winked and held up his beer glass, pointing it down the half-lit street. 'That way. Sheep Court.'

The rattling of an unseen train across the overhead viaduct relieved Cora of any need to thank him.

She turned her back to the ale-house and walked from one smoky circle of lamplight to the next as quickly as the raw blisters on her heel would allow. In a beam from an alley lamp, a chalk sheep was drawn roughly on to damp bricks. The same beam lit up a skinny dog laid flat on the pavement. Cora wondered if the dog was dead but as she stepped over it the mangy tail twitched.

Squeals funnelled along the entry. The din got worse as the passage widened to a space between tall dilapidated houses. The court was heaving with kids and not a clean face on any of them. The loudest yelps came from three boys hurling themselves around on ropes hung from the lamp post topped by a leaping yellow flame. The air reeked of privies.

At Cora's feet, a small girl seemed deaf to the wails of the baby trying to pull itself upright on her dirty pinny. Cora shouted over the bawling.

'Which is Mrs Small's?'

The girl's wizened face looked up at her. 'Got anything to eat?'

The baby stopped crying and looked up too, wobbling on fat little toes that squelched into the mud. There was no telling if it was a girl or a boy but it wasn't as big as Cora's own child should be by now. He'd be walking properly. Running, even. Cora shivered. For a second, she sensed the exact pressure of a child that size on her hip, although she had never, as far as she could remember, held one. She blinked the thought away.

'No, I haven't.'

The little girl shrugged. 'Don't know then.'

'Grasping little blighters round here, aren't you?'

Cora felt inside her skirt and into the pocket for a farthing but could find nothing less than a penny. She held it out to the girl who snatched the coin and scooped up the baby. Cora followed them across the court. The boys, sensing something happening, left their scuffling around the rope swings and ran after them squawking like seagulls behind a night-soil wagon.

'Oi Missus! Missus where y'going?'

The girl with the baby was pushing against a door. Wood scraped and paint flaked. The baby started to yowl. Cora placed herself in the doorway to keep the other kids out.

A throaty voice came from the darkness of a passageway. 'Who is it?'

Then a woman's head appeared from an inside doorway; metal curlers flopped on to her shoulders and swung around her ears.

'I've come about the situation.'

'What situation? Who sent you?'

'Mr Thripp. The photographer.'

'Oh, him. Come in then if you like. But tell them kids to go to hell.'

The children seemed already to have melted away.

Cora followed the woman into a dingy parlour but stayed by the doorway and tried to ease the weight off the throbbing on her heel. The woman sat at a round table covered with a threadbare Turkey carpet. On an upright chair, a girl about Cora's age stared into the empty grate. The women's frocks, now faded and frayed, must once have dazzled. Neither of them seemed to be wearing stays. The older woman with the curlers, Mrs Small presumably, let her gaze drift over Cora.

'Done it before, have you?'

'Laundry, do you mean?'

'Is that what you think the situation is for?'

'Isn't it?'

'Well, there's always washing to do. And we don't seem to get round to it very often.'

The girl at the fireplace tittered but Mrs Small's face stayed straight.

'Where have you worked before?'

'In a big laundry.'

'Which one?'

Cora hesitated, but couldn't see much reason to lie. 'At the Borough Asylum.'

'Was you an inmate there?'

'No!'

The woman smirked. 'All right. Keep your hairpiece on. Why'd you leave?'

'I… I couldn't work any more.'

'Was you ill?'

'Yes. That's right.'

'Did they give you a character?'

'Yes, but I seem to have lost it.'

'Oh well. We don't care about characters here. Just the opposite in fact.'

She exchanged a glance with the girl at the fireplace who giggled louder and Mrs Small joined in with a strange gurgling noise. It was the indecency of their laughter more than anything else that suddenly made Cora realise what sort of work really went on at Mrs Small's. She winced at the pain inside her boot.

'How much would you pay me for the other work, besides the laundry?'

'No, no. It doesn't operate like that. You'd be welcome to use one of my bedrooms, but you'd pay me rent, see, each time.'

'How much?'

'Three shillings an hour. Arrangements made inside the bedroom is between you and your visitor.'

Cora kept her face still. That's what it was then. A bawdy house. On Bordesley Street. That bastard photographer would get his reward for this lousy joke. She could almost hear the smash of the cobble through the fancy sign-writing on his window.

Mrs Small put her hands on her knees and leaned forward. 'What do you say then? You seem like a tough sort of girl who's not going to go sissy on me.'

Cora wondered if that was how the rest of the world saw her. Perhaps she looked to Mr Thripp as hard and slatternly as these women.

The girl by the empty fire turned her grin to Cora as she waited for the reply. But at the sight of the girl's pale oval face, Cora's heart dropped in her chest.

'Alice? Alice Salt? Is that you?'

The girl turned to Mrs Small and frowned. 'Why's she calling me that? She must be one of them loonies from the mad-house. Don't let her work here.'

The girl's features looked suddenly shrunken, her skin dimpled by pocks. No, not Alice. Nothing like. Cora almost felt herself lunge towards the fireplace. She imagined the heaviness of the girl's head between her hands and the crunch of her face against the grate until blood dripped on to cold ash. But Cora gulped down the quiver in her throat.

'Well, don't trouble yourselves on that score. I wouldn't work for you filthy whores if it was the last job of work in England.'

Paradise Street

Cora caught hold of a stone balustrade as her boot rubbed the skin from another blister. Tobacco and beer fumes blasted from open mahogany doors and she shrank away from the drum-roll of empty beer casks along the pavement.

No one had given her anything to eat since the skilly she'd later thrown up on the towing path. Her head was light as a soap bubble. She reached inside the sacking pocket to feel what coins were left. Two and sixpence. But she had no notion whether that was enough for a pie as well as lodging. Cold panic rippled through her empty stomach.

'"Taters! Hot 'taters!'

The street seller didn't look old but was bent double beside his cart. When he saw Cora stop, he reached up to creak open the iron hatch. A velvety whiff of coal smoke and baked potatoes wafted out.

'Tuppence a 'tater.'

'Let me see them first.'

He put his hand straight into the oven then held the potato in front of Cora's face. 'Cooked right through. Guaranteed.'

They usually weren't but Cora was too hungry to argue. Sixpence was the smallest coin she had and she handed it to the seller in exchange for the hot, sticky potato. Even before her teeth went into it she knew it was bad. She spat a mouthful of black slimy muck into the road.

'Bleedin' hell! I'll have my sixpence back if you please.'

'No you won't. Swearing like that. And you've eaten my 'tater.'

'You can't call that a 'tater. And it was supposed to be tuppence.'

'Well, I've got no change.'

'You bastard.'

'Watch your mouth, girly. There's a copper over there.'

'I'll go and get him for you, shall I? Tell him about your swindling?'

'Go on then. Or are you frit he'll know you for a bad 'un?'

The potato man's smirk tightened the knot in Cora's belly. Could he smell the prison stink of carbolic and drains still hanging about her clothes?

She turned her back on him and went to the edge of the wooden pavement. Iron-rimmed wheels rumbled past and the brisk trot of a cab blew her skirt against her legs. She'd get her own back on that bleeding 'tater man if she ever saw him again. Kick his cart over and watch it crumble into the flames.

A carthorse strained past, its metal shoes skating on slippery cobbles. From under its belly, a murky face appeared, and then a whole boy, scuttling close to the ground and wielding a long-handled shovel to fling manure on to a soil heap. Then he noticed Cora.

'Shall I see you across the road, missus?'

Irish. She might have known. A flat cap was pulled down over the sweeper-boy's ears and one of his boots was clearly bigger than the other. Cora ignored him and launched herself off the pavement. A cart thundered by. But she kept her eyes on a beacon of yellow light beside the black stillness of a boarded-up church. Rickety piano tunes pulled her through the traffic. A pub was just what she needed to cloak herself in beery warmth, and a pint of porter would fill her up and take away the taste of rotten potato.

The Waterloo Bar's heavy door swung open easily. Cora leaned into the crush at the tap room counter, wedging herself between two men with drooping moustaches who shouted for ale and whisky. Her face, in the engraved mirror behind the bar, was a ghostly oval. She scanned the reflections of the other female faces; a woman with sagging feathers in a week-old hairdo, a flower-seller holding out a fist of limp violets, her hair loose and matted about her shawl. By the wall in the jug-and-bottle queue, a girl with the grey complexion of a maid-of-all-work clutched a bucket. But there was no trace of Alice in any of their faces.

'Bitter?' The young barman bounced his fist on the counter.

'No.'

'What then?'

A line of bottles glistened against the mirror.

'Gin.'

He banged down a zinc measure and reached below the bar for an earthenware bottle.

'Threepence.'

Cora drank it in one gulp and closed her eyes. Heat flared from her throat into her chest and her gut.

'Another. Double.'

The barman eyed her as he swept the coins off the counter and poured more spirit into the cloudy glass. Cora went to the back of the room, clutching the glass. She ignored the *Evening, my lovely*, from a swell with side-whiskers and a checked suit and kept the glass close to her lips as she drank. The Irish sweeper was bobbing around below the bar, emptying the slops pails into a milk can. He took a swig from each pail as he went.

Gin started to work into Cora's brain. She tried to count the gilt burners flaring across the mirror but they circulated so fast she couldn't tell real from reflection. Brass hand-pumps whirled along the bar. Her eyelids drooped.

As the sweeper went past, she reached out to him and caught his sleeve.

'Where can I sleep round here?'

'I'll take you, missus. Only a penny.'

'You charge, do you? For a bit of friendly advice? Bastard...'

But he was already at the door, beckoning her like a stallholder at Michaelmas Fair.

She stumbled towards him and clung on to the boy's greasy sleeve as they left the tawny light of the pub and went into blackness. She blinked lazily. The air was so dark it was hardly worth prising her eyelids open. Her bad foot banged against stone and the shiver of pain opened her eyes. A sheer wall soared up.

'In here.'

He was climbing up steps and into a tight opening in the wall. Cora followed. Her petticoat snagged on metal; sharp masonry grazed her palm. Then she popped through the block-work opening into cold still air. A cavernous void opened up around her.

'What's this?'

'Christ Church.'

'Tha's no good... tomorrow's Sunday.'

'It's all right, missus. Nobody comes in here any more.'

Cora slumped down between the wall and a dust-coated pew. Arched windows of silvery glass swirled like a kaleidoscope. As she reached down to unfasten her damned boots, her eyes closed.

When they opened again, the chancel was filled with light. Cora squinted into piercing whiteness at painted clouds that floated above the high wooden galleries. Her tongue was fat and slimy; her neck ached. God, she needed a pail. As she pressed numbed fingers against damp stone floor, cloth tightened around her legs. Her skirt was open at the waist and pulled down over her petticoat, almost to her knees. Jesus. What had happened last night? The pub, the man in the checked suit, that sweeper-boy, the loosened bootlaces...

And then, suddenly clear-headed, she felt for her pocket. She stood up shaking her skirts, then crouched down to look under the pews. The soles of her feet pressed on icy flagstones. She was barefoot as a gypsy. God in heaven. It wasn't just the pocket with her last shilling that had gone, but her boots too. And the birth certificate with her mother's name. She would never see it again.

The laugh that welled up in her echoed into a strangled moan. She stood up, clinging on to the pew with one hand. With the other, she pulled open her jacket and felt inside her stays. The rubbed-smooth edge of the half-medal was still there. For all the bloody good that would do.

Where in the world would she go? There was no one to tell her. No one even to ask. The workhouse would take her in, but she'd sleep in the canal before going back through that grim archway. Or there was Mrs Small's. It wouldn't take long to earn a new pair of boots there. That other place, the gentleman's residence, was so far off her feet would be in shreds by the time she got there, and she had no notion which way to go. But she could remember directions for the house and the name of the gentleman.

FOUR

THE
WYVERN
QUARTERLY

SUMMER

1885

PRINTED BY
CORNISH BROS,
37 NEW ST, BIRMINGHAM

FROM: Thomas Jerwood Esq.
An Essay on Character, Crime and Composite Photography

I am indebted to Capt McCall, Governor of Her Majesty's Prison Birmingham, for his kind invitation to capture the likenesses of prisoners, male and female, who reside under his jurisdiction.

His offer was made consequent to my previous contribution to these pages (viz. **An Essay on Criminal Physiognomy** *The Wyvern Quarterly*, Winter edition 1884). This essay piqued the interest of the governor (and other discerning readers) in the connection between physical appearance and felony. Do murderers, for example, always possess sunken eyes (as many have conjectured), or bigamists a weak chin?

In some quarters, however, my words stirred up not a little controversy. I had assumed, perhaps naively, that the foundation of my thesis (as proven by Prof Lombroso and others) was unquestionable. Surely all that remained for this theory to be put into practical usage was identification of specific links between each type of facial feature and particular offences. I therefore decided, as a man of science, to take this urgent endeavour upon myself. For, once these links have been catalogued, the crimes of any villain will be revealed by a study of his face.

'Not so,' says, amongst others, Mr JW Armstrong of Erdington (see **Letters**, *WQ* Spring 1885). This gentleman's objection rests upon his doubt that criminal tendencies are rooted in *biology*. 'Crime,' he says, 'is simply a skill which may be learnt through instruction and practice in the same way as playing the piano. A baby is no more likely to be born to crime than he is to emerge from his mother's womb able to play a polka.' Mr Armstrong's witticism lays bare the full extent of his ignorance. For crime, unlike performance on a musical instrument, requires a felon to contravene the civilising codes of his society. The convict must, therefore, be possessed of a criminal *character*.

Thanks to Governor McCall's generous invitation, my growing collection of prisoner portraits will soon allow me to rebut Mr

Armstrong once and for all. The process of establishing correlation between particular facial features and common criminal offences has required me to perfect a vital technique (resting upon remarkable recent advances in photography) which allows the photographic portraits of several individuals to be merged into one. This technique, namely *composite photography*, requires much delicate work but if done well, the composite likeness becomes a *pictorial average* of many individuals.

I have already been able to produce several prisoner composites categorised by crime. When perpetrators of the same offence are merged into one image, a dominant facial feature tends to become apparent. My investigations seem to prove, for example, that house burglars are marked out by the prominence of their jaws, ruffians by the luxuriance of their eyebrows and fraudsters by the thinness of their lips. These early results are tentative only due to the still limited extent of my prisoner portrait collection.

There is no doubt that composite photography will, more generally, produce all manner of unforeseen breakthroughs in the study of the human species. It may, for example, come to be used as a reliable test of consanguinity. Where parentage or a sibling relationship is in doubt, the ease with which faces (e.g. father/ mother + child) are melded into one could determine the closeness of their blood ties.

Indeed, I believe that composite photography can be used to show the transmission of criminal physiognomy *down the generations*. I now have in mind a single experiment that will harness my twin preoccupations with *character* and *heredity* to prove beyond doubt the hereditary nature of crime. I trust that readers of this journal (other than Mr Armstrong and his ilk) will have no difficulty understanding that criminality, as a facet of character, is subject to the same *biological* rules of heredity as bodily physique. An addiction to crime runs through the generations of a family as surely as short stature or red hair.

Mr Armstrong will, I daresay, argue that temperament is separate from anatomy but his predictable scepticism has done me a service by stimulating my imagination. Through unceasing contemplation of these questions, I have devised a rigorous method for the study of criminal character using *moral tests* combined with the *numerical measurement* of human behaviour. The method proceeds thus: a convict is released into a normal domestic setting and presented (under clandestine observation) with a range of dilemmas designed to probe moral fibre. These choices may be trivial or more perplexing. Traps, as it were, can be laid. The 'captive' subject's reactions are recorded and then assessed on a scale of *one* to *ten*.

I know full well that my raw material is the human being and so this experiment is fraught with difficulty. Its exercise is also dependent upon the possibility (perhaps slight) of finding a suitable individual who may be photographed and secretly observed. Furthermore, the study will have weight in the field of heredity only if a similar investigation has been carried out on his criminal parent.

This whole endeavour is hampered by the laboriousness of the composite photographic process and my own nervous fatigue. In recent weeks, my ideas have proliferated at an exhausting rate and my camera has hardly been idle. Should I, however, retain sufficient mental strength to continue, I am confident that my labours will uncover clear evidence for the *biological heritability* not only of criminality, but of the chief attributes of character within us all.

T Jerwood Esq.
Spark Hill, Warks.

FIVE

October 1885

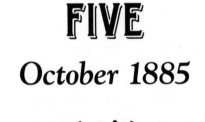

leaves

The Larches was a square white house, neither old nor new, with tall windows and a shallow slate roof. Across the lane from the entrance gate, an open field was scarred by rickety scaffolding and piles of new bricks. But once Cora was on to the curving carriage drive, holly thickets cloaked the disagreeable outlook.

Gravel clung to the rag bindings on her feet as she crunched towards the house. Earlier, when she'd stopped at a wrought-iron drinking fountain, some boys had pointed and jeered: *Clodhopper!* She'd cursed and sprayed them with water from the steel cup. The mud-crusted sacking had done its job, though. Her feet, like her head, throbbed but she was still walking.

She stopped at the wide front door. Her fist seemed to make no noise against black lacquer so shiny that she could almost see herself. No one came. Cora peered into a gap in the gauzy curtain covering a nearby window. The crush of furniture, upholstery and ornaments seemed to leave no room for people. But an orange fire blazed in the tiled hearth. Someone must be there.

The driveway led to a jumble of roofs and outbuildings at the rear of the house. Mustard-bright trees ringed a metal-fenced paddock where a pony cropped lush grass and threw Cora an indifferent glance. Damp petticoats wrapped her legs and her head pounded with each step. No one had seen her yet. It wasn't too late to turn back to the familiar flat greyness of the town. But her feet, screaming for rest, led her to a half-open back door.

The brass handle was brown with wear. Cora pushed on it and pungent warmth drew her into the dim passageway.

'Hello.'

She coughed but couldn't quite make herself speak again. To her right, the corridor widened into a parquet-laid hall where a long-case clock ticked. To the left, the narrow passage was lined by doors; one half-open on to a windowless pantry, another, covered in green baize, oozed a smell of meat dinners. Heart pulsing, Cora pushed her thumb against it.

The lime-washed kitchen looked dingy in the weak light from an overshadowed window. A scrubbed table covered in bowls and knives filled the centre of the room; plate-crowded shelves lined the walls. At the far end, a long black kitchener spewed heat and a whiff of gravy into the stuffy air. Two copper pans bubbled on the top-plate. And next to the range, in a Windsor chair, a girl in a print dress was quietly snoring.

Cora moved closer. The girl's mouth dribbled against the chair's wooden spokes. Her skin was pale as milk. Even asleep, she got on Cora's nerves. Cora picked up a fork from the table and held it over the girl's head. The weight felt expensive and Cora glanced at the door, half-wondering whether to make a run for it. But she wouldn't get far on a fork, even a silver one.

She moved her hand sideways, then let go. Metal clattered on stone. The girl stretched her arms and slowly opened one eye. Then she sprang out of the chair.

'Oh, Lor'! Who're you?'

'Cora Burns.'

'What are you doing in here?'

'I've come about the situation.'

'What situation? There isn't one.'

'Between maid.'

'A tweeny? We don't have one of those.'

'I think you'll find, if you ask Mrs Dix, that you do now.' Cora nodded at the range. 'Don't let them pots catch.'

The girl gave her a sideways look as she picked up the silver fork from the floor. Then she went to stir the pans. Apple sauce. Beef gravy. Cora's stomach groaned. The girl turned and stood awkwardly.

'Did Mrs Dix send for you?'

'Yes.'

'So why'd you come on a Sunday afternoon?'

Cora shrugged and took a step nearer. 'Is she here?'

'I believe so.'

'Will you fetch her for me?'

'She doesn't like being disturbed on a Sunday.'

'If you tell me where she is I'll do the disturbing.'

'No, no. I can knock at her door for you. But she might not come down.'

'I'll wait here till she does.'

Alarm flashed in the girl's eye. 'Not in here, no. Outside.'

'As you wish.'

The girl ushered Cora out along the passageway and shut the door behind her. Cora waited in the cold shadow of the house and listened. A faint trail of footsteps pattered up the stairs. There was a murmur of voices; one shriller than the other. Somewhere in the house, if she wasn't mistaken, a child laughed.

Footsteps, louder, were coming back down. The door opened.

'Yes?'

The woman wore black crêpe, shiny as a fly. A row of stiff curls rimmed her forehead. Cora looked her in the eye.

'I've come about the place. Between maid. The letter said to ask for you.'

Mrs Dix put out her hand. 'Do you have the letter?'

'No.'

'Or a character?'

'No.'

She rolled her eyes. 'Then you could be anybody.'

'I have walked all this way on the understanding that there would be a situation here for me as between maid on eight pounds a year. Even without a character.'

The woman glanced at Cora's mud-crusted feet and sniffed. 'What work have you done before?'

'Laundry. Rough and fancy.'

'We only boil linens here. The rest is sent out. Anything else?'

Cora guessed that unpicking old bits of tarred rope wouldn't strengthen her prospects, and if Mrs Dix didn't already know where Cora had come from, the mention of oakum would instantly tell her.

'I can sew quite good.'

'Nothing of use then. Let me see your hands.'

Mrs Dix peered at Cora's toughened palms.

'I shall confer with the master. And I shall have to explain to him the inadequacy of your things. He may not be prepared to provide you with apparel in advance of employment.'

'So is there a place for me or not?'

'There most certainly will not be if you continue to address your betters in that fashion. You may wait in the wash-house until the matter is decided. Ellen will escort you.'

Cora followed the girl in the print dress alongside a glasshouse built against a high wall. A smell of horse wafted out of the red-brick stables. Ellen pushed on an outhouse door, scraping the wood against worn tiles. At one end of the dank room a huge copper sat on a curved brick burner. Cora went in and leaned on the wall by the cobwebbed window but the girl stayed at the door, a smile wavering across her face.

'I'm Ellen Beamish. The scullery maid. Are you hungry?'

'A bit.'

Ellen put a hand in her skirt and held out an apple. Cora took it but kept it tight in her fist. She was so hungry that if she started to eat, she'd gobble like an old sow.

'I hope they take you on. We've not had a tweeny before. It would be a boon.'

Oh, it would, would it? Cora saw how things were going to be; she'd get all the lousy jobs that no one else could face. Somewhere nearby a horse whinnied and Ellen looked over her shoulder.

'I had better go back and see to the range.'

Cora waited until Ellen had gone before sinking down to the floor. Her swollen feet pulsed inside the dirty bindings. The apple was sour but she ate every bit, even the pips.

Despite the lingering scent of soap, the closeness of the wash-house walls brought to mind her prison cell. Outside, the whispering of brittle leaves through towering branches tightened the unease in her stomach. There seemed something queer about this house and the people in it. But perhaps all gentlemen's residences were the same. There'd be rough work and sharp words wherever she ended up.

Before long, footsteps crunched on gravel and a man's voice, well-spoken, threaded into a woman's. Then the fading light at the doorway was eclipsed by a black silhouette.

'Cora Burns?'

She stood up blinking. It was a man, a gentleman, but jacketless and with the sleeves of his shirt rolled up above the elbows. He stepped inside the wash-house. Pale light fell on to one side of face.

'Ah, yes. That's her, Mrs Dix. Fear not.' He turned to Cora. 'Do you remember me?'

'No, sir.'

Cora dropped her gaze to the floor but already sensed that he knew she was lying. Because despite the briefness of her glance and the dimness of the light, she had recognised very well the searching grey eyes of the prison photographer.

brick dust

'You'd do better to pin them up.'

Cora guessed it was her sleeves that were at fault. She'd been given an old-fashioned cotton frock, finely made, but too big. The full sleeves hung down over her hands and the cuffs were already grubby from a morning carrying coal boxes. Cook raised her eyes from the floury innards of a stoneware bowl.

'I'll lend you a couple of pins if you wish.'

'No. Thank you. I can roll them.'

'Just take care to unroll them if you go upstairs.'

'Yes, Cook.'

'You can go up now, in fact. Put on your good apron and take this dinner tray to the missus.'

The cook was a thin woman in early middle-age. Her words weren't exactly friendly, but they weren't over-sharp. She gave no sign of knowing where Cora had come from. Maybe word hadn't yet got around. But it couldn't be long until all of the servants started clutching their valuables a bit tighter as Cora went by.

The tray was laid out with a bone-handled knife and fork on a lace cloth. Gravy curled around chops and potatoes on the gold-rimmed plate along with some green vegetable that Cora couldn't name. It must be dinnertime here even though the long-case clock had not yet struck eleven.

'Where do I take it?'

'Up the back stairs, to the second door after the sink room. Put the tray on the floor, knock twice and say "tray" loud as you like. Then turn around and come back down the stairs without looking into the room. Herself doesn't like it.'

Cora had already been up the back stairs, but only as far as the sink room to leave the coal boxes. She'd seen an assortment of doors leading off the landing at both sides of the main stairs. The front of the house seemed crammed with things but empty of people. The back of the house, the servants' part, was full of both.

With all available beds filled by the upper servants, Cora had slept last night in the kitchen. Ellen didn't seem to think there was anything odd about the arrangement. She had pulled out a truckle bed and her own night things from under the kitchen dresser without comment. But Cora was shocked. Even in gaol she'd had her own cell.

At the mistress's door, Cora knelt down to place the tray on the carpet runner. There were voices somewhere across the landing; a man talking, the master, by the sound of it. But behind his wife's bedroom door, all was silent. Cora stood up and knocked firmly.

'Tray!'

Inside the room, skirts rustled. There were footsteps and then a call of *Helen! Helen!* The tone was shrill, but unmistakably the voice of a lady. As a key twisted in the lock, Cora spun round and was at the top of the stairs before the door fully opened. Mrs Dix's face as she bent to pick up the tray was grey as wash-water. She didn't seem to notice Cora.

In the scullery, Cora put on a rough striped apron and rolled her trailing sleeves above her elbows. Rain beat at the small window and smeared plates filled the deep sink. Although it was the middle of the day, the gas mantle fizzed yellow light on to a heap of dirty green vegetables. Cora began to scoop slops from the sink into a bucket on the floor, each movement hindered by the yards of soft cotton around her legs.

A draught blew on to her neck as the scullery door half opened. Ellen's face appeared at the crack.

'Cook says I'm to get on with the wash. You're to do in here alone.'

'Do?'

'All this. Dishes, boots, sprouts.'

Sprouts would be the mouldy-looking vegetables, Cora supposed. She followed Ellen's glance to the muddy boots beneath the bench; a man's pair in knee-length brown leather with laces and buckles and much smaller wine-coloured button-ups; a girl's. Cora had no definite notion of what to do with any of it.

'Do you mean wash these dishes?'

'Yes. What else would you do with them? And polish the cutlery.' Ellen nodded to a tray of dusty orange stones with a small hammer laid alongside on the wooden draining board. 'Do you know what to do?'

'Yes.'

Ellen certainly didn't believe her but was too wary to contradict. Ellen nodded and closed the door.

The tap ran cold into the big wooden bowl beside the sink. Cora scraped off each of the dinner dishes into the bucket and then dipped them in the bowl. The plates came out of the cold cabbagey water almost clean, and dripped greasily from the rack on the wall. But the cutlery looked more tarnished by the wash-bowl than when it went in. Cora rummaged in the wet pile by the sink and picked out a round, bladed knife with a creamy handle. The stony orange dust, she could now see, was crushed from a house brick. She picked up a fragment and rubbed it along the knife. A streak of silver scored the blade. Harder rubbing with the stone brought up more of the metal to a shine but seemed to loosen the handle. The brick left rusty spots in the pitted skin of Cora's fingertips. She'd no doubt that she was doing everything wrong.

At eleven that night, after a cold supper of pork pie thick with meat jelly, Cook turned off the gas, lit a candle and climbed the back stairs to her bed. From below the dresser, Ellen pulled out the narrow truckle bed for herself and unfolded the horsehair mattress on to the floor for Cora. Ellen undressed to her shimmy then slipped under the covers to take it off and wriggle into her nightdress. In the light of a smoky candle she watched Cora unbutton the long row of buttons on the old-fashioned bodice. Before unfastening her stays, Cora blew out the flame but she felt Ellen's wide-open eyes still on her.

'Are you from round here, Cora?'

'From town.'

'Where did you come from yesterday? Another situation?'

'Yes.'

'So what happened to your things, your boots...?'

'I had an unfortunate accident on the way.'

'Oh! What happened?'

'I'd rather not describe it.'

'Oh my!'

Ellen was quiet for a moment. Cora could almost hear the whisper of her speculation.

'Was it a house grander than this, where you was before?'

'It wasn't a house.'

'Oh? What then?'

'A steam laundry.'

'Oh! Which one? Not Hardman's on Ladypool Road? My sister works there. I bet you'd know her. She talks to anyone. Never stops!'

'No. Not that one.'

'Or Palmer's at Digbeth?'

'No. A different one. Smethwick way.'

'Oh.'

Ellen twisted her head to look at Cora in the whitening moonlight from the bare window.

'Do you think you'll stay here?'

Cora was quiet for a moment. 'They may not keep me.'

'Oh, don't fret. Cook doesn't mind about the mess you made today.'

'What mess?'

'The crockery. It was hardly washed. As if you hadn't used soap and soda or any hot water at all. And the knives!'

Cora cursed silently. Nobody told her to light the scullery copper. Or to use soap and soda. Well, she'd remember for next time. And put her mind to the best way of applying brick dust to metal.

'I should have done the laundry instead. I know what to do with that.'

'That's what I thought, but Cook said it wasn't fair to make you do battle with the wash-house copper on your first day. It nearly did explode too. Lor'! It made me scream. Samuel came running. He will think me a right ninny!'

She giggled in a way that made Cora want to pinch her.

'Is Samuel your fancy man?'

'Cora! No! He's too good for me.'

But Ellen's protests were so threaded with breathiness that she clearly believed the opposite to be true.

'I hope you do stay, Cora.'

'Well, I shall have to, at least until these boots are paid for.'

'They're good ones too. Buttons not laces.'

It'd be two pounds at least, Cora reckoned, for the print dress, two flannel petticoats, two bib aprons, cap, boots and underthings. Three months' work. So she'd not be able to leave until spring was on the way. Ellen's voice became a whisper.

'They belonged to the missus I shouldn't wonder. Bet she hasn't worn boots for years.'

'Because she's an invalid?'

'That's one word for it.'

'What ails her?'

'I don't know. I've never seen her.'

Cora realised that all of her new clothes had probably once been worn by her new mistress.

'Mrs Dix looks after her then?'

'Yes.'

'What about the master, what's he like?'

Ellen was quiet for a second. 'He's an odd one, but is fair to the staff.'

'And his daughter?'

'Daughter?'

'I heard him talking to a child, a girl.'

'That'll be Violet. Not his daughter.'

'Who is she then?'

'Some relative of theirs, I think. But not Mr Jerwood's child. He has no children of his own.'

Ellen said no more and Cora sensed her already falling into sleep. The grey outlines of table and dresser pressed through the darkness. How easy it would be to get tangled up here in the sentiments of the back stairs; the petty jealousies, the lightening strikes of passion. Cora must keep herself to herself, especially when it came to Ellen and her intended. If she couldn't, she'd walk, boots or no boots, back to the smoky streets of the town. Because nothing of what went on in the servants' hall at the asylum must ever happen here. She'd die first.

the cabinet of curiosity

Towards the end of the week, in the late afternoon, Cora was sent upstairs to lay a fire in a grate. She didn't let on that she'd never before lived anywhere with a proper fireplace; the asylum had been warmed by hot water pipes and the Union workhouse by the mass of small sweating bodies. There'd been no heat at all in her gaol cell. But she'd lit a fire under the copper in the asylum laundry plenty of times. A fireplace couldn't be that different.

The library was at the front of the house by the top of the main staircase. Cora listened at the door then knocked. A creak of furniture that might have signalled someone inside was drowned by the cawing of rooks on the lawn. Once inside, though, Cora seemed to be alone.

The library air oozed mustiness from old books lining the shelves along the back wall. Tranklements of all sorts crammed the cabinets. Cora went to the fireplace, the metal pail clanking against her legs, and kneeled on the hearth rug. Behind her, something seemed to swish between the furniture and she looked around. But, apart from the spinning of one of the coloured balls on the wire contraption by the window, nothing moved.

She turned back to the ashy grate, heart tapping. Knots of scrap paper went in first, then sticks and coal from the pail. She struck a match and sat back. Flames licked at the kindling and she willed the coal to catch. Above the fireplace, a row of pointy skulls glistened white against the brown velvet mantel. Cora looked at each skull in turn trying to re-clothe it with flesh, skin and fur. She wondered if they were from animals she would recognise; a dog, a cat, a rat, or perhaps from creatures she couldn't even imagine.

'Who are you?

Cora flinched then slowly turned. Standing over her was a girl of about ten in a green dress. She must have been here all along, perhaps hiding behind the box of tiny glistening birds, frozen in flight. Unease pricked the back of Cora's neck.

'The tweeny.'

'What's your name?'

'Cora Burns.'

'That's a funny one.'

'Is it?'

'It sounds like the middle of you is on fire.' The girl started to smile then changed her mind. 'My name is Violet Poole.'

'That's funny too.'

'Why?'

'You're a purple pond.'

The girl's smile broke through. Despite the genteel voice and well-brushed hair, something about her pale face, with its small lips and dark brows, made Cora's heart catch in her chest.

A latch clicked and Violet turned sharply, her thin auburn plait slapping the back of her dress. Cora was not quite on her feet when Susan Gill came into the room.

'Nothing to do, Burns?'

The housemaid was the only servant who seemed to wear a uniform; a mauve afternoon dress with a frilled white apron and starched cap. And she was the only one who called the other maids by their second names.

'I just laid a fire.'

'But you haven't cleared the ash.'

'No.'

'What sort of household have you been used to? The grate should be cleared completely before a fire is lit. Not to do so would be slovenly.'

Cora thought, fleetingly, of how Susan Gill's face might look if her head were rammed against the wire thing by the window, one of those coloured glass balls gouging into her cheek. Blood would pool on the patterned carpet and spatter the armchair's cracked leather.

'Clear the ash now and take it to the midden. And Violet, you're wanted in the laboratory.'

The girl folded her hands across her stomach and went to the door. Susan Gill held it open.

'I'm sure you've been told, Burns, not to touch anything in this room without particular instruction.'

'No. I haven't.'

'Well, you have now.'

Cora curled her lip at the closing door then tipped coal dregs from the pail on to the fire. Black dust bloomed over yellow flames.

She raked out the hearth, shovelling ash and hot cinders into the pail. Chips of burning coal fell through the grate and glowed red in the grey embers. That girl was about the same age as Alice had been when Cora last saw her. Apart from that they were not much alike; Violet's eyes were blue not hazel and her hair sleeker and more coppery than Alice's had ever been. But Cora's throat still tightened with longing.

She grabbed the bucket half-filled with ash and went on to the landing. The next door was open far enough to reveal a thin slice of workbench and a man's arm in a dark blue sleeve protector laying out chain scales and rubber tubing. An unseen child, who must be Violet, coughed.

Outside, thin grey clouds bruised the reddening sun. Cora took a long breath of damp air. She mustn't let herself get accustomed to the richness of the food here or to the quietness of night hours. It couldn't be long until they threw her out. Nothing she did in the house seemed to be right, but she'd never known how to live except with hundreds of others.

She crossed sodden grass to the smouldering midden and emptied the bucket. Fine white ash clouded up.

'The between girl, is it?'

Across the waste heap, a young man with wayward light hair leaned on a pitch-fork. He pulled at an imaginary cap and gave a teasing smile.

'How do.'

Then he drove the points of the pitchfork into the ground and stood, feet apart, with his thumbs tucked into the little pockets of his waistcoat. His smile widened.

'Samuel Shepherd. Under-gardener. Pleased to make your acquaintance.'

Cora nodded but did not reply. She disliked his brash stance, although it was clear from his broad shoulders and twinkling eyes why Ellen was sweet on him. Cora imagined that if she went up to him there would be a smell of saddle leather and clean straw. She turned away sharply making sure not to lift her skirts too high over the wet grass.

Samuel shouted after her. 'Don't go! Stop here wi' me a while. Just to be friendly, like.'

Cora didn't look round but could sense his eyes following her to the door.

In the library, flames had begun to crackle in the grate. Cora took up the short poker, but as she stabbed air into the coals, one of her ears seemed to go deaf with a sudden whoosh of air. She blinked and looked around. The sharp noise had come, she felt sure, not from the fire but from somewhere behind the bookshelves. Another sound, like a high-pitched cry, was coming from the same place.

Quietly, Cora went to the wall of books and breathed in their odour of papery staleness. Her finger skimmed the tooled lettering on the spines: *Infant Nursing and the Management of Young Children; A Manual of Photographic Manipulation*. So many unimaginable combinations of words must be behind each one.

'I can't do it, I just can't.'

Violet's voice was as clear as if she were in the room. Cora held her breath and listened for Mr Jerwood's reply but none came. Gently, she pulled out a volume of *Travels in the African Interior* and put her ear to the empty slot on the shelf. Through the wall, metal clunked against wood and a long whistling sound grew higher in pitch until it disappeared into silence.

Cold air whispered out as Cora pushed the book back into place. Then she hurried across the room towards the hearth where the leaping orange flames had already died to black. But before Cora got to the grate, something made her stop dead.

It was in the middle of the room, in a dark wood cabinet displaying outlandish figurines with oversized private parts. But Cora's eyes were drawn to an open velvet-lined box near the base. It held a collection of shiny coins slightly bigger than half-crowns. Engraved on each was an object; a boat, an open book, or some queer instrument that Cora couldn't make out, and each was circled by a band of capital letters.

Cora bent closer but then, in a flash of lilac and white, the library door burst open. She sprang upright and hurried to the fireplace, hardly able to breathe. Although she'd need a closer look to be sure, the tightness in her chest was telling her that she was right. For, despite each one being so luminous and still a circular whole, the coins in the box looked like brothers and sisters to the tarnished half-medal that was tucked inside Cora's stays next to her heart.

SIX

1874

sisters

Keeping Alice by her turned out to be easy. Each day, Alice moved forward in the schoolroom until she sat at the same desk as Cora right in front of Mr Bowyer. No one seemed to think it odd.

As Cora wrote on the blackboard, she developed a habit of glancing over her shoulder after every three chalk loops. Alice's encouraging smile was always there. Mr Bowyer seemed a little irritated by this new habit and asked Cora more than once what in heaven she was doing but he never gave her much of a telling off. She knew too many of his secrets.

In the dining hall, Cora always saved a narrow place on her bench for Alice. When it was Cora's turn to give out bread and dripping, Alice always got the freshest slice. That summer in the workroom, when all the girls were learning to knit socks, Alice seemed to get away with just holding Cora's wool. Together, Cora and Alice chanted the stitches out loud almost in one voice until their overseer Millie Leggatt, a girl of fifteen who could knit as fast as a loom, told Cora to shut her mouth.

The other girls, click-clacking with their steel needles, sneered but weren't bold enough to say anything. They were jealous because Cora and Alice had become as close as sisters. Cora patted Alice's hand and smiled at her sweetly, ignoring the puzzled looks and the giggles. The others no longer mattered.

As the year went by and the air in the dormitory turned from damp to stuffy, the two girls' need to speak when the others were around seemed to evaporate. Language became not words but a glance or the turn of a head. When the other girls came close, Cora and Alice would both scowl. Alice learned quickly how to make even the biggest girls back off with the stamp of her foot. Cora started to dare Alice to be bolder; to rub a muddy finger down Emma Jeake's clean pinny or spit in Mary Smith's water cup. Alice never refused a dare and Cora burned with pride as her friend became stronger and more fearless. The thrill of mischief bound them closer. They would entwine their fingers and press their bodies together, standing on tiptoes and beaming, delirious with the triumph of getting away with it.

Soon, in order to preserve the excitement, the dares had to become riskier. On a rainy day in May they hung back in the corridor by the schoolroom as the others filed in a crocodile towards the dining hall. Cora pulled at Alice's sleeve and asked her if she needed the privy.

'I'll wait,' Alice replied.

'But could you go, if you had to?'

Alice's eyes widened. 'What are you on about, Cora?'

But Cora could see by Alice's furtive smile that she knew. As Alice lifted up her skirt to squat down right there in the corridor, Cora pressed both hands over her mouth to stop herself screaming with laughter. She almost laughed herself into a faint.

Alice was giggling uncontrollably too by the time she'd finished and wiped herself on her petticoat. The classroom door was shut but Mr Bowyer was still in there and might have come out at any moment. The girls clasped each others' hands as they ran squealing to the back of the dining hall queue.

No one owned up to the mess in the corridor. So Molly Pearce who was known as a habitual bed-wetter got the blame. Mr Bowyer gave her six raps of the ruler on her palm and made her stand, snivelling, at the front of the class for the rest of the afternoon.

As summer began to steam, Cora and Alice pulled themselves further away from the other girls. They liked to loiter on their own at the far end of the schoolyard especially when the infants were still out at play. Cora would tell Alice about what she could remember about being in the infants' quarters herself. None of the girls from that time were still in the Union house. A couple of the boys she recognised at chapel, but they never made any sign from their pews that they remembered Cora.

On a July morning that made the asphalt sparkle, Cora and Alice stood with their faces pressed into the railings of the infants' yard. They could almost touch the toddling, pinafored figures on the other side who prodded each other and sucked snotty thumbs. One of them, an ugly ginger thing, tried to pick up a stone and fell backwards, his brown skirt flying up to expose his tiny parts. He righted himself clumsily and burst into retching sobs.

Alice giggled. 'I thought that one was a girl. Why do they all wear the same? You can't tell lads from lasses.'

'It's always like that, isn't it, with little ones?'

'Not in our house! Ma always put Arthur in a little red flannel waistcoat. He had to have skirts on account of getting caught short, but it didn't seem right to put him in frilly pinnies as well.'

Cora looked away not wanting Alice to see her confusion. Was everything, even the way that small children were dressed, entirely different beyond the Union house walls? A huddle of shaven-headed toddlers in clumpy ankle boots and rumpled stockings surrounded the screaming boy who was ignored entirely by the two bent old women in workhouse bonnets who sat on a nearby bench.

Then the asphalt by Cora's feet began to squeak. A baby bird, quite large but featherless, was slumped on its bloated belly, a tiny blue heart beating under translucent skin.

'Alice, look.'

But in a swirl of air, the sole of Alice's boot ground down on to the gasping bird. Cora stared at the fledgling's lifeless hooded eyes.

'Oh Alice! I thought we'd look after it and feed it scraps until it could fly.'

Alice picked up the dead thing by its claw. 'Da always said it was kindest to kill them quicker than a cat would.'

Tears pricked at the top of Cora's nose. She would never know as much about the world as Alice already did. Then a cold finger touched Cora's cheek.

'Don't fret, Cora. I've killed all sorts. Pigeons, hens. A rabbit once. As soon as you've done it, you feel so brave and strong that you get a lovely tingle all over.' Alice's eyes glistened. 'I bet you could do it too, Cora, as long as the thing wasn't too big.'

Cora swallowed. 'Like a cat?'

'They're too scratchy. Best try on something that can't fight you off.'

'A lamb?'

'Where would you find a lamb around here, you ninny?'

Alice's gaze had drifted to the smallest children on the other side of the railings and Cora felt an ache of unease.

'Do you mean… a babby? But that would be wicked.'

Alice giggled. 'You are wicked though, aren't you, Cora?'

The shiver that went through Cora was electric. 'Am I?'

'Well, you won't know for sure whether you are or you're not until you try. Maybe...' Alice nodded towards the crying boy, '... try on that one who just tripped over and showed us his fella.'

Alice began to laugh. Then she took hold of Cora's hands and their fingers locked together, excitement fizzing between them. And, as the dreadful course they had set became suddenly inevitable, Cora laughed too, harder and harder, until trickles of hot tears squeezed out of her eyes and creased her cheeks with salt.

SEVEN

October 1885

focus

Outside the scullery window, hooves crunched on gravel and Ellen's laugh trickled through Samuel's low utterings. Although Cora couldn't make out the words or see them all climbing on to the pony trap, she could picture Ellen squashed between Samuel and Cook on the narrow rocking seat. As they picked up speed and the trap began to vibrate, Ellen's leg beneath her skirts would knock against Samuel's and then stick to it like flypaper. Cook would pretend not to notice. And Ellen was dull enough not to realise how badly all that sort of thing was likely to end.

The hooves stamped then quickened and grew fainter. Cora felt a needle of envy that Ellen was included on the excursion for Cook's messages. But at least that got her out of the way. Cora stood to one side of the window before opening the top buttons of her bodice and slipping the half-medal over her head. Its drab surface was spattered with black spots around the lettering. She laid it on the wooden counter and dipped a scrap of dampened hessian into the tray of brick dust. Whenever she'd tried before to clean it, soap and water seemed to make the metal duller than ever. Now, as she rubbed with dust, tarnish turned to shine. The bronze glinted with new-penny lustre and the fine etching became vivid; spindly rods rested on grass and poking out from a swathe of drapery was a dainty toe.

Outside in the passage, Cora listened for a second but the house was quiet. Earlier, she had seen Susan Gill go towards the parlour with a basket of dusters. The master, she suspected, was downstairs in his study. What he did all day, she couldn't imagine. It was an odd sort of photographer who had no customers and rarely left the house. Maybe being a gentleman was a job in itself.

She tip-toed up the back stairs and kept to the carpet runners along the landing. The doors were tight shut. At the library, she put her ear to the panel. If someone caught her inside she was ready with a story about looking for a lost pin from her sleeve that might have become lodged in tufts of carpet ready to pierce the soft sole of an indoor shoe. Cora's hand went to the doorknob. She twisted and pushed but the door didn't budge. She tried again, rattling the metal latch against the frame.

'Would you mind?'

Mr Jerwood was standing behind her on the landing, navy blue sleeve protectors covering his white shirt to the elbow. Cora's hand flew away from the door but too late, he must have seen. Her stomach flipped.

'Beg pardon, sir, I was just looking for my pin. You see, I…'

'Do you have a moment?'

'Sir?'

'Come this way, if you would. I need your assistance. It will not take long.'

He put his arm to the open laboratory door, beckoning her in. She could think of no way to refuse.

The laboratory was a narrow room but tall and bathed in light. Jars filled with floating dead things lined the shelves along one wall; a workbench ran along the other. At the far end, beside the tall window framed by black curtains, was the mahogany camera that Cora had last seen in Birmingham Gaol. Mr Jerwood closed the door.

'Very good. I merely require some assistance with focus.'

He turned his back to her and moved aside a large pair of pincers with sliding metal pointers and a wooden gauge. Cora thought again of Violet's anguished voice: *I just can't…* She felt her pulse quicken.

'And so,' Mr Jerwood went to the tripod, 'if you would stand again with your feet inside the chalk marks.'

'Sir…?'

His eyes darted around the room and then locked on to hers. 'As you did before.'

The same camera. The same photographer. She could still picture the shadow of window bars against a glossy brown wall. He smiled, gesturing to the pair of white loops chalked on the linoleum.

'You remember our first meeting now?'

She nodded. It seemed stupid to lie. The master bent to look into the back of the camera and turned a brass screw at the side of the device that seemed to compress the leather bellows behind the lens.

'Good. I expect you were somewhat confused when you first arrived here. And our perception of other people can be much affected by setting and attire. The change in your own demeanour demonstrates this remarkably well.'

As he was talking, his hand had moved to the lens-flap and lifted it for a second or two. Cora's heart missed a beat. Perhaps he had taken her likeness.

'Very good.' The master's hands rubbed together. 'And I have your likeness from… before, if you wish to see it.'

He didn't wait for an answer but reached to the shelf above the workbench and lifted down a pasteboard box labelled: *Composites 1884 –*. Removing the lid, he pulled out a stiffened photographic print. Cora's own face, wary and flint-eyed, stared back at her from the ugly prison bonnet.

Mr Jerwood made a noise that was almost a cough. 'What do you think of yourself?'

Cora shrugged but her lips were pressed together tight enough to stop her yelling at him to burn the thing that very minute. Anyone in the house who saw it would know instantly what she really was.

The master continued, almost merry. 'What, I mean, do you see in this face? A victim of fate and of the depravity of men? Or someone determined to have her own way however heavy the cost to others?'

Cora felt herself flinch. He knew. The details of her conviction must have been revealed to him as readily as a stationmaster's pocket watch. Rage swelled in her chest but her voice compressed to a whisper.

'I couldn't say, sir.'

But Mr Jerwood was leaning over the workbench examining the print. Cora eyed the length of rubber tubing beside him and could almost see it around his neck, his face swelling purple as she yanked it tight.

He caught her sideways look, but seemed only curious.

'You would agree though, would you not, that your crime may, in a moral sense, have several different interpretations.'

'I don't understand you, sir.'

'Come, try. What does this face tell us about the character of the person behind it?'

It was perfectly clear. She was an evil bitch. Anyone could see that in the white pinpricks of those monochrome eyes.

'It is the face I was born with, sir.'

The master sighed and went to put the likeness back into the box, flicking through numerous striped bodices and white bows tied under chins until he found the place. As the lid closed down, Cora made sure to remember the position, more or less, of her own likeness within the box of convicts.

Then Mr Jerwood picked up a pencil. His fingers drummed on the bench as his other hand flew back and forth across a loose sheet of paper filling it with scrawl. He seemed to have forgotten that Cora, humiliated and seething, was still standing with her feet inside the chalk loops.

Then, without looking up, he spoke. 'That will be all. I trust that you will find the library to be open.'

the japanned frame

The door opened easily. Perhaps it hadn't been locked at all. Cora slipped inside the library, blood pulsing in her ears. There was no telling now who else in the house knew that their tweeny had come direct from Birmingham Gaol. Mrs Dix almost certainly did, and maybe Cook too. The master might have told them all.

Cora wished that she'd smashed one of those creepy-crawly jars into his self-satisfied face. The master must be on friendly terms with the prison's governor. Perhaps he knew the Poor Law Guardians too, and they may even have told him of those long-ago goings-on that Cora hardly knew about herself.

A tapestry curtain flapped at the open window and anger fidgeted in Cora's throat. She went unsteadily to the cabinet, fists itching to lash at the rude figurines and smash them against the glass. But instead, breathing hard, she knelt down beside the display box and ran her hand over the lid. The wooden inlay was fashioned into two pigeons perched amongst branches. The box alone might be worth more than she could earn in a year. If she picked it up and walked out, no one might notice. And Mr Jerwood would not be surprised by the theft. He had only employed her because she was a criminal.

The lid was secured with a catch that flipped up easily. Inside, the shiny coins were pressed into perfectly sized indentations in the black velvet lining. Each one had on it an engraving of an object; an arithmetic equation, or a map of some unknown country. They had the same bronze tint as Cora's newly polished half-medal, and the same rim of lettering. But none of the medallions showed the words *IMAGINEM SALT,* only gibberish that ended with a random assortment of capitals: *M, C, V*… Nothing in the box could lead her to Alice.

She put her fingernail on a coin and eased it from the soft, tight niche. Fine etching on the moulded metal captured a perfect likeness of a rabbit. The expensive weight of the coin in her hand made its connection to a back-street japanner's smithy seem remote.

Then at the edge of Cora's vision, a green movement turned into Violet standing up behind the armchair and grappling with a large book that must have been on her lap. She grinned.

'I hoped it might be you.'

Cora fumbled the medal back into its indent and snapped down the lid. Violet came closer, a finger wedged inside her book.

'What are you doing, Cora?'

'Looking for my pin.'

'Inside the medallion collection?'

Cora glanced at the bookshelves as if Mr Jerwood might somehow be listening but there were only rows of leather spines.

'I was just…'

'Shall I help you?'

The binding crackled as Violet laid her book open on the carpet and kneeled by the cabinet, but Cora stood up, brushing her hands on her apron.

'I'd best go.'

'Can't you stay a while?'

'I have things to do.'

'You've not yet found your pin.'

Violet's brow creased and her chin wrinkled. Cora wondered for a moment if the child was about to bawl and bring Susan Gill from the parlour, scowling and full of questions.

Cora made her voice softer. 'I won't interrupt you, miss. You can go back to reading your book.'

'I've read most of it already.'

'Is it good?

Violet shrugged. 'It has all different things in it. Poems, pictures, stories and the like.' She held out an open page. A girl in a low-cut bodice stared, terrified, from the title: *Transformation By the author of Frankenstein.* 'This one is meant to make your blood run cold.'

'How does it do that?'

'A man in it sees his own face on someone else. But that wouldn't bother me.'

'Wouldn't it?'

Violet shook her head. 'A girl who looked like me might become my friend.'

Cora's neck prickled as she thought of herself beside Alice. In their workhouse uniforms, they had looked almost like twins.

Violet closed the book with a thud and bounded to the side table by the armchair. She picked up a decorated picture frame then thrust it at Cora.

'Does this face resemble mine?'

The woman in the faded photograph sat with a book on her lap. Her fairish hair was pulled into a chignon; the toe of one shoe rested on a footstool. Unfashionably wide skirts rippled with weak light.

'No.'

Violet clasped the frame to her chest and bit the inside of her lip. 'Are you sure? Most people say she does.'

'Who is she?'

'My mamma.'

'Oh. Perhaps you look more like your father.'

'Perhaps, but I've never seen his likeness. Or him, that I can remember.'

'I'm sorry.'

'No, no, they are not dead. He and Mamma are in India.'

'And you can't remember what they look like?'

Violet sighed and stared at the photograph. 'Sometimes I think I can. I remember the feel of Mamma's cold cheek against mine. And the buzzing of fat flies in very sour air. But that is all.'

'Well, you remember more than I.'

'Why? Are your parents in India too?'

Cora gave a snort but then Violet's arm shifted and she saw a small white label on the back of the frame:

Salt & Co. BIRMm
Japanners and Tin-platers

Without speaking, Cora reached out and took hold of the frame. It felt curiously light. Under a thick gloss of lacquer, golden leaves scrolled around the black edge. Luminous pink and blue buds threaded through a garland so delicate that it must have been painted by a child. Perhaps it was the firing of a piece such as this that had left the scar on Alice's wrist. Cora rubbed her thumb across the painted blossom and felt her throat tightening.

Violet smiled and reached up to touch a finger, light as air, to Cora's cheek. 'Oh Cora, have I made you fret for your mamma?'

'Lord no. It's not that.'

'What then?'

'This frame. It's japanned ware, isn't it?'

'Yes. Why should that upset you?'

'I knew someone once, who made it.'

Violet's eyes widened. 'A young man?'

'No. A girl. Like you.'

She handed back the photograph and Violet put it on the table then sighed.

'Your friend? How I should love to have a real friend. More even than seeing my mamma. Where is she now, Cora?'

'I don't know.'

Cora felt a small cold hand squeeze her knuckles. Violet's white face looked up at her earnestly.

'You should look for her. You must not lose her forever.'

Cora shook her head and swallowed. 'I have not seen her since… since we were children.'

'But you would recognise her if you saw her?'

'I would.'

'Then perhaps I can help you.'

'How?'

'I have a talent for charcoal portraits. Mrs Dix says she has never seen any so good. If you describe to me how your friend should look, I will draw her. Then you can put the likeness in an advertisement on the "Wanted" page of the *Birmingham Gazette*.'

Violet was excited now, gripping Cora's hand tightly and bouncing up and down on the toes of her soft-soled shoes. Cora stepped back and pulled her hand free.

'I must go.'

'But next time you're in here we can make a start on the drawing.'

'I am not often sent upstairs.'

'Or I will bring my charcoal sticks into the morning room. At any rate, we will need to do it shortly, before I leave.'

As Cora turned towards the door, she glanced down at the inlaid lid of the medallion box. Salt & Co must have also made those coins; the coincidence was too great. And as soon as she was allowed out of this peculiar house, she would get back to town, not only to check that Thripp the photographer had kept his promise, but also somehow, to track down Salt the japanner's smithy.

veal

For a while, the only sound was the screech of cutlery on china. Cora ate slowly, studying her plate to avoid the eyes of the others around the table. But it was hard not to gobble. As she bit through crumbly pastry to the soft meat and thick gravy inside, she thought that she'd never in her life tasted anything so good.

Perhaps because it was Saturday, everyone seemed cheery. Even Susan Gill was gulping her half-glass of flat beer. The outdoor men had come in laughing together at twelve o'clock sharp and when his plate was clean, Timothy, the gardener and useful man, gave a smile that showed the black gaps between his yellow teeth. He raised his glass.

'A very fine veal pudding, Cook. My compliments.'

Cook almost smiled back. 'Compliments should go to Mr Todd the butcher. I take back all I said. And compliments to the garden staff on these kidney beans. Still very tender.'

Cora blinked and wondered why vegetables had so many names. They'd been runner beans at the asylum although she couldn't recall ever eating beans, or anything green, at the workhouse or the gaol. But veal was entirely new. She wondered what it might look like when it was alive.

Ellen leaned across the table, the fork raised in her hand. 'You should have seen Mr Todd's shop, Cora. The mirrors! And a mechanical slicer!'

Cora already knew all about it. Ellen had talked of nothing else since her return from yesterday's trip to the Stratford road.

'The slab was pure marble wasn't it, Samuel?'

Somehow Cora had found herself sitting beside Samuel Shepherd but Ellen was doing her best to keep his head turned in her direction. As she began to recount the variety of jars in the sweet shop, she picked up her glass too quickly and beer sloshed on to the white cloth.

As Ellen jumped up, mopping the stain with her apron, Samuel seemed to take her distraction as an opportunity. Cora felt him lean in towards her. He didn't exactly whisper but spoke too quietly for Ellen to hear.

'Would you like to see the shops, Cora? I could take you in the pony trap tomorrow afternoon.'

The warmth of his breath on her neck was an irritation. What gave him the licence to get so close? But Cora could not make herself pull away. She gripped her knife harder as it dripped gravy on to her plate.

'They'll be shut.'

She stabbed a chunk of veal with her fork and began to chew on it. Samuel Shepherd was even dimmer than he looked if he thought she'd be lured so easily into that sort of thing, no matter how good the smell of his smooth-shaved cheek, or how satisfying it would be to wipe the silly smile off Ellen's face.

As she sat down, Ellen leaned across her plate with the look on her face twisted between eagerness and resentment. Perhaps she had heard after all.

'And the confectioner's display! I have never seen the like. Samuel was kind enough to purchase two of the fondant fancies I so admired. We ate them on the pony trap on the way back didn't we, Cook?'

Cook's eyes narrowed. 'Yes. Very nice.'

Samuel put his knife and fork together on the empty plate and sat back, running a hand through his hair. Cora wasn't sure it was an accident that his knee lolled against hers. But at that moment, a bang on the ceiling like a flat iron dropping made everyone at the table look up. The gas burner quivered. Cook rolled her eyes.

'We'd better have our bramble pie sharpish, before herself wants something. Cora, bring that jug of custard to the table.'

Cora scraped her chair back roughly, banging it against Samuel's leg.

When she placed the warm earthenware jug on the table, Cook was already slicing pastry that sparkled with sugar. A tang of sharp fruit wafted up from the hot pie as the knife went in. Purple juice oozed out. Cora hovered behind the chair, not quite wanting to sit back down next to Samuel, but her mouth watered for the brambles, whatever they might be.

One of the bells on wires above the door gave an abrupt jangle.

Cook shook her head. 'What did I say? Mrs Dix'll be wanting warm milk for the missus. Acting up again, I expect.'

Ellen giggled. 'Funny how warm milk puts her to sleep. It never has that effect on me.'

Samuel beamed at her with his clean white teeth. 'Need something a bit stronger than milk, don't you, Ellen?'

Ellen's face flushed to the colour of the fruit bleeding from the pie. 'You rascal, Samuel Shepherd.'

Cora pushed in her chair. 'I'll see to it, Cook.'

'Would you? Good girl. Use the small copper pan for the milk and only fill the cup halfway. Blood warm.'

The tray seemed pointless for just a small cup of milk but, on the landing, Cora placed it as usual in front of the mistress's door and then knocked.

'Tray!'

Instantly, a voice inside replied. 'Bring it in.'

Mrs Dix sounded breathless. Something about her tone made Cora's heart pump faster as she opened the door.

The curtains were closed and the mantles unlit. Sourness blanketed the room. As Cora's eyes grew accustomed to the dim light, she saw that the dark mound at the centre of the room was a heap of furniture; an assortment of chairs, ottomans and footstools loaded around the bed. And on top of the mattress in the middle of the heap, in her customary black crêpe but, hunched on hands and knees, was Mrs Dix.

Her face shone with sweat. 'Over there. On the sideboard.'

Cora picked her way around the barricaded bed. Spread out across a countertop against the wall, were dark glass bottles, and jugs with weighted lace covers. She threw a glance to the bed. Mrs Dix, still kneeling, was whispering to a figure lying under the covers. Then, without looking round, she raised her voice.

'Cora? Take the light brown bottle before you marked *Chloral Hydrate*. Put three crystals from it into the milk and stir them vigorously. Can you do it?'

'Yes, Mrs Dix.'

The odd familiarity of the room's stench made sense now. Certain parts of the asylum had reeked with the foul breath of inmates dosed up on chloral.

'Now bring it here.'

Cora carried the cup towards the bed. A shaking voice came from the depth of the pile.

'Do not let me fall, Helen.'

'Fear not, madam, I have you fast in my grip. But I must sit you up a little now, for your milk.'

Mrs Dix reached to the bottom of the bed for a cushion and as she turned, cast a fierce eye at Cora. Her face was white and her coiled hair dishevelled. She jerked her head indicating for Cora to bring the milk forward.

Cora squeezed between a stool and a pot-cupboard that were rammed against the bed and held out the cup. As Mrs Dix reached for it she let go of the mistress's arm and Mrs Jerwood lifted her head. Her bed-cap and nightgown glowed white, but her skin had the grey pallor of a lunatic. The twin spots of light in her eyes were full of dread.

'Helen? What is she doing here?'

'It is Cora, our new between maid.'

'Cora?'

'Yes, madam.'

'That is not her name.'

Mrs Dix held the cup to Mrs Jerwood's lips, but she pushed it away, her terrified eyes trained on to Cora's face.

Again, Mrs Dix brought the cup to the mistress's lips. 'I'm sure you have not seen her before, madam.'

Then Mrs Dix turned her head to Cora and hissed, *leave!* But as Cora manoeuvred backwards between the furniture, Mrs Jerwood raised herself up on an elbow, watching. Something about the recognition in her eyes made Cora's skin crawl. The mistress's voice became suddenly commanding.

'Tell me, Helen, who let her into this house?'

'She is going now, madam.'

Mrs Dix moved across the bed trying to shield Cora from the mistress's mad-eyed stare. But with sudden strength, the woman lurched forward and stood upright on the bed. Towering above Cora, she pointed down at her with an outstretched arm, her voice cracking with rage.

'Why have you come back? Is it just to gloat at me in this state?'

Cora reached the door with the empty tray, the handles slippery in her grasp. She fumbled with the doorknob and tripped out of the room. But just before the door banged behind her, Cora glimpsed the stricken face of the woman standing on the bed, her lips mouthing over and over the same word.

'You!'

EIGHT

Research Journal of

David Farley MD
Assistant Medical Officer
Birmingham asylum
October 1885

<u>Sat 10th</u>

My superior is a most contradictory fellow. This morning, when I put to him my research proposal, he regarded me over the top of his spectacles with a look of such disdainful amusement that I steeled myself for disappointment. He then surprised me with the enthusiasm of his support.

It seems that Dr Grainger is already familiar with the technique of hypnosis as a treatment for lunacy and is well versed in current thinking amongst the Continental experts. Indeed, he seemed pleased that a younger medical man with the energy to test out this new method had arrived under his supervision in the Borough Asylum.

Dr Grainger went on to provide useful advice on the selection of patients for my experiments. His only stipulation regarding the research was that it should be done in my own time and must not distress the subjects or those around them. I thanked him for his unexpected kindness but as I rose to leave his office he was determined to have the last word. 'I have no doubt,' he said, 'that you will succeed in getting them under but it remains to be seen whether, even in a trance, a monomaniac kept indoors by fear can be persuaded to exit the building, or a morbidly thin hysteric can be induced to eat.'

I nodded (I hope sagely) and, as I made for the door, replied with some platitude about enriching scientific progress in this field regardless of the experiments' outcomes. He chuckled and made a final attempt to dampen my spirits, 'I am afraid to say, dear boy, that the act of talking, hypnotic or otherwise, can never on its own be a cure for insanity.' From the curtness of my parting nod he may have inferred my determination to prove him wrong.

I am not surprised, of course, by Dr Grainger's scepticism. He shares the general view of the medical establishment in assuming the root causes of madness to be <u>Biological</u>. He looks for the origin of mental distress only in physical or chemical defects of the brain, and so the role of misfortune is ignored. Yet, every day of the week, patients are admitted to the Borough Asylum because their lives have driven them mad. Poverty, disappointment and grief may cause insanity as surely as heredity, germs or disease.

My own exposure to new experiences here at the Asylum has reinforced my adherence to a <u>Political</u> theory of insanity. Can it be a coincidence that ever-larger borough and county asylums have sprouted across our towns and countryside in direct parallel to the proliferation of manufactories, collieries and mills? These *monsters of industry devour the working classes and spit them out; exhausted, broken and insane. Capitalism is designed to create discontent, and despair is a tool used by the rich to keep the poor in chains.*

I will for now, however, keep this theory of the link between mental instability and social inequality to myself. Dr Grainger, for all I know, may be a true disciple of Socialism, but I doubt it. I shall await evidence from the practical application of my theory to convince him. For my (as yet undisclosed) aim is to convince each mental patient, whilst in the grip of a hypnotic trance, that the key to their recovery lies in the creation of a fairer society. Who can say whether the lunatic, once given confidence to join the swelling ranks of the labour movement and strive for a better future, may find his own Political purpose to be as good as a cure?

<u>*Sun 11th*</u>

I considered several patients for my first experiment but thankfully, before making my final selection, I consulted Matron. Previously I had encountered this lady only on my rounds of the women's wards when she seemed a rather formidable personage. So after chapel this morning, I had to gather some courage to ask her if she might have any interest in assisting with a private research project into the therapeutic effects of hypnosis. Her response was instantly affirmative and her manner far more agreeable than the stiff Nightingale that I had unfairly presumed her to be.

Mrs Abbott (for, incredibly 'Matron' is not her actual name!) considered the several placid inmates I suggested, then enquired whether, in my short time here, I had ever visited the asylum kitchen. I confessed that I had not and she replied that I would not then be aware of the lamentable change in the patient whom I will call Mary B. Despite her twenty-year residence here in the asylum, this inmate's symptoms were until very recently minimal. Aphonia was the only apparent residue of whatever maladies had brought about her admission all those years ago. Some attendants were not even aware that Mary B was an actual inmate. For as long as anyone could remember, she had worked in the asylum kitchen and been so diligent and apparently content that she was allowed to sleep there (despite the proximity of sharp instruments). Then, eight days ago, without any obvious cause, the patient suffered a dramatic relapse and inflicted injury upon herself with a knife. Since then she has been in the infirmary and made a good physical recovery but her former cheerful spirits have deserted her. Matron reports that Mary B's aphonia continues and whilst awake she is entirely silent. Once asleep, however, or when waking from the grip of medicinal

85

stupor Mary B has, apparently for the first time in two decades, uttered spoken words. Matron Abbott could give only sketchy details but she had already fired me with optimism that a hypnotic trance could be the way to unlock Mary B's tongue from the straitcoat of silence.

Mon 12th
This afternoon I spent a few hours in the asylum's record office on a hunt for the case history of Mary B. It took a good while trawling through the cabinets, but my perseverance was repaid with her medical admission certificate. The information contained in it shocked and intrigued me in equal measure. It is here transcribed in full:

Mary B – Age (circa)18 Admitted: 23rd June 1865 Female
Single, Married or Widowed .... Single
Previous Occupation .... Prisoner
Religious Persuasion .... Unknown
If First Attack .... No
When and where under previous care and
    treatment .... Birmingham Gaol
Duration of existing attack .... six weeks
Supposed cause .... lactational insanity
Whether suicidal .... SEVERE risk
Whether dangerous to others .... Yes
Name and abode of nearest known relative .... Unknown

Facts upon which the opinion of Insanity is founded following observation by Medical Man:
She has been admitted directly from the Borough Gaol and is chargeable to the Aston Union. The prison doctor reports that her condition appeared stable until mania was brought on by excessive nursing of a child. Became prone to alternate bouts of raving and taciturnity. Melancholic. Attempted to hide the child under a mattress. May also have caused it injury. She has induced bleeding by rubbing repeatedly at her breasts with a handkerchief. Was then introduced to the padded room and the strait waistcoat. Malnourished. Eats sparingly but clean in habits. Regular menstruation not yet re-established.

Attached to the top of the certificate was a photographic likeness showing an interesting-looking young woman with striking eyes. Sadly, as was often the case during this era of more rudimentary care for the insane, the most salient fact about Mary B, namely her crime, has been omitted from the record.

Matron Abbott was as shocked as I to discover this patient's history. When I told her of the details, she replied; 'Blow me!' at which I gave a laugh (I hope she did not find any disrespect in my reaction, for none was meant). I must say that I was impressed with Mrs Abbott's refusal to jump to any opinionated conclusion about Mary B's youthful predicament. Instead she showed a sisterly sympathy which warmed my faith in humanity. Later today Mrs Abbott reported that she had (very kindly) spoken on my behalf to the most long-standing attendants here. Their reaction was the same as ours; none knew of Mary B's criminal past nor of her child, and all were dismayed.

More time in the record office will be needed to scour the casebooks for information about Mary B's subsequent treatment and the likely cause of her muteness. Given the lack of reference to aphonia on her admission certificate, she must have had the power of speech at this time and I am unable to ascertain when this ended. A full medical examination may be required to rule out physical damage to her vocal chords or respiratory tract but, in view of her nocturnal outbursts, I think I am safe to conclude that her mute state results solely from the pathology of mania. I am extremely hopeful that my curative suggestions to this unfortunate woman under hypnosis will allow her voice once again to be heard.

NINE

October 1885

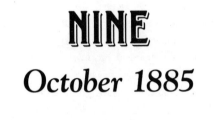

a trick of the light

Her own clothes were as near as Cora could get to Sunday best. Once breakfast was cleared, Ellen went into the pantry to change and was transformed by a pale blue Holland jacket, cut tight across her hips over draped skirts. No one on the street would guess her a scullery maid.

When Cora asked if she was going to the church, Ellen laughed. 'I know Sunday is meant to be for chapel or church but I don't think many go. Except Mrs Dix. As long as you're back by dark no one will bother about where you've been.'

'Where are you going?'

'Home, of course.'

Queasiness rippled through Cora's stomach. *Home* was not a word she could ever imagine herself saying.

Cora waited at the scullery window until she could see Ellen's petite blue bonnet and big silk bow bobbing towards the lane. Then, Cora wrapped herself in her plaid shawl and went to the stables.

Samuel was in the tack room scooping grain from a barrel. Through a haze of bran dust, she could not help admiring the muscular confidence of his movements. When she stepped through the doorway and said his name, he froze briefly before turning around. Cora could not quite read his face. He might have been alarmed, eager or ashamed. Perhaps all three.

'Aye?'

'You said you'd take me out in the pony trap.'

He folded his arms and leaned a shoulder against the wall. His eyes seemed to sparkle but he did not smile. 'Aye.'

'Will you take me now? To town?'

He snorted and shook his head, running a hand through straw-like hair. 'I only said to the shops on Stratford Road.'

She took a step towards him. 'Well, take me there, then. I can walk the rest.'

'You'll not be back in time if you walk.'

'Take me anyway.'

He smiled lazily. 'What's the rush? We can take a bit of leisure here.'

'You shouldn't make promises you can't keep.'

Samuel's face darkened. He stood straight, his arms falling to his sides.

'It wasn't a promise, just a friendly invite. And I will take you, but not today.'

Red warmth began to curdle in Cora's throat. Why should he have the say in what they did? He wasn't her better. Her fists clenched on to the wool of her skirt and she took another step towards him lifting her petticoat above the top of her boot. Samuel's eye dropped, as she knew it would, to the lick of black stocking. She took a breath full of saddle soap and horse.

'Is there anything I can do to get you to take me?'

His face coloured, but he didn't move. 'Maybe next Sunday.'

'No, now.'

'What's the rush?'

'I'm looking for someone.'

One side of his mouth raised into a smile. 'A sweetheart, eh?'

In her next heartbeat, Cora went for him. And she didn't know whether it was to lash his face with her nails or to kiss him until her tongue was inside his mouth. He tasted warm and sour as beer. One of her hands slipped beneath his jacket. His skin radiated heat through the damp shirt. She felt her limbs begin to soften and mould to his tensed body. His lips slackened against hers.

Then, he reeled back. 'Cora... Not here. Anyone might see us.'

'Ellen has gone.'

'But at any rate... not here.'

'Will you help me though? I have to get into town.'

He stepped back from her, his face crimson, and began to fumble into the pocket of his trousers.

'Aye, aye. Have this.'

'Sixpence? What for?'

'The steam tram. The stop's not far.'

Cora stood for a moment, breathing hard. The skin around her mouth stung from the irritation of his bristles. She snatched the coin.

'I'll pay you back. When I see some wages.'

He opened his mouth but she made sure not to hear his reply as she stamped out into the stableyard then hurried along the drive.

He was right. At a fast walk in good boots, it didn't take long to the stark new church and the terminus. Steam hummed from the engine tram as it waited. On account of the mild weather they'd pulled back the canvas roof. The passenger car rocked and creaked as Cora climbed the spindly staircase to the top deck. She had expected to be terrified by the wobbling height of the upper floor and the brushing of tree branches into the open sides but as a whistle tooted and they set off, she found herself filled with a white-hot impatience to go faster.

The engine tram, hooked on behind, belched black smoke as it pushed the passenger car up the hill. Tar and sulphur laced the warm air. They picked up speed past the parade of shops; the butcher's, counters swathed in grey sheets, was not nearly so grand as Ellen had made out and the confectioners' display was pasteboard.

As the road flattened, Cora closed her eyes into the howl of noise and air. It helped to blank an inner gnaw of reproach for getting what she'd wanted out of Samuel Shepherd like a Bordesley Street whore. Except that now she was beholden to him, not just because she owed him sixpence but because he'd stirred a ripple of heat inside her that she thought she was finished with for good.

Houses thickened into long straight streets. Weak sunlight glinted off slate. The tram slowed to a huff past a recreation ground where men in white shirts rolled heavy balls over grass as flat and glossy as linoleum. Cora realised that she must have passed this way only last Sunday but she'd been too blinded by desperation and gin-dregs to notice anything except her rag-bound feet. She flexed her toes inside the button boots, and put a hand into her newly made pocket to reassure herself that the return ticket was safe inside.

The tram clipped along between the red-brick houses. The air grew sooty. She must have breathed that bad air every day of her life until last week. Then they were into Deritend with its iron-barred warehouses and gated foundries that buzzed and clanked even on a Sunday. They passed enamel works and rolling mills. Cora craned her head looking for a painted sign that might say *Salt & Co* but factory gates and archways rattled past in a blur.

Up ahead, a lone figure in a narrow grey skirt and perched bonnet leaned against the bridge over the canal. Something about the slope of the woman's shoulders and the way her face was turned to the sun made Cora hold on to the bar of the upper deck and lean over. As the tram approached the bridge, the engine gave a blast of the steam whistle and the woman looked up. Briefly, her eyes met Cora's in a hard blue stare that turned into a smirk.

Cora pushed herself up to half-standing then cleared her throat. She waited until she was level with the woman then spat over the side of the tram. The gob of phlegm almost made it on to the hard-eyed woman's dress but she'd deserved it; the coarse shout of *whore!* that followed the tram showed that. Cora slumped down vexed with herself, not just for missing her target but for allowing her hopes to be raised with every trick of the light.

stereoscope

Corporation Street's pavements thrummed with the sturdy boots of housemaids and factory apprentices out for a Sunday jaunt. Cora hurried through the throng and, as she neared the photographer's shop, her stomach twisted at the sight of what seemed to be her likeness against the dark backcloth. But it was a cabinet portrait of some woman, much older, in a high-necked gown. Only their stance was the same.

Cora put her fingertips against the glass. She should have known, as soon as she saw Bordesley Street, that Mr Thripp was not to be trusted. The two shillings she'd paid him might as well have been posted into a storm drain. It was no use trying to tell herself that the coins would have gone anyway into the thieving hand of an Irish sweeper. Vexation still simmered in her throat. Then, the velvet backcloth quivered and her fury boiled.

'Oi! You swindler. Open up!' She hammered on the window then flew at the door. The *CLOSED* sign shuddered behind it. 'Let me in, you bastard! Give me back my shillings.'

A crowd was gathering on the pavement. Cora stepped backwards into the road and peered at the curtained windows above the shopfront. Putting her hands to each side of her mouth, she bellowed up.

'I'll have the police on you, Thripp, if you don't open this door. I want my money back!'

The throng on the pavement began to join in. There were shouts of *Open up!* and *Constable!* A couple of lads came up behind Cora, asking if she wanted them to fetch an officer. They all crowded around the door. Then Cora heard the handle rattle and the lock turn.

'Come in then, come in. Not you lot. Just the young lady.'

A man's hand grabbed her elbow and pulled her forward. The boys' faces pressed up against the glass as the door closed. Cora shook herself and straightened her shawl as her eyes adjusted to the shaded light.

'I want to see Mr Thripp.'

'I am Mr Thripp.'

But the man was young and slight, a reddish beard trimmed close to his face.

'Not you. The old one.'

His face relaxed into a slight smile. 'I hardly dare ask what it might be about.'

'It's about my money that I gave him. Two shillings to put my likeness in your window. He said he would.'

'A photograph? Of you?'

'Yes.'

'Why would you pay to put it in our window?'

'So that someone I have lost touch with might see it and find me. Mr Thripp said he would keep a note of anyone who enquired. But that can't have happened if the likeness is still in the drawer. So I'll have my money back thank you very much. And the likeness.'

The man smoothed a hand across his beard. There was a resemblance to old Mr Thripp about the mouth and nose, but this one had a detached, straightforward gaze.

Cora shifted under his stare. 'Well?'

He put out his hand. 'I'm Mr Alfred Thripp. How do you do?'

Cora could not remember that anyone had ever before sought to shake hands with her. She eyed his hand suspiciously as she put her own limply inside its grip. In spite of his well-cut suit and the gold ring on his littlest finger, young Mr Thripp had the hands of a workman. It was the photographic chemicals, Cora supposed, that had hardened the scars of blisters and made his hand as rough as her own. But its movement was firm and businesslike. She found her anger deflated by the contact.

'And you are?'

'Cora Burns.'

'Well, Miss Burns. I shall do my best to make amends for my father's oversight. Shall we try to locate the likeness? When was it that you came in?'

'Last Saturday. Late in the day.'

She watched him lift a box on to the glass counter and sort through prints of all sizes inside. Rough as his hands were, he picked up each portrait lightly by the edges so that his fingers never once touched a glossy surface.

'Let me try another box.'

'Perhaps I'll come back and see the other Mr Thripp.'

'I'm afraid my father can be a little... unreliable at times. You'd do better to stick with me.'

Cora glanced up warily expecting something saucy to have crept into his expression but it remained plain.

'Let me look in the studio.' He pulled back the curtain. 'You are lucky to find someone here. I'm usually out and about with my camera on a Sunday but the light is poor today.'

In the corner of the studio, the camera on its tripod was covered by a pink dust sheet. Alfred went to the shelf beside it and pulled forward a box labelled *STEREOSCOPICS*. As before, he lifted the prints out gently. Each one showed two apparently identical scenes joined together on the same piece of card.

Cora shook her head. 'I paid only for one likeness not two.'

'My father may have wanted it for a stereograph.'

'What's that?'

'Have you not seen one before?' He picked up from the shelf a device on a metal rod then clipped a twin-image to one end. The other end of the rod was attached to a pair of heavy wooden spectacles.

'Here.' Alfred held the spectacles gently to Cora's face. 'Put your hand on this screw and turn it forwards until you see one single picture clearly.'

Intrigued, Cora wound the knob on the side of the eyepiece and the photographs moved towards her. The duplicate views of New Street Station merged miraculously into one; ironwork shifted into sharp relief under the vaulted glass roof and a locomotive seemed to move forward in a soft puff of steam. The two pictures in merging, took on the detail and depth of real life.

'Oh.'

'Good, isn't it? I took that one. The images look like copies but they are not. The difference between them is almost invisible to the naked eye but each one is taken exactly two and three quarter inches apart, the same distance as between your eyes. Would you like to see another?'

Cora felt his breath on her cheek. She had a sense, for a vivid second, of how his mouth might taste; not of beer, like Samuel's, but of something sweeter, perhaps like the Rowntree's fruit pastille she'd once had.

'No. I have to get back.'

'Do you?' He lowered the stereoscope. 'No matter. I'll look through the negatives later and make a print if I find yours.'

'And put it in the window?'

'Yes. I promise.'

He smiled and began to file the stereographs back into the box. One of the double images showed a lady with a sly smile raising voluminous skirts by a fireplace to warm her bare legs. In another, a girl not much bigger than Violet looked into a stereoscope wearing only a transparent chemise. Cora's pulse quickened. Had old Mr Thripp been behind the camera when those likenesses were taken, or his son?

'Oh my word.'

Alfred had pulled a glass negative from the end of the box and was holding it up to the light. Cora's nasty stare shimmered, ghost-like, from the plate.

'This is... striking.'

She felt suddenly unsure about putting the fiendish person in that likeness on public display but changing her mind would mean losing face.

'And you'll put a print of it in the window?'

'Gladly. I expect many will stop for a closer look. And if your friend does, to where should we direct her... or him?'

Cora hesitated for a second, but then put into words the thought that had remained in her head but been unspoken for so long.

'It's a she. My sister, in fact.'

'And the directions?'

'The Larches, Spark Hill.'

'Mr Jerwood's house?'

Cora flinched. 'You know him?'

'A customer. He has a very fine collection of photographic equipment.' Alfred was smiling. 'And will you come back next week to view the print?'

Cora shrugged. 'Not without the tram fare.'

'Oh, yes.' Alfred took out a pocket book from his jacket and fumbled with the flap on the pouch. He held out two silver coins. 'Please… accept this reimbursement, with apologies on my father's behalf and compliments on my own.'

Cora shook her head. 'You don't have to pay me off. I'm not going to the police.'

'No, no. Please take it. Your likeness is such a fine character study that I am grateful to put it in our display. And, of course, pleased to help you find your sister.'

Cora frowned but took the shillings, closing her fist to feel their imprint on her palm. She saw then, beneath the glass counter, a display of fancy frames, some ornately wrought in silvery metal, others lacquered black and delicately painted.

'Are any of those from Salt & Co?'

'Would you like to inspect one of them? I could offer a discount.'

'No. I just want to know the whereabouts of Salt & Co, the japanners.'

'I'm sorry, I don't know. We used to stock a wide range of japanned ware but there's not so much call for it nowadays.'

'Where could I find their directions?'

He shrugged. 'Kelly's Trades Directory perhaps. Was it a particular thing that you wanted from them? Perhaps I have something similar.'

'No. It comes only from Salt.'

the trap

On the way back, the steam tram terminated at the recreation ground and then Cora had to walk. When the pavement ran out, she kept to the hard top of the cart ruts so that her boots would not get spoiled. Once off the main road, the lane was lined with dense hedgerows. Strings of red berries wound through the dark leaves.

Two girls with baskets over their arms were picking fruit that left purple stains on their white pinafores. Nestled between them, a small child, hardly more than a baby, burbled as Cora went by and held out a fat berry in juice-smudged fingers. Cora looked back blankly. She tried not to see the baby's slippery red cheeks or to hear the chatter of the little girls looking after him.

She walked, head down, as quickly as the road surface would allow until a thud of hooves made her pull into a gateway across a stubble field. The pony slowed as it approached and Cora recognised its flattened ears and bad-tempered eye. She put her hand to her brow. Low sunlight outlined the two men sitting close together on the front seat of the trap.

Samuel Shepherd slid her a furtive look as he pulled on the reins. The master, smartly dressed in a dark suit and polka-dot bow tie, tipped his hat.

'Hello there! Can I offer you a ride?'

Cora tried to give a deferential bob of the knee. 'I'll walk, sir. It's not far.'

'No, no. Samuel can make room for you. I shall drive.'

'Sir, I'd rather walk I...'

'No, Cora. I insist.'

The edge in his voice suggested that if she was to return to The Larches at all, it would have to be on the pony trap.

Samuel passed over the reins and made to climb into the back but Mr Jerwood, smiling, shook his head.

'I think we should not over-tax Hector's legs, Samuel.'

Cora puzzled for a moment before realising that the horse had a name.

'Right, sir.'

Samuel climbed down and stood awkwardly, smoothing his hand over the pony's shiny flank. His face had reddened but whether from embarrassment or irritation, Cora couldn't tell. She felt his eyes on her ankles as she clambered on to the swaying seat. The leather was still warm where he had been sitting.

'Trot on!'

Mr Jerwood flapped the reins and the pony trap lurched forward, leaving Samuel standing in the road. From the high seat, Cora could see across the hedge-tops and ploughed fields to the reddish-grey fringe of the town. The whip swished across the pony's conker-brown rump and the trap clipped around the bends. Mr Jerwood sat in the middle of the driving seat and, although Cora tried to keep a gap between them, she could not help her arm brushing against his.

Then, after a minute or two, he pulled up the pony to a walk.

'We should let the animal cool off before we reach home.'

Mr Jerwood put the reins in one hand and straightened his homburg hat with the other. The air fell quiet. Cora had the sense of him preparing to speak and she stiffened at the thought of what he might say.

'You have met my ward, I believe.'

'Sir?'

'My young charge, Violet.'

Cora blinked with surprise. All she could imagine might be coming next was a reprimand for talking to the girl which must be one of those rules that everyone knew about except her. The pony's ears flicked as if it was listening.

'I have seen her, sir.'

'And talked to her?'

Here it was then, the inevitable knuckle-rap.

Cora's grip on the seat tightened. 'It would have been rude not to.'

'What do you think of her?'

'Sir?'

'How did you find her? Was she shy or talkative, polite or rude?'

Cora faltered. 'She is a child.'

'Indeed. But she still has a character of her own. And some might say that the character of a child is more pronounced than that of an adult.'

He turned to look at her briefly but with intent. 'Would you be willing, I wonder, to assist me in a small experiment?'

'Experiment?'

He nodded. 'I would say that I know Violet, but I see only how she behaves towards me. If I am to understand her true character, by which I mean the pattern of traits and reactions which we call "the self", I must see how she reacts to others.'

'To me?'

'Indeed.'

'How, sir?'

'By setting Violet a small dilemma. Nothing dangerous or difficult. But a choice that requires her to reveal something of her nature.'

'How would I do that?'

'By suggesting that Violet break a rule.'

Cora stayed silent. Her instant instinct was to refuse. But if she did, he might turn her out without even a week's paltry wages. Yet the thought of entering a secret pact with the master to deceive Violet made her squirm.

He glanced at her sideways. 'Fear not. I have in mind merely some trifling transgression that would not cast the girl into any real trouble. She might simply fail to confess to a smudge on a newly polished fender, or eat a left-over biscuit from the pantry without asking. Whatever small misdemeanour of your choosing that you think might pose her with a conundrum.'

'Why would she listen to me?'

'She may not. That is also part of the test. I wish merely to gauge how readily she agrees to the suggested mischief when it is put to her by a person of, forgive me, low station who is unlikely to chastise her. With me, Violet always appears to be docile and compliant. My study requires that we see if this remains so with you.'

The pony shook its head, jerking at the traces and Mr Jerwood pulled the slack from the reins. Cora could not bring herself to agree.

'I don't wish to get anyone into trouble.'

'No, no of course not. This is merely an experiment. And so if you were able to engineer an eventuality such as I have described, perhaps you could, for my scientific purposes, time Violet's response.'

'What, sir?'

'Count slowly, as if exposing a photographic plate, from the time of inviting the wrongdoing to the moment of Violet's acquiescence. And note the willingness of her response on a scale of one to ten; one being refusal, ten being eagerness.'

Cora moved her head in a way that might look from his angle like a nod. But if he imagined she'd get mixed up with him in any of that sly nonsense he could stick his photographic plate up his arse.

Half-built walls scarred the mud-churned field that faced The Larches. The pony started again to pull but Mr Jerwood kept a tight hold on the reins.

'So, you understand my request?'

'Yes, sir.'

'And once you have carried out the task, I'd be obliged if you would come to me when I am alone in my laboratory and advise me of the result.'

TEN

1874

a lark

As soon as the littlest Union house inmates could walk, they were kept most of the morning in the airing yard. So Cora and Alice spent every recreation time at the schoolyard railings calling to the infants. The girls found a place where the wrought metal was bent wide enough for Alice to get her arm and shoulder through. She seemed to have a special language of *dickies* and *sleepy-byes* and *din-dins* that the little ones instinctively understood. They crowded round her arm as it protruded through the railings, pushing each other out of the way to feel the soft touch of her fingers.

Sometimes the old female inmates who watched the infants outdoors would raise themselves off the bench and totter towards Cora and Alice at the gap in the fence, clapping their clawed hands and screeching *off with you!*. The little ones reached out and blubbered as the girls went back towards the school room. But they always returned.

To Cora, all of the infants looked the same, but Alice seemed to remember which little boy it was who had fallen over just before she'd stamped on the baby bird. The boy had gingery hair and a habit of scratching at the back of his collar. He made plenty of noise but couldn't say any proper words.

'Hey little laddie. Come here. Cat got your tongue?' Alice called out to him then punched him lightly in the stomach until he smiled. She looked up at Cora. 'We should give him a name. What would you call him if he was yours?'

Cora shrugged. 'I dunno. Percy?'

Alice laughed like a tinkle of broken glass. 'Percy, Percy come and suck on my sticky.'

Cora watched, transfixed, as Alice licked her thumb and then put it, dripping, into Percy's mouth. The boy began to suck hard and stared, unblinking, into Alice's eyes. She reached down with her free fingers and tickled him under the chin but after a while he pushed her thumb away and tottered off in his oversized boots.

Cora watched Alice wipe her wet hand on her pinny.

'What did you do that for?'

'To get him used to me putting something in his mouth.'

'Why?'

Alice rolled her eyes. 'We'll have to shut him up somehow, won't we? So you can do you-know-what to him.'

Cora's stomach did a somersault. She took hold of Alice's arm and marched her away from the small children.

'Listen, we're not doing anything until we've made a plan. And had a practice.'

Alice screwed up her face. 'How can we practice for... that?'

Cora felt like she was standing on tippy-toes on top of a high wall. 'We'll have to test ourselves first to find out if we're brave enough to go through with it.'

'How?'

'By doing something that's bound to get us put in the bleak.'

Alice blinked slowly. 'Get caught on purpose?'

Cora nodded. 'But I'm the one who'll think up how.'

She considered several possible routes into the bleak. They might tear up Lottie Bolger's bedsheet, but that would be too easy and might look like an accident. They could, when they were allowed to stay behind in class to clean the board, empty Mr Bowyer's lacquered ink-stand over his desk. Cora had examined the shiny inkwell each time she was at the blackboard and knew it would be easy to overturn. But the punishment would be severe and it was not easy to see how both Cora and Alice would get equal blame.

On a day when the sun was shining especially bright through the high classroom window, Cora scrutinised the ink-stand from her place by the board. Perhaps they could lift it together, one of their hands on each side of the small pot... then her eyes widened as she saw near the inkwell's base, a maker's stamp: *Salt & Co BIRMm*. She could not wait to tell Alice.

'Is it one of your Da's?'

But Alice seemed unimpressed and just shrugged. 'There's lots of japanners and tin-platers in Birmingham.'

'Called Salt?'

When Alice shrugged again, Cora gave a sharp pull on one of the long tufts of hair sprouting from her scalp. Cora knew she was lying and did not sit next to her at dinner that day. And although by bedtime they were talking once more, the ink-stand was never again mentioned.

In the end, Cora decided on the new hymnals. When piles of the small black books had appeared in chapel, the Chaplain had given the children a very stern talk. The godly paper was frail and must be treated gently, especially when turning a page. Fingers must be as clean as the angels'.

Each Sunday since then Cora had loved to feel the surprising weight of the leather-bound book in her hand. The pages made a satisfying squeak as she bent them back and forth.

'While we're singing, we'll tear one up,' Cora declared.

Alice stared at her for a moment. 'But they'll see us.'

'That's the whole point, isn't it? We'll find out how bad we really are. But if we inflict exactly the same amount of damage, they'll give us the same punishment.'

As it turned out though, despite their crimes being identical, Cora was treated worse. The Chaplain's face turned puce beneath his whiskers when he noticed the confetti of printed words around the girls' feet. Lottie Bolger smirked as Cora and Alice were hauled out of the line and marched to the superintendent's office.

'But why did you do it?'

The superintendent's expression above his clean white collar and knotted tie was puzzled. He was a youngish man with children of his own and he seemed more curious than annoyed.

Cora bit her lip to kill a grin. 'It was just for a lark, sir.'

She felt the warmth of Alice standing next to her but didn't dare look. A snigger was already simmering and if their eyes met, she knew that they would both dissolve into hiccupping, bladder-loosening hilarity.

The superintendent shook his head. 'My goodness, Cora Burns, you have been here long enough to know better. You will spend the daylight hours of next week alone in the refractory cell and endure a potato diet for the rest of this month.'

Alice seemed to get away without any time at all in the bleak. And potatoes were her favourite so she didn't mind the short rations. Perhaps the superintendent thought that Cora must have led Alice astray. There was no point Cora trying to tell him that it was the other way round.

That stretch in the bleak gave Cora time to think about the plan. The first thing she'd do was accidentally drop a dinner bowl in the dining hall and stamp on it to make sure that it smashed. She'd pick out a good big fragment with a sharp edge and hide it between her skirt and her petticoat. Then, maybe the next day, she and Alice would get Percy through the railings while no one was watching. What would happen next was not so clear, but that was the point of the dare; it would tell her how brave she really was, and how bad. She did not like to admit even to herself about the place of sharp china in her plan except that she could not now rid from her mind an image of two letters, *A* and *C,* entwined together and glistening red against a background of soft white skin.

ELEVEN

October 1885

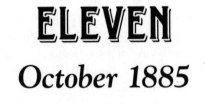

reflection

Cora had imagined the morning room to be a place draped with black crêpe, the curtains permanently closed but as she opened the door from the entrance hall and squinted against the brightness, she realised her mistake. A high bay window, looped with muslin curtains, flooded the room with sunlight. The comfortable-looking armchairs were covered in pale flowery print as faded and old-fashioned as Cora's frock.

Cora was not surprised to see Violet bent over the writing table beside the curved window. She'd seen the girl enter the room just before Susan Gill thrust a bowl full of dirty brushes into Cora's hands and told her to go in there too. There was something guarded in Susan Gill's eye as she gave out her instructions for black-leading the grate but Cora took this as another sign of the housemaid's condescension.

Cora put the enamel bowl of brushes on the hearth and unscrewed a glass jar. A heady waft of turpentine leaked into the room. Violet, with the end of her plait pressed between her lips, looked up from the spread of white paper. Then she jumped off the chair.

'Oh, Cora! I thought you were Susan.'

'Good day, miss.'

'I'm so glad it's you. I'd thought there mayn't be time before I go.'

'Time?'

'To make my sketch of your friend.'

Cora put the turpentine jar back into the bowl. A stick of leading left a black smudge on her fingers.

'Oh, you must forget about that, miss. It might get you into trouble.'

'No it wouldn't! I am meant to do my drawing practice this morning anyway. I have my charcoals here. Sir won't mind if I do portraiture instead of still life. Please Cora, let me try.'

She kneeled down beside Cora, their skirts touching. The girl's widened pleading eyes and soft white skin caught at something in Cora's gut.

'All right. If it's quick.'

'Yes, I promise. Here, come and sit by me.'

Violet pulled another chair to the narrow table and Cora perched on the edge of the cushioned seat. Clearing the loose sheets, Violet pulled forward a large wire-bound pad with plywood covers and turned to an empty page.

'First, the outline. What was the shape of her face?'

'It's hard to say.'

'Was it a round face, or square? Or something in-between; an oval, like yours?

'An oval, yes.'

Picking a spindly black stick from a metal tray, Violet sketched two curving lines on the blank paper.

'And her eyes, were they like yours too?'

'It has been a long time.'

'Think back.'

Cora seemed to feel the chair spin beneath her. 'She looked a little like you, I suppose.'

'But she is a grown-up now, like you?'

'Yes. Just like me.' Cora's voice thickened. 'She was my sister.'

'Your sister? Oh Cora, you should have said. It makes everything so much easier.' Picking up the sketch pad and the stick, Violet bounded to a walnut sideboard in the window alcove. 'Come over here.'

Cora had to lean down to see Violet's reflection in the wide mirror. The sight of her own face next to it stopped her heart. She had seen herself only in shop windows or public bars. The looking glass at the asylum was a grainy thing that had never revealed, as this one did, the creaminess of her skin or auburn tint in her dark hair. But it was her own eyes that astounded Cora. They were so full of pigments; dove-grey flecked with hazel and lilac, that she could not put a name to their true colour.

Violet picked up the charcoal stick and addressed Cora's reflection. 'I shall draw our two faces into one; the girl and the grown-up.'

She glanced from Cora back to herself and then to the stick on the page. Lightly, then with more definition, she sketched curving lines across the paper. The tip of her tongue slipped out of the corner of her mouth as shapes began to emerge; a clear outline of the cheek and chin, deft shading around the eyes and lips. The drawing was done with a child's boldness but was recognisable as a real person. The face was not quite Cora and not quite Violet; neither a girl nor a woman. Was it Alice? Cora couldn't say.

'You draw well, miss.'

'Do you think so? Could this be her?'

'Maybe.'

'What was her name?'

Violet was bent over the paper, smudging the shadows with a fingertip. She looked up when Cora didn't reply.

'Alice Salt.'

'But your name is Burns, isn't it?'

'She was boarded out to the Salt family and took their name.'

A look of pain shot across Violet's eyes. 'I will help you find her, I promise. We'll write this minute to the *Gazette*.'

'No.'

'Why not?'

'I… I don't have any money.'

'It's only threepence a line.'

'Even so…'

Violet's eyes roamed the ceiling for ideas. 'We could ask if they would print it for free because I am a child with no funds of my own but seeking a long-lost sister who was last seen… where was she last seen?'

'In the Birmingham Poor Law Union Workhouse. Eleven years ago.'

Violet bounced on her toes. 'A sister last seen in the poor house? How could they refuse? I will look in the *Gazette* for the directions of their office.'

'Do you have an envelope? And a stamp?'

'Oh, I don't.' Violet looked suddenly crestfallen. She tore the sketch from the pad and held it up, her chin quivering. 'And it seems such a good likeness.'

But Cora's gaze had dropped to the new top sheet of the sketch pad. 'What's this other drawing?'

'My still lifes. The medallion collection.'

Cora leaned closer. 'Can I see?'

'Do you like it? This is my favourite medallion, with the rabbit.'

Violet pointed to the sketched roundel on the page. 'And I like the boat. But not the mechanical equipment.'

'Are these the coins that are in the box in the library?'

Violet nodded.

'What are they?'

'Mr Jerwood's annual medallions. He has designed one for each year of his married life. See, this shows the boat he sailed along the Bosphorus and the year: 1875.'

'The year? Where does it say that?'

'Here at the bottom, of course. In Roman numerals.'

Violet pointed to the jumble of charcoal letters: *M, C, X…* copied with a slight slant around the curve of the coin's circle. Roman numbers. Cora had never heard of such a thing.

'What year is this one? With the rabbit?'

Violet's lips moved silently as she counted on her fingers. '1881.'

'And why a rabbit?'

'Some experiment he was pleased with that year. It involved rabbits.'

'And what are the words around the edge?'

'I don't know what they mean but I copied the letters exactly. It is Latin.'

Cora stared at the neat pencil drawings. Perhaps *IMAGINEM SALT* had a Latin meaning too.

'And Mr Jerwood had these medallions made for himself? You can't buy them from a shop?'

'Oh no, they mark something special that he did himself.'

'Which foundry made them?'

Violet giggled. 'How should I know?'

Cora took a step back and checked in the mirror that her expression appeared blank. But her heart was racing. Mr Jerwood's medals looked so similar to the half-moon of metal around her neck that they must, surely, have all been made by Salt & Co. Perhaps the master would be able to direct Cora to the foundry. Cora promised herself that she'd somehow find the courage to show him her half-medal and ask. She just needed to find a reason to converse with him in private.

Then Violet lifted up the charcoal portrait and turned to Cora. 'Shall I keep this safe until you get the money for a postage stamp and an envelope?'

Cora put her head on one side and her mouth into a smile. 'Can you not help me a little more? Mr Jerwood must have lots of writing things. Would he even miss just one envelope and one stamp?'

'But they are in a drawer in his study. And he keeps it locked.'

'Susan Gill has a key. Perhaps, you could test how brave you are by asking her to let you in and say it's on the master's instructions.'

'And then steal an envelope and a postage stamp?'

'It isn't really stealing, is it? It's just using an everyday item from the house where you live. Otherwise, you would be stealing the lead from your pencil every time you wrote, or the paper from the hook whenever you used the lavatory.'

For a moment Violet's face was serious. She pushed herself on to the tips of her toes. Cora began to count. Then Violet's heels dipped down and she burst out laughing, holding her stomach as she giggled.

'You are so funny, Cora. And I suppose you're right.'

'I am.'

With a mischievous grin, Violet set off at a skip out of the morning room.

Cora stared at the charcoal face on the table, hardly able to breathe. Alice seemed suddenly closer than she had been in a dozen years. Cora needed only to ask Thomas Jerwood for the missing piece and the puzzle of her half-medal would be solved. Perhaps the master would be glad to assist, because Cora could also convey to him, quite truthfully, the result of the experiment on Violet.

*Eagerness to do wrong on a scale of one to ten – **seven and a half**. Time – **five seconds**.*

feathers

With the copper unlit, the scullery air was jagged with cold. Early morning fog beaded the spider's web on the outside of the pane. At the sink, Ellen was ripping downy feathers from a white-eyed bird but she kept looking up, flushed and restless, through the misted glass to the curve of the drive beyond.

Cora rose, irritated, from the low stool in the corner where she was knifing mud from boots.

'I thought I was meant to be cleaning those birds.'

'You don't know how.'

'How can I learn unless you show me?'

Ellen shrugged. 'All right.'

She moved aside so that they could both stand on the raised wooden duckboard at the sink. Even with its feathers, the pigeon in Cora's hand was solid and heavy; more like meat than a living thing.

'Just get a good grip on a few feathers at a time and pull quick, like, but don't yank at it or you'll rip the skin.'

Cora began to pick at the grey feathers but even the softest were reluctant to pop out of the bird's flesh. The exposed skin was spotted with blood.

'Is this right?'

Ellen was looking out of the window. 'Take care with the pheasant. It's been in the larder a few days. And keep the head nice. Master likes to see plumage on the table.'

'Like this?'

'What?'

'Why do you keep looking outside, Ellen? For Samuel?'

'No!'

'Why then?'

'My brother may call.'

'Oh.'

'Look! That's him now.'

Ellen's hand flew to the strings at her waist. She bundled off her apron and ran out of the door making a draught that floated wispy feathers on to the sink's wet grime.

A stocky man in a brown bowler hat and corduroy jacket was crunching toward the house. In his arms was a baby about a year old with corn-coloured curls. Their voices moved inside; the baby's grizzle, Ellen bleating something about a bonnet and a deep laugh that must be her brother. Then, over a shuffle of boots, Samuel's voice was at the back door too. Cora's insides tugged. She hadn't seen him since the ride on the pony trap and hadn't spoken to him since the tack room. She'd keep away.

A mound of blood-tipped feathers covered the half-stripped creature in the sink. The eyes were tight closed and the beak slightly open. Cora jabbed at the wing and it moved as if still alive but the skin was purplish and loose. It tore in two places as Cora pulled on a feather. She folded the bird belly-side down on the tray to cover her mistake.

The big rust-coloured game bird gave off a musty smell as she lifted it into the sink, the head drooping forlornly to one side. The long tail-feather cut into her hand but Cora kept pulling it and pressing down on the body until something seemed to crack and squash inside. She looked closer, and inside the soft nest of down was a writhing knot of maggots. With a gulp of air, she let the pheasant drop into the sink. Then, grabbing the tray of naked headless birds, she fled from the scullery.

In the kitchen, everyone was crowded into the warmth belching from the range. Ellen's brother stood to one side with a teacup in his hand while Ellen bounced the wary-eyed baby on her hip. No one looked round as Cora came in. Not even Samuel.

Timothy, sitting on the Windsor chair in his stocking feet, chewed his pipe as he spoke.

'Still on the railways then?'

Ellen's brother took a slow sip from his cup and shook his head. 'I had a much better offer from Mr Dawson, the brick merchant. He supplies all the builders round here. Said I was the best man for the job by a mile. I'm the only one he trusts to come and see the foreman at the site across the way. So I thought I'd bring young William along for a ride on the wagon.'

Ellen bounced the baby more vigorously. 'Aww! Did he like it? Did he like the gee-gees?'

The baby's bottom lip stuck out above the shiny dribble across his chin. Ellen swung him towards Samuel.

'Say hello to Samuel, he took your da's place in the stableyard. Perhaps he'll take us to see the pony.'

Samuel flicked his cap on to his head and pulled the brim low. 'I wouldn't get too close to that pony till he's had his mash. You best stay here where it's warm.'

For a second, as they watched Samuel leave, Ellen's face and the baby's appeared identical; the same golden curls and china-blue eyes, the same expression of dismay. The baby looked around the room and caught Cora's eye, then burst into a wail of tears.

Everyone around the kitchener joined into a general cooing and ahh-ing as Ellen bounced William into quietness. Cora left the tray of waxy game birds on a corner of the table and slipped out of the room. In the scullery, she took a long breath and lifted the pheasant up by two fingers around its neck then dropped it on to the board.

Her heart was ablaze. How did she not recall anything about her own child's hair? She had only seen him in darkness but should still have been left with some recollection of what he'd looked like; whether his hair had been thick or thin, black or fair. Perhaps she had not even bothered to look.

The cloying air rising from dead game again threatened to choke her. Taking care to avoid the creeping maggots, Cora scooped the loose feathers into a bucket and went outside. A white sun pressed through the fog. Cold air bit her throat. Something about the scene in the kitchen had made her feel desolate but whether it was the closeness of the family resemblances or the accusing look in that baby's eye, she couldn't say.

Cora went towards the midden, wet grass darkening the hem of her skirt. At the edge of the smoulder she stopped and looked into the bucket, uncertain if this was the right way to get rid of the waste. The feathers might simply fly off and cover the cold frames with their mess.

'Not one for babbies either?'

Samuel was leaning against the wall, an orange-tipped cigarette in his hand.

Cora kept her voice steady. 'Do you have any use for these feathers?'

He came over and put his hand on the bucket tipping it forward to look inside. Cigarette smoke rose between them. The tobacco had a harsh, tarry edge and she caught herself holding a breathful of it in her lungs, waiting for its heat to loosen her veins.

The bucket handle rattled as Samuel let it go. 'Aye. Don't throw them out. I'll use 'em to bulk up the muck in the mushroom shed.'

Each bristle around his mouth had a different shade of gold.

'Thank you for the loan of that sixpence.'

'Did you find who you was looking for?'

'No.'

'Can't say I'm sorry.'

'I told you, I'm not looking for a sweetheart.'

'Then maybe you'll come to town wi' me Sunday next?'

'Like I said...'

'Well, we could just have a few laughs, a few drinks.'

'You know I've got no money.'

She wouldn't be giving him any of the coin from Thripp. That would only raise suspicion about how she'd got it.

Samuel smiled and patted his jacket with the hand still holding the cigarette. 'Don't worry about that. It's payday for the rest of us, isn't it? That's why Billy Beamish came over bright and early, and grinning like an organ grinder's monkey once he'd got all Ellen's wages.'

'Ellen wouldn't speak to me if I went out with you.'

'Well then, we won't tell her. We'll wait till she's set off for Yardley, then go to Moore's Oyster Rooms on New Street. All on me.'

His voice quietened as he spoke and his eyes did not leave hers. Cora hardly breathed. Might he, right here in the open, put his arm around her back and press his mouth to hers? If he did, she'd not push him away.

She took a sharp breath of manure-laced air. 'When I see some wages, I'll pay you back.'

'You'll come then? On Sunday?'

'I didn't say that.'

Samuel took a long drag on the cigarette before throwing it on to the midden. Then he stretched out his hand, work-hardened and steady, as if to shake Cora's and seal their pact for a Sunday outing. But instead he took hold of the pail.

'Here. Let me take them feathers out of your way.'

a matching pair

Only Cook was still in the kitchen, holding a blue and white dinner plate up to the light.

She nodded as Cora back came in. 'Better.'

'I put some bran in the cold rinse bowl like you said.'

'Good.'

Then Cook picked up the box of cutlery that Cora had brought in from the scullery and put it on to the dresser. She did not pull out the knives to scrutinise their shine and Cora took this as a compliment.

'Are those birds done?'

Cora nodded. 'Except I couldn't rightly manage the pheasant.'

'I'd best do that one. You can make a start on scouring the pantry shelves. But first, take up this tray.'

The bone-handled knife and fork was already laid on the lace cloth. Cora's chest tightened.

'Can someone else take it?'

'Why?'

'I don't think the missus likes me.'

'She doesn't like anyone.'

'But she shouted at me last time I went up and got herself into a tizzy.'

'Don't take any notice, Cora. You can see she's not right in the head. Just leave the tray outside and come back down.'

Cora opened her mouth to protest, to tell Cook that there was more to it than that; the missus thought Cora was someone else, someone who she knew well and hated. But saying it was likely to make her seem as mad as the missus.

'Yes, Cook.'

At the top of the back stairs, Cora stood for a second and listened. From the kitchen, where Cook was sieving soup, came the faint back and forth of a wooden spoon against a tammy cloth. The long-case clock by the front door ticked. She took a breath and went to the bedroom. An odour of mutton fat wafted up as she put the tray down.

'Tray!'

She jumped aside and flattened herself against the wall before the door clicked open and Mrs Dix's arms came out. The tray disappeared, but just before the door closed a peculiar screeching writhed through the gap. Cora let go her breath but flinched. From across the landing, behind the laboratory door, came a loud rattle, hollow and metallic, like the locking of a cage.

The master must be in his laboratory. Perhaps Cora should take her chance to tell him about the experiment on Violet and, if she could drum up the nerve, unbutton her bodice, pull out the half-medal and ask if he knew the whereabouts of the smithy that had made it.

Cora listened for a moment then crossed the landing and knocked lightly on the laboratory door. It opened almost instantly.

For a second, a look of horror flashed across the master's features but woven through it was a mix of other sentiments: sadness, recognition, and perhaps, joy. Then, before Cora was sure whether she had seen it at all, the expression was gone.

'Yes?'

'Sir, I did what you asked. With Violet.'

'The moral test? Ah yes, come in then and tell me the result.'

He closed the door. Cora put her back to the shelves lined with specimen jars so that she would not have to look at the dead things inside them. On the floor by the big window, two straw-scattered cages held a pair of rabbits. They sat, noses twitching, staring at the wall. Both were pure white except for the black tip of a left ear and a right foot. They seemed, in fact, to be entirely identical, except that one had a fresh bloodstain on its back.

'Very good, then. Tell me.'

'She wanted to send a letter and I said she should get an envelope and a postage stamp from your study.'

'Which was locked?'

Cora nodded.

'And she agreed?'

'Yes.'

'How readily?'

'Within five seconds.'

'And her score for eagerness?'

'I would say seven and a half.'

Mr Jerwood opened a marbled notebook on the workbench and wrote in it with a silver pencil. His shirtsleeves were rolled up and lightly spotted with blood. He tapped the pencil against his brow.

'And how did she accomplish this mischief?'

'By lying to Susan Gill so that she would open the room.'

'Lying and stealing? Excellent.'

He smiled and nodded. She wondered if he was about to ask her how she had fixed on this task or where the letter was now, but he turned back to write in the notebook and said nothing.

Cora's eyes went to the shelf above his head and the pasteboard box labelled *Composites 1884 –*. If the master would only leave the room for minute she could open the lid, pluck out her own prison likeness and, as soon as she was able, feed it into the flames under the wash-house copper.

Mr Jerwood turned and Cora, too late, dropped her gaze.

'You are interested in photography?'

'I… I don't know, sir.'

'Or at least interested in your own likeness? I would be happy to take another, in more becoming attire, if you'd care to sit for me.'

'I…'

'And I would let you have a print to keep.'

'I don't want one, sir, thank you.'

'Really? You would not then have to spend money in a photographer's shop.'

She froze. He must somehow know that she'd gone to Mr Thripp's. Perhaps he'd seen her face against the window backcloth. He was, after all, a customer. With a thump in her chest she realised what a witless mistake it had been to put herself on display like that.

Mr Jerwood smiled. 'You could send your likeness as a keepsake to a relative.'

It seemed more like an instruction than an invitation. Cora did not know quite how to arrange her face as she replied.

'I have no family, sir.'

'Ah yes. Your mother left you to the Board of Guardians.'

'Yes.'

'And you know nothing of her except the name she gave which was Mary Burns.'

'That's right, sir.'

Cora's unease tightened.

'Do you imagine that you look anything like her?'

His eyes were examining her face so intently, that Cora had the sudden impression that he already knew the answer to his question.

'Sir, I know nothing…'

At that moment, a volley of hard knocks struck the door. Cora flinched but Mr Jerwood merely shook his head in irritation as he went to open it.

'Mrs Dix, I thought I'd…'

'I must have a word, sir.'

The faintly foreign accent in Mrs Dix's voice strengthened.

'Is Mrs Jerwood unattended?'

'Almost asleep, sir.'

Mrs Dix threw Cora an anguished glance.

Mr Jerwood sighed, his head still shaking. 'Very well, Cora, that will be all.'

Cora gave a bend of the knee. Mrs Dix stepped inside the laboratory as Cora left. As soon as the door closed, the low juddering sound that came from behind it could only have been a woman collapsing in tears.

Cora stood on the landing, frustration boiling in her chest. She'd missed her chance to ask him who'd made the medallions. The half-medal seemed to burn against her skin like a tally iron.

Across the landing, the door to the mistress's bedroom was slightly ajar and as Cora looked, the gap seemed to widen. A pale nightdress shimmered at the opening, and then a glistening eye. The voice behind it was no more than a hiss, but in the heavy stillness of the air Cora heard each word that was spat in her direction.

'I know it's you there, Annie. You harlot. You murderess!'

TWELVE

THE
WYVERN
QUARTERLY

AUTUMN

1885

PRINTED BY
CORNISH BROS,
37 NEW ST, BIRMINGHAM

FROM: Thomas Jerwood Esq.
An Essay on Experiments in Human Nature

Following my latest contribution to this journal (viz. **An Essay on Character, Crime and Composite Photography** *WQ* Summer 1885), I have received letters from several Midlands men of (amateur) science enthused by my suggestion for the study of human character through clandestine observation. Could this technique be applied to any human subject, they ask, not just the criminal? Happily, I can confirm to interested readers that the notion of experimentation upon humans in everyday settings does indeed provide a powerful and, as yet, largely unused tool for study of the human condition.

Few others have entered this new field of endeavour, and so I myself have devised a means for the investigation of character by way of the *moral test*. This test may comprise nothing more than an ordinary incident in an individual's life but one which is apt to make him betray his essential temperament. Through the observation of his choices, a lone experimenter, or better yet, two acting as secret accomplices, can collect abundant statistics of human conduct and character.

The simplest explanation may be to describe a particular *moral test* which I have used, namely one designed to measure *forbearance of gratification* amongst children. Particular cunning is required in the observance of the young and I have learnt that experiments are most revealing when the method they employ is simple yet enjoyable. In this one, the experimenter must befriend a child to the extent that they might, quite naturally, play together an artless game (such as noughts and crosses). The child should be allowed to win, and when he does, a prize will be offered: <u>one</u> boiled sweet now, or <u>three</u> boiled sweets if the child can wait until the following day to collect his reward.

The strength of character required to forego an aniseed drop or a sherbet lemon, in the faint hope of acquiring two more at a future time, is not inconsiderable, and the decision reveals a great deal not only about the individual child but also about society in general.

Are children of the lower orders more likely to succumb to the lure of an instant but inferior prize? Are girls more likely to do so than boys? Common sense may decree that the obvious answer to both questions is 'yes'. How many poor families are reduced to eating scraps by Thursday because the weekly earnings were spent in the public house on Saturday? And no young lady of my acquaintance has ever foregone a frivolous summer bonnet in favour of a warm winter cloak.

Social assumptions such as these can be *proven*, however, only by the results of scientifically validated experiments. Unfortunately, my own opportunities for exploring forbearance of gratification by application of a moral test have been too limited to be conclusive. I nevertheless have hope of one day directing a large investigation (perhaps in conjunction with the municipal School Boards) using multiple tests and consistent statistical reckoning. I have no doubt that such an endeavour would harvest irrefutable proofs.

My interest in character is, however, deeper than mere comparison between the classes and the sexes. What is it that makes each person unique, regardless of who they are? Character traits and behaviours can vary enormously even amongst siblings of the same family. Is this the result of some as yet unexplained variation in the transmission of *heredity*? Or do the subtle differences in childhood *experience* have a magnified influence upon character?

The man of science is often asked to pronounce upon these slippery theories. I have, therefore, expended much mental energy in the creation of scientific methods to test hypotheses of human behaviour. A perceptive reader of this journal might have already deduced that the supreme demonstration in this field of science would be a *living experiment*, conducted by subjecting one or more human specimens to a full range of moral tests and measurements throughout their life.

Furthermore, the experiment could be extended by experimental attempts to *induce* particular character traits within the 'captive' individual. A long and arduous experiment of this sort would be, believe me, full of hidden risk. Anyone who embarks on such an enterprise will have to steel himself for the many unforeseen difficulties which will present themselves along the way.

By way of illustration, I shall provide just one example. Many years ago, a young friend of mine became obsessed with these same questions of the varying effects of *heredity* versus *upbringing* upon the individual. In a flush of youthful optimism, he adhered to the strong belief that education was the primary sculptor of character. Therefore, he reasoned, in selecting a wife, he need not be overly concerned with her intellect or temperament. Once married, his educative endeavours would be sufficient to mould the young lady's personality into one entirely compatible with his own. Regrettably, despite increasingly pressing exertions over a number of years, his efforts to turn a dull person into a more interesting one failed. Yet still our young friend would not give up his belief in the power of *nurture*. Frustration or perhaps arrogance inclined him to believe that a determined man of science might overcome the influences of the rest of the world and shape a young human to his own design. He became inclined to think that people, especially females, from the bottom of society would provide more malleable matter upon which he might work his own design. He was convinced that he could make a lowly soul into one more refined. Thus, he told himself, would the ascendancy of *nurture* over *nature* be proven.

Sadly, our young friend's second human experiment ended even less happily than his first, and so his scientific outlook began to change. This young scientist's difficulties helped to shape my own belief in the *ascendancy of heredity* and thus, in the primacy of *nature* over *nurture*. His failures planted the seed for my highly successful laboratory work using the transfusing of blood between rabbits to discredit the notion of the *heritability of acquired traits* in animals. More importantly, it was my young friend's travails that laid the foundations for my work on human nature and the invention of the *moral test*. The results of <u>my</u> experiments, though complex and sometimes contradictory, are steadily formulating a new branch of science that deals with the *statistical measurement of character*. From this pioneering discipline will arise, in the fullness of time, an overarching *theory of human nature*. I have no doubt that this *human science* will lay bare the roots of man's behaviour as surely as mathematics reveals the cosmic truths of the universe.

Thomas Jerwood Esq.
Spark Hill, Warks.

THIRTEEN

November 1885

a model

Workmen laying pipes had left a mound of soil and rubble in the middle of Corporation Street. As Cora crossed the road, she considered stooping to pick up a smooth cobble and then lobbing it through Mr Thripp's window. That way, if her likeness was behind the glass, she could whip it out. If it wasn't, she'd have paid back the younger Mr Thripp for being as dishonest as his father.

But on the corner, a constable was rocking back and forth on his heels and rubbing his hands beneath his cape. So Cora walked onwards to the shop window and there, on the velvet backcloth, was her face. It was hard, though, to think of the person behind that flat grey stare as herself. Perhaps just the breathing of country air was making her into someone else.

The sign on the door said *CLOSED* but the handle yielded under her hand. A bell tinkled as she entered the paraffin-warmth of the shop. Alfred Thripp looked down from a short stepladder that allowed him to reach the top shelves behind the counter.

'Miss Burns.'

He climbed down and pulled back his oatmeal jacket putting both thumbs in the little pockets of his waistcoat. The self-satisfied smile gave him the look of his father.

'Did you see the print? I hope its position in our display meets with your approval.'

'I want you to take it out.'

His hands dropped to his sides. 'Would you rather it was mounted in a frame, or placed further to the front?'

'No. I don't want it on display at all.'

'But I have made special provisions. Let me show you.' He pulled back the curtain and reached into the window display, then laid Cora's likeness on the glass counter. 'It is a fine image. Several customers have commented. Don't you like it?'

'Not much.'

'Why?'

'I look hard as a steel pin.'

She realised as she spoke that she must look like that now.

But Alfred smiled. 'Steel can be beautiful.' He coloured slightly and reached below the counter to pull out a hard-bound notebook. 'You have not yet found your sister?'

'No.'

'Well then, why not leave your portrait on display? It can do no harm. Look, I wrote down your particulars in our day-book.'

He opened it for her to see. The ruled lines were covered in a precise shrunken hand. Standing apart from the dates and messages was an entry in red; *Window display bottom right – details of any person enquiring regarding the identity of the sitter to be noted and kept for Miss C Burns c/o The Larches, Spark Hill.* A stretch of the page below was ruled off, presumably to record the details of anyone who might enquire. But the space was blank.

Cora shook her head slowly. 'I don't wish my employer to see my face in your window. And I have found another way to look for my sister.'

'I see. Would you care to keep the portrait then? Without charge.'

'Not looking like that.'

'I cannot agree with your opinion of yourself. In fact, I have you in mind as a model.'

'What do you mean?'

'To sit for some private shots, including stereographic images like those I showed you last week. It's a commercial venture on behalf of a friend.'

Cora took a step away from the counter. One of those filthy pictures, he must mean. Like father, like son.

'Well, you can wash that idea out of your dirty mind with soap.'

The colour bleached from Alfred's face. 'No, no, you misunderstand me. Nothing like that, I promise.'

Cora reached for the door handle but Alfred jumped around the counter and put a hand on her arm.

'Please, Miss Burns, you must believe me. This is an entirely respectable venture for an engineering works at Coventry. They have made a breakthrough which will change the world and they have asked me to help them tell the world about it.'

'What's that to me?'

Cora wondered why she had not already shaken her arm free.

'Please, Miss Burns, if you have time, allow me to show you the invention.'

'In here?'

'Not far off. My Coventry friend will pay handsomely for photographic assistance. If you would agree to pose, I can give you at least a guinea for an hour or two of your time.'

Her eyes narrowed. A guinea. That made it sound even more likely to be something obscene, especially if he was wanting to take her to an out-of-the-way place. Alfred flushed as he finally took his hand from her arm. His eyes were level with hers. Cora had no doubt that if there was any funny business she would easily fight him off.

'All right.'

He pushed the portrait of Cora into a drawer, grabbed his hat from a shelf and locked the shop door behind them. Feathers bobbed on his Tyrolean hat as they walked into the swirling air. The traffic was sparse but when they crossed towards Union Street, he put his arm out behind her as a shield against a trotting cab. Cora imagined Samuel in town with her and felt a twinge of guilt. Before she'd set off from The Larches, she'd made sure that he was busy in the stableyard and wouldn't see her hurrying down the drive. It didn't seem likely that Samuel would go alone to the Oyster Rooms but she couldn't help scanning the scattered figures along the street for his broad outline.

'Did you have an easy journey from Spark Hill?'

'I came on the steam tram.'

'Ah yes. There's a new stop not far from Mr Jerwood's.'

'Do you know his house?'

'I have been once, to deliver his Dallmeyer. A top-notch device.'

Cora thought of the polished brass bindings and shiny dark wood on Mr Jerwood's camera. She slid a look sideways at Alfred.

'What is a composite?'

'A *com*posite photograph, do you mean?'

She'd said it wrong and now wished she hadn't said it at all.

'Interesting that you have heard of it. I'd say it's an excessively fiddly process for blending many likenesses into one. I've heard exaggerated claims for the possibilities of the technique but can't see that it's anything more than a fad myself.'

'What sort of possibilities?'

'Oh, I don't know. Like discovering a person's true racial origins, or pinpointing a criminal. A lot of tosh, I'd say.'

Cora felt a flutter of understanding, and then unease.

Alfred's eyes widened. 'Is that Jerwood's line? Composites? Oh dear. Don't tell him what I said about them, will you?'

'As if!'

Cora laughed then Alfred caught her eye and laughed too. A sour-sweet memory of Jimmy flashed across her mind but she blinked it away.

Alfred's hand touched the small of her back. 'Oops. Nearly missed our turning.'

They entered a covered brick passageway and then a yard, open to the sky, that backed on to a hotel. With a key, Alfred opened a lean-to outhouse that was stacked with stepladders, buckets and porters' trolleys. The air smelled of paint and ash. Alfred took hold of a protective sheet and whipped it into the air.

'Here it is.'

Cora shrugged. 'A bicycle?'

'No, *the* Rover Safety Bicycle! Believe me, this is the future of travel. It has covered a hundred miles in just seven hours!'

The bicycle certainly looked different to an ordinary high-wheeler. Both wheels were the same size and the seat was low enough for a cyclist to keep his feet comfortably on the ground whilst sitting down. The pedals were connected not to the front wheel but to a cogged chain at the rear.

Alfred rubbed a white hand across his sandy beard. 'My friend at the factory thinks that ladies should be able to ride this type of bicycle almost as easily as men. That, of course, doubles his potential for sales. So he wishes to circulate far and wide pictures of ladies using the bicycle. Stereoscopic images as well as hand-drawn advertisements.'

'You want me to ride it?'

Alfred's eyes gleamed. 'I could photograph you just sitting on it. But if I could get a shot of you in motion it would be, well, it would be an absolute first. Here, come and sit on the saddle.'

'All right.'

Cora couldn't see how there'd be any harm in it but as she took hold of the handles and lifted her leg awkwardly across the bar, her skirt became stuck above her knees. Dragging it down, she managed to sit on the moulded seat whilst balancing on the toecaps of her boots. The complicated frame and rubber wheels beneath her seemed to fidget with the possibility of speed.

'I'll never be able to ride it.'

'Whyever not? I managed all right. It just takes a bit of determination, and I think I can safely say, from what I've already seen of you, that grit is not something you're short of.'

another half

Cora whacked harder with the plaited cane and puffs of dirt billowed from the carpet on to wilted wet grass. She stopped to rub the ache at the back of her neck and looked at the house. Her place here was not bad; better in fact than most she could imagine. The master's attention was unnerving but did not seem malicious and the missus's behaviour no more queer than what had come to seem normal at the asylum. The air was more wholesome and the food more plentiful than she'd ever known. It wouldn't do to lose this position. And as long as the other servants didn't find out where she'd come from, she'd stick with it for as long as she could.

Cora dragged the carpet from the line and dug her knuckles into the stiff woollen tufts as she rolled it up. In the front hall, she stood for a moment with the carpet roll on her shoulder and listened at the dining room door before knocking. There was no response but as Cora heaved the carpet to the hearth, Violet looked up from the table, startled. She was wearing the green day dress; her hair woven as usual into a plait. Cora started to smile, but the girl jerked her head back down to the sketchbook. A stick of charcoal lay beside it and in front of her, on the tablecloth, four dull brown apples were piled into a pyramid. The page was blank.

The breakfast things had been cleared away but the dining room air was still stewed with bacon fat. As she unrolled the carpet by the fireplace, Cora could see Violet's profile, pale and motionless against the dark wallpaper. Cora kept her voice low enough not to be heard in the hall.

'Do you still have the sketch of Alice?'

Violet was silent.

'You know, for the *Birmingham Gazette*? Because I'm not sure now that it would be right to send it.' She dropped to a whisper. 'I don't think it's worth us getting into trouble over. Violet? Do you see?'

For a short moment, the girl turned to her blank-eyed, then looked down at the charcoal. Cora gave a start. That brief look had been enough. Violet's left eye was its normal blue, but the other eye was completely black. Cora darted a sideways look to check but there was no question. Violet's eyes had become mismatched.

'Are you unwell, Violet? Shall I fetch Mrs Dix?'

The girl shook her head.

'Are you sure?'

'Aye.'

Aye? She'd not heard Violet use that word before. And in her voice was the guttural undertone of the town.

Cora straightened the carpet, wiped her hands on her apron and went to the door. Violet remained staring, not at her drawing nor the pile of apples, but at a tray of condiments on the sideboard. Cora's hand stiffened with an urge to give Violet's cheek a hard slap.

Anger still pulsed as Cora climbed the back stairs. Violet had not only ignored her, she'd seemed to mock Cora by imitating her way of speaking. Rage simmered as Cora wondered whether her previous opinion of Violet had been entirely wrong. The girl had never before seemed haughty or spiteful but perhaps that was a clever act. Violet's true nature might be not just mischievous but wicked. But Cora remembered the blackness in her eye and was suddenly unsure. Could Violet be ill? Perhaps she'd suffered a fall or a blow to the head and no one had realised.

Cora knelt to the landing floor and folded back the faded woven runner. The floorboards beneath it were much darker than the surrounding wood. Behind the laboratory door, glass clinked. The master was in there, doing something peculiar no doubt, like measuring a rabbit's ear or making a cabinet portrait of some hag in prison stripes. Perhaps this was Cora's chance. If she knocked on the door and explained her concern about Violet looking poorly, she might at the same time show Mr Jerwood her half-medal and ask about his connection to Salt & Co.

From the other side of the main stairs came an abrupt shout, high-pitched and agitated. Cora almost ignored it. She was becoming used to the asylum noises from the missus's room. But then the door was flung open and Mrs Dix bolted across the landing to flatten herself, arms aloft, against the laboratory door. A rumpled white gap opened between her jacket and skirts as her fists banged on wood.

The door opened. There was a dark smudge across the master's brow and his wiry hair stuck out like uncombed wool.

'Yes? What now?'

Mrs Dix's voice trembled. 'You should come, sir. She has taken a bad turn.'

Mr Jerwood shook his head. His jacket seemed wet with stains. 'Can you not manage it with chloral?'

'No, sir, she will not abide it today.'

Cora crouched on the floor. Perhaps they had not noticed her. Or perhaps they did not care whether she was there or not. Then, from the mistress's bedroom, came a noise like the howl of an animal in the night. Mrs Dix's head jerked around and her face crumpled. With a loud sigh, the master side-stepped her and, licking each palm in turn, stroked his hair to pull the wayward tufts into place. Then he strode across the landing leaving the laboratory open. Mrs Dix followed him into the mistress's room and closed the door.

A caustic smell seeped from the laboratory. Cora crept to the threshold and peered at the disorder inside. The jars on the shelves were jumbled out of order; the species no longer logically arranged. Insects, lizards and birds mingled with a cat in mid-yowl. At the back, the body in the biggest jar of all was obscured by the others except for a tiny hand.

The workbench was covered in tubes and apparatus. A thick slimy substance had spilled over a good part of the countertop. At the centre of the mess, an unsealed jar was half-filled with clear liquid. Floating inside, nose pointing towards air, was a stiff white rabbit with black patches on its ear and foot. Above it on the shelf, was the box labelled *Composites 1884 –*. Voices came from Mrs Jerwood's room and then muffled wailing. Cora took a breath and stepped into the laboratory, pulling the door behind her.

Taking care not to touch the spill that gave off a choking whiff of ammonia, she reached for the box of photographs. It was heavy and as she lowered it on to the floor, one end thumped against the linoleum. Cora stopped and listened for footsteps on the landing but heard only her own heartbeat.

Quickly, she removed the pasteboard lid and began to flick through the likenesses. Most of the faces were men's and boys', but amongst the women's were some she remembered from the exercise yard or the oakum room. All were in convict stripes. A few images seemed bland and blurry, but most of the faces whether angry or gormless, pock-marked or under-fed, were recognisably those of prisoners. The human rubbish of the town. And then came her own face. It fitted so snugly amongst the other criminals that she might have missed it. Turning the box to the light, Cora could almost feel the itch of that prison bonnet on her brow, the lumpiness of the stays on her breasts.

She pulled the print out of the box with no idea for an excuse when Mr Jerwood discovered it gone and came asking. Now the prison likeness was in her hands, she could not bear for it to stay any longer in this house, or to exist at all. She folded it and stuffed it inside her bodice over the half-medal.

As she went to replace the lid, Cora noticed the portrait behind the place in the box where her own had been and thought it might be a copy. The surly set of the mouth seemed a reflection of hers. But the brows were too dark and unruly, the eyes too inky. In fact, if Cora were to say who the face might resemble, other than herself, she could think of only one person – her employer, Thomas Jerwood.

brambles

Timothy slurped a saucer of tea and raised his eyes to the kitchen ceiling.

'She's in a paddy today, all right.'

Cora looked up too. The gas mantle above the kitchen table shook with each thump from the continuing commotion in Mrs Jerwood's bedroom. Timothy's eyes twinkled above the brown slosh in the saucer.

'Who's this Annie she keeps yelling about?'

Cora's heart gave a hollow beat. She could imagine the queer look he'd give if she said that she was Annie, or at least that's who the missus thought she was.

Cook glanced up from a ball of pummelled dough. 'Take no notice. It's all nonsense.'

But as Cook's fists returned to kneading, she shot Cora a look seeming to suggest, nonsense or not, that subjects like this should be kept well away from Timothy. Another notch tightened on the unease in Cora's chest.

Timothy dipped a bread crust into the saucer. 'What was the missus like when she was in her right mind?'

'When she used to get out of bed, you mean?' Cook walloped the bread dough against the table. 'It's so long ago I can hardly remember.'

'What does she fancy will befall her if she gets up?'

'Oh, it's not getting up that afears her. It's falling out of bed. So she stays in it, barricaded with furniture and cushions to keep her safe.'

Timothy chuckled and cast a sly look at Cora as he held out his empty teacup towards her.

'I wish someone would barricade me in my bed. As long as my wife wasn't in it with me.'

Cora lifted the teapot. How easily she might slip the spout and gush scalding tea on to his hand, but she poured carefully and then put the pot down. Inside her bodice, the prison likeness buckled with a snap that she hoped no one else had heard.

'I should get back outside to them carpets. You didn't want me for anything else did you, Cook?'

Raising a sticky hand into the air, Cook wiped her forearm across her brow.

'Yes, Cora, take that tin bowl with you and see if you can find any brambles for our pie.'

Timothy winked. 'I'd look behind the stableyard if you want something juicy.'

Cora's tongue was fighting to be stuck out and perhaps if Cook hadn't been there she'd have let it. But Timothy, she realised, might be more vexed by being ignored. She picked up the bowl without any notion of what a bramble might be but she was not about to give Timothy further chance for lewdness by asking.

'Yes, Cook.'

A squint of sunlight burnished the yellow grass alongside the outhouse path and old spiders' webs matted the hedge around the bonfire. Cora crouched down beside the warm ash. A black twig still smouldered at the edge of the cinders and she poked it until a few embers throbbed into orange life. A handful of dead leaves brought up a billow of wood-smoke and then a leap of flame.

Cora stood. As far as she could see, across the paddock and along the path to the glasshouse, nothing moved. Timothy was still supping tea in the house and she hadn't seen Samuel since Saturday. Perhaps he was out on the pony trap.

Squatting down, Cora unhooked her bodice and pulled out the photographic likeness of a face that no longer seemed like hers. She placed the creased image on to the ashy fire. For a moment, it seemed as if the thickness of the card might smother the flame, but then the striped prison jacket began to darken and the edge of the print buckled. Cora poked at the ash to cover the whole surface of her convict's scowl.

She picked up the enamel bowl and heard a grinding on gravel. On the drive beyond the paddock Samuel was leading the pony back to the yard. Cora ducked below the hedge top, only straightening once she was shielded by the wall and was out of Samuel's sight. If she was quick, she might make it to the back of the stable block without Samuel noticing she was there.

Low bushes, stiff with thorns, straggled across the unused ground. Most of the berries had wizened to brown husks, but some still gleamed fat and black. Brambles and blackberries must be the same thing Cora decided even though people called them, for no good reason, by different names.

The plumpest ones were hard to reach. Cora pulled up her skirts above the tugging of spikes in leaves as well as stems, and waded into the tangle. A sudden waft of smoke caught in her throat. Perhaps she'd breathed in her own likeness, consumed by the flames into vapour.

In the stableyard, hooves scraped on stone and Samuel barked some command to the pony. Cora was not close enough to hear his words only the roughness in his voice. Why was she hiding from him? She'd done nothing to apologise for and she should tell him straight that if he was holding out any hopes where she was concerned he'd be disappointed. Perhaps it'd be best to give him that sixpence back before she got paid and think up some story to go with it.

Dark juice stained Cora's hands and she licked a tang of fruit and charred wood from her thumb. The base of the tin bowl was not yet covered by berries and some of them were shrunken and wound around with spider's threads. Cora chose the fattest shiniest berry and put it in her mouth. Sweetness burst on to her tongue but as she bit down on the carcass, the flesh of the fruit slipped away and she was left only with hard seeds embedded in her teeth.

'Bit sharp, aren't they?'

It was Samuel, standing just behind her, arms folded. He smiled but his eyes were icy. There was an edge in his voice that she hadn't heard before and it kindled something inside her, although whether temper or passion she couldn't tell. Her skirts dragged on the brambles as she went to him. It wouldn't do to raise her voice, at least not yet.

'Timothy said there was plenty here. But he was wrong.'

'Maybe you're not looking in the right place. You have to lift up the prickles to get a good one.'

She pulled at her petticoat and heard a rip of cotton. 'They hurt.'

'Not if you're careful.'

He took a step towards her but didn't put out his hand to help her on to the grass. Instead, he unbuttoned his work jacket. His shirt beneath was collarless; a brown handkerchief was knotted around his neck. Cora felt his size above her and a shade of menace in his strength.

Samuel smiled, but not pleasantly. 'Had a nice jaunt yesterday, did you, on the steam tram?'

Cora tensed. 'What's it to you?'

'Nothing. Except you used my money on it. And on your fancy man I suppose.'

'You don't know what you're talking about.'

'I know you owe me sixpence.'

'All right, then. Have it back. Have it now.'

Cora reached into the seam of the print dress and to her pocket. Her hand went to a coin that she knew to be a shilling but she pulled it out anyway and held it up, shining, to Samuel.

'What's this? My sixpence seems to have swelled up with excitement.' His attempt at a chuckle turned into a snort.

'It's the smallest I've got. Have it anyway. Call it a payment for your loan and then we're quits.'

'My, flush today, aren't we? Had a win on the horses?'

Cora shrugged and looked at the ground. She did not want to look at him or speak because she could feel an itch of fury laced with passion worming through her insides.

'Well? Do you want my money or not?'

'Depends where you got it.'

'What do you mean?'

'Was it by fair means or something a bit more foul?'

'What?'

He reached down into his trouser pocket and then held out a scrap of paper pinched between his thumb and forefinger. The fragment was charred around the edges but there was no doubt what he was holding; Cora's face, brown now from the fire but still recognisable beneath the starched prison bonnet.

Samuel's voice crackled with fake jollity. 'Nice hat.'

'You bastard…'

Swimming through rage, she lunged at him with the full force of her body. Samuel, shocked and wrong-footed, reeled back then fell sideways into the brambles.

Cora never knew quite what happened next or how she found the strength to inflict so much damage on a tall, muscular young man. All she could later bring clearly to mind was Samuel lying face down in the bushes and herself sitting astride him, riding his buttocks like a saddle as he bucked and writhed amongst the needle-sharp thorns. Both of her hands had grasped on to clumps of his hair and she'd had such a firm grip on his head that she was able to swipe his face from side to side through the bramble-barbs until he was bellowing like a cow in the slaughterhouse and his face was mashed into blood-drenched shreds.

FOURTEEN

1874

china

Cora didn't feel the gash until a red blob popped out of her skin. She put the finger in her mouth and sucked hard, wondering why she wanted to cry. The cut hadn't hurt; she'd hardly felt it. Maybe that was because the china was so sharp.

She still couldn't believe quite how neatly the dinner bowl had smashed against the wooden boards of the dining hall, nor how easily, right under the nose of the overseer, she had concealed the sharpest isosceles of it inside her skirt. And because of the blood on her hand, the breakage had looked so much like an accident that she'd got away with two quick slaps around the head. Those hadn't hurt either.

Cora managed to find a way to carry the shard around, wedged into a hole in her petticoat. It stayed there all morning, even though Mr Bowyer asked her twice to write on the blackboard with the whole class looking at her. In the recreation time she and Alice went together to the privies and shut themselves inside a stall.

Their nostrils pounded with the sweet-sour smell of dung. Cora lifted her skirt and extracted the china knife from the petticoat. Alice put out her hand to feel the edge but Cora pulled it away.

'Careful! It'll cut you to ribbons.'

'But I want you to cut me.'

Cora shook her head. 'There'd be too much mess.'

'Please, Cora. Just a little one.'

Again Cora shook her head, but as usual, she could not refuse her friend.

'All right, then. Just so I can get a feel for how to hold it.'

Alice lifted her skirt high enough for Cora to see all of her black stockings tied over her knees and the tops of her thin white legs. Alice's breath was shallow and quick. She licked her lips.

'Where shall you cut me?'

Cora placed her fingertip, the one with the raw scar, to the inside of Alice's thigh. Alice spread her legs wider and braced her back against the wooden partition. Then Cora kneeled on to yellowed sawdust and held the razored china between her fingers like a stick of chalk. The greasy hem of Alice's skirts brushed the top of her head.

Gently, she touched the china point to the softest part of the leg and drew a line about an inch long. Alice flinched. A trickle of blood, brilliant and quivering, spilled out of the cut and down the leg. The crimson lattice on Alice's ghostly flesh transfixed Cora. She could not bring herself to wipe it away or to press the cut and stop the flow.

'Did it hurt?'

Alice's eyes were half-closed. 'A bit. But it was nice. Shall you do my other leg as well?'

Cora shook her head and felt an unbearable urge to become Alice, or at least to be her reflection. If they looked the same, they'd be as brave and strong as each other. Together, nothing would be too daunting for them, even the dreadful task that they'd set themselves.

'I'll do one just the same on my leg. Hold my skirt.'

Alice helped pull the skirt aside and Cora bent forward to find the same fleshy part of her own leg. Just then, the outside door opened and Alice, wide-eyed, put her finger to her lips. But the door banged shut again without anyone seeming to come in. Cora's heart beat faster. It was harder to get a good grip of the china when it was slippery with blood and she could not quite see the inside of her own thigh as she cut. A blind wave of numbness washed through her. And then pulses of pain almost made her fall over. Blood cascaded down her leg.

Still holding Cora's skirt, Alice bent down and stared at the wound.

'Oh my. How shall we stop it?'

Cora stood rigid against the splintery door, too scared to touch the cut.

'Don't get it on our clothes. Find a rag.'

They both looked at the wooden bench with the hole in it. Sometimes scraps of torn paper or rags were left there for the children to wipe themselves. But usually they just used their hands. Today the bench around the earth closet was bare. With the skirt still in one hand, Alice pressed her other against Cora's thigh.

'Don't.' Cora tried to push her away. 'The blood'll stain your sleeve.'

'I don't mind getting into trouble to keep you safe.'

Cora looked into the coloured part of Alice's left eye and began to count the tiny hazel flecks. She had no sense of how long they both stood there without blinking but the trickles into her stockings began to ease and Alice pulled away her hand, scarlet and dripping. She stretched it over the privy hole until the dripping stopped.

Cora took a long breath. 'If you wash yourself at the pump, they'll see you.'

'Don't fret Cora. I'll not give us away.'

Alice turned to her with the sweetest of smiles and Cora watched, mesmerised, as Alice's purple tongue licked back and forth across her red hand until it was white.

Once she was back in the school room, Cora began to feel ill. Her head throbbed each time Mr Bowyer's cane rapped against the lines of the prayer they were chanting.

'Not only for the past I grieve,
The future fills me with dismay,
Unless Thou hasten to relieve,
Thy suppliant is a castaway.'

Each time Cora thought of the cut on her thigh, her stomach pitched. A black void grew inside her. She stood up and walked in a daze towards the door. Mr Bowyer turned, scowling, and left off his cane from the blackboard. Then his expression flushed into what might have been embarrassment, or even shame.

'Cora Burns, what is amiss?'

His eyes were no longer on Cora but on the trail of bloody footprints staining the floor behind her.

Late that night, under the grey blanket, Alice inspected the cut on Cora's thigh and pronounced the scab to be sound. The reassurance made Cora breath properly again.

'I can't believe Mr Bowyer let me leave class on my own.'

Alice shrugged. 'He thought you had a curse.'

'A what?'

'Curse. It's what women get. Bleeding.'

Even in the dark, Alice must have seen the horror on Cora's face.

'I'm a girl not a woman.'

Alice gave a quiet chuckle. 'He's not to know when it starts, is he? And now he thinks it, he'll let you go out on your own again.'

'To the infirmary?'

'He wouldn't expect you to go there. Only to the privy.'

Cora caught the shine in Alice's eye and there was no need to say more. Tomorrow they would do it.

As Alice had predicted, Cora only had to raise her hand next morning for Mr Bowyer to nod her towards the door. He didn't even seem to notice when Alice ran after her saying she would go too and make sure that Cora was all right. As soon as the sharp sun hit their faces they began to giggle like lunatics, pressing their hands over each others' mouths which only made their laughter more frantic.

Once they'd got to the end of the yard their giggling was drowned by the wail and shriek of the infants. Percy seemed to be waiting for them by the gap in the railings. He was scratching his scabby head with one hand and holding his skirt where his tinkler must be with the other.

Alice licked her thumb and held it towards the child. 'Here, my pet lamb! Come suck on my sticky.'

Frowning, Percy wobbled forward and latched his mouth on to the dripping thumb. Alice reeled him closer to the railings.

Inside the fence, an old woman was slumbering on the bench. Cora put herself in front of Alice to screen her. It was a tight squeeze getting him through the gap but Percy was sucking so hard that he seemed to forget to cry. Alice scooped the little boy up and, with Cora still shielding them, they hurried to the side of the yard and to the privies. All the time, Alice cooed and clucked at the child. He smelled of milk and shit. Cora's heart was beating so hard that she could scarce breathe.

Once the privy block door shut behind them the air was suddenly still. Percy left off his sucking and looked first to Alice and then to Cora. Alice put her mouth to Cora's ear, in case the boy might understand.

'First, we'll take off our clothes.'

'All of them?'

Alice nodded. 'Otherwise they'll get messed up. And the babby won't think it so strange when we take his off.'

Alice was right, of course. Cora should have thought of that too. Percy did not smile as Alice stripped off his pinafore and his stiff dress but neither did he complain.

'That's it, darlin'. Hot today, isn't it? This'll make you feel more comfy.'

Alice lifted off her own dress, and then her stockings and even her shift, and she signalled for Cora to do the same. Cora had never seen anyone completely naked, even herself, and now all three of them were bare as they'd been born. Cora felt the soft reeking air bathe her skin and thought she never wanted to wear anything ever again. Intoxicated, and sure at last of her strength, she picked up the china knife.

What happened next was never clear in Cora's mind. If a memory ever wormed through, or if the scene came back to her in a dream, the sequence would vary each time. The events inside the privy block were ever afterwards cloaked in haziness.

The first thing that she remembered bursting through that haze was the bang of the outside door and Lottie Bolger's finger pointing. Mr Bowyer was there too, eyes darting, his face as grey as the wall.

'What in God's name…?'

Only then did Cora blink and follow his horrified stare to the small body on the floor. Percy's head was turned sideways, his eyes half-closed. Cora's petticoat bloomed from his mouth like a chapel flower. There was hardly any blood on the floor, but carved on the inside of his thigh, just below his shrivelled private parts, was an unmistakable red A.

Cora's insides seemed suddenly to move into the wrong place.

'It wasn't me, sir. I didn't do it. I swear. It was her. It was Alice.'

But her voice was drowned out by the clanging of the chapel bell, and Mr Bowyer was already inside the stall heaving up the contents of his stomach.

Cora ran then, to search in every corner of the privy block and, naked as she was, out into the yard. Yet Alice was nowhere. She had evaporated it seemed, as completely as a scrap of schoolyard mist on a hot summer morning.

146

FIFTEEN
November 1885

outhouse

The wash-house pump shrieked like a crow in a trap and Cora's hand quivered under the lash of icy water. The tremor worked into her shoulder, her stomach, her teeth. Bramble juice mixed with blood, some of it her own, in red streams across her knuckles. What in the name of heaven had she done?

Before she ran, she'd seen Samuel's face so dripping and raw that if he came looking for her now she'd not fight back but take his punches gladly. She deserved them, and more. He'd not go to the police, though, she knew that. Attacked by a woman? No man would take that shame.

There were bloodstains on her sleeves. Too much to pass off as some accident with game birds in the meat larder. Her fingers groped at the buttons of the print dress. She peeled it off and let the tang of chill air ripple through her shift. The pump screeched as a freezing drench ran through the thin cotton bodice. But cold water was the best thing for blood. And the red was still vivid, the spots not yet dry. With luck, the taint would come out and not leave a mark.

Her fingers grew numb as she bundled the bodice to the back of the room and slumped it over the indoor line. It wouldn't dry of course, but she'd rather stay undressed than have its wet folds cling to her skin. If Samuel came in now and got an eyeful of her underwear it was only what he was due.

He'd get his revenge somehow, she had no doubt. Lord, if it had been the other way round, Cora would have relished thinking up the ways; a poisonous word in Ellen's ear, a gob of spit in his greens, a cigarette jumping back to life in the hay shed. That other way round was the normal order of things; a girl leads a lad on, rejects his advances, gets thumped and then exacts her sly revenge. No one could argue with that. But for Cora to set about a strapping under-gardener and get the better of him was unnatural.

The water petered to a drip. Cora leaned on the sink edge and shivered through her sweat. A mannish odour seeped over her stays.

This nastiness wasn't all her doing, though. Samuel shouldn't have provoked; once he'd seen the prison bonnet he should have known better than to rile her. Even a milk and white-bread lad like him should have realised then that Cora was not one to be messed with.

And the cruel irony of her outburst was that the prison likeness was probably still inside Samuel's pocket. If only she'd applied some cunning she'd have got it back from him easily, with an upward flick of her petticoat and a lick of her lips. Then he'd have been slavering for a feel of her whenever he came near the kitchen, and perhaps she would have been too. And he'd have guarded the secret of her convict past. Instead, she'd half-killed him; had scarred him anyway. Maybe for life. He'd think of the crazed gaolbird who did that to him every time he saw his reflection.

In the yard, metal scraped against stone. Taking care to stay in shadow, Cora moved nearer to the window but she could see no sign of Samuel through the grime. The stable doors were still shut and the water in the trough was unrippled. She caught the ghost of her face in the glass; scratched, bedraggled, mad-eyed. Yes, that was who she was, and who she had been for as long as she could remember. A troublemaker and a bully. Unreliable. Unhinged.

Cora began to pace, back and forth across the brick floor of the wash-house. Six paces one way, six the other. The same number, she realised, as the breadth of her cell. In those first days in prison, as she'd paced, she'd let herself recall the crime that had brought about her conviction. But the pacing had worsened the drip of blood down her leg and the soak of thin milk through her prison jacket. The ceaseless motion had made thoughts of the Union house leak out too; a recurring vision of a small girl carrying a smaller boy across the schoolyard. It might have been Alice, but Cora could feel, like a missing limb, the weight of a child on her hip. And was it Cora too, who'd pushed the petticoat into his mouth? She could not say if he'd squirmed or bitten or kicked. She had no sense, either, of how long it had been until he was still. Surely if she'd been the one who'd done it, she would remember all this. She knew for certain that her own child had made no fuss. Perhaps he'd been too little.

Cora's breath shivered on to the wash-house pane. She put her hand inside her stays and pulled out the half-medal. It had dulled since she cleaned it but the markings were still clear, as were the words: *IMAGINEM SALT.* Perhaps in that distant time before Alice came, Cora had been a meek and docile child, unwilling to hurt so much as a featherless starling. Or perhaps, like the severed coin, Cora had been made wrong from the start; cursed by her place of birth and her mother's blood.

The scene in the Union house privies was a blank blot in her memory like a hole in vision that came from looking at the sun. The only person who might colour in the blank was Alice. Cora went to the washing line and wiped the half-medal on the soaked sleeve of the print dress. And as she pushed metal and twine back inside her stays, her hands no longer shook.

vinegar

Cora slipped inside the scullery, wet sleeves slapping against her arms. She struck a Vesta and the gas mantle fizzed into an orange flame. Shadows jumped around the plate rack. She leaned against the wall, too numb to shiver. If anyone came in, she could try to make out that she had been in here all along, scouring the tin lining of copper pots, but before she had time to pick up the bowl of soap and flour paste, a draught of gravy-soaked air blew into the scullery.

Cook's face was red, her voice quiet. 'Where've you been?'

Cora saw that her soaking bodice required some sort of explanation. 'In the wash-house. My dress had got stained with bird mess.'

'All afternoon?'

'And I was looking for brambles, like you asked.'

'Did you find any?'

'No, Cook.'

'Where's the bowl?'

Cora's heart quickened as a lie began to form in her mouth. But Cook cast a look over the wet bodice and clicked her tongue.

'Save your excuses. I need you to come now and take the girl her tea.'

The tray on the kitchen table was already made up with a plate of thickly buttered white bread, tea in a china cup and a hot egg wrapped in linen. There was a teaspoon beside a tiny silver cup and a metal lever with a hole in one end.

'You'd best help with the egg. Take the top off for her. Or she's like to make an almighty mess.'

Cora's teeth had begun to chatter so fast she could not ask if the top was the same as the shell.

As Cora entered the parlour, Violet looked up wide-eyed and silent. Thin light hissed from the overhead mantle and flames licked across the orange coals in the grate.

'Shall I pull this table forward for you?'

Violet blinked but did not otherwise move. She sat on the worn edge of the leather armchair, her green dress almost hidden by an overlarge white apron. Her eyes did not leave Cora. One of the pupils was still larger than the other, making the eye look black. Her gaze seemed widened with suspicion. Perhaps word of the prison bonnet had already spread.

The tray rattled as Cora set it down on the card table, too far from the armchair for Violet to reach. But if she was going to play Miss Hoity-Toity, that's where it would stay. The egg, as Cora unwrapped it from the linen cloth, was almost too hot to touch.

'Cook says I'm to help you with this egg. How do you want it?' Violet stared at her in silence. 'Shall I peel off the shell?'

At this, Violet lowered her eyes to the egg, squinting as if it was a thing she had never seen before then she raised one shoulder in an indifferent shrug. Cora clenched the hand that was itching to give Violet a clip around the ear.

'Well, I can't help you if you won't tell me what to do. There's this spoon here. Maybe you could eat it with that. And this thing here…'

Cora picked up the implement with the hole and the lever then dropped it back on to the tray when the girl refused to respond.

Cora sniffed. 'Is that all, then?'

Without looking up, Violet gave a quick nod of her head and Cora shut the parlour door harder than was proper. The girl, who had so recently seemed to want Cora for a friend, now hated her. Cora told herself she should not care nor even be surprised. That was what always happened once anyone saw her true character. Just as Samuel now had. And perhaps that was also why Alice had disappeared.

Yellow light spilled under the kitchen door into the dusk of the passage. Cora took the tray in one hand as she went in then reeled from a reek of vinegar. Ellen stood holding a saucer beside a large figure reclining, head back and eyes closed, in the Windsor chair. Ellen looked up at Cora and her jaw tightened. Then she went back to dabbing an acrid handkerchief from the saucer of vinegar to the seeping wheals across Samuel Shepherd's face.

A chink opened in Samuel's eye, then widened as it came to rest on Cora. She stood, frozen by his gaze, just inside the door.

He winced. 'God damn it!'

The vinegar-soaked handkerchief leapt up in Ellen's hand. 'I'm sorry. There's a thorn.' Her face reddened as if about to crumple with tears. She turned to Cora. 'Get me a needle, can you?'

Cook, stirring at a copper stew-pan on the range, watched Cora open the dresser and take out the mending box. Neither her expression nor Ellen's gave a clear sign of what Samuel might have told them. Cora's cold hand trembled as she pulled out the needle with the finest point. A glint in Samuel's half-open eye followed her as she brought it towards him.

Ellen laid the handkerchief down and flattened her hand for the needle. 'You know what happened, don't you?'

The needle hovered. Ellen's palm was as good as a pincushion to stick it in. 'What?'

'To Samuel. Behind the stables?'

Samuel shut the slit of his eye. 'Leave it, Ellen.'

'No, I won't. Why did she not try to help you or go to find Timothy? She must have heard the commotion.'

The thump of Cora's heart warmed her and the lie came easily. 'I didn't.'

Samuel's eye flashed from Cora to Ellen. 'Well, I'm all right now. Just get on with your surgery, Doctor Beamish.'

Ellen's head shook as she bent over Samuel's face with the needle. 'I don't think you are all right, Samuel. And how could she not have known? There must have been a fearful noise when he attacked you.'

He. Cora's heart skipped a beat. So Samuel had also lied. To protect her, or to protect his pride? Either way, Cook and Ellen did not know what Cora had done.

Painfully, Samuel licked his lips. 'Aye well. It would have made no difference. That pony won't take no notice of anything when he gets the devil inside him.'

Cook rapped her metal spoon on the edge of the stew-pan then pointed it at Cora. 'If you was in the wash-house you must have heard the racket.'

Cora shrugged. 'That old pump makes a racket as well.'

'Not as much as a crazed horse trampling a man into thorn bushes.'

'Jesus!' Samuel pushed Ellen's hand with the needle away from his face. 'That'll do!'

He sat upright and rubbed his neck. Cora saw that his hands, like his face were covered in a web of raised cuts, but most of the scratches were shallow. In a few days, they should have healed without a mark.

Ellen held up the needle with its tiny black trophy on the point. 'I'm sorry, Samuel. It was a deep one. But I think I've got it all out now. Let me just dab that last bit with vinegar.'

'No thank you. I'll live.' He stood up and pulled a crusted oil can from the shelf below the table. 'I'll take the storm lamp to the stables so I can check the pony over for scratches.'

Ellen folded her arms. 'You must tell the master to get rid of that Hector. He's vicious.'

'He's a beast, Ellen. Savagery is in his nature. If something riles him, like an over-tight harness or a horsefly bite, he'll turn nasty and he doesn't care who is in his way.' Samuel shot Cora a look that flickered with disgust. 'He's too tangled up in his own selfish desires to consider the upshot of his violence.'

Cora had seen that look all her life; in the eyes of the workhouse orderlies, the female attendant at the asylum, the wardresses at the gaol. Her voice, steely and remote, seemed to come from a different part of the room.

'And what is the upshot of violence? For the horse?'

'I shall put him in a nose twitch and hope it teaches him better manners.'

'You think cruelty will make him gentler?'

'If he can't learn to be civil he'll find himself at Bristol Street horse fair.'

Samuel began pouring oil into the storm lamp but his hand faltered as Cook emptied the vinegar from the saucer into the slops bucket on the floor beside him. She spoke sharply.

'It's up to the master what happens to that horse, Samuel Shepherd, not you. And it will pay you to treat that animal with respect or the damage he could do you might be a sight worse than those scratches on your face.'

Samuel winced and his face looked even redder. Perhaps he, like Cora, suspected that Cook knew more of the truth than she was letting on. She raised her chin at Samuel as he lit the oil and pulled his cap low over his brow.

'And keep an eye out for that enamel bowl. There's no telling what might have happened to it.'

transformation

As the print-covered buttons slipped, one by one, out of each damp hole, exhaustion slid through Cora's limbs. Apart from a few grazes to her hands and more than usually dishevelled hair, she looked the same as she had when she'd got dressed that morning. But she no longer felt like herself; her mind seemed liquid; her body no longer whole.

She looked away blankly as Ellen came in from the scullery and put her night things on the table in a neat pile. As Ellen began lighting a candle, Cora felt a sudden stab of fury.

'Is even my candle not good enough for you, Ellen?'

Ellen kept her eyes on the flame before her. 'I need one of my own tonight. To go upstairs.'

'Upstairs?'

'I'll be sleeping there from now on.'

There was only one reason that Ellen would want to sleep in a cold cramped attic room instead of the warm kitchen.

'Can't even stand to be in the same room as me?'

'Well, I'm not really a scullery maid any more, am I? Mrs Dix said that part of my recompense for the extra kitchen work would be to sleep with the upper servants.'

Cora stepped out of her petticoats and dropped them over the blanket on her bed. In their usual contortionist's jig of dressing and undressing beneath a nightdress, neither Cora nor Ellen had seen more than a brief flash of white flesh on the other.

'Where? There's no spare bed up there.'

'I'll be sharing Susan Gill's for now.'

Cora snorted. 'Does she not object?'

Ellen shrugged. 'Weather's turned so she doesn't mind.'

'And you don't mind being a human hot water bottle?'

'At least I shall be away from your nastiness.'

Cora felt her thoughts dissolve into rage. 'If you think I've been nasty, you haven't seen the half of it.'

Before Cora quite knew what she was doing, her stays were unhooked and her drawers loosed. Then, in a cloud of white-hot fury, she tugged her shimmy over her head and stood naked before Ellen in the candlelight. Not even her hair, still coiled under her cap, covered her breasts. The only thing against her white flesh was the half-medal hanging on its greasy twist of twine.

'Is this nasty enough for you?'

Ellen scrabbled her night things from the dresser and went to the door, tears filling her eyes. 'There's something very wrong with you, Cora Burns.'

The door closed in a draught of mould-spiced air. Without bothering to spit on her fingers, Cora squeezed out the candle's flame then dropped, still naked, to the mattress, wrapping herself in the mound of cheap blanket and petticoats and hoping she would never again have to come out.

Cora struggled to fix her eyes on the orange light ebbing behind the bars of the kitchener. Usually, she could stare at it for only a minute before her aching limbs relaxed and her eyelids closed. But tonight, the room started to peel apart like a smashed mirror. She seemed to be falling into a waking nightmare with madness dancing at the fringes of her mind. If it took over, as it had before, she would not want to ever wake up. The orange coals in the burner became suddenly darker and, in what seemed no more than a blink, the glow was swallowed into blackness.

Then Cora jolted awake. There'd been a sudden noise; perhaps the chimes of the long-case clock or a lump of grey coal shifting in the grate. But it moved again. There was something in the room; closer than a crumble of ash, bigger than a rodent. And there was breathing; a thin inhalation followed by a shuddering breath out.

The sound was too light and womanly to be a male intruder. Was it Ellen? Perhaps Susan Gill had kicked her out and she'd come creeping back to her old bed. But the breathing seemed fixed in one place a few paces from Cora's face.

Cora inched the blanket away from her ear. Every nerve concentrated on the silence. Was that another breath? A footstep? Someone or something was standing just beside her. Cora listened, for seconds, or perhaps minutes, eyes trained towards the sound. Slowly, the black kitchen turned to grey. And a dull white shape emerged from the gloom.

It was a woman. With long thin hair loose over her nightdress and her hands before her, clasping and unclasping. As Cora's eyes strained on to the hazy outline, an icy tremor slipped through her. Was this ghostly visitor someone she knew? Was it Alice? Cora looked harder into the dimness, stifling the horror rising in her gut. Because there was another with good reason to haunt her. Cora's mouth began to open. *I didn't kill him,* she wanted to say, *it was Alice.* But if the mother of that poor little boy in the Union house was now a spirit, she would know truth from lie.

Cora gripped the bedclothes as the woman's whimpering grew into words.

'Why?' Dull eyes stared as the mouth quivered. 'Why did you take what was not yours? You must have known the harm it would do.' The shady figure shuffled closer, the voice firmer. 'Why have you come back? Can you not see how you torment me?'

Cora's limbs locked stiff as she recognised the voice, and saw too the outline of the woman's long nose. Not a ghost; just the missus. She must have slipped down the back stairs without Mrs Dix seeing her. And now she was in the kitchen, weeping.

'You ended my life, Annie. Killed it. As good as a murderess. Evil you are. Bad through and through. A vile serpent...'

The voice choked. She seemed suddenly to be beside the kitchen table where the knives, rubbed in mutton fat to keep their shine, were laid out for the night. The mistress's hands folded and unfolded above them like a trapped bird.

Then, in a rush of air that made Cora's eyes snap shut, the mistress swooped down at her. Cora expected to feel a carve of red warmth across her skin, but when she opened her eyes she realised that she was not harmed, and the mistress, muttering and sniffling, had turned towards the door. Then she was gone. Cora listened, frozen, to the creak of each tread on the back stairs. The footsteps stopped. A door upstairs clicked. And then there was silence.

A lump of anguish wedged in Cora's throat. The missus might be deranged but her words held truth. *Bad through and through.* Cora had done damage to so many people that the words could have been spoken by any of them. And it was only right that she should be tormented by a lunatic because she was as good as one herself. Why else would she have wanted to kill that little boy, or her own babe?

She turned on to her side and a trail of tears slid across her nose. It wouldn't be long until she'd hear Cook stirring. Then Cora would need to be up and raking the grate into the ash bucket; laying sticks and fresh coal into the range. She shut her eyes. How could she carry on scouring pots and polishing boots as if nothing had changed? How would she even raise herself from this mattress? As Cora thought of the day ahead, she forced her face against the greasy pillow, but the howl that choked out of her lungs was too savage to smother.

SIXTEEN

Research Journal of

David Farley MD
Assistant Medical Officer
Birmingham asylum
October 1885

I received Matron Abbott (who seems so different without her starched apron and tall nurse's bonnet!) in my rooms this afternoon, and in the course of arranging for the delivery of Mary B from the infirmary to my office, we enjoyed a most stimulating discussion about the conduct of hypnosis upon the insane. Mrs Abbott asked pertinent questions regarding what I imagined might transpire. I then outlined Dr Voisin's methods for hypnotising lunatics by simply addressing the subject with a repeated verbal instruction to stare into the instructor's eyes. Sleep, he says, almost always descends voluntarily. If it does not, hand-passes may be made across the subject's head (without touching). This process should be continued for at least thirty minutes. Should it not be successful, Dr Voisin recommends restraining the lunatic in order for the eyes forcibly to be kept open whilst they look into a magnesium lamp for up to three hours if necessary (however, I do not think that I could in conscience employ this method). Mrs Abbott then made the excellent suggestion that, after bringing Mary B to my office, she herself might stay on to act as a note-taker. I had not previously considered the benefits of having a witness present but I immediately accepted. What luck to have chanced upon such an intelligent associate for my research!

I suspect that Mrs Abbott may be only a few years older than I, but her life, from the few facts she told me about it, has been turbulent. Her pleasant West Country lilt originates not from the rolling hills of Devonshire (as I had fondly imagined) but from Bristol's grimy docks. It was there that her late husband met his end in a ship's hold. She told me (with great bravery) of this event; of the pressure upon the dockers to unload the valuable cargo of tobacco bales swiftly; of how the stevedores all knew the crane's rope to be rotten but the dock owners, consumed by their love of profit, refused to replace it. The result was Mr Abbott's tragic (nay, unlawful) death at the age of just 26 years. Mrs Abbott then realised that she must make her own way in the world and took up a situation as an attendant in the asylum at Wells, studying Nursing in her own time and by her own efforts fitting herself for the responsible position she now holds.

Sun 18th

I have set up a therapeutic area within my office along the lines recommended by the French experts. Being unable to procure a couch, I have pulled in an old wing-back chair and placed my stool directly in front of it. As arranged,

Matron Abbott brought Mary B to my office directly after chapel. The patient is a small neat woman in early middle age who at first glance appears sane, if a little pale and nervous-looking. Her countenance is moderately grey and her eyes dull. They are, nevertheless, the same striking eyes that I had seen in the likeness appended to her admission certificate. The likeness did not, of course, reveal their remarkable porcelain blue.

Mary B sat in the large chair somewhat reluctantly. Perhaps it was my proximity which unsettled her as our knees were almost touching, but I judged her sufficiently compos mentis to proceed. Mrs Abbotts's discreet presence in the corner with her notebook was, I think, reassuring. Thenceforth the session proceeded more dramatically than I could have imagined. My hand, indeed, shakes as I here transcribe Mrs Abbott's notes.

10.30am

Dr F uses a quiet, sonorous voice. He instructs Mary B to relax each part of her body into the chair.

Dr F says: 'Look at me. Think of nothing but sleep. Your eyelids begin to feel heavy; your eyelids are tired; your eyes are getting moist; you cannot see clearly.'

Mary B's eyelids droop but she remains awake.

Dr F makes some passes of hands over her face.

The eyelids quiver.

Dr F says: 'Can you still hear me, Mary?'

She nods. Her movements are slow and deliberate, her lids flutter.

Dr F says: 'You have now regained the power of speech. You will retain this power even after you wake up.'

10.45am

Dr F asks Mary B to tell him about her work in the kitchen.

She sighs loudly and then yawns. Her eyes are closed.

Dr F talks a little more about the kitchens; how pleasant it must be to work in the warmth, preparing the wholesome ingredients which are pleasing to the patients and aid their recovery.

Mary B's mouth flickers into a trance-like smile and her chin slowly nods. Dr F continues in a low rhythmic voice: 'The quality of the pastry at the asylum is better than I have tasted anywhere. There must be a special recipe that is followed here to make it so light and tasty.'

Then, Mary speaks: 'Tis the table, sir.'

Dr F: (after a slight pause) 'How do you mean?'

Mary B: 'It is a marble-topped table that we use to roll out the dough. The coolness of it is good for pastry.'

Her voice is a little hoarse but the words, in a north-country accent, are clear.

Dr F: 'Do tell me, Mary, how you prepare your pastry.'

Mary B: 'The flour should be sieved, the beef fat and butter kept in the larder to stay hard. The rolling must be quick.'

Dr F: 'I see you are an expert. Where did you learn these skills?'

Mary B: 'My mother taught me.'

Dr F: 'On a marble-topped table?'

Mary B: (slight chuckle) 'Nay, sir. There be nowt of that sort in our village.'

Dr F: 'And what village was that?'

Mary B: 'Salt.'

Dr F: 'The village of Salt?'

Mary B: 'Aye, sir.'

Dr F: 'In Staffordshire?'

Mary B: 'Aye.'

Dr F: 'And when did you leave the village?'

Mary B: (eyes crimp into a frown) 'I was sent as a scullery maid when I was fifteen…'

Dr F: 'To Birmingham?'

At this, Mary B's face begins to redden and her lips press together. Her head turns from side to side.

Dr F: (his upturned hands pass across her face without touching) 'Mary, do not tire yourself. Sleep now, a deep refreshing sleep. When I clap my hands you will awake and remember the ease with which you have spoken. Your difficulty with speech will disappear.'

11.10am

Mary B is calm now, with eyes closed; breathing deep and steady. At the clap of Dr F's hands, Mary B blinks and yawns.

Dr F: 'Tell me what you remember about our talk.'

Mary B coughs then shakes her head.

Dr F: 'Do you remember anything?'

Mary B: No response.

Sun pm

I had agreed with Mrs Abbott that we should take a turn around the asylum meadow after luncheon in order to discuss the morning's events. She met me by the main entrance door. In her knitted red scarf and tam o'shanter, she seemed almost girlish. Indeed we were both giddy as schoolchildren as we talked of the near-miraculous breakthrough we had witnessed a few hours before.

I confessed that I had been a little overwhelmed by the effectiveness of Dr Voisin's method, having used it only once before on a friend (and I did not tell her that I suspected the trance induced on that occasion was faked to keep me happy!). I admitted that I should have thought harder about how to encourage Mary B to talk. The nonsense about pastry-making was entirely thought up on the spur of the moment – my main object being simply to hear Mary B's voice. Nevertheless, my embarrassing chitter-chatter seemed to work.

Mrs Abbott then asked whether I have any theory regarding the cause of Mary B's insanity. I took a deep breath and ventured to explain a little of my <u>Political </u> *theory of madness. This was prefaced, as it must be, by a vignette of my own rather miserable childhood – the failure of my father's business, my mother's subsequent incapacity – and how, early on in my medical studies, I had decided to specialise in malfunctions of the mind. Insanity, I explained, may express itself in many bizarre modes of behaviour – peculiar delusions, religious mania, an obsession with cleanliness, self-starvation – but at the root of all symptoms lies the despair of* <u>inequality</u>*. That, as any disinterested person must see, is why the Borough Asylum is more stuffed with paupers than any other category of lunatic.*

I think I found a receptive audience. Mrs Abbott confided that my ideas chimed very much with her own. Indeed, she wondered if Mary B may be a personification of my theory. Then, somewhat haltingly, she began to describe one of Mary B's verbal episodes upon emerging from the stupor of chloral hydrate in the infirmary. Matron Abbott witnessed Mary B falling, at the point of consciousness, into a sudden terror akin to a fit. The words wailed by the patient at this point seemed to describe the terrifying birth of a child upon the floor of a gaol cell. Naturally, Mrs Abbott judged the details too indelicate to relate to me exactly. My face must have conveyed my fluster at the subject matter because Mrs Abbott briefly laid a reassuring hand on my sleeve. I was torn by a desire to know exactly what had been said and an embarrassment at the thought of it coming from Mrs Abbott's lips. I then ventured a suggestion that, although she would not wish to relate this unseemly anecdote to me directly, she might instead write it down as best she could remember and keep this testimony safe. It may

*form an aid (as yet unforeseen) to Mary B's recovery. Mrs Abbott agreed gladly
to do so.*

*I was so affected by our conversation that I asked if Mrs Abbott would do me
the courtesy of calling me by my first name, at least when we are out of earshot of
the staff. Again, she quickly agreed and asked if I would return the compliment
by calling her Miriam.*

SEVENTEEN
November 1885

face

When Cora woke, the babe was in her bed. She felt the warm hard ball of his head tucked below her breast and the soft smell of his new skin wafted up between the stale sheets. But when she put her hand to him, there was nothing. Then the dream came back to her; he'd been laughing and gurgling, a dark-eyed child of six months or more. Nothing like the tiny bloodied scrap she last saw.

She opened her eyes on to the beginnings of thin wintry light and wiped at the tear that had slipped into her hair. Her legs ached under the weight of blanket and clothes. She had forgotten the toll that fighting took. Her eyelids sagged but she would not let them close. The boy might still be there in the darkness to tear at the knot of sorrow in her throat. She thought of the day ahead and could not see her way through it; her limbs would be too feeble to take her from one vigorous task to the next. By now, she should be dressed, her hair brushed and bound under a fresh cap. Cook expected the range to be aglow by the time she came down and the kettle already in a hiss.

Cora pulled herself up, one limb at a time and sat on the mattress. Her head throbbed. Yesterday seemed more dream than real. Had she really mashed Samuel's face into the brambles and put her naked parts on show to Ellen? And had the missus, mad as you like, been crying over her in the night and calling her Annie? Yet it must be so, for she was still naked apart from the half-medal around her neck.

She took a long breath and reached for her nightdress amongst the rumpled bedclothes. As she pulled it free, a rectangle of speckled paper fell on to the floor. Cora picked it up and a woman's face looked back. She dragged on the nightgown and scrabbled for a Vesta, striking one to the candle's blackened wick. Then she held the stiff paper beside the flame that tongued through the smoke and her heart gave a beat so hollow that she felt it might stop for good.

The girl in the small cabinet portrait was dressed in an expensive, if outdated gown with a full skirt and a high waist. Her thick, dark hair hung in coils about her shoulders and her face was a pale oval with thin cheeks and rounded brows. The face could not have been more familiar, because it was Cora's own.

Unsteadily, she stood up, still clutching the portrait to the light. It must be a trick; some photographic sorcery that could paste her face on to another woman's body. The master must have done it. But the angle of the face looking away from the camera was unfamiliar. Cora had never before seen her head from the side. And there was no line or join between her own pale cheek in the likeness and the woman's complicated twists of hair and jewel-drop earrings.

A shiver prickled into Cora's scalp and she dropped the print to the bed. It must have been left here, unseen, as the missus came towards her in that pale shimmer of distress. Perhaps the woman in the photograph was Annie, the imagined foe who just happened to look like Cora. That would explain everything. And perhaps Cora should, right now, march upstairs and bang on the bedroom door to tell the missus what was what. And warn her to leave Cora alone.

But Mrs Jerwood was a mad-woman. She would believe what she wanted and no proof of anything solid would persuade her to change her mind. Cora knew enough about lunatics to know that. And no good could be done by drawing attention to herself. Neither would it do to leave this picture where it might be seen. Any of the other servants who saw the likeness would surely think it showed Cora and then wonder by what means she could have decked herself in such finery. There was only one way. The gown's swags were as scandalous as prison stripes.

Cora tucked the cabinet portrait into her nightdress sleeve and wrapped the blanket around her. Boiled wool itched through her nightdress as her bare feet twisted into the slippery leather of the button boots. Outside, damp air reeked of earth and dead fires. White mist lightened the brick path past the coal house to the servants' privy. Cora banged the privy door to warn off rats and went in.

Dirty light from the dripping window showed up the O of the bowl but not much else. The seat was icy against Cora's thighs; the uneven floor pitted with small puddles. She kept her foot against the door. Samuel might already have heard her come this way and know that she was alone, the rest of the house still abed. Who could blame him if he tried to get some revenge? She'd almost think better of him if he did.

She pulled the likeness from her sleeve but the light was too weak to see more than an outline of the ballooning crinoline. The stiff paper creased to a sharp point as she balled it in her fist. She squeezed harder, pressing with her thumb until it had crumpled into a soft lump. Then she dropped it into the lavatory and pulled the chain.

The grey ball of card bobbed around in the roll of water and piss, reluctant to sink. Perhaps water would destroy this likeness no better than fire had worked on the last. If she had to, she'd put her hand in the bowl and scoop it, then try something else. But then the water settled to smooth emptiness and the fine lady with Cora's face was gone.

temper

When Cora got back to the kitchen, black tufts already smoked between the bars of the range. Cook sat in the Windsor chair with a sour look watching a silent kettle on the hotplate and didn't turn around when Cora came in.

'Sorry, Cook. I had to visit the privy.'

'Are you poorly?'

'Maybe.'

'Not something you've eaten, I hope. Like brambles?'

Cora shook her head. 'Time of the month that's all.'

'Is it?'

Cook's eyes narrowed. Perhaps she thought Cora was hiding some other complaint; one that gave her good reason to beat Samuel Shepherd to a bloody mess.

Cora tried to move and speak as she normally would. 'I'll be right presently.'

'Good. Master has specially asked for you to take up his tea.'

Cora stiffened. He must by now have spotted the gap in his box of prisoner portraits. Perhaps he also knew about the mishap in the brambles. She could not bear the thought of facing him.

'If my stomach is out of sorts it might be catching.'

Cook raised her voice just enough to quash further discussion. 'He particularly asked for you. So you'd best get your clothes on sharpish.'

The four-legged tray weighed heavy on Cora's arms as she

climbed the back stairs. Halfway up, she stumbled on the print dress and thought that the whole thing, steaming silver teapot, flower-edged china and fishy-smelling toast, was about to fly into the air and crash on to the treads. She was almost disappointed when it didn't. The print dress seemed to drag on the floor as if to press home the notion that Cora would never again wear it. The master would no doubt want her changed back into her own clothes and gone from his house before he was even up for the day.

Well, he could stuff his tweeny position between his bare arse cheeks. And once he'd sacked her, Cora would give him a piece of her mind; tell him to keep his damned eight pounds and his button boots and stop taking pictures of her face to do Lord knows what with without so much as asking. A hollow lightness started to rise inside her. Perhaps it would be a relief to be away from this house and all of the black looks that would be coming her way from Samuel and Ellen and Violet if she stayed. She could do with keeping the boots though, and a blanket. Her prospects in town were no better than they'd been last month, and the weather was colder.

'Come!'

Mr Jerwood seemed to answer before she'd even knocked. Inside his chamber, dark velvet curtains were still closed and two gas wall-burners hissed. Stacks of books sprouted from the patterned carpets. He sat in the middle of the brass bedstead, propped against pillows, a brocade dressing gown over his nightshirt. The shiny coverlet was almost hidden by a spread of white paper, each sheet covered in dense pencil handwriting. He must have been awake half the night.

Cora stood inside the door. 'Tray, sir.'

'Ah yes. Put it here, over me, if you would.'

'On the bed, sir?'

'Yes, yes.'

He scrabbled some of the paper away from his knees and Cora felt the unexpected rise of a blush as she placed the tray across his legs. A slightly rank smell came up from the bed although Cora knew the sheets were not long changed; she'd washed them herself. She stepped backwards with her eyes firmly on the Turkey carpet, narrowly avoiding a pile of books.

'Would that be all, sir?'

She knew that it wouldn't. The ticking off would start any second now, and then the good riddance. But the master was so quiet that she looked up again. His gaze was on her, scrutinising.

'Come forward again, closer to the bed...'

She took a half a step.

'... and whilst I pour my tea, do me the favour of looking at this chart.'

He leaned forward across the tray and held out a stiff sheet of pasteboard. Disconcerted by his mildness, Cora took it. On the left side of the sheet, words were listed in a column. Each described a character or temperament: *Sulky, Fretful, Proud, Fiery.* And each temper was joined by a red ink line to its opposite at the other side of the page: *Sunny, Calm, Yielding, Timid.*

Mr Jerwood took a small bite from his toast and swallowed without chewing.

'What do you think it is?'

'I can't say, sir.'

'Come now. You are not a dull person. I know that much of you.'

'Opposites, sir. Of temper.'

'There. Quite so.'

He slurped a mouthful of tea then put down the cup and held out a sheet of thin, almost transparent parchment.

'Be so good as to lay this sheet across the chart exactly.'

Marked on the parchment in pencil were a row of crosses. When the corners of the parchment lined up exactly with those of the chart, the crosses fell upon the red ink lines. All of them were closer to the right-hand column, with the more agreeable traits.

'Can you imagine a person with this sort of character? Does it belong to anyone you might know?'

'Sir, I... I don't know what you mean, sir.'

'Violet perhaps?'

'No. Not Violet.'

'Why not?'

'Her temper changes. Sometimes she is gay and lively, and other times solemn and...'

'And...?'

Cora could not bring herself to say *rude* and *haughty*. 'Silent.'

'I see.'

'So I couldn't rightly put just one cross on each line for Violet. There would have to be two.'

Mr Jerwood blinked. 'Two?'

'Yes. Sir.'

He put down his teacup and, with precise movements that made very little scraping or clinking, he removed the lid from the sugar bowl, lifted out a lump with the tongs, and stirred it into his tea.

'And what of yourself, Cora Burns? Where would the crosses lie upon your own chart of temper? To the left or to the right? More agreeable than these here, or less so?'

For the sake of appearance, Cora looked again at the descriptions on the left. *Sulky, Fretful, Proud, Fiery.* It might have been a list of distinguishing marks on her criminal record. But the master must have formed his own opinion of her character by now. Why should he care what she thought of herself?

'In the middle, perhaps.'

'For every pair of tempers?

'Yes, sir.'

Mr Jerwood took a sip of the sweetened tea and turned to Cora with a gaze like granite.

'I think that you owe me a little more than that, Cora Burns. I have, after all, employed you in circumstances which few others would countenance. And I am prepared to overlook certain misdemeanours, even theft and assault, which most employers would hold to be heinous. All I ask in return is a little transparency about your own circumstances.'

For a second, Cora's muscles seemed to dilute, but then she dug her fingernails into her palms and a pulse of heat flowed through her.

'I wanted only to get back what was rightly mine. Sir.'

Mr Jerwood smiled with one side of his mouth and then nodded. 'Steal it, you mean?'

Cora squeezed her fists and the nails dug deeper. She looked at the floor. If she saw the master's self-satisfied smile, she couldn't be answerable for what those fists might do. He did not seem to want a response.

'I think we might place your temper closer to the left side of the chart. And perhaps you would indulge me by revealing whether your character has always been as it is now? Or have you changed according to the experiences of your life?'

'How could I know?'

'Well, if you think back to your childhood – in the Union workhouse, wasn't it – was your temper then as fiery as it seems now?'

Cora returned a look as hard and unblinking as his own. 'Yes.'

'So we might say that your temper has been passed to you, unchanged, from Mary Burns. Or indeed, from Mr Burns.'

'Who?'

The word was out of Cora's mouth before she could stop it but she instantly saw the stupidity of her question. The smugness of the master's expression made her want to lunge for the silver teapot and bring it down, scalding, on to his head. Instead she stood frozen and waited for his reply.

'Why, Mr Burns, your mother's husband, of course. Your father.'

an empty egg

Violet did not look up as Cora came into the library for the breakfast tray. Cora waited by the door, watching the girl scrape out the last slips of white from the shell and spoon them hungrily into her mouth. Violet closed one eye then lifted the empty egg from its silver cup and peered inside it. She seemed entirely unlike the stiff, wary child of yesterday. Perhaps once she noticed Cora, the stony watchfulness would return.

But as she lowered the eggshell and opened both eyes, Violet beamed.

'Cora!' She jumped off the upholstered stool, an orange drip of yolk on her chin. 'Have you ever been to the Free Library?'

Cora blinked. 'No, miss.'

'Oh! You should go. The central reference hall is the biggest room you could possibly imagine. It would make your mouth gape. Like it is now.'

Violet put her hand over her own mouth and giggled. Cora tried to straighten her expression as she picked up the tray.

'I don't suppose it's open on a Sunday, miss.'

'Perhaps not.'

Violet bounced up and reached out to the breakfast things in Cora's hands, turning over the hollowed-out eggshell in the small cup so that it appeared whole and uneaten. There was fresh colour in the girl's cheeks and a new lightness in her step.

'You are looking better, Miss Violet.'

'Better than what?'

'Better than yesterday.'

'Did I see you yesterday?'

'Yes. I brought you your egg.'

Violet frowned. 'I think you are mistaken.'

'Mistaken? No. I brought you an egg for your high tea.'

'Perhaps you are unwell, Cora. You do look a bit peaky.'

Cora gave the child a sideways glance as she turned for the door. How could she have forgotten that Cora had brought her tea last night? Had she been in some sort of stupor? Perhaps Mrs Dix had mixed up the milks and given Violet a draught of chloral intended for the missus. But as she looked, Cora saw that Violet's eyes once again contained identically sized discs of clear blue.

'Your eye is healed.'

'My eye?' Violet laughed. 'You do say the funniest things, Cora.' She began to rock back and forth on her heels with a mischievous look. 'I wonder what you'd say if I told you what else I did yesterday.'

Cora shrugged. 'Depends what it was.'

Throwing a quick look at the bookshelves, Violet lowered her voice almost to a whisper. 'Well, it's sort of a secret.'

She reached out her arm and beckoned Cora towards her with a theatrical curl of her forefinger. As Cora put down the tray, she felt sure that the master was listening behind the books. Violet stepped on to the stool so that their faces were level and put her mouth to Cora's ear, cupping it with her hand. Her breath was hot and faintly eggy.

'Alice has gone to the *Gazette*.'

Cora pulled her head away. 'What?'

Violet put a taut finger to her lips then whispered again in Cora's ear. 'I delivered the sketch myself with a letter in my best handwriting.'

'Lord in heaven.'

'Are you not pleased?'

'What did the letter say?'

'It asked if they would publish an advertisement free of charge for a respectable but poor child seeking her long-lost sister.'

'What name did you give for a reply?'

'My own. "Miss V Poole, The Larches, Spark Hill".'

Cora closed her eyes.

Violet whispered louder. 'It was done only to help you. I thought we had agreed.'

'I did not expect it to happen.'

Although Cora had, miraculously, kept her position here despite yesterday's outbursts, she'd no doubt that from now on any small misdemeanour would be enough to make her lose it. Becoming over-familiar with Miss Violet and causing the child's name and directions to be printed in the press for anyone to see, was more than enough reason to be dismissed.

Violet stepped back and the colour dropped from her face. Then she whispered again, her breath brushing Cora's ear.

'Did I do wrong? Will you forgive me?'

Cora sighed and could not summon the energy for anger. And anyway, perhaps it would come to nothing. It was far-fetched to imagine that a newspaper would print an advertisement that was not paid for.

'Don't think on it. 'Tis done now. And I doubt anyone will respond.'

Violet's eyes glazed with tears. 'Are you not pleased at all, Cora?'

The child's heartfelt look made Cora suddenly sigh. Her voice softened. 'It was a clever idea, Violet. I'm obliged to you.'

Again Violet beamed. Cora thought of the master's chart of temper and how easily any person's mood might swing from one side to the other. How might Samuel or Ellen describe her own temperament? Cold-hearted, vicious, deranged? She had no real idea of how she might define herself.

Cora bent for the tray and Violet jumped down from the stool.

'Don't go yet, Cora. I'm supposed to amuse myself in here all morning.'

'I could lay the fire, I suppose.'

'Oh yes. And maybe you could help me with my still lifes again.'

'I don't think so.'

But Violet had already rushed to the what-not and was opening a drawer. She brought her sketchbook to the cabinet and sank down in front of the glass shelves, the white pages open on her lap.

'Here. I can show you my medallion sketches against the real things and you can tell me how true they are.'

Violet pulled forward the inlaid medallion box and flipped open the lid. Cora gave a start. Here, suddenly, was a chance to examine the collection. She knelt beside Violet. A glinting bronze disc was already inside the child's cupped hand.

'Look. Here's the boat on the Bosphorus. Do you think I made the oars long enough in my drawing?'

But Cora's gaze fixed on the line of randomly arranged capitals at the bottom of the coins. 'How do you work out the years from the letters?'

'Don't you know your Roman numerals?'

'No.'

'Have you not seen them on grand buildings in town? I can work them out perfectly now.'

'How?'

'*M* for a thousand, *D* for five hundred, and so on. Here, like on this ship medallion; *MD* then three *CCC*s that's the century, eighteen hundred, then *LXXIV* for seventy-four.'

'Seventy-four? So the one goes before the five to subtract it.'

'Exactly! You are clever, Cora. It took me ages to get the hang of that.'

The medallions seemed to shine brighter. Maybe Susan Gill had polished them with something more delicate than brick dust. Cora took the ship medallion from Violet and laid it on her palm. It had a familiar length and thickness although heavy. She turned it over. The back was as smooth and empty as her half-medal except, at the top rim, there was a neat band of capitals: *W.TONKS&SONS*. It was a maker's mark. A cold shiver passed down Cora's back.

Pushing the medallion back into its velvet roundel, she stood up. 'I need to get a bucket of coal.'

Violet grabbed hold of her skirt. 'Don't go, Cora. You haven't compared my sketches with the medallions yet.'

'I'll be back presently.'

Once inside the coal-house, Cora made sure there was no sign of Ellen or the outdoor men, then she stood with her back to the opening and undid the two top buttons of her bodice. The letters at the base of the half-medal made instant sense: *MDCCCLXI. 1861*. But the cut through the middle had sliced almost into the last *I*. Perhaps originally the whole coin showed more numerals. Perhaps another *I*, or a *V*. The coin might actually show a full date of *1862* or *1863*. Or *1864*.

Cora turned her half-medal over. She had not cleaned the reverse as thoroughly as the decorated front but apart from the hole for the twine, there was nothing to see on the plain half-moon of metal. If it had been made by W Tonks and Sons, his mark would surely be there as it was on the medallions in the library. Cora breathed out. Just because the master's collection was made by someone else did not mean that her own was not from Salt & Co. Perhaps this sort of coin was a common product amongst Birmingham's many metalworkers.

Then, as her eyes adjusted to the light in the dirty lean-to, she noticed a chip on the reverse of the half-medal near the top of the point. Cora spat gently on the metal and rubbed it with her apron. She had never before noticed this blemish on the back, or perhaps she'd just discounted it as a slip of the saw when the medal was cut in two. But now that she'd seen another mark so similar she realised that she had been wrong. Because the mark was not an accidental dent, nor the chip from a saw, it was a slightly severed but perfectly crafted *W*.

EIGHTEEN

1881

the cut

Mrs Catch said the asylum wasn't far from the Union house. You could just about see it from the gatehouse. Cora followed her along the big corridor from the dormitory, past the women's receiving ward and into the porters' lodge. There, they told Cora to write her name on a piece of paper. As she wrote, her eyes flickered over a list of all the clothes that she was wearing and the others in her bundle right down to the hanky.

Then Mrs Catch held out a brown envelope. *'Cora Burns'* was written on it in spidery faded ink.

'Here are your own things.'

Cora blinked. 'What things?'

'From when you were admitted.'

Cora shook her head. 'I've always been here.'

'No. You came as a babe in arms.' Mrs Catch glanced down at the ledger. 'Twenty-third of June 1865. Brought by a wardress.'

Cora had no notion of what a wardress might be but would not give Mrs Catch the satisfaction of asking. The flap on the envelope was not sealed and she lifted it to see a piece of stiff paper furred along the folds. Mrs Catch tapped her on the shoulder.

'Come now, don't dither. Put it safely in your bundle.'

They went outside into the gatehouse archway where whitewashed columns separated the covered pavement from the cartway. Even though it was Sunday, a line of vagrants, men and women, stood patiently by the receiving door. Cora had only ever seen the casuals in their workhouse clothes. She couldn't help staring at the filthy rags they wore on this side of the gatehouse. One old man's white belly flashed through a rip in the greasy blanket he had wrapped around himself. Cora looked away in case she saw more.

Mrs Catch walked briskly into the swirl of crisp air then stopped by the railings and pointed towards the cut. In the distance, pointed brick gables jutted out of bare trees.

'Follow the canal until you see an entranceway. The sign is quite clear. It will not take you long.' The railing gate squeaked open. 'Off you go then. And don't speak to anyone until you get there.'

Mrs Catch had already turned her back. The black frill on her tall bonnet quivered as she strode back to the archway.

Weak sunlight silvered the puddles on the empty road. Cora began to walk, her feet in time with a muffled banging somewhere inside the boiler-works across the way. She tried to feel hopeful. When Mrs Catch had come to the dormitory after chapel and told her to gather her things, Cora had done her best to make out that she didn't care one way or another. But she knew that this meant that she was going, finally, to a situation. She seemed to have waited for this day longer than any of the other girls and should have been giddy to get away at long last, but the notion of walking alone out of the gatehouse scrambled her stomach.

She'd hardly ever been out. Some years ago, the workhouse foundlings and orphans had performed in an Easter tableau at St Philip's Church and she'd been a handmaiden, whatever that was. And last October, in the gilded banqueting hall of the new Council House, she'd been one of the hundred pauper children given fruit punch and a pie. On each occasion, the gaggle of chattering workhouse kids cocooned her so tightly that she hardly noticed the outside world.

The road narrowed on to a bridge and Cora stopped to look at the cut. A hard breeze funnelled off the water. Both ways, the canal was empty of barge boats; towards the town, the waterway curved out of sight into crammed rows of grey houses and slender belching chimneys. In the other direction, it followed a straight course alongside an open field. Beyond that, the long building with fancy brickwork must be the asylum. And looming over its pointed red gables was the black roofline of the gaol.

A muddy trail dropped from the bridge to the towing path and Cora stopped at the edge of the water. If she was to do what she'd been told, she'd turn along the field, up the tree-lined drive to the asylum and into a life she could imagine very well. There'd be wages and a day off but it would be the same washerwoman drudgery they'd been skilling her for at the Union house, except for the longer hours and the fouler sheets.

In the other direction, lay the town. She mightn't need to walk that way for long until she'd come to the wide sweeping streets and stone facades. Why shouldn't she? Surely she was strong and clever enough to make her own way in the world. And, for the very first time, there was no one around who could stop her.

Cora sat down under the bridge and let her boots dangle above the canal. A fat drip fell from the damp curve of brickwork and sent rings rippling across the sluggish surface. Perhaps the envelope inside her bundle would help her decide which way to go.

The apron was slackly tied but Cora's fingers fumbled on the knot. Her nightdress and spare shimmy spilled on to the dirt. Then paper fluttered in her hands. The white rectangle had been folded for so long that the print had worn away along each crease. Printed columns revealed themselves one by one; under **Name and Maiden Surname of Mother**, a greyish copperplate hand had written *Mary Burns*.

It was Cora's birth certificate. And there at last was her mother's name; a name so obvious that Cora felt suddenly sick. There were more Marys than anything else in the workhouse so if she had given the matter even a minute's thought she could have guessed her mother's name years ago. The next column: **Name and Surname of Father** was blank. And then, under **When and Where Born**, a cluster of words that made Cora's eyes swim black as the canal: *Third April 1865, Birmingham Gaol, Female Wing*.

Gaol. She was born in gaol. To a convict? There seemed nothing else that Mary Burns might be. Of course her offence could have been trivial; a drunken insult or the theft of a crust. But it might have been something much worse; a crime so wicked that Mary Burns could still be there, under that distant black roof.

A crack echoed off the bridge and it was a second or two before Cora realised that the noise was a laugh that had come from her own throat. It barked again. *Gaol.* Yes, that was funny. And completely obvious. She should have known all along what her mother would be. How many times had Cora been told that she was a bad lot, the wickedest girl in the workhouse? And then there was that business with Alice…

For a short minute, Cora let her mind skitter over the place in her memory that was usually sealed. The place where something bad had happened to a little boy. Percy they'd called him, although she never knew his real name. She could still see his face; dull-eyed and still, with something she thought of as a flower coming out of his mouth.

She could not fathom what had happened next. Had she been taken straight from the privy block to the infirmary? If she'd gone somewhere else, the superintendent's office or the Bridewell, she could not remember it. And she had no notion of how long she'd then stayed in the workhouse infirmary. Many months. Perhaps years. She'd become so used to the rough-fingered orderlies and the runny food that she was almost fond of the place. Sometimes she'd even been ill.

When, finally, Cora had left the infirmary and returned to the dormitory, everyone she'd known before had gone. Not just Alice, but the whole Bolger tribe. And Mr Bowyer. The new teachers never again asked Cora to write on the blackboard. When she'd got too old for lessons, she'd been sent to the laundry. Others came and went from the girls' dormitory until Cora seemed to be the oldest as – she could now see from the birth certificate – she certainly was. Because, although she hadn't known it until two minutes earlier, today, the third of April, was her sixteenth birthday.

The paper in Cora's hand felt suddenly caustic, as if covered in lye. She flung it away from her and watched it drop, twitching, over the lip of the canal before drifting down. Brackish water began to seep over the words.

Cora cried out. Those faded copperplate words, however hateful their story, were all that she had to tell her who she was. She scooped up the birth certificate, drying it quickly on the apron bundle and refolding the paper along the creases. Then as she opened the envelope to replace it, something weighty fell out. A dirty half-moon of metal landed on Cora's palm.

It was a coin cut through the middle; bigger, she thought, than the half-crown that Mr Bowyer had once showed the class when they were adding up money, but brown like an old penny. The straight-cut edge was slightly jagged but the back, apart from a small hole bored near the point, seemed entirely smooth. The front showed no sign of the Queen's head which Cora knew to be on all proper coins. Instead, there were some folds that looked like badly pegged-out sheets and a tiny raised hand that pointed at the letters around the border. At the bottom, *M*s and *C*s spelt out nothing that

Cora could pronounce. But above them, elegant capitals carved two words: *IMAGINEM SALT.*

SALT. Her heart leapt. What else could this be but a gift from Alice Salt? Alice must have come back to the workhouse asking for Cora but got no further than the porters' lodge. So Alice had left instead this keepsake. Alice had, after all, lived with a family of japanners and metalworkers, so the coin must have been made in the workshop of Salt & Co. Alice might have retained the other half herself, giving Cora the portion that would act as an instruction to keep faith in her friend. If she could no longer see Alice every day, Cora must at least imagine her. And when the two halves were reunited, the girls would be sure to know each other, however much they might have grown up and changed.

Cora folded her hand over the thing, squeezing until the points dug into flesh. Alice had not forgotten her. And perhaps she'd come looking for Cora with a confession about what had happened in the privy block. A few heartfelt words from Alice would instantly release Cora from the unsettling gnaw of guilt.

She now had no choice about which direction to take along the towing path. If Alice again went to the workhouse to ask for Cora, they would direct her to the laundry at Birmingham Lunatic Asylum. So that was where Cora must go. She secured the half-coin back inside the envelope and retied the bundle. Then as she jumped up, a dark figure seemed to glide across the mirrored surface of the canal. Gooseflesh rose on Cora's arms.

But it was a reflection of a dark figure on the path; a man, well-dressed with a parson's collar, marching towards her. The path beneath the bridge was narrow and in avoiding Cora, he tripped on the coping of the water's edge. His words bit the air.

'Out of my way, girl. Know your place.'

Fury filled Cora with sudden strength and she felt her body swerve towards the parson. One firm shove from behind and he would be in the cut, flailing and sinking. With any luck, he'd never get out. But already the man was beyond the bridge and striding towards the town, his long black coat flapping at the back of his knees.

Cora floundered into the light. Lord in heaven. She'd almost pushed a man, a gentleman priest, into the canal. Almost murdered him. And she'd no idea why, except for Mary Burns' savage blood running through her veins.

The smell from the workhouse piggeries, or maybe the gasworks, blew across the canal as Cora stumbled along a path that pointed to the lunatic asylum. Black and white birds dived over the yellow field with plaintive whooping calls. Then the path forked on to a tree-lined track that widened to a carriage turn. Black diamonds patterned the red-brick facade behind the thin trunks. Stone steps led to entrance doors beneath a mullion window set with coloured glass.

Uncertain whether to knock, Cora clutched her bundle to her chest. As she reached out to touch the brass handle, the door seemed to open on its own.

'Yes?'

The man wore a blue calico suit with matching cap. His bushy grey eyebrows scuttled into a frown as he looked over Cora's head and across the field. He seemed as like to be a lunatic as one of the staff.

'Are you seeking admission?'

Cora's brain was blank.

The man bent closer. 'Who brought you?'

'No one. I've come for a position. In the laundry.'

'You've picked a funny time for it. They've knocked off till Monday. Why've you come today?'

'I had to come today. It's my birthday.'

The man's look was suspicious. If he thought she was an imbecile she couldn't blame him. But he pulled open the door and it was only then as she entered the cavernous white hall that Cora realised, with the unmistakeable punch of truth, that she shared her birthday, and indeed, the very day of her birth with Alice Salt.

NINETEEN

December 1885

cycle

Alfred Thripp, in shirtsleeves and fancy waistcoat, was rolling up his cuffs and whistling. Cora listened through the crack at the door. The tune was familiar, although the words escaped her. She stepped further back into the studio to slip off her Melton jacket and then her linsey skirt. Winter light lanced through the roof window, turning her bare arms the colour of newly skimmed milk.

The outfit he had laid out for her on a chair was more handsome than anything she had ever held. It was fine wool, cashmere she guessed, that was soft as down. Stripes of dark purple and heathery mauve ran head to toe through the fabric. She guessed that the pattern would draw the eye and intensify the vividness of the stereograph.

The skirt tied snug at the waist. An apron pleat at the front swept up to a drooping mound of fabric behind which needed a bustle for support. But only the walking-dress had been left out. Alfred cannot have thought too deeply about the detail of ladies' underwear. Which was a blessing, she supposed.

As she began to fasten the gilt buttons on the jacket, the whistling stopped and Alfred called out.

'Nearly there?'

'Yes, nearly.'

Cora took a breath and looked down at herself. The dress was too long in the skirt and too tight under the arms but it more or less fitted. A faint tidemark along the hem and some wear on the cuffs showed that it was not entirely new. Perhaps Alfred had a sister to whom it belonged, or even a wife, although the dress seemed too grand. Cora itched to see her reflection but there was no mirror in the studio. The stereographic likeness alone would show how she might look as a lady.

'I'm ready.'

The door then sprang open as if he'd been waiting behind it.

'My goodness! You look fine.'

Alfred brought with him into the room a clean waft of tar soap.

186

His face was flushed and Cora sensed that he was trying not to smile too wide.

Cora breathed in. 'It doesn't fit exactly right.'

'But it looks grand. I'll arrange the fabric once you are in place with the safety bicycle.'

The Rover was leaning against a stool, cramped into the corner of the studio. Carefully, Alfred lifted the bicycle forward, casting an eye at the camera lens as he placed it in front of a wobbly screen painted to show a faded woodland glade.

'Here, Miss Burns, if you could put your hand on the saddle to balance the machine, like this.'

'Oh, just call me Cora.'

'Would you not mind?'

She shook her head. Being called *Miss* made her feel as though there was someone else standing beside her who was too close to be seen. Her hand replaced Alfred's on the stitched leather saddle and in the changeover their smallest fingers stroked against each other. Cora sensed Alfred's eyes flicker up but she kept her gaze on the Rover's seat. He went to the camera and looked into the back of it.

'There. Yes. A little more towards this way. Yes. Good. And if you would just permit me…'

He came towards her across the room, his eyes shining with purpose, and bent almost to one knee behind her. Before Cora could look round, she felt her skirts being lifted and a rush of air move up her legs.

'What are you doing?'

'I'm sorry, I'm just arranging your attire into a more fashionable aspect. Do you mind?'

Getting intimate with ladies' garments must be a normal part of his work. She shrugged and looked over her shoulder as he lifted the mound of unbustled fabric from her behind and tried to balance it on the Rover's back wheel. It took several attempts to make the skirt stay where he wanted. As he manipulated the woollen folds, Cora felt her underthings rub back and forth across her buttocks. A little needle of heat jumped up inside her.

'If you could stay, Cora, exactly there and not move…' Alfred put out both hands as if commanding the walking-dress to do as it was told and jumped back behind the camera. 'And now, as you look into the lens, imagine yourself outside of the town on a country lane. You are about to mount yourself on to the saddle and glide the machine down a gentle hill.'

The heat inside Cora spread to her gut and then up to her throat. She stared into the camera, her breath quickening. The shutter made a faint click. Alfred raised the flat of his hand in a sign to stay where she was.

'Please, now if you can, do not move a muscle. Just for two minutes whilst I reset the device.'

Cora did as he said and kept her eyes forward and her hand clamped on the bicycle seat. But her insides churned. She watched Alfred change the camera box that held the plate and then, hurriedly but deftly, he moved the device a few inches to the left. She admired the confidence and precision of his actions. His body was compact and wiry beneath his shirt. She breathed lightly but the jacket of the walking-dress felt even tighter than when she had put it on and her heart pulsed against her stays.

Alfred looked up from the camera and nodded. 'Right then. Again, you're at the top of that hill, a light breeze blowing into your face.' The shutter snapped and Alfred smiled. 'Very good. You are a natural. Not many can hold still so well.'

Cora could have told him that it must be due to the many hours she'd sat motionless in her cell thinking of nothing except the passing seconds and a resolve not to go mad. But that was something she hoped no one would ever know.

'Are we done now?'

Her heart dipped at the thought of replacing the sleek walking-dress with her coarse Melton jacket.

Alfred, still scrutinising her, put his hand to his cheek. 'Might we try another pose? Whilst the light is good?'

'All right.'

'I would like to see you sit upon the bicycle, if you dare.'

'The seat looks too tall.'

'Here, I can adjust it.'

He came forward with a small spanner and bent over the Rover, twisting and pushing on the seat. The muscles on his forearms tensed into shadow lines as he took a firm hold of the handlebars.

'That should do it. And here is a stool to step on. Perhaps you may wish to place a hand on my shoulder to help you mount the machine.'

For a moment Cora looked straight at him. There was such a mix of seriousness and shyness in his eyes that she almost laughed out loud. She'd lay a pound, if she ever had one, on him never having done it with a woman.

Bending her head to hide her amusement, Cora gathered the skirt away from the bicycle's oily mechanisms then stepped on to the low wooden stool. She held on to Alfred to steady herself. His shoulder beneath the waistcoat felt tight and warm. Cora raised her leg and lifted it over the crossbar. Her stocking flashed black between her petticoats and she gripped Alfred hard. His breath was on her neck and he was willing her to fall against him, she could tell. The choice now was hers.

'No. I'm sorry, Mr Thripp. I won't be able to keep myself still like this.'

She flung her leg back over the bar in a flurry of white cotton and purple stripes.

'Please, it's Alfred. And that's perfectly all right. I think we have some excellent shots already. Would you mind waiting for me to develop the plates? Just to check? You can change, if you like, whilst I'm in the developing room.'

He opened the door to the orange-lit cupboard that she had seen his father use on her first visit to the shop. His cheeks were crimson.

The construction of cleverly cut seams and tiny darts allowed the walking-dress bodice to keep its shape even after Cora had taken it off. She'd have liked to take a closer look at the needlework to see how it was done, but couldn't delay getting her own clothes back on. There was no telling how long he'd be in that cupboard. But as she walked out of the studio and back into the shop she let her hand linger on the soft woollen fabric of the walking-dress.

In fact, Alfred did not reappear for quite some time. When he came into the shop, his face was glowing. He wiped the shine from his brow with a handkerchief.

'Excellent results, I think. I shall just give the plates two further minutes. Let me pay you for your time as we agreed.'

He went behind the glass counter and opened a wooden drawer with a small key from his waistcoat pocket. Cora heard coins dropping one on to another. Then he placed a neat pile of silver on the glass top and folded his arms.

'There. A guinea.'

'It's too much.'

'I thought we'd agreed.'

'But I've done so little. It seems… improper.'

Alfred flinched. 'Believe me, there'll be plenty of money changing hands in this Rover business. Why should you not have your share?'

The coins squeaked against the glass as he pushed them forward. Cora licked her lips. She was due something, she supposed.

'I'll take ten shillings. To cover the trams and such.'

'Yes. But take the rest next time.'

'Next time?'

'Of course. I still have in my mind that you should learn to ride the Rover. Perhaps over the darker months you could come back to practise. And when spring comes, try for an action shot out of doors.'

'I don't think…'

He raised both hands to silence her. 'Just wait. Don't say anything until you have seen the plate.'

He rushed back into the studio and emerged a minute later holding a wet plate by its edges. The glass, when he laid it on top of a sheet of white blotting paper, looked as detailed as a print although black where it should be white. Cora could see why he was pleased. The bicycle might really have been out on a country lane with a striking woman in a fancy outfit poised to mount it for an exhilarating ride. The woman's dark face gave off such confidence that no one viewing it through a stereoscope could have had any doubt that she was capable of such a feat.

Cora counted four half-crowns from the pile of silver and slipped them into the laundered flour-sack pocket. Then she pulled her shawl tightly about her head.

'Thank you for your kindness today, Mr Thripp. But I have to tell you that I shall not be coming back here again.'

doll

A chill gust whipped Cora's face as she turned into Bull Street but she let her shawl drop and hang loose about her arms. Inside she was boiling. It was her own stupid weakness that had forced her to wave goodbye to the prospect of so much easy money. All she'd have needed to do was let herself be helped on to a safety bicycle and then keep still. But she knew, if she ever went back to the photographer's shop, that she'd never manage it.

She'd be unable to resist Alfred Thripp for long. His mix of yearning and sheepishness would soon make her crack, as much from impatience as desire. Then she'd be the one egging him on to do things that were ever more unspeakable and delicious. With each increasingly shocking suggestion she'd relish his initial outrage. But then, like Mr Jerwood perhaps, she'd examine his reaction and perhaps even count the seconds that it would take for his shock to melt, as it inevitably would, into lust.

With Jimmy, the count wouldn't even have reached one second. His appetites were almost as urgent as Cora's, although not so inventive. The only time Jimmy had ever looked shocked was when she'd waylaid him, that first time, on the tree-shaded path beside the boiler house. He'd probably never seen anything so brazen as her standing there, petticoats above her ankles, asking whether he wanted to do it with her or not.

Cora, in her ignorance, had been unable to see how the urge could be wrong if she felt it so strongly. The words 'ventilation tunnel' were hardly out of her mouth before he'd pulled her inside the brick duct beneath the asylum. They were so well hidden in there that even though she'd never done it before, and guessed that he hadn't either, both of them ended up entirely unclothed. Afterwards, for what seemed like hours, they'd remained naked, unable to take their eyes off each other's secret parts.

And if she went with Alfred Thripp, it would end up just as it had with Jimmy. She'd bleed in the same nasty snare as before. All for the sake of ten shillings every Sunday and the scratching of an itch between her legs. She may as well go and work on Bordesley Street.

Past the Market Hall, the street began to widen out and the soot-caked spire of St Martin's Church brooded behind the mist. In the middle of the roadway, stalls were scrubbed bare and piled up; a few empty handcarts chained to railings around the statue. A roast-chestnut man, with a covered tray slung around his neck, stood silent by the drinking fountain, his eyes scanning the High

Street for constables. A one-handed woman sat on the plinth, her knees spread wide to display a row of used clay pipes on her stained apron.

Cora felt a tug at her skirt and a shifty-looking boy in a flat cap opened his fist in front of her.

'Ha'penny for the lot, missus.'

Three grubby monkey nuts lay on the boy's outstretched palm. Before any thought came into Cora's head, the flat of her hand had sprung up towards his cheek. The satisfying sting of a slap would have him scuttling off like a skittle in an alley. But with her hand in the air, she clenched her fingers and stopped herself. He was a child, after all. Cora shivered and dropped a penny into the street-lad's hand.

'Keep the nuts.'

The boy swiped the coin into his fist and sneered at Cora as he would a simpleton. Then he ran off.

Cora pulled her shawl tighter. When the flower market was there, the Bull Ring had an air of liveliness and colour but on a Sunday nothing masked the grime. The roadway was ground down with hardened horse shit and slimy scraps. As she hurried on to the stone pavement by the church, a street-seller, apparently heedless of any nearby constables, was calling out her wares.

'Kitty-cats! Bow-wows! Babbies!'

Cora began to veer away from the girl with her home-made trinkets laid out on a sack, but she could not help looking. The figurines were roughly made from paper and paste, all painted in unlikely colours; yellow dogs, orange cats and a red-faced doll with black pinhead eyes.

'Want a doggy, missus?'

Then Cora saw the girl's face and froze.

'Violet?'

The girl's expression fell into a scowl.

Cora took a step closer. 'Violet? Is that you? What are you doing?'

'Don't know what you're on about.'

The girl's voice was laced through with the drawling vowels of the town's rookeries. Her coppery hair was loose about her shoulders but the face, the dark brows and rounded cheeks, was

Violet's. Blood rushed to Cora's brain. This girl could not be Violet and yet she was.

'How did you get here?'

'What's it to you, missus?'

The girl stuck out her chin, and in that moment the misty light must have reflected across her eyes, because Cora saw that although one was blue, the other was almost entirely black. A thought flashed through her mind like a spill in a gas jet.

'That was you at The Larches last week, wasn't it? I saw you there.'

The look of sudden recognition and panic that flooded the girl's face was enough to let Cora know that she was right.

Cora took a quick breath and told herself to walk away. She should ignore the unsavoury goings-on in the Jerwood household just as Cook and the other servants with wit enough to notice must have already decided to do. If Cora gave in to curiosity, the consequences were unlikely to do her any good. Yet, she might learn something that would give her some sway over the master and perhaps oblige him to point her towards Alice. And a bitter taste came into Cora's mouth as she imagined the master in some way taking advantage of Violet.

Cora cast an eye at the girl, then bent down beside the sacking and put out a finger, lightly stroking a lopsided yellow terrier.

'This is a dear little thing. Did you make it?'

The girl's face was still fixed in a scowl but her fingers were twisting into her filthy cotton apron that had probably never been white.

She shook her head. 'Florrie made that one.'

'Which did you make then?'

The girl pointed at the paste-head doll with pin eyes. A few black lines had been painted on for hair; the body was no more than a stuffed bag made from a calico sack.

'Oh, that's the best one of all! But I suppose it costs the most. How much do you want for it?'

'A shilling?'

The girl probably didn't expect more than sixpence. Her eyes followed Cora's hand as it came out of her pocket with a big silver coin pinched between thumb and forefinger.

'Here. She's so pretty I'll give you half a crown for her...' Cora held the coin over the girl's cupped hand and looked into her darkened eye. '… if you tell me your name.'

The girl hesitated and licked her lips. 'Letty. Letty Flynn.'

'And where do you live, Letty?'

The girl shook her head but Cora dropped the coin in her hand anyway.

'All right. But tell me a bit more. Is Florrie your sister?'

Letty nodded.

'Do you have any other sisters?

'Aye. Plenty.'

Cora gave a laugh. 'Any close to you in age?'

'What d'you mean?'

'A sister who looks just like you.'

With a shrug Letty raised herself up on to her tiptoes and held herself there for a moment, a look of concentration on her face. Hairs prickled at the back of Cora's neck because, apart from the tattered shawl and the flapping boots, it might have been Violet, raising herself on to the toes of her indoor shoes to consider stealing an envelope.

Letty lowered her heels back to the ground. 'There was one but she died.'

The tingle slipped into Cora's spine. 'Oh, that's sad. Do you remember her?'

Again Letty shrugged then scratched the back of her head. Cora took a quick breath.

'I know it was you at The Larches last week. I don't mean to pry but I'm shook to see you here, like this. Will you let me see where you live?'

Letty shook her head fiercely. 'It's all to be kept a secret. Ma says it would cost us dear if anyone finds out.'

'Why?'

'I don't know.'

'Well, I've found out now. Why should I keep it a secret if I don't know what for? Your Ma can explain it to me. I just mean to be sure that you're safe.'

Letty's brows furrowed as if the words were foreign. Cora reached into her pocket and felt through the coins. Why hadn't she, damn it, taken that single shilling that made up the guinea? All she had left to offer was another half-crown. Letty's eyes widened as Cora held it out to her.

Both of the silver coins went inside Letty's sack along with the tatty paste toys. Cora felt her shoulders tense as she imagined where Letty might take her and what might be said. But the trepidation was warming her up. She was ready for a fight.

Letty hauled the bulging sack over her shoulder and nodded her head towards Digbeth. One of the paste toys, the ugly doll, was still in her hand. She held it out to Cora.

'Here, missus. Don't forget your babby.'

court

Boot soles gaped and flapped like hungry fish but didn't seem to slow Letty down. She weaved over cobbles and kerbs, steering Cora against a wall at the tight corner of Meriden Street as a horse tram clipped by. Cora sensed that the girl was more at home amongst the carts and costermongers and dingy corner shops than she would ever be.

They turned into Coventry Street and even though it was Sunday, a sour breeze blew up from the vinegar brewery. Deftly, Letty pushed Cora aside saving her foot from a steaming pile of dog mess. The girl laughed and looked so like Violet that bumps rose through Cora's flesh.

'Is it far?'

Letty shook her head and smiled. The blackness in her right eye seemed darker.

'What happened to your eye?'

Letty shrugged.

'Has it always been like that?'

'I don't know.'

'Does it trouble you?'

'Oh no. Ma says it's a blessing because it helps her see that it's me.'

'What does she mean?'

Again the girl shrugged. Then she began to skip and pointed.

'That's our entry.'

From the street, the houses didn't look too bad; a three-storey brick terrace with solid chimney stacks and tall sash windows. But once through the whitewashed passage to the back of the row, their true condition was clear. Other rows of almost identical houses had been built at tight right angles to the street and the high featureless wall of a factory or warehouse formed the back of the enclosed court. The yard looked worse even than the one Cora had seen on Bordesley Street. Perhaps there, the thin glare of gaslight hadn't revealed the squalid detail, but here, there was enough bleak light to expose every pane of broken glass and gutter stain.

At the back of the yard, a boy smaller than Letty was sitting at the edge of an overflowing ash heap beside the privy hut. He saw them and rushed over, his fists caked with ashes.

'What you got, Letty?'

'Nothing.'

'Who's this?'

'Nobody.'

Letty was heading towards a door that was piled about with huge sacks, as high as Cora's shoulder, brimming with rags. The whiff of rotten clothes blotted out the reek of the privy. Cora's grip on the paste-head doll tightened.

They went inside and up a narrow wooden staircase. As the boy squeezed past Cora, his hand left an ashy smear on her skirt. At the landing, Letty pushed open a door and went in. Warily, Cora followed over the threshold then caught her breath. The room was not much bigger than the scullery at The Larches. In one corner, a bed was piled high with dirty rags and, below the window, two grubby-faced little girls were tearing paper into a wooden tub. In a poor effort to cheer the place up, yellowed pages from illustrated newspapers were stuck haphazardly around the walls.

At the small iron stove, a woman was on her hands and knees, her head almost inside the open door, rattling the grate with a poker.

'Is that Robbie?' Her voice was breathy with Irishness. 'Did y'get any?'

The boy dipped past Letty and went to the stove. 'Here, Ma.'

Delicately, the boy opened his fists and laid a few nuggets of charcoal on to the chipped tiles of the hearth.

'Good boy.'

'Letty's back an'all. With a woman.'

Mrs Flynn's head jerked round. As she registered Cora standing at the half-open door, her expression hardened to a blank mask. She stood up, hands on her waist.

'What's she doing here?'

Letty delved a hand into the bulging sack. 'She's from The Larches, Ma. She saw me at the Bull Ring. Look.'

Her hand thrust the silver half-crowns towards her mother. The woman's eyes went from the coins to Cora. Her face was hollowed with shadows; a thin line of soot cut across her forehead.

'What d'y want?'

The woman was just about old enough, Cora reckoned, to be her own mother. And if Cora ever met her, she imagined that this was how Mary Burns would likely look. A bitter little flame leapt through Cora's stomach.

'I've come to give you Mr Jerwood's compliments.'

Mrs Flynn snorted. 'And?'

'And to ask Letty to visit The Larches again next week.'

The woman's eyes narrowed. 'Next week?'

Letty gave out a throaty wail and dropped her sack to the floor. Then she jumped at her mother, both hands gripping on to the woman's fraying sleeve.

'I'm not going back any more. I don't like it.'

'Shish! Hold your tongue, child.'

Mrs Flynn's hand glanced across the top of Letty's head. Then she folded her arms and stared at Cora.

'Why's he sent you?'

'Mr Jerwood is busy.'

'But I don't see him anyways. Haven't seen him for years.'

Cora took a breath and steeled herself. 'Not since you sold your daughter to him, do you mean?'

Mrs Flynn lunged. Cora put up her hands ready to make a grab at the lank hair but the woman stopped herself before they touched and her mouth hovered by Cora's cheek. The breath was rancid as month-old pork dripping.

'You'll say not another word.'

In the far corner of the room, a wail had started up. Until then Cora hadn't noticed a red-cheeked baby sitting on a rolled-out mattress. Its arms were thrown wide as it hiccupped and sobbed, a thick sheen of slobber across its chin. Mrs Flynn reached for a knitted shawl hanging on the door knob and flung it around her head and shoulders.

'Letty, see to Peg. Robbie, make some knots for the fire.'

She held the door wide for Cora to leave and pressed her thin lips together. Cora glanced at Letty whose face was suddenly pale as she heaved the baby on to her hip.

Cora followed Mrs Flynn down to the yard, through the passageway and out on to Coventry Street. Dusk was blowing a grimy mist down from the chimneys. With a sudden grip on Cora's elbow Mrs Flynn pulled her into the boarded doorway of a grocer's shop.

'What is it you want from us?'

'Only to know about Violet. He gave you money for her, didn't he?'

'He still does, Missus whatever-your-name-is. So that's why you have to keep your trap shut. Because if that money stops, all them kids you see in there will be in the workhouse.'

'But why did he want her, Mrs Flynn? Have you not asked yourself what he might be doing to her? And to Letty?'

'Well, it's nothing like that.'

'How do you know what he's up to?'

'If there was any funny business Letty would tell me. She's going up there a few times a year.'

'And Violet? How could she tell you what he does to her? She doesn't even know you exist.'

'Now missus, you hold your dirty tongue. It's nothing sordid that's going on but 'tis all for science. To measure them both and see the difference fresh air makes to a child.'

'That's why you sold your little one to a stranger?'

'And how does she look then, missus know-it-all? Is she better fed than her sister? Better clothed?'

Cora faltered. 'Yes.'

'So I did right then, didn't I?'

'But Violet feels very alone, Mrs Flynn.'

'Well, so do many of us. But the pain is not so great when your belly is full.'

'Where is Mr Flynn?'

Her look was shifty. 'He's away. Him and my eldest lads. Navigators.'

Cora took a breath. 'Listen, Mrs Flynn. Violet carries inside her the ache of losing a family, of losing a sister who was like a second self. You may not understand.'

'And you do, do you?'

'Yes.'

Mrs Flynn's face, framed by the black shawl, was drained of colour. The woman's mouth twisted with contempt and her sour breath blew into Cora's face.

'A housemaid like you can't have any idea of what it means to bring a child into the world knowing that you have sentenced her to a life of misery.'

Cora felt herself sway forward, fist clenched. She could strike away the woman's easy assumptions with one hard punch. But instead she twisted her heels and blindly marched away.

Thomas Jerwood must have gone looking for a pair of twins and found them easily in the Digbeth rookeries where every family, Irish or not, had too many kids. Perhaps he'd left this same place, or a dirty street just like it, carrying little Violet not long after Cora and Alice had carried the little boy across the Union house schoolyard.

How had Mrs Flynn chosen between the two little girls that were so alike? Was Violet quieter and more timid; more likely to go along with what would be wanted of her by the gentleman? Or did Letty, more fiery and funny, hold a secret place in her mother's heart? Perhaps the babies were so alike that even their mother couldn't tell them apart.

Cora looked up. The gables of Smithfield Market seemed to shudder and close in on her. If only she'd been delivered of two babies. She'd gladly have given one up if that meant she could keep the other. At the edge of the high pavement, as she went to lift her skirts, Cora realised that the paste-head doll was still in her hand. She stumbled up the kerb then stopped and felt suddenly empty of everything. Her hands opened and the garbage-doll dropped into the gutter. As it fell, the sacking arms seemed to fling up, reaching out to her before the whole misshapen body settled into the stone channel. Black pin eyes stared up.

The sight of the forlorn bundle suddenly made Cora buckle. Her throat tightened and she crouched down to scoop it up, shaking her head as she dried the rags and the painted head gently on her skirt.

How she could be so cruel, even to a child that was not real?

Through the fading light, a steam tram went past in a yellow glow, its bell clanking. Cora wiped her cheek and, cradling the papery doll in a careful embrace, she set off at a run towards the terminus.

TWENTY

THE
WYVERN
QUARTERLY

WINTER
1885

PRINTED BY
CORNISH BROS,
37 NEW ST, BIRMINGHAM

FROM: Thomas Jerwood Esq.
An Essay on the Measurement of Man

A mathematical man of my acquaintance, fired with a desire to prove the usefulness of statistics in the study of human biology, took it upon himself to measure the circumference of his children's heads. Throughout their early years, as my friend laid down the dimensions of each child's cranium, he noticed how interludes in growth coincided with an episode of common childhood illness: scarlet fever, diphtheria, measles or the like. Thus, by way of his *living experiment,* my friend contributed to a deeper understanding of the effect of disease upon bone growth.

Man's body is, however, only one component of the human machine, although the easiest to measure. To survey an individual in his entirety, intellect and character must also be gauged, and if the measurements are to be rigorous and capable of accurate comparisons, they must be given *numerical* values. For intellect, examinations (such as those set by the Grammar Schools or the Imperial Civil Service) provide clearly quantifiable scores. Character, as attentive readers will know, may be evaluated numerically by means of the *moral test* (viz. **Experiments in Human Nature** *WQ* Autumn 1885).

All very good, the sceptical reader may say, but how can a person, even a child, be studied as if he were a captive zoological specimen? I would reply that the scientific study of children requires no more than careful observation and record-keeping, along with the application of well-chosen tests. Consider again my mathematical friend and his offspring. How easily he might have measured his own children in their entirety; body, intellect and character rather than simply their skulls, and how much more instructive his endeavour might consequently have been. Indeed, I would even venture to suggest that my friend might have elevated his work to a higher level still had he taken it upon himself to create a *comparative* study by measuring not just his own offspring but also the urchins who habitually called at his kitchen door seeking a cupful of leftover dripping. For, armed with an arsenal of numerical facts detailing the physical, mental and moral capacity of children from contrasting stations in life, my mathematical friend would have been equipped to detect and demonstrate, not merely the effect of disease upon the skeleton, but the entire impact of all manner of influences, stemming from both *heredity* and *upbringing*, upon human development.

Yes, yes, doubters may cry, but what new would be proved? Is it not self-evident that the lower orders are smaller, duller and less morally robust that their betters in society? To which I would reply: where is your statistical proof for such assertions? We may assume, for example, that inadequate nutrition stunts the growth of the lower orders but perhaps some other factor is at work. Only rigorous measurement and statistical analysis can tell us if it is diet that gives the public schoolboy his head and shoulders above a street-seller. Perhaps, in fact, the poor are naturally smaller than the rich, just as some of the African races are shorter than neighbouring tribes.

The perspicacious reader may still be wondering how rigour can be brought to this investigation. Height, for instance, varies even within the classes; every Eton rowing crew has its diminutive coxswain. Can we ever disentangle the multifarious influences that make each person who they are? I believe that we can. Think again of my mathematical friend and imagine, if you will, that he has invited one of those urchins from his kitchen door to share the nursery and education of his son. Both children are then regularly measured in character, intellect and physical traits and their progress plotted by means of statistical tables and graphs. More importantly, another child is also measured; a child who is a peer of the erstwhile urchin, perhaps even his close relative, but one who continues to inhabit the degradation of the slums.

It seems an incontrovertible truth that the 'rescued' boy growing up in my friend's genteel household would emerge taller, cleverer and more civilised than his former companion in the rookeries, but a scientific experiment upon the validity of this apparent 'truth' has never, to my knowledge, been completed. Even if it were, the unconvinced reader might still argue that any unexpected divergences in development were simply a result of the measured individuals being from different stock. How, indeed, can we ever know definitively that a person has been 'changed' by the manner of his upbringing?

This question goes to the heart of my thesis and my answer requires further consideration of the erstwhile slum-dweller, now a young gentleman, and his comparator who still lives in poverty. The two children might not be simply related by blood, they could be chosen for a similarity which is as close in age, body and circumstances as two humans can be; they would, in other words, be a matching pair of twins. With one twin in his keeping (and access allowed to the slum 'double'), my friend might scientifically test the *origin* of any divergence in growth, capability and character. The respective effects of *nature (heredity)* versus *nurture (upbringing)* upon any individual would then be beyond doubt.

Of course, the likelihood is low, to say the least, that a set of twins might be separated at an early age to be brought up in contrasting circumstances and measured throughout their childhoods. Some readers of a more delicate sensibility might baulk at the very idea of a *living experiment* such as this. Can it ever be right, they might say, to extract a child, however disadvantaged, from their natural family? Any person putting forward such an objection has probably never visited the worst habitations in one of England's industrial towns. Had they done so, their response might be rather to rescue as many unfortunate children as possible from the noxious air, adulterated fodder and vermin-infested beds of such places.

The same righteous reader might also object to the separation of twin siblings who, it is commonly held, share a bond so intimate that each feels an almost supernatural attachment to the other. Who has the right to shear such a cord of natural affection? My answer would be that a man of science must keep his eyes upon his lofty ideals and steel himself against any ensuing scenes of maternal heartache and childish distress. The demands of scientific endeavour must prevail. For, once we have obtained incontrovertible evidence of the relative effects of *nature* and *nurture* upon human biology, intelligence and character, a clear path may be prepared towards the complete physical, intellectual and moral improvement of our species.

Thomas Jerwood Esq.
Spark Hill, Warks.

TWENTY-ONE

December 1885

muslin

There was so much dried fruit to pick over and chop that Cook called Cora into the kitchen for the morning. Ellen was there too, as usual; she might as well be a kitchen maid during Christmastide. Everything in the scullery as well as the heavy lifting and dirty upstairs work was now left to Cora, although nothing had been said about additional recompense for her trouble.

Cook cleared a space on the scrubbed table and put out a flour dredger and a cup of dripping. Then she laid out a circle of flimsy white cloth.

'First, get your whole hand greased and wipe it across the muslin. Then, flour the cloth lightly and shake off the crumbs. We don't like a thick skin on our plum puddings here.'

Cora ran her finger up the pile of muslins. 'How many shall I do?'

'All of them. The master likes a pudding to go to the tradesman and to various village folk with a connection to the house. Now, let me see you do one.'

Cora scooped a lump of pale fat from the cup and smeared it over the delicate fabric. Flour fell like soft snow from the dredger on to the white roundels.

Cook nodded. 'Make a pile of them, floured sides together. Then you can help Ellen with the fruit. Miss Violet will have to wait for her ox tongue.'

Ellen, at the meat grinder, laughed. ''Bout time that girl got her tongue back!'

Cora shot a look over her shoulder. 'What do you mean?'

'Well. You know what she's like; sometimes mardy and moon-eyed, other times you can't shut her up.'

'Why is that, then, do you think?'

'How should I know? I thought you were thick with her.'

At the kitchener, Cook rapped a metal spoon against the edge of a stew-pan.

'That's enough chatter.' She shot a look at Cora. 'You've no

206

concern being friendly with Miss Violet, you need only see that her tea trays are delivered sharpish and the library scuttle doesn't run out of coal.'

'Yes, Cook.'

Cora's eyes dropped to the muslin. Cook must know the truth about Violet. Why else would she flash that warning look? Ellen might think there was nothing behind Violet's extremes of temper apart from childish moods. Only yesterday Cora had thought the same. The Flynn sisters were so alike that anyone might be taken in. Although now that she had seen Letty in her street rags, Cora realised their subtle differences. The green dress and the plaited hair disguised the poorer girl's slighter frame and paler complexion. Her voice, though, could not be covered up. The girl might have been told not to say anything during her visits to The Larches but of course, she did. So Cook can't have been the only servant to suspect something untoward going on, even if Ellen was oblivious.

Cora's greased fingers pushed across another skin of muslin. As they pulled back, a gash of floured tabletop appeared through a rip in the cloth. Cora winced then looked up at Cook who was staring into the bubbling stew-pan that filled the whole kitchen with the scent of cinnamon spice, raisins and beer. If Cora stuffed the ripped muslin into her pocket Cook might not count up the rest to know that one was missing. But slyness would only increase her fault. She took a quick breath of the intoxicating air.

'Cook. This muslin has torn. I'm sorry…'

Cook tapped the stew-pan then came to the table with the spoon held out in front of her like a teacher's cane. It pointed, no doubt, to a deduction from Cora's miserable wages.

'Let me see the damage.' Cook sniffed. 'No matter. It's one of last year's. And not much use even for dusting.'

A sudden thought flew into Cora's head. 'Can I have it?'

'If you wish. Are you needle-working?'

Cora nodded. 'I thought I might make something useful. Are there other scraps about the place?'

'Susan Gill keeps a rag-bag for mending. I daresay she'll let you look through it and have anything she can't use. Especially at this time of year.'

It wouldn't take much to prettify the ugly paste-head doll that

207

Cora had unexpectedly bought from Letty. A new set of clothes might be enough to tempt someone wanting a Christmas toy to pay over the half-crown it had cost her.

'Thank you, Cook.'

'Now finish these off then help Ellen with the mincemeat. You can stir up.'

Ellen was dropping bloody handfuls of shredded beef into the earthenware basin. She flinched as Cora's bare arm, pushing a wooden spoon into the meat, brushed hers. If she was still wary Cora could not blame her. When Cora thought of what had happened amongst the brambles and afterwards when she'd stood naked in the kitchen, she wondered if she'd gone briefly mad. Maybe Ellen thought she still was.

'Is this right?'

Ellen did not look up. 'Aye. Just keep stirring, slow like, while I drop in the fruit.'

'On to the meat? But it's raw.'

'You don't heat mincemeat. The sugar and spirit will cook the meat whilst it rests in the jar. That's why we're making it in good time for Christmas. Have you never had a mince pie?'

Cora shook her head and Ellen gave her a queer look as if she was about to ask which foreign place she had been living in until now. Instead she shouted over to Cook.

'It's ready for the brandy.'

Cook took a key from the belt beneath her apron and dragged a chair toward the high corner cupboard. Her heeled boots clacked up on to the seat and she reached into a huddle of dark bottles. The cork squeaked out of a bulbous bottle and amber liquid glugged into the bowl across the mix of currants, chopped apple and fatty beef. The smell that came off the mixture was better than anything Cora could ever remember.

Cook pushed the cork back into the bottle. 'Cora, you'd better go to find Miss Violet and ask her if she is to have her cold meats in the dining room or on a tray.'

Cora's pulse quickened. 'Yes, Cook. Where should I find her?'

'Downstairs, I think. In the morning room.'

a letter from Sun Street

Thin flurries of snow whipped across the windows giving the morning room a hard, empty brightness. Violet was standing by the fire with her back to the door and fidgeting with something in her hands. Cora never quite knew whether to curtsey. It seemed especially absurd now that she'd seen the dirt and degradation of Violet's natural home.

'Cook sent me to ask where you'd like your meats.'

As Violet wheeled around, her face broke into a tangle of nervous excitement. She ran to Cora waving a stamped envelope and, bouncing on her toes, breathed a whisper into Cora's ear.

'Oh Cora, I've been praying that you'd come!'

'Why?'

'To show you this.'

Violet flapped the envelope. It was addressed to *Miss V Poole* in a neat cramped hand.

'What is it?'

'From the *Gazette*. It must be.'

'Have you not opened it?'

'Of course not. It's for you.'

'It has your name on it.'

Violet shook her head. 'No one would write to me. It'd be thought odd if I got a letter. That's why I've been running out to catch the postman every day, just in case something came with my name on.'

'What about your mother? Or father? Are you not expecting a Christmas greeting from them?'

Cora's stomach churned. She hadn't realised quite how queasy this particular lie would make her.

Violet rolled her eyes. 'Then it'd have an Indian stamp, wouldn't it?'

'Perhaps your parents have returned from abroad. Or maybe one of your sisters or brothers has written to you.'

'I don't have any sisters or brothers, silly! And I'd have been told if my parents were to return. No. This is from your sister, from Alice. I just know. Please open it.'

Cora swallowed and took the envelope turning it over in her

hand. The cream paper was plain, neither cheap nor fancy and there was no name on the back for any return. Could this really be from Alice Salt? After so many years? Cora's mind was suddenly numb as she tried to imagine what the message might say.

'All right.'

Her nails fumbled into the gummed lip of the envelope. She should have taken it to read elsewhere. If the letter really was from Alice she would not be able to keep herself in check.

She opened out the single folded sheet. The page was covered in the same small neat hand as the envelope. Alice had never mastered so much as a slate pencil at the Union house but if she could read well enough for the *Birmingham Gazette*, she must also have learned to write a plain note. Cora felt sure that she would recognise Alice's hand as easily as her own. And so her heart dipped when she saw that the sender was someone who found writing with an ink pen as natural as speech.

12th Dec.

43 Sun Street
Edgbaston

Dear Miss Poole,

I write in reply to the 'Missing Persons' advertisement which appears in the current edition of the Birmingham Gazette. *I do, indeed, recognise the face in the sketch, though whether the child that I remember from the Birmingham Union Workhouse is the person you seek, I could not say. The girl I am thinking of went by a different name. Yet the resemblance is so strong, and the date you mention so significant, that I feel drawn to offer my help. It would assuage much in my own mind if I were able to assist with your search and perhaps impart some important* advice.

I would prefer not to correspond further in writing but should the weather be clement, I intend to spend the early part of this coming Sunday afternoon in Council House Square, close to the statue of Joseph Priestley. I shall be reading the Birmingham Gazette. *Perhaps, if you pass by, you would introduce yourself.*

Yours most sincerely,
George Bowyer

For a second, Cora's eyes fixed on the name. And then, as her mind slithered on to a half-remembered face, she was hit by a school-room reek of scoured wood and sweaty wool. *Mr Bowyer.* Cora's knees crumpled and she reached out for the armchair. Her body slumped on to the horsehair cushion, winded by the turbulence in her chest. She told herself distantly that she must get up, but she could no more stand than crawl across the ceiling.

'What is it?' Violet was plucking at Cora's sleeve, her face twisted with concern. 'Is it from Alice?'

'No.'

'Who then?'

'From someone we knew. A schoolmaster.'

Mr Bowyer's face became sharper in her mind; his thin white cheeks with freckles the same colour as his hair. There were places in her memory where his face should be clear; the time when he gave Bet Fulton ten raps on her open palm and looked as if he would burst into tears himself; the time Cora noticed him fall asleep even though he was standing bolt upright at the blackboard; and the time he'd winked and slipped a Peek Frean Pearl into her hand. But in all of those recollections, his face was partly clouded; she could see his watery eyes but not his long nose; the greased-down hair but not the slight chin. Her only memory of his whole face in sharp focus was when it froze in horror beside the defaced body of a lifeless boy.

Violet was leaning over Cora's arm, her eyes skimming the letter. 'Oh, he wishes to see you. But that's good, isn't it? He might help you.'

Cora clawed the letter into a tight lump. 'No. No. I can't see him.'

Then, with a sudden burning inside her, Cora sprang from the armchair towards the fireplace. Her skirt almost brushed the flames as she cast the letter into their blaze.

'Oh! Cora.' Violet stood with her hands pressed against her cheeks. 'I thought you'd be pleased.'

'I should have known. Only upset comes from stirring up the past.'

'No, Cora. You are wrong. I should love more than anything to meet my mamma and papa and if I did have a sister...'

Cora turned to Violet, her eyes flaring.

'You do. A sister who is as like you as Alice was like me.'

'What?'

'I've seen her and I could tell you all about how she lives and how you came to be separated. But believe me, you do not wish to know.'

'What? What are you talking about?'

'If you've got any sense you'll not ask me again.'

Violet's chin crumpled and her eyes glazed with tears. 'I thought you were my friend, Cora Burns. But you are the nastiest person I've ever met.' Teardrops slipped down Violet's cheeks. 'Go away. And don't ever speak to me again.'

'Very good, miss.'

Cora's curtsey swept over the hearthrug but she was not quite out of the room before bitter regret washed through her. What had possessed her to say anything at all, let alone something so vicious? Violet was right. Cora might sometimes seem like a decent person, but her true, hateful self would always burn through. The morning room door slammed behind her but the mahogany could not entirely drown the sobs of the child on the other side.

jars

Brandied steam fogged the kitchen as Cook lowered a dark and dripping muslin ball into the big copper pan. Boiling water seethed, spitting around the pudding's innards and muffling the click of the door as Cora slipped in and to began to ladle mincemeat into jars.

Cook didn't look round. 'Well?'

Violet's luncheon meats, Cora realised, had been forgotten entirely.

'She does not want anything.'

'Why not?'

'Said she wasn't hungry.'

'Is she ill?'

'Maybe.'

Cook released the pudding's muslin tail and turned towards Cora, wiping her hands on her apron.

'You look none too well neither. Is it something catching?'

'I'm all right.'

Cook came closer. 'You'd best go and tell the master if the child is unwell. He wants to know directly about anything like that.'

'Me?'

'Why not? Lord, you look white as yon muslins.'

Firmly, but with surprising gentleness, Cook clamped her hand to Cora's forehead and kept it there. She looked so searchingly into Cora's eyes that she must surely, Cora thought, have seen the turmoil behind them. Until ten minutes before, Cora had entirely forgotten that Mr Bowyer ever existed. But now the picture of his stricken face in the privy block would not leave her mind. Might he have seen who did what to the little boy? Or had he come in too late to know of anything except the child's death? A sudden heave of guilt clamped Cora's heart. For a second, she thought she would dissolve into a snivelling heap and cling to Cook's skirts.

Cook took her hand away. 'You feel cool. But I'm hot as a stoker's shovel so I can't tell. What have you eaten?'

'Not much.'

'Directly you come back from upstairs, have one of those crusts I've been keeping along with a spoonful of new mincemeat. Kill or cure.'

'Yes, Cook.'

'Off you go then.'

At the top of the back stairs, Cora gripped the banister. With each breath, it felt as if something sharp was pressing into the bottom of her lungs. Violet must be told, as soon as could be, that Cora had spouted a lot of nonsense in the morning room on account of a sort of fit she'd had, brought on by the shock of the letter, and in truth, she knew nothing at all of Violet's family.

Cora hovered at the top of the stairs, waiting for a minute to pass before going back to the kitchen. At this moment, she'd sooner flounce to the stables and tap Samuel for a sixpenny loan than confront the master with a lie about Violet. A rustling at the bottom of the stairs made her look down. Susan Gill's coiled hair and the top of her starched cap wavered above a basket of folded sheets. Cora jerked away from the banisters towards the sink room then realised it was too late. She pressed herself against the wall to let Susan up.

'Burns. Have you anything pressing in hand?'

Susan rested the wicker basket on the banister.

'Cook wants me to bottle the mincemeat.'

'Well, I'll have you for ten minutes to help with the master's bed.'

'Cook…'

'She'll not mind for ten minutes. Put a hand to this basket with me.'

Cora took hold of the woven handle and helped lug the basket along the landing. Was Susan one of those in the house who'd guessed that Violet had a street urchin for a twin? She was sharp enough to have worked it out, and selfish enough not to have done anything about it. The basket jabbed into Cora's waist as Susan stopped at the laboratory door. Cora's heart quickened.

'I thought...'

But Susan had already rapped on the door with her free hand. It sprung open. Despite the chill air, Mr Jerwood's face was flushed and glossy. The near-white strands of hair that habitually covered his scalp had fallen over and stuck out like a railway signal. His eyes flickered from Susan to Cora and back again.

'Yes?'

'If you please, sir. Am I in order to do your sheets?'

'Yes, yes. But remove the papers carefully from the bedcover and replace them exactly.'

The linen basket creaked as Susan made a quick bob of assent before turning towards the landing window.

'Wait.' There was a squeak of urgency in his voice. 'Cora Burns. I should like your assistance in here. I am sure that Susan can manage the bed alone.'

Mr Jerwood opened the door to the laboratory. Susan nodded quickly and pursed her lips as she took the full weight of the basket.

The laboratory door closed behind Cora. Perhaps Violet had already told the master what she'd heard of her origins and from whom. He might not even deny the truth of it, he'd just tell Cora to change out of her clothes and leave. For a moment, Mr Jerwood pulled at a pointer of wayward hair and stared at the floor. He seemed to have forgotten that Cora was there.

The laboratory was more orderly than Cora had before seen it; the bench scrubbed clean, the apparatus folded neatly at one end. Amongst the measuring sticks and chain-link scales, her gaze fixed on an appliance that appeared to be a stereoscope. It had the same long stick frame but this one was marked off in inches, and fixed to it was a card with a single sentence in printed type which became smaller and more difficult to read as the sentence progressed... *the light-haired men in America were more affected than the dark-haired by every form of disease except chronic rheumatism...*

Mr Jerwood patted the loose hair to his skull and seemed suddenly roused.

'Yes, that's it. Heavy lifting.'

'Sir?'

His grey eyes focused on her. 'The job I have for you.'

'In here?'

'Yes. Look behind you at all of those specimen jars.'

Cora turned to the four rows of shelves, one on top of another, that held an array of differently sized jars. Inside each one, bathed in yellowy liquid, was something dead. Mr Jerwood's arm swept across the display.

'You will notice that they are arranged by phylum: mammals, birds, reptilia, amphibia, fish. But I am concerned for... for the strain upon the joinery and wish them to be rearranged by weight.'

'Sir?'

'Come it is simple. All I wish is for you to put the vessels in order of weight; heaviest here at the bottom continuing in a line left to right, and then proceed to the next shelf until you have the lightest there at the very top.'

'Yes, sir.'

Mr Jerwood went to the window and wheeled forward a set of short library steps.

'I shall first remove all of the jars, and then you may begin your task of rearrangement.'

'Shall I not lift them down, sir? I'll take good care.'

'No, no. You must gauge their weight purely by eye as you replace them. Some of the vessels are wide and squat, others tall and thin, and you must apply your mind to the volume of liquid in each one in order to divine its relative weight.'

Hairs needled at the back of Cora's neck. What did it matter to him how she did the job as long as it was done? She watched him scoot up the steps and come down cradling the jars. Each dead creature was whitened by the fluid and bent out of shape by the curve of the glass. She recognised the snake folded inside a tall cylinder, and the black and white rabbit which had so recently been chewing on hay in the now empty cage on the floor.

Was Violet also one of the master's specimens to be measured and tested? Once his experiment was over, the child could not be put into a glass jar but she still could be cast out as coldly as Mr Jerwood had dispatched the rabbit. And sending a girl like that to Coventry Street was as good as doing away with her.

The last jar containing a bloated spiny fish was positioned on the table. A label glued to the glass read: *diodon antennatus*. Mr Jerwood's hand again went to his hair.

'There. Now be quick about it. Quick as you can.'

'Yes, sir.'

He went to the workbench by the door, opened a notebook and leaned over it with a silver pencil in his hand, but did not start to write.

As he'd said, the task was easy. Cora concentrated on the size of each specimen jar hard enough to banish thoughts of Violet and Mr Bowyer. She reached up first to the high shelf with the lightest jars of unnameable creatures. The labels were no help. Even when she found an animal that she recognised, like the rabbit, the inked words meant nothing: *oryctolagus cuniculus*. Science must have a language of its own.

The rabbit was not quite the heaviest of the jars. There was one left on the floor, pushed against the wall. As Cora bent to take hold of it, she cast a sideways look at the master. He was still leaning over the bench, silver pencil poised and pretending, she sensed, not be looking in her direction. The last jar was a fat, thick-glassed thing as heavy as a bucket of coal. Cora had already pulled it out and cradled it in her arms before she looked into the liquid. The small floating face wore an expression of resignation that deadened Cora's brain. She opened her arms and let the child go.

The jar hit the linoleum with a gunshot crack. Vinegary sourness wafted from the seeping fluid. Mr Jerwood was already running to his stack of photographic equipment by the window and returned, muttering, with an earthenware bowl. Gently, he lifted into it the fractured jar and the miniature baby. The tiny preserved face, now open to air, seemed almost set to break into a wail. Cora clutched the edge of the table and could not take her gaze from the half-closed eyes and opening mouth: *homo sapiens 8 mens. gest.* The child had once had life, if not breath.

Mr Jerwood looked up at her from the floor, his eyebrow raised. 'It had a particular effect upon you, this specimen?'

'I'm sorry, sir. It slipped out of my hand.'

'Was it the shock? Of seeing something so close to your own sensibilities?'

'No, sir. The glass was greasy.'

But his half-smile showed that he did not believe her, and that he knew full well the cause of her prison term. Rage spurted suddenly inside her. What right did he have to mock or to judge?

His smile quivered. 'Perhaps you were distracted by fellow feelings for the poor woman who brought a doomed child into the world.'

Cora made a lunge for the door. 'I'll go to the scullery now, for a floor cloth.'

And before he could reply, she had stepped around the bowl with a too-small baby boy in the shards of his glass coffin and fled from the laboratory with no intention to return.

TWENTY-TWO
1881-82

laundered

On her first walk through the asylum, the place had not seemed so different from the workhouse. Cora had glanced to each side of the attendant's blue jacket as she followed him along the wide central corridor. Smaller white-walled passages connected the maze of wards and workrooms; a familiar smell of cabbage and drains was spiked with polish and disinfectant.

Male and female seemed as separated here as they had been across the canal at the Union house. The inmates that Cora saw did not look especially mad. In a day room a girl in a brown linsey dress, not much older than Cora, sat on a wicker chair staring at a pile of crochet on her lap. As Cora passed the door, the girl glanced up and gave a faint smile.

Beyond the attendants' mess room, the dispensary and the china store, they arrived at a door marked *Housekeeper*. The whiskery attendant gave a firm rap and a stout but neat woman appeared. She looked Cora up and down then confirmed that yes, she had arranged with Mrs Catch for the new girl to come today. She was to share a room with the other laundry maid.

They showed Cora the servants' hall, the flushing lavatories and heated washrooms and then the small clean room with two iron beds that she was now to inhabit. Cora sat on the thin mattress and felt a shivering swoop of hope. This was a situation she might be proud of, a comfortable place where she would have to work hard but would be looked after and treated fairly.

Then, Jane Chilvers returned from her afternoon off. She was a tallish girl with dark hair who said that she was nineteen, but Cora didn't believe her. Jane tinged her every utterance with sly condescension. She made out that she'd never before known anyone from the workhouse and widened her eyes with astonishment and fake concern when Cora admitted that she had always lived there. Cora soon realised that this was part of Jane's intention always to be, in her own mind at least, one rung higher than everyone around her. She spoke of her family home as a villa although Cora suspected

220

there was no dwelling of that description on Pitsford Street.

The icy sheets smelled faintly of mould. Cora climbed between them with the half-medal clutched in her fist. *IMAGINEM SALT.* Yes, she could easily imagine Alice lying, instead of Jane, in the other squeaky bed across the narrow room. Did she have any family? Jane asked in the darkness. Only a sister, Cora replied, a twin sister, but they had been separated as children.

Perhaps that was the truth. As she tied the half-medal on a string, Cora realised that if it helped her to find Alice she might at last know for sure. And Alice might not be far away. She could even be working at the asylum as an indoor servant or female attendant. But as the weeks passed and Cora came to know all of the staff, she realised that she would have to look for Alice elsewhere.

On the first Monday, Jane introduced Cora, in her new navy blue dress and white bib apron, to the laundry. A predictable reek of dirty clothes and stagnant water greeted her as they entered the block. It was not much bigger than the workhouse washrooms but noisier and more complicated. The building was split into a honeycomb of smaller rooms; a foul-linen receiving room, male wash-house, female wash-house, mangle room, steam drying-horse closets, and a repeat of the whole arrangement for the staff laundry. The servants' things were to be laundered entirely apart from those of the lunatics.

Jane said that she and Cora, overseen by the laundress-in-charge, were the only paid servants in the laundry. The rest of the women there were inmates, though quiet ones who should not give any trouble. Some of them grinned at Cora, toothless and stupid; others stared at her blank-eyed. The bigger rooms were noisy. Any conversation amongst the women at the soaping troughs was impossible when the revolving machine was in motion. Cora thought that it must run on electricity, as did the mechanical wringer in the mangle room. Both made a racket like a brewery dray across cobbles.

Cora must have looked as horror-struck as a piglet at the slaughterhouse, when Jane, nastily, put her first off in the receiving room. Cora's assistant there was a bug-eyed woman who could not speak for constantly sucking her thumb. All morning, the porter brought dirty washing in wheeled wooden trugs and emptied it on to the floor to be sorted into male and female, soiled and foul. Cora's permanently startled assistant could use only one hand for the task as the other was in her mouth. Cora had not smelt so much puke, shit and piss in all her time at the workhouse laundry as she did in that first morning at the asylum. She saw very clearly then what kind of companion Jane Chilvers would be and vowed not to let the bitch take advantage again. Before long, she would feel the acid sting of Cora's true nature.

As months went by, the asylum shrank in Cora's mind from a vast warren of odd-smelling wards and bath-houses, to the few well-trod rooms where she had some sway. She got the measure of the laundry. When it was her turn in the receiving room, she never touched the foul linen herself. Instead, she ordered the inmates about from a downdraught of fresh air at the doorway. The imbeciles eyed her warily as they knew how sharp her tongue could lash.

Gradually, Cora began to speak more freely in the servants' hall. In the early days she had been overwhelmed by the thought of conversation with grown women or, even more alarmingly, with the men. She had never really known any of the opposite sex, apart from Mr Bowyer and a particularly kind medical man who had examined her during her months in the workhouse infirmary and manipulated her chest. At the Union house, all of the overseers and paupers that she saw were female. So, it was in the servants' hall at the asylum that she had her first chance to observe the male of the species. And, on the whole, she liked what she saw. Very much.

The outdoor workmen, in particular, always commanded her attention. They seemed like a breed apart from any of the people she had so far known in her life. They would come into the servants' hall in their sweat-stained shirts and moustaches, frisking and braying to each other like young horses released into a spring paddock. They laughed and cuffed each other around the head, eyes twinkling. She started to smile at their improper jokes, sometimes directed at her, and then to laugh out loud. Smithson, the stoker, was burly as a Suffolk Punch but had the sharpest wit. It was Jimmy though, the gasman, who she waited for most expectantly each dinnertime. He was not especially tall and he had the same drooping moustache as the rest of them, but his every movement was as lithe and powerful as a rich man's riding horse; one that you couldn't take your eyes off as it swept by.

Once, Smithson came in unwashed and complained that the coal dust was turning him into an African. An African elephant more like, Jimmy said. Cora giggled and asked Smithson how long was his trunk. Everyone roared. When Jimmy nodded at her and winked, her stomach squeezed in on itself like a wrung-out soap-bag. That night when the gas was turned off but the bedroom mantle was still glowing, Jane revealed that Jimmy had already asked her to accompany him to Michaelmas fair. The darkness seemed to heighten the smugness in Jane's voice. Cora lay awake, listening to the lunatics' shrieks and muffled obscenities, and imagined what she might do to prevent the outing.

And so, she came to be waiting in the shrubbery for Jimmy to finish his shift. As soon as she stepped towards him and raised her petticoats just a little too high, she saw the look in his eye and knew that she had won. An actual bead of dribble ran down his chin. Already undressing, she followed him into the ventilation duct. By the heaving end of it, the half-medal, moist with sweat, was all that she still had on.

This was only the first of countless frantic couplings in all manner of places around the asylum in the months that followed. Sometimes they couldn't stop laughing with the outrageousness of what they were doing and the unspeakable thrill of it. Sometimes, behind the coal-house or in the dead space beneath the water tower, she'd make him crawl to her like a dog, panting and licking, as she lifted her petticoat higher, inch by inch, above her stocking-tops. Sometimes he would put his hand over her mouth and press it hard saying 'someone will hear', but she would laugh and shriek all the louder.

She took her own enjoyment in what they did together, and liked to think up ways for him to increase her pleasure. But a good part of her satisfaction in the affair came from the look on Jane's face whenever she saw Jimmy and Cora smirking at each other across the servants' hall. Jane's hoity-toitiness began to dissolve and her eyes sometimes glazed with the blankness of a melancholic.

It was Jimmy who noticed before Cora herself when the inevitable happened.

'Your tits look bigger,' he said to her after they'd finished an especially acrobatic congress and were lying sticky and entwined in the dust of a tool shed. 'And your belly,' he added.

'It's them custard puddings,' Cora replied, laughing. 'I can't stop myself.'

But Jimmy's eyes suddenly lost their greediness for her. He no longer winked and threw bits of crust at her across the table. And when her courses still refused to flow he stopped turning up at the usual places. One Tuesday, when the summer blossom was starting to turn into hard little fruits, he did not appear at all. Smithson told Cora, his face reddening through the coal dust, that Jimmy had got himself a plum position with the Corporation. Cora knew she'd never see him again.

Her belly did not seem to care about the anguish inside her. It took no notice of all the food that she was pushing aside. Bigger and rounder it got. She told the housekeeper that her navy bodice was too small and she was given a roomy Melton jacket without any question. Perhaps the housekeeper put it down to the effect of the asylum's very superior fare over that of the workhouse. But soon the new jacket was tight. Cora let out the seams one evening and Jane was too pasty and distracted to ask why she was altering it already. Cora knew that, eventually, the Melton jacket would not fit her at all. And then, she had no earthly idea of what she would do.

TWENTY-THREE
December 1885

an engagement

Because the afternoon was so crisp and the mud ruts on the track would be rock-hard, Cook had paid a call at Tyseley Farm to deliver a plum pudding and select a goose from their yard for the Christmas table. Ellen had gone with her. And so, with Susan Gill occupied by the dining room silverware, Cora found herself alone in the kitchen for the afternoon. In the cold scullery there were potatoes to peel and boots to polish but they could wait.

Cora's breath gauzed the window pane. Outside, clipped bushes threw frost-filled shadows on to the bright lawn and rooks squabbled in the naked branches. She went to the dresser and felt for her bundle stuffed beside the truckle bed. The paste-head doll was wrapped in fresh-laundered pudding muslins and an assortment of cotton print scraps. Susan Gill had shrugged and pulled a face but had nevertheless handed them over along with a few short lengths of white ribbon. Cora sat in the Windsor chair with the mending box on her lap and began to sew the oddments together to make a dress for the paste-head doll.

It was to be after the fashion of a christening robe, although she had only ever seen one once in an illustrated newspaper's pen and ink sketch. The baby princess's gown seemed to fall from the Queen's stocky lap right to the floor. There was not enough muslin to make the doll's robe so outlandishly long, but the print strips would make flounces to cover the feet. And she could decorate the yoke with ribbon. Her clever needlework would turn the home-made doll into a gift that any little girl might be pleased to receive. She should get a few shillings for it, at least, on the Bull Ring. The doll's head rested against Cora's stomach as she sewed muslin pieces around the lumpy sacking torso. Dense with clotted glue, the head had a lifelike weight to it and the pinhead eyes reflected a prick of light from the window. Cora's scalp crept up and she covered the doll's face with her apron.

It had been Christmas time when she'd first felt that the lump inside her was indeed a real child. After Christmas Eve supper, the asylum servants had been gathered around the piano singing *oh! bring us a figgy pudding...* and Cora felt a kick inside her belly that was so queerly separate from herself it made her cry out. The housekeeper's eyes turned to her and narrowed. So she'd said she was going for an early night and had spent Christmas Day in her bed. By the following Christmas, she'd been inside Birmingham Gaol for most of the year. Christmas now seemed like a festivity designed only to rub the noses of poor incarcerated wretches into the mire.

The kitchen door rattled suddenly with a pull of outdoor air. Boots too heavy for Cook or Ellen pounded the passage floor. Then the kitchen door sprang open, pushed by a thicket of green foliage and behind it, as she had feared, was Samuel Shepherd's face, beaming. As his eyes fell on Cora, the smile died.

'I thought it was Cook in here.'

'She's paying a call at the farm. Ellen too.'

'Oh. I just... Susan Gill asked for Christmas greenery. I thought to bring it in here and see if Cook wanted mistletoe for the kitchen.'

'She might.'

He took a few steps forward then hesitated and stayed by the table, his arms filled with the ball of waxy leaves and translucent berries. The cuts to his cheeks and brow had healed to no more than scratches. His eyes skittered across the room.

'Shall I leave it on the table?'

'On the floor would be better.'

'Aye, sorry.'

Cora wondered as he bent down what she had ever seen in him. It was true that he was tall and broad-shouldered but everything else about him was dull. He had none of Jimmy's mesmerising physical grace, nor his easy confidence. Samuel's jokes were rarely funny. But Jimmy's wit had been intoxicating enough to have her shedding her clothes for him even without his firm muscles and dark eyes.

Samuel stood up with such a lame attempt to avoid Cora's gaze that she almost laughed. But she'd do better not to rile him. He knew too much about her. And she needed him to keep what he knew to himself.

'I hope your wounds are no longer painful.'

Samuel shot her a wary look. 'They was only scratches.'

'Even so, I'm sorry you were hurt. It was a shock to me. I mean, the likeness...'

'I meant nothing by it, you know. I was not even sure it was prison garb you had on until you flew at me like a banshee.'

Samuel's scratches reddened but there seemed more anger in his face than embarrassment. Cora clutched at the doll on her lap, the head still hidden in her apron.

'Do you still have the likeness?'

He shook his head. 'It went into the tack room grate.'

'I'm obliged.'

'Give no thought to it.'

He cleared his throat and Cora wondered if he might try to spit through the bars of the kitchener but instead he turned to go.

'Wait, Samuel.'

Cora rose up, sticking the needle into the doll's body and bundling it with the fabric on to the seat of the chair. Samuel seemed to flinch as he saw her come towards him and Cora put up her hands in reassurance.

'I'm glad there is no bad blood between us, Samuel. And just to make full amends, please let me pay back what I owe you. I have a sixpence amongst my things.'

'No, don't...'

As she swept past him to the dresser, he took a pronounced step back so that her skirt would not touch him.

Her coins were folded into the pocket that she kept inside the Melton jacket. She rummaged amongst her night things, keeping them shielded from his sight. Then she turned around with the silver sixpence between her thumb and forefinger.

'Here. Take it.'

'I don't care about your pennies.'

'Please. I don't wish to be in your debt. Have the kindness to accept it.'

His eyes narrowed as he regarded her for a moment and then put out his flattened hand. Cora bowed her head as she placed the sixpence on his palm.

'Thank you, Samuel.'

'It's nothing.'

Now that she was close to him his voice seemed gentler. His hand with the sixpence moved up towards hers.

'Samuel!'

They both looked round at the burst of air and light. Ellen stood at the doorway, her blue bonnet haloed by wisps of fair hair and her cheeks rosy from the cold. Her mouth was smiling, but dismay lined her brow. Samuel sidled away from Cora, flushing.

'I just brought in some greenery...'

Ellen came towards them. Two bunches of shiny brown onions tied together by their dried stalks, were hanging around her neck. She gave Cora a sideways look and lifted the stringed onions over her head, laying them on the table. Then she went to Samuel and slipped her arm around his. Her dark gloved hand twined around his wrist.

Then, huffing and blowing, Cook swept through the open door and closed it behind her.

'Coldest we've had all year.' She dropped a swede, big as a football, on to the table and chuckled as she took the pin from her hat. 'He wanted us to bring carrots and parsnips too but this was as much as we could carry.'

Cora thought how much younger and almost pretty Cook seemed with a smile on her face.

Then Ellen stepped forward, pressing her lips into a simper and pulling Samuel with her so that they both stood square to the dresser. Her mouth wavered into a frown and back again before she spoke.

'Samuel and I think it's time for our announcement.'

Cora bit her cheek. What a stuck-up little trollop Ellen could be, for all her simpering. Cook hung her bonnet on the back of the chair and sat down, her smile fading.

'I see. What have you planned?'

'Well...' Ellen looked at Samuel and her voice rallied. 'We are to be married at New Year.'

Cook seemed unimpressed. 'Congratulations. And how shall you live?'

Ellen gave Samuel's arm a slight but distinct squeeze with her brown glove. Samuel's face twitched and he looked up from the heap of leaves and berries on the floor.

'I was to tell Timothy today, but it will not matter if you know first. Ellen's brother put in a word for me and I have an offer from Mr Podesta the furniture remover and haulier at Handsworth. It is a good position. In charge of the stables. And it comes with a room above.'

Cook put her elbow on the table and rubbed her forehead with two fingers.

'So that will be enough, will it? To keep you both?'

'Ellen has some savings put by.'

'Yes. I do.'

The room seemed to throb with unsaid resentments.

Cook sighed. 'Well. Good luck to you both.' She turned to Cora. 'I shall ask Mrs Dix to contact the registry regarding a scullery maid but this is a poor time of year. Ellen may be gone before we find anyone else. We shall be very grateful to have you in place as tweeny in the meantime.'

Cora nodded and tried to smile and say, *yes, Cook*, then wish joy to the seemingly happy couple but she found that her heart was so unexpectedly leaden at the news of the engagement that her voice had clotted in her throat.

game

Susan Gill had instructed Cora to bring the basket of fireside brushes and cloths to the library *directly*, yet the hearth was hardly dirty. A quick wipe over to remove some feathery ash and a few charred nuggets of coal was all that was needed. Cora wondered why the master, according to Susan, had been most particular in wanting Cora to do it straight away. His reason, she suspected, would be connected in some queer way to the presence of Violet, who sat sullen in the leather armchair.

The girl was shuffling, sulkily, through a handful of visiting cards on her lap. Cora ran the floor cloth over the tiles with the weight of watching eyes on her back. As she turned to repack the basket, she expected Violet to be observing her from the armchair but the girl did not look her way until Cora rose to go.

'Are you done?'

'There wasn't much to do, miss.'

'Can you not stay a short while?'

'I suppose.'

Cora wondered if her outburst in the morning room had been forgiven, but Violet's cool manner suggested otherwise.

'I have a game. My guardian said I might play it with any of the servants who came to the library this morning.'

And he knew, Cora thought, that she would be the only one. She threw an involuntary look at the bookshelves.

'Very good, miss. I'm glad to assist.'

Violet's face softened as she pulled a footstool in front of the armchair. 'It is a word game. You must take a turn to pick up a word card and then write down as many other connected words as occur to you within the minute. Whoever writes the most wins.'

The visiting cards seemed only to have one word written on each. Cora stopped herself protesting that Violet had already seen all of the words and would therefore have an advantage. The point was not to win but to be seen, by the master, to be playing. Cora nodded and kneeled by the stool.

Violet went to the cluttered side table by the window, returning with a pencil, paper and a small brass cylinder. The hollow centre of the cylinder revealed glass bulbs at each end, one half-filled with white sand. Violet placed a pile of scrap paper at either side of the footstool and the cards, face-down, between them.

'The hourglass is set for one minute exactly. I shall go first and show you what to do.' Violet took hold of the brass cylinder with one hand and the stack of cards with the other. 'Ready? One, two, three...'

The hourglass and the first card were flipped over together. On the word card, *Bee* was written in a careful adult hand.

Violet grabbed the pencil and began to scribble on her scrap of paper. White sand, almost noiseless, swished through the hourglass. Then the pencil stopped and Violet put the end of it between her teeth as she looked up at the window. Cora frowned at the upside-down list: *honey, flower, hum, fly, hive, comb, nectar.* But words, surely obvious, like sting, pain, swat, queen, worker, grub, forage, were missing. The last grain of white sand fell.

'Time's up.'

Violet hit the pencil-end against the footstool. 'Oh, bother! I've just thought of another.'

'How many do you have?'

'If you'll let me have *petal*, twelve.'

'All right.'

'Your turn now.'

Cora took up the pencil and Violet, shuffling with eagerness, turned both hourglass and a word card. The word was *Ladder.*

As Cora began to write, she found that her hand could not keep up with her thoughts; *step, up, down, climb, rung, fall, sway, grasp, downwards, upwards, backwards, reach, clutch...* She filled one side of the paper then turned it over. The blank space was squeezed out by a partly cut-through column of printed type:

...HEARING (Highest audible note...)

...EYESIGHT (Colour sense............)

...SPAN OF ARMS (...feet...inches)

...EXPIRATION (.........cubic inches)

A corner of Cora's brain wondered at the purpose of these classifications but multiplying words were still pouring from her into the empty space around the type: *grasp, slip, fireman, sway, bang, steep, jump, floor, wall...*

'Minute over!' Violet's eyebrows arched as she came around to Cora's side of the footstool. 'Goodness! Have you done this before?'

'No.'

'Twenty! I've never got that many.'

'You should have another go.'

Violet shot a sideways glance towards the bookshelves then went to perch on the edge of the armchair's cracked leather seat where she could not be seen from the back of the room. Cora had no doubt now that the master must be listening, and perhaps watching, from the laboratory.

'No. You go first this time, Cora.'

'If you like.'

Violet bit her bottom lip and then, instead of turning over a card, she placed a warning forefinger to her lips and then wrote on a scrap in childish spidery capitals:

WHO IS MY SISTER?

Cora sniffed. She should have realised that what she'd said in the morning room would not be forgotten. She began to shake her head but Violet, lips tight-pressed and eyes glaring, thrust the written question at her. Cora did not blink as Violet waggled the slip of paper angrily in her face, but the girl's darkly furrowed brow and quivering chin filled her with sadness. She'd almost forgotten how much rage and yearning could be compressed into the small frame of an unloved child.

Cora sighed then pulled forward another blank scrap and began to write:

Her name is Letty Flynn
She lives in a poor part of town.
She looks just like you.

Violet's eyes followed every loop of the pencil. Then she snatched it out of Cora's hand. Hourglass and word cards were forgotten as Violet's pencil scrawled:

Does she know anything about Me?
Can you find a way to take me to her?
How did she come to be in the Slums?
Do you think she would like to borrow The Keepsake?
Does she know that our Parents are in India?
Is she my Twin?

Cora took the slip. 'Minute's up, Miss Violet. Very good. Now I think this had better be my last turn, or Cook will be wondering where I have got to.'

Slowly and deliberately, so that it might be seen from the bookshelves, Violet inverted the brass hourglass. Sand slithered as the pencil remained hovering in Cora's hand. Should she tell Violet more? But she had already revealed too much. The pencil formed slow deliberate loops: *I cannot say.*

Violet did not wait for the sand to run out. She stamped her foot.

'Three words? Can you not do better? I'll give you another chance.'

'No. I can't think of anything else. Giving me more time won't help. It's too hard for me. You'd do better to play with someone who can give more useful answers.'

'Like who?'

Cora shrugged. 'Mrs Dix?'

Violet's plait whipped from one shoulder to the other as she shook her head and set her face in a sulk. She began to gather the loose paper into a pile.

'All right then, I shall. I shall quiz everyone until I find someone who puts down enough words to satisfy me.'

'Maybe nobody knows that many, Miss Violet.'

'Someone does.'

With this, Violet turned a pointed gaze to the bookshelves and Cora pictured the master behind the leather spines, standing in the laboratory with his eye to a peephole.

Violet carried the slips of paper to the hearth rug and sank down next to the ash bucket. Cora touched the girl's shoulder but she did not look up. Instead, with her back to the bookshelves, Violet ripped at the paper until every word fragmented into a meaningless scribble on shreds scattering across the ash.

specimens

Later that night, when Ellen had gone up to the attic room but Cook had not yet turned off the gas, Cora brought out the doll with its half-sewn robe and sat at the table under the light. She hoped that upstairs in the narrow bed, Susan Gill would be getting an earful about the joys of Handsworth; how pleasant and varied were the shops on Soho Road, how large and modern was Mr Podesta's yard. Ellen's life must stretch out ahead of her, in her own mind at least, as comfortable and predictable; a husband, a home, a child. Cora had never allowed herself to imagine any future at all.

As Cora sewed, Cook stood at the other end of the table beside a wire rack covered in candied peel. A heavy, fragrant bag of oranges had been delivered that morning by the grocer's lad. The orange flesh had gone into the big stockpot to make marmalade jelly, and the skin was sliced then boiled all afternoon in sugar syrup. When Cook laid the hot drizzling strips of peel on to the rack, the kitchen had fizzed with orangey sweetness. Even Cora's Christmas oranges from the Guardians had never smelt that good.

Cook was using a spatula to lift the cooled peel into a high-sided biscuit tin lined with brown paper. She glanced across at the doll.

'You're handy with a needle, Cora.'

'I should be. All the hours I spent sewing as a child.'

'At the Union house?'

'Yes.'

'How long was you there?'

Cora took a breath. She had avoided the servants' questions about her past except for once telling Cook, because she couldn't seem to avoid it, that she was an orphan from the Birmingham Union Workhouse. She knew Cook better now.

'I was always there.'

'Was you not boarded out? Or put into service for some of the time?'

'No. Not until I was sixteen.'

'Was that not odd? I thought they try nowadays to give the kiddies, especially the orphans and foundlings, a bit more of a life…'

Cora's needle remained suspended above the muslin and ribbon. The doll's pinhead eyes looked up at her.

'Not me.'

Cook sighed. 'Forgive me, Cora, I don't mean to pry. Or to stir up bad memories.'

'No, I don't mind. They're not bad memories on the whole. I never starved or froze. I learned to read and write, and to wield a needle as you see.'

'But did they care for you? And treat you kindly?'

Cook's face suddenly knotted into a look of such pitiful concern that Cora realised, with a jolt, it could not have been provoked by Cora's own childhood predicament. Cook's keen interest in the Union house was clearly much closer to her heart than that.

Cora tried to appear indifferent. 'Some of the overseers were kind.'

'But not all?'

'It was like anywhere. There was both good and bad.'

Cook looked down at the peel on the rack. Her breath seemed to stutter.

'You've done all right though, Cora, haven't you, in the end?'

Cora could not answer. What would she say? *Yes, apart from having a child out of wedlock* or *yes, apart from nineteen months in gaol*? At least Cook's question showed that she was still ignorant about the worst of Cora's past. But her unanswered question hardened the air between them.

Cook broke the silence by clanking open the biscuit tin and picking out a stick of sugary peel. She shook the tin towards Cora.

'Here, have one. Take a few. I think we deserve 'em.'

The tin was decorated with a hunting scene; a red-coated huntsman offered up the dead fox's tail to a thin-lipped lady riding side-saddle in a blue habit. Cora bit into the orange peel and her mouth burst with citrus sharpness through soft flakes of sugar. It was better than any shop-bought sweet she had tasted. Perhaps it was the sharp-sourness that caused Cook to wipe a finger across the corner of her eye.

Cora pushed the needle into the cloth, still unsettled by Cook's question. Had she done all right? Apart from being a hard worker and quick on the uptake, Cora could not say what sort of person she really was. Sometimes, there was no telling what she would do next, as Samuel Shepherd had found out. Perhaps only Alice Salt, or George Bowyer, could tell Cora the truth about herself.

She felt a prick into her thumb and jerked her hand away from the muslin. One drop of blood and the pure whiteness of the dress would be ruined.

'Cook, do you have a thimble? I will return it directly.'

Cook was blowing her nose on a lace-edged handkerchief. She nodded and went to the dresser. As the drawer creaked open, they heard the first thud. Cook rolled her eyes at the ceiling. Then there was another, louder bang. Something as heavy as a water jug, or a lamp, must have been dropped from a height. There was a shout too; a woman's voice: shrill but indistinct. It might have been the missus or Mrs Dix.

Cora's eyes rose to the ceiling. 'Who was that?'

Cook shook her head. 'It'll be herself. Creating.'

'Should we do something?'

'Aye, put on the milk pan. No doubt Mrs Dix'll ring for milk if she thinks we're still up.'

Outside the kitchen door, Cora stopped in the passage with the pan in her hand. There were still noises from above; voices slightly raised and footsteps, but calmer. In the larder, she poured milk from the covered jug. A warm bodily smell oozed from the cuts of meat hanging from hooks against the walls. Perhaps Ellen would be happy spending her days cleaning a room that smelled of horse and cooking poor imitations of the dishes that Samuel was so fond of here. But Cora would rather unpick oakum than act as an unpaid skivvy to a man. She knew that, at least, about herself.

There was another thud upstairs before the real crashing began. Bang after bang. China ornaments perhaps? And then something as heavy as the potted fern on the landing. Another crash came, just as heavy, but with the shatter of glass. A bottle? A window pane? Cora glanced up as hard footsteps, running, shook the ceiling. Then came a scream.

Cora hurried back to the kitchen, milk slopping. 'Should we go up? Could it be an intruder?'

Cook wiped her hands on her apron. 'We'll both go. You take the rolling pin.'

Cook picked up the poker from the stand by the range and Cora followed her out of the door. As they climbed haltingly up the back stairs, a clamour erupted; doors slammed, glass shattered. Through it all a woman screamed obscenities that Cora could only just make out.

'Fiend... Judas... devil!'

And then, at the top of the stairs Cora heard the master's voice raised and agitated.

'Stop, damn you. Stop, I say.'

All of the doors leading on to the landing were open but it was from the laboratory that the dull half-light of an oil lamp burned. Cook edged towards it, the poker held up in front of her but as she reached the open doorway, her hand lowered to her side. The sour-sharp odour of the specimen jars wafted from the laboratory. Cora gripped the glass rolling pin so hard that her wrist throbbed but when she too reached the door, it almost dropped from her hand.

The room had been ravaged; the camera and its tripod knocked to the floor, the specimen jars all pulled from the shelves and smashed. The linoleum swam with preserving fluid and dead creatures. And at the back of the laboratory, both in billowing white nightgowns, were Mr and Mrs Jerwood. The mistress's face was ashen and wild-eyed, straggled with greying hair. Her arms were pinned behind her back by the master. Blood ran freely from his cheek on to his neck. His chest heaved as he shouted to Cook.

'See to Mrs Dix. Make sure she is all right. Quick, woman. Go!'

Cook shook herself and dashed across the landing into the

mistress's bedroom. Cora could not think what to do or say. Then from the attic stairs, Susan Gill and Ellen appeared wrapped in shawls, their faces white as their nightdresses. And behind them came another smaller figure in white. Violet pushed herself forward until she stood on the threshold of the laboratory. The girl's lips were moving but the words almost soundless.

'Mamma... Oh Mamma...'

Cora stared uncomprehending at Violet. But then her voice was drowned by a hollow laugh that grew shriller and more sinister until it was eerie as a vixen's howl. Words screeched through strangled gasps.

'See her? There she is. The girl. The harlot. The murderess. There! There!'

The master struggled to keep a grip on his wife's arm and force it to her side but he lacked the strength to stop it from rising; a rigid finger extended to point straight at Cora.

TWENTY-FOUR

Research Journal of

David Farley MD
Assistant Medical Officer
Birmingham asylum
December 1885

<u>Weds 16th</u>

My research into hypnotherapeutic treatment for the insane has been interrupted by a relapse in the condition of Mary B. In the weeks since her last trance, she has fallen in and out of a melancholic stupor and, having refused to eat, has had to be fed on several occasions by the stomach pump. When I examined her in the infirmary last week, she presented a sorry sight; very thin and her nose reddened from the introduction of the tube. For the past few days, however, her meals have become more regular and she has responded well to my prescription for daily doses of 2gr quinine and 4oz brandy. The knife wounds to her upper legs have all but healed.

Matron Abbott advises that there has been no further speech from Mary B, either conscious or whilst asleep, but having discussed her condition at length, we have agreed that Mary B should again be fit for hypnosis this coming Sunday. The trance may produce distress, but Matron and I agree that this catharsis could be ultimately beneficial to Mary B's cure. I prescribed beef tea and custard to be added to the patient's diet.

<u>Thurs 17th</u>

I slept little last night as my mind cantered around the likely aetiology of Mary B's condition. Might her insanity be rooted in the poverty and rural squalor of her childhood? Yet the few words she spoke about this time, and of her mother, seemed fond. Was her lunacy instead the result of overwork and exploitation at the 'fine house' she mentioned? Yet it is hard to imagine how a young girl might have lapsed from respectable domestic service to a life of crime. The father of Mary B's child, whoever he might be, is no doubt the villain of this story, although I cannot ignore the evidence of the admission certificate which declared Mary B to be a violent prisoner; a danger to herself and those around her. Our more recent experience of her self-inflicted harm with the kitchen knife would seem to confirm her inherent tendency to viciousness at moments of distress.

Having thrashed about in my bedclothes long enough, I resolved to further research Mary B's past and in particular the nature of the crime that resulted in her conviction. As soon as is practicable, I will take an afternoon stroll along the canal and introduce myself to the medical authorities at Birmingham Gaol. With this hopeful plan in my head, I was finally able to sleep.

Fri 18th

I find myself quite shaken by my visit to Birmingham Gaol. Dr Grainger had kindly supplied me with a letter of introduction to Dr Tomlinson, the prison's medical officer and this peculiarly genial fellow gave up more than an hour of his time to show me into the gaol and to look through the records (such as they were) which might pertain to Mary B.

Once I had passed through the castellated gatehouse (as impressive and foreboding as any medieval citadel) and been welcomed by Dr Tomlinson, we entered the record office. At first, the prison's atmosphere was akin to any public building that caters for the poor. Asylum, workhouse and infirmary all have the same dull corridors that smell of cabbage and drains. The administrative portion of the gaol was no different.

Dr Tomlinson helped me to look through the cabinets for a female admission prior to June 1865 that showed the name Mary B—. Alas we could find nothing. Dr Tomlinson explained that this period fell before the incorporation of the gaol into the control of Her Majesty's government. In the sixties, the Borough Gaol, as it was then, operated on rather slap-dash lines and he was not surprised that I was unable to locate information about my patient.

By way of consolation, Dr Tomlinson offered to give me a brief tour of the wings. As we climbed the echoing metal stairways and surveyed the galleries that radiate from the gaol's fan-lit core, I struggled to suppress the rage growing inside me. Miserable stripe-clad figures shuffled along the hollow walkways. Some were shackled and hooded; all appeared weighed down by humiliation. Dr Tomlinson cheerfully outlined the regime; how little contact each prisoner has with any other, how meals are passed through a slot in each cell door, how prisoners are made to face away from each other even during services in the chapel. The female prisoners too, are subject to a regime of isolation and minimal communication.

I strived to keep my composure in the face of the good doctor's obvious pride in this barbaric regime. How can Man, already doomed to a short life dominated by illness and grief, inflict such purposeless brutality upon his fellow Man? If any place on earth was designed to produce lunatics, then this gaol must be it.

At that point, pleading a little queasiness, I thanked Dr Tomlinson for his informative tour and promised to repay the favour at the asylum.

Sun 20th

After chapel, Matron Abbott brought Mary B to my office as arranged. I must say I felt a little wary of continuing the session when I saw the look in the patient's eyes. They had the classic dullness of extreme melancholia, as if their twin points of light had been touched out with grey paint. Mrs Abbott assured me, however, that Mary B had been much brighter upon waking this morning; almost her old self. So, we decided to proceed with the hypnosis and Mary B made no sign of complaint. The patient eventually fell under with the same method as before, but her descent was more halting.

Here transcribed are Matron Abbott's notes:

10.40am

Dr F says: 'You told me before of your happy childhood in Staffordshire and of your situation as a servant in a pleasant house near Birmingham. What then happened that led you to gaol?'

Mary B: looks surly and shakes her head.

Dr F: 'But something must have caused you to fall into crime.'

Mary B: 'I fell only into the canal.'

Dr F: 'What do you mean, Mary?'

Mary B: (opens her eyes and looks at the doctor as if the trance has broken) 'Do not call me that.'

Dr F: 'Is Mary not your name?'

Mary B: a shake of the head and the eyes close.

Dr F: 'What is it then?'

Mary B: a vigorous shaking of the head. Grips the arms of the chair.

Dr F: 'And Burns? Is that your not your name neither?'

Mary B: continues to shake her head. Lips pressed. Eyes closed. Feet tapping rapidly against thin air.

Dr F: 'And how far gone were you in the family way when you arrived at the gaol?'

Mary B: the eyes open but do not seem to see. Then she speaks: 'My babe…'

Dr F: 'Tell me about your child…'

Mary B: (very distressed and thrashing in the chair, begins to weep) 'Sir, oh sir, I beg you, I beg you! Please, please, do not take my babe, do not take my Cora from me…'

Dr F rises urgently from his stool and passes (without touching) both upturned hands across Mary B's face.

Dr F: 'Your eyelids are again heavy, very heavy, they are closing and you are falling again into a deep refreshing sleep. Once you*

have slept your fill, and heard the clap of my hands, you will
awaken and be untroubled by painful memories. Your appetite
will be good and you will feel confident to speak. You will find
the strength to bring about change in your own life and in the
world.'
Mary B relaxes into a deep trance.

At this point, as I recall, Miriam and I both looked at each other, somewhat
in shock. We whispered low together with a plan to restrain the patient should
she become unmanageable upon waking but once I had (with some trepidation)
clapped my hands, Mary B opened her eyes without fuss. She seemed subdued,
indeed exhausted. Miriam returned the patient to the infirmary and I await
with eagerness our next discussion.

<u>Sun pm</u>
Although the weather was pleasant this afternoon, I received a note from Matron
to say that she would be unable to accompany me on a meadow walk owing to
some other pressing duties. She would not be free until after 4pm and by then the
light would be gone. I replied by inviting her instead to take tea in my rooms.
I must confess to my anxiety that Mrs Abbott had already decided against
continuing to aid my research following the distress it seemed to have provoked
in Mary B this morning. However, a few anxious minutes after 4pm Miriam
Abbott appeared at my sitting room door.

I welcomed her in and once I had poured the tea, expressed my dismay that
hypnosis did not seem to be having a therapeutic effect upon Mary B. Miriam
concurred and asked what I had made of Mary B's utterances today. I replied
that it is not uncommon for criminals to give a false name upon arrest, and her
outburst regarding the removal of her child had a horrible ring of truth. I had,
indeed, felt a shudder as Mary B seemed to beg me not to take away her baby.

Miriam agreed. Then her face quite blanched. 'Did you hear her say the
name of her child – Cora?' I went to reply but Miriam's hand had already flown
over her mouth. She bolted upright out of the armchair. 'What is it?' I asked,
but she was already pacing the room, a hand at her forehead, repeating 'Oh my!
Cora B–! She was here, all along. And no one knew!'

Eventually, I got her to sit down and explain the source of her consternation.
It seems that Cora B– is the name of a young woman who was for some years
employed here at the asylum as a laundry maid. Matron knew her only vaguely
but became entangled in an unfortunate incident which precipitated this young

243

woman's departure. Miriam would not say much about this incident, whether from delicacy or distress I could not tell. All she would confide was that, following the unexpected birth of a child to Cora B— (a little boy), the young woman was arrested upon a charge of attempted murder. Miriam must have noticed me recoil at the word and she looked away, as if about to weep. I was too sensible of her feelings to press her about whether the victim of this crime was the child or someone else. Miriam volunteered that Cora had received a lengthy sentence in that dreadful place which I visited only last week.

I tried to comfort Miriam by suggesting that 'B—' is not an uncommon name (although 'Cora' is more so). The girl she remembered might have had no relationship to Mary B. But Miriam shook her head. She knew that the young laundress had come from the workhouse and, now that Miriam came to think on it, her resemblance to our Mary B was strong. 'Sometimes in life,' Miriam said with great authority, 'the truth of a thing hits you with bodily force. It is not a feeling that occurs very often but when it does you know you may rely upon it.'

<u>Mon 21st</u>
This afternoon's visit to the record office at the gaol proved far more productive. The warder welcomed me, unsurprised by my second visit and guided me to the most recent (and far more efficiently kept) admissions and discharge details of female convicts. I found those for Cora B— without much difficulty. They showed a sentence of nineteen months following a guilty verdict for attempted murder (again omitting any details of a victim). She was discharged to a situation in a gentleman's residence: The Larches, Spark Hill, Warks. Less than three months ago.

As I walked back to the asylum along the dirty canal and the bleak winter fields, I mused upon the effect that finding her daughter might have on Mary B. Would knowledge of her daughter's survival rally her spirits, or would the sensibility of the years they had missed add to her sadness? I should like to imagine that a happy reunion between mother and daughter might bring about a cathartic cure for Mary B. Yet the few details gathered about the daughter, indicate a life no less troubled than the mother's. Cora's very serious criminal record, along with Mary B's known outbursts of violence make me wonder if the mother's and the daughter's crimes were similar. Indeed, despite my theoretical reservations, I cannot deny the indication of a hereditary origin of crime (and perhaps also of lunacy) in this case.

Upon my return to the asylum, it was my turn to be stunned by an uncanny coincidence concerning Cora B—. At the main desk, I consulted the day book *and noted that a private patient, cared for at home, has experienced a relapse so violent that urgent medical assistance has been requested. The day book informs me that a visit to the house is required with the likelihood of an admission to the private female ward. An attendant should accompany the duty medical officer in the closed carriage and take a straitcoat. It was with a trembling hand that I wrote my own name in the column as the attending doctor, for the house to be visited in order to remove the lunatic occupant was none other than: The Larches, Spark Hill.*

TWENTY-FIVE

December 1885

the shortest day

A tiny bonnet's gathered muslin frills covered most of the doll's badly painted head. Black pin-dot eyes stared up from a red circle of face as Cora knotted a bow under the paste chin. The doll no longer seemed quite so home-made. The long white christening robe and frilled bonnet made it into a proper Christmas gift. If Cora could get to town, there'd be no trouble selling it.

She took her clean apron and laid it out on the floor. Cook sipped from a teacup as she watched Cora wrap the doll.

'It's finished then?'

'Yes.'

'You've made a grand job.'

'Thank you. How much do you think it'd fetch?'

'Ten bob, I'd say. At least. There's a lot of hours and care gone into that needlework. And here…'

Cook went to the drawer of the dresser. On the countertop, she flattened out a crumpled ball of tin foil and tore off a strip, folding it into a tiny circlet. Then she bent to the floor and pinched the foil on to the doll's wrist.

'There. A christening bracelet.'

Cora gave a quick smile. 'Well, it looks the part. Although I've never seen one before.'

'Have you not? All babies are given something silver for their christening, even if it's just a sixpence.'

'Are they? I don't suppose I was. I don't even know that I had a christening.'

'Oh, you would have done. The Union house Guardians baptise all babies in their care. I know this for a fact.'

Cook glanced down at the doll and then at Cora and, as their eyes met, Cora understood that Cook was trusting her with a secret which was from long ago but the memory of it was still raw. Cora had no wish to say that, if she'd ever had a christening, it would not have been in the workhouse but the prison chapel.

She covered the doll's head with the apron. 'It's my last chance to get this sold before Christmas. Am I still all right to go out this afternoon?'

'Yes. Why wouldn't you be?'

Cora lowered her voice. 'Am I not needed to clear the mess, upstairs?'

'It's already done. Master asked Susan to help him with it last night. She didn't get to bed till three. He said she could have the whole day off today to make up.'

'Oh. But do you not want someone else to stay with you in the house?'

'Mrs Dix is here. And judging by the amount of warm milk I've sent up herself'll be asleep till Christmas.'

Cora's stomach tightened as she put the wrapped doll by her shawl. The air was cold but the sky clear. So, there was no reason to doubt that Mr Bowyer would be there by the statue, reading the *Birmingham Gazette*. And it was entirely possible that he would be able to tell her, with a nod of his head, whether she'd been a normal child or a monster.

Cook picked up the flattened tin foil from the dresser and began to fold it into a neat square.

'Where did you get that dolly?'

'I found it near the Bull Ring. In a gutter.'

'A gutter? That was lucky.'

Cora didn't need to see Cook's face to know that she didn't believe it for a second.

Cook slurped at her cold tea. 'Watch it doesn't get dropped again. The pavements are filthy. Anyways, once you've washed and put away the breakfast things, you can get off. Make sure you're back before dark. And today's the shortest day.'

Cora had wrapped a flannel towel between her shimmy and her stays but the outside air bit right through the layers. She pulled her shawl up round her neck and was tempted to wrap it over her head like a costermonger but stopped herself. Mr Bowyer might know that she wasn't respectable but she'd do her best to look it.

The button-boots crunched so loud on frost-wrapped gravel they muffled lighter footsteps that came up behind Cora on the drive. Violet wore only her thin dress and indoor shoes. Twin spots of pink flushed her pale cheeks.

'I've been watching from my room hoping you'd be going out.'

'You should go back in Miss Violet. You'll catch your death.'

'I'm allowed to the gate.'

'In those shoes?'

Violet's face slipped into surliness but she walked on, arms swinging. 'I wanted to speak to you before you went.'

'Why?'

'To make sure that you'll be going to Council House Square.'

Cora took a quick breath. 'It depends.'

'On what?'

Cora nodded at the apron bundle in her hand. 'On how long it takes to sell this.'

'What is it?'

'Something I made. A dolly.'

'Oh! May I see?'

'It's all wrapped up.'

'Oh.'

The girl's eyes glittered with dismay and Cora sighed.

'All right then.'

But as she pulled at the string, she realised how proud she was to show Violet her handiwork. Violet, shivering, put her hands to the bundle and the painted face stared back blankly.

Violet's mouth fell open. 'Oh, Cora. Did you make it all yourself?'

'Only the clothes. From scraps and old cloths.'

'But they're beautiful! And look, she has a little christening bracelet. I've always wanted one of those.'

'Do you not have one?'

'No, I have nothing from when I was a baby.' Violet stroked the doll's paste cheek with a forefinger then her face puckered. 'But I think maybe, I used to have a babby just like this one.'

Cora blinked at the unlikely word *babby* in Violet's mouth. Perhaps she had.

'I must get on now. Let me wrap it up again.'

'Yes, Cora, sorry.'

Violet began to hop from one foot to the other, her jaws wobbling with the cold as Cora shrouded the doll in white cotton. They were almost at the gate.

'You will go, won't you, Cora? To see your teacher? I couldn't bear it if you gave up on Alice. She may be waiting for you, hoping every morning that this will be the day that you find her.'

Cora tried to reply but found herself unable to speak. All she could do, as she took hold of Violet's cold hands to rub a little warmth into them before she left, was to give a quick nod of her head.

monster

Cora stood in the shadow of the Town Hall arcade. From there, she could see across the roadway to the square without being noticed. Two marble statues on plinths gleamed in front of the sooty stonework of the Council House. Cora knew that Joseph Priestley was the nearest. The statue had an unusual hairdo and such a kindly look on his stone face that she always peered up at it if she passed by. Today though, she looked only at the faces of men loitering below his feet.

A small throng in bowler hats and Sunday suits jostled to lean their shoulders against the smooth white slab of Priestley's plinth. The statue must be a habitual meeting place. Several men wore over-sized blooms in their buttonholes as if they wished to be recognised by a stranger. One extravagantly bearded man was reading a newspaper as he stood. But Cora could tell, even from across the street, that he was too old to be Mr Bowyer.

She took a quick step forward out of the archway's shadow and glanced up at the clock tower. Quarter to two. Ten minutes she'd been here already. Maybe she was too late. *The early part of the afternoon* could mean all sorts of times. But she could not stand still much longer. The cold was starting to numb her and an attendant in some sort of uniform by the Town Hall entrance was giving her suspicious looks. Perhaps she should take a circling walk of the square, staying outside of the iron bollards that protected the statues and fancy lamp posts from the traffic. But she could not quite bear to put herself into the light. She needed to observe Mr Bowyer unseen before deciding what to do. His face, even from a distance, would tell her what sort of man he was.

Would he remember Cora Burns? The advertisement in the *Birmingham Gazette* had, after all, mentioned only Alice Salt. If he did remember Cora, it would be as a cheeky brat too clever for her own good, or a schoolyard bully always itching for a fight, or more likely, as a killer of a little red-haired lad not much more than a baby. Cora clamped her eyes shut. No. That had been Alice. Cora might have looked on, and maybe tried to copy but she could never have taken the lead. And Mr Bowyer might be able to tell her, once and for all, that this had indeed been so.

Cora's eyes opened on to a rearranged pattern of figures around the statue. The bearded man with the newspaper had gone; one of the chrysanthemum button-hole men was linking arms with a woman in a bustle so protruding and severe that it gave her the look of a pantomime horse. Just behind them, Cora noticed a newcomer in a dark jacket with a knitted muffler tied tightly under his chin. Something about the slope of his shoulders made her eyes stay on him as he came nearer to Priestley's plinth. A neat brown moustache partly obscured his face but when he undid a button on his jacket and pulled out the *Birmingham Gazette*, Cora had to put a hand on the wall to steady herself.

He did not look at all like the domineering figure that Cora remembered. There was no sternness in his face and his build was slight rather than tall. She watched him unfold the *Gazette* and pretend to read but his eyes darted in all directions. Cora took a step backwards into the shadows. If he did recognise her, what was the worst he might do? Strike her? Spit? Nothing she wasn't used to. This was the only chance she might ever have to find out what she had done and what had happened to Alice. And even if he told her the worst, she didn't have to believe him. Clutching the apron-swaddled doll in front of her like a shield, Cora set off across the road.

She got as far as the first iron bollard when his eyes locked on hers and she saw that he had recognised her. His whole demeanour seemed to slacken; colour blanched from his face. A tight pain twinged under Cora's lungs.

'Mr Bowyer.'

The newspaper collapsed to his side. 'Yes.'

'I got your letter.'

'You did?'

'Yes.'

His eyes were the same watery blue. One of them twitched. 'But... but it was meant for Miss Poole.'

'She's a young friend who placed the advertisement on my behalf.'

'Oh.'

The open newspaper flapped at Mr Bowyer's leg. For a peculiar moment Cora expected him to bark a command for the quantity of threepenny loaves that might be bought for a florin. Yet the man in front of her seemed like a limp shadow of the terrifying schoolmaster who had loved to rap the blackboard with his cane. She took a breath shallow enough not to hurt her ribs.

'Do you remember me?'

'Oh yes. I remember you.' His face flushed suddenly. He put two gloved fingers to his brow and rubbed them hard across the faded freckles. 'I'm afraid I don't understand. Why would you place the advertisement?'

'To find Alice Salt.'

'I thought that must be a pseudonym you had adopted.'

'A what?'

'A false name. Because of the opprobrium attached to your own.'

Cora frowned. A few people had stopped close by and were staring unabashed in her direction.

'I'm sorry, Mr Bowyer. I don't follow what you mean. Shall we walk for a bit?'

She nodded in the direction of the colonnaded facade of the Council House. Mr Bowyer folded the *Gazette* untidily and limped slightly as they walked. He coughed before he spoke.

'I must tell you that I replied to the advertisement mainly because I felt it my duty to protect Miss Poole.'

'Protect?

'I feared for her, a child presumably, who would not be aware of your... history.'

Ice seemed to tighten around Cora's chest. She was not sure she could bear to hear more. 'I should go...'

'Let me finish please. My health is not good and I have been sorely afflicted since I saw the newspaper drawing. Memories came flooding back of the dreadful event which I had strived so hard to banish from my mind. I knew I must reply to the advertisement. It seemed like fate. But as soon as my letter slipped into the mouth of the posting box, I was full of anguish that I had done the wrong thing. I have slept very little since.'

Cora felt a needle of anger. 'So why are you here?'

'I am sure that the only thing which might allay my disquiet is if you can tell me now, after all these years, why you did it.'

Cora was quiet. A feverish stew of shame, disgust and rage began to swirl through her head. She would make him say it.

'Did what?'

'To that little boy…'

'Yes?'

'Why did you… do what you did to him?'

'And what was that?'

'Do you not remember?'

'You tell me, Mr Bowyer. Tell me what I did.'

'I found you with him by the privies. His mouth had been suffocated with your underthings and his legs cut with strange marks. Both of you were naked as the day you were born.'

His hand went to his mouth and his shoulders heaved a little as he seemed to retch.

Cora's voice trembled. 'How do you know it was me?'

'What?'

'It might not have been me that did it.'

'Who else could it have been?'

'Why, Alice Salt of course. You said her and me were both there, naked.'

'No. I said you and the boy. Both of you were bare.'

'And Alice too. She was there. That's why I put her picture in the advertisement. That's why I am seeking her, to find out what really happened.'

'Until I saw your advertisement, I had never heard of anyone called Alice Salt.'

'You must remember her. She came to the Union house that summer and we could not be parted. She looked just like me. I have no doubt now that she is my twin.'

'I can assure you, Miss Burns, that whatever the diseased content of your head might be telling you, you never had any sister at the workhouse, nor indeed any friend that I can recall. And I can also tell you, without any shadow of a doubt, that when I found you and the body of that poor little boy in the privies, you were entirely alone.'

A fist of air punched at Cora's ribcage. She felt herself sway.

'No. No. You are wrong. Alice was there with me. She was the one who did it.'

'I'm sorry, Miss Burns, to shatter your convenient delusion. But there is no such person as Alice Salt and there never was.'

He lifted up the newspaper and crackled it open to the advertisement page, tapping his finger against the small printed copy of Violet's charcoal sketch.

'No one can have any doubt about who is depicted here. Anyone standing hereabouts could tell you. It is you, Miss Burns. This Alice Salt is you.'

Cora's knees and ankles seemed to liquefy. She reached out for smooth stone but her hand did not quite make it to the pillar and she fell heavily on to the steps, grazing her palm and twisting her wrist. Mr Bowyer looked down, his face ashen. Then he threw the folded newspaper on to her with some force before turning away and breaking into a lopsided run as he crossed the road.

With one hand still clutching the wrapped doll, Cora pulled the *Gazette* towards her and as she stared down at her own carefully depicted features amongst the tight columns of black type, she understood with the force of a body blow that Mr Bowyer was right.

babby

Cora blinkered out the clop and roll of traffic, the swish of passers-by. Hop-scotch paving wavered beneath her feet. In a shop window, she saw a Cora-shaped shadow drifting past but it was empty of any features. She was no longer cold or aching or thirsty. She was no longer anything.

It made sudden sense now, that time she'd spent in the workhouse infirmary when there was nothing wrong with her. What else might they do with a little murderess; too young to hang, too old to be ignored? The whole Board of Guardians would probably have been sacked if the scandal had got out. And so they covered it up with an excuse of infantile lunacy or some such that had kept her, forcibly on occasion, in bed. Eventually so much time passed that anyone who'd heard about the bad goings-on in the schoolyard privy no longer cared. It was then, perhaps a whole year later, that she was allowed to get up on to her muscle-wasted legs and totter back to the girls' dormitory.

Further up the street, shouting broke out over a clatter of hooves and wheels. Four brawny cobs were pulling an empty dray down the hill far too fast. The driver, cursing, grappled with the reins. The horses pranced and slavered at their bits. If Cora stepped into their path now, they could not miss her. One hoof amongst the sixteen that clipped and sparked on the cobbles would be enough to finish her off. It would hurt, but it couldn't fail to be over quick. Iron shoes and bone-hard hooves would strike her skull then mash her to a pulpy mess beneath the horses' steaming bellies.

And no one would care. The carter would simply blame the mad-woman for flinging herself at his team. Cook would be hard-pressed in the scullery for a while but she'd soon find another tweeny. And Cora wouldn't care either. She'd have already passed from this teeming street into nothingness.

Although, at the very last minute, when it was too late to save herself, would she change her mind? Maybe she'd remember, just as the first iron horseshoe touched her hair, how good it had felt to wear a cashmere walking-dress, or to bite into a veal pudding or to have Jimmy's sweating limbs wrapped around hers. With her last breath she might cry out: *No! It's too soon for everything to be gone!*

Had the little boy cried out? Perhaps she could remember if she really tried. Cora knew that he'd been too little to say much. *Shoe, dickies, ta-ra*, had been about it. His whole sense of what life was couldn't have amounted to much more than the scratch of an itchy sock, a mouthful of semolina or a rag wiped roughly across a runny nose. But those small things had woven together into an existence that she, Cora Burns, had robbed from him.

Cora stood frozen on the kerb as the straining horses pounded past her and away towards the High Street. Then, without realising how, she was crossing the wide roadway of the Bull Ring. The doll-bundle flapped against her skirts as she walked but her legs and every other part of her were numb. Should she stop or keep walking? Live or die? She hadn't the strength to choose.

At the sailor statue, an ancient woman hobbled past with a

tray of gingerbread. A ragged girl sat by the water fountain with a few bunches of red-berried holly. Cora stood between them and unwrapped the paste-head doll. She did not want it. Perhaps no one would.

The sun was beginning to sink behind the Market Hall. Cora stood motionless until she was gripped by a sudden fit of shivering. But she knew she could not move on until someone had taken the baby. A small girl in a cape-shouldered coat let her eyes linger on the doll as she was pulled past. A boy at the tail end of a plainly dressed family group stuck out his tongue.

Then a woman stopped. She was youngish but had a stern look. The high crown of her bonnet was piled with dark ribbons; a gauzy half-veil covered her eyes.

'How much for the dolly?'

'Ten shillings?'

'Let me see.'

Cora held it out. Her hand was shaking. The woman turned the doll over and lifted up the white muslin robe. Cora winced at the rough handiwork on the sacking body underneath. The woman passed it back.

'No thank you.'

'Five shillings?'

'No.'

'You can just have it if you like.'

'Well, the costume is pleasant but the doll itself is quite hopeless. So, no.'

The woman walked off with polished heels kicking up the hems of her complicated skirts.

Cora rotated the doll around and around in her hands. The woman was right. It was ridiculous to think that a thing so horrible could be made nice. How could you turn bad into good? It couldn't be done. Cora had been idiotic to try.

She took a few steps to the edge of the stone pavement above a deep rut of wet mud and rotting paper. Then she dropped the doll into it. Brown slime spattered the white christening robe. The sparkle of a tin foil bracelet sank into the slurry. Cora lifted her foot and let the sole of her boot hover above the red face. And then she stamped down on it hard. There was a cracking and crumpling of brittle paste and then a satisfying expulsion of air as the head flattened against dirt-soaked asphalt. Cora placed her other boot on the muslin dress and wiped both soles on the doll as if it was a coir mat at a doorway. Then she stepped back to see what she had done.

The doll lay splintered and mashed into the sludge. Filth smeared the white dress and the head, part of it still inside the embroidered bonnet, was shattered into many pieces. All of the time that she had spent thinking up patterns and sewing the tiny garments had come only to this. A sharp pain shot through Cora's gut.

She bounded on to the roadway and kneeled down beside the broken toy. Maybe it was not too late to salvage the clothes. She could launder them after all, and then make her own ragdoll to wear them. But when she lifted it up, the christening robe seemed to fall apart in her hands. Fragments of hard paste and of dirty muslin fell through her fingers into the dirt. It was too late. Damage this bad could never be undone.

A strange braying filled her ears. Then her stomach heaved, once and then twice, as if she was about to vomit. But all that she retched up was a throat-burning wail. She buried her face into the raggy mess of muslin and filth that had been her baby. A faint scent of orange peel in the cloth brought up another howl from the depths of her insides. Tears were flowing now and her face was slimy with mud and snot. She, Cora, had done this. No one else could be blamed. No matter how hard she tried, she'd never change. And no child, not even a paste-head doll, would ever be safe with her.

She bent over, crouching on the road and shuddering with ugly hacking sobs that would not stop. Her shawl flapped at her shoulders as she wept. The flapping became firmer and after a while Cora sensed, through the racking of her body, the pat of a tiny wizened hand.

'There, lass, there.'

Cora looked up, her chin dripping. Through the throbbing blur, was a woman's face, brown and wrinkled as a walnut, as old as the century.

'That's it lass. Weep. Weep yourself dry.' The gingerbread-seller did not cease her patting, rhythmic as a heartbeat, on Cora's heaving shoulder. 'But you'll get by, lass. You'll get by.'

TWENTY-SIX

1883

plum

She told them she had dropsy. Not bad, but enough to make her shuffle and put on weight. Jane Chilvers looked sideways at Cora as she was pulling on her nightdress over where her stays should be. Jane knew what was up all right but her lifeless eyes didn't care one way or another.

Towards the end of her time at the Union house, Cora had once asked a woman in the laundry about babies. The washerwoman was loud and friendly, not afraid to get a slap for loose talk. Cora had seen enough pauper women in the family way, hobbling about with one hand at their back, the other stroking a huge belly, to know something of their state. One morning when she and the woman were alone at the soaping-tub, Cora took a deep breath.

'I know babbies grow inside your belly, but how do they get out?'

The washerwoman laughed her rudest, throatiest laugh. 'Same way they got in pet, same way they got in!'

So, as Cora went about her work at the asylum in an ever-tighter Melton jacket, she had an inkling of what lay in store. But she could not imagine how it might happen. Not for a second. As winter strangled the cold-water taps and stiffened the drying courts with February winds, Cora had to leave her jacket open and wrap her shawl around like a bodice. No, she insisted, she wasn't cold; the dropsy must be keeping her warm. She almost believed it herself.

The baby was there, of course, making himself felt. Sometimes his somersaults were so acrobatic that Cora felt sure they must be visible through her shawl. She knew it would be a boy. That seemed as obvious as her own name. But still, she could not really believe that there was another person inside her. Nor could she imagine what she would do with him when he came out.

The choice, if you could call it that, was not hard. Even if she begged a baby-farmer to take the child, any wage she could get would never be enough to pay for his keep. And the asylum would sack her on the spot and without a character. The workhouse would be all that was left; her choice was simply whether to seek admission for both of them or to send the child, if he lived, on his own. She would avoid that decision as long as she could.

But when he came, choice seemed to disappear. It started on a day as raw as winter even though the birds and the daffodils had begun to think it was spring. As she heaved herself out of bed that morning, the skin of her belly felt as stretched as an overripe plum. One prick of a knife seemed like all that would be needed to split it open and push out the stone.

In the afternoon, she was set to oversee the mangle room, but the whirr of the centrifugal wringer burrowed into her head. As soon as the shift was over she went to the bedroom. There was no point taking tea. The thought of eating anything made her stomach turn. As she lay all evening on the bed, feeling pulses of pain tighten her middle, she told herself it was gripe or something she ate. And as she managed, again and again, to waddle to the water closet, her stomach did indeed seem to be in a foul state. But after the last bout on the lavatory she knew that she could not go back to her bed. She was feeling so poorly that she would not be able to keep a smooth face once Jane came up for the night. And that could not be long. The door next to the lavatory was the linen store. She made sure that no one saw her slip inside.

The waves of pain kept coming, throbbing through her belly. Her shawl fell to the floor. Her shimmy, already soaked with sweat, clung to her bosom. The painted shelves were set at a convenient height for her to cling on to and bury her face in the piles of clean sheets and towels to stifle her groans. She knew then what was going to happen and the dark, soap-scented cupboard seemed about the best place she could have chosen.

In the end, her body folded over on itself and she sank down on to the floor to push him out. She reached up and grabbed a flannel, stuffing it into her mouth, as much to protect her teeth from the grinding as to soak up the noise. Her palms slipped on the watery mess that now covered the linoleum. She was glad it was too dark to see the colour of the liquid. A bloody, earthy odour filled the airless cupboard. Then a burning tightness flared between her legs. Muscles ripped. Skin tore open. And, with a pop, something inside her gave. A heavy object flopped on to the floor.

Groaning softly, she spat the flannel from her mouth and

gathered up her petticoats. A wide shaft of light from the crack under the door illuminated the slick of fluids that had come from her body. Inside the puddle lay a ghostly-white child. Cora leaned over on all fours and put her face beside his. He had the sweetest cleanest smell. His arm seemed to move, but not his chest. Cora reached up for a bedsheet and laid it around him, mopping up the wetness. She used a clean corner to wipe away the lardy muck filling his nostrils and mouth. And then, still on her knees, she leaned down and kissed his cheek.

His little ribs began, magically, to rise and fall. In the glow from beneath the door, his greased, silvery limbs seemed to have their own brightness. He was the strangest but most beautiful creature that Cora could imagine. And he was hers alone. As she watched, his eyes tugged open and showed, for the very first time, white pinpricks of life. He cried a thin shuddering mewl. Then it got louder.

They must not be found; at least, not yet.

'Hush, baby, hush.'

She put one hand beneath his slippery head, the other under his thin bottom. As she lifted him, she felt that she was still connected to him in some way, but could think only of stopping his noise. Her shimmy would not quite open far enough. She bit hold of the top of it and clamped her teeth, pulling down on the neckline with three fingers until the cotton ripped enough to let one bosom through. His mouth was already open in a wide shivery wail. But as his lips felt her flesh they closed around the nipple and began to suck.

He was strong. His mouth pulled at her; he wanted as much as she could give. If only time could stop now, and forever. Cora leaned back against the shelf, to ease the discomfort underneath her. She looked down at the little head on her breast and saw a dark shape across it. The half-medal, still around her neck on its twine had drifted on to his cheek.

Then, something inside her began to slip. She felt a pang, hot as flame, shoot through her insides. Her stomach hardened. Lord, it was happening again. Was there another child still inside her? A twin? Would her boy have another just like him, as she had had Alice? She laid him down on the floor as she strained again, bearing down to push out what was there. This time, the pain was so sharp she could not help but cry out. But what was left inside slithered out quickly. Would it be another boy? At least then they might grow up together in the same workhouse dormitory and never be alone.

Cora wiped hot sweat from her eyes and sat back to look at the new baby. The slice of light from under the door fell across the wiggle of white, rubbery rope that fastened her boy's soft belly to the other child. But while the first boy lay peaceful and perfect at one end of the rope, his twin, at the other, was nothing more than a ghastly lump of bloody brown meat.

In that instant, everything was spoiled. Cora rocked back and forth over what she had produced, shaking her head and moaning. But how could she have expected to create anything good? Her offspring were always bound to be as disgusting, in body or in spirit, as she was herself. None of them would ever have a life worth living.

Why didn't Mary Burns, when she'd had the chance, put a bootlace around newborn Cora's neck and pull it tight? That quick act would have prevented an ocean of heartache. And it would have meant that Cora's whole life, even if it had only been a few breaths long, would have been entirely spent with her mother.

Tears fell on to Cora's soiled boots as she began to untie the laces. It was a struggle, shot through with stomach-churning pain, to pull her feet free without disturbing the loosely aching softness underneath her. One black lace would be for the boy, the other, once he was gone, for herself. She longed to feed him again, for one last moment of bliss in this world but if they were found too soon, she would not get another chance to do what she must.

Keeping clear of the dead meaty thing and the white rope, Cora threaded the bootlace behind her baby's downy neck and tied it in a loose knot. Again, she kissed his cheek, smooth and glossy as silk and found his tiny seashell ear with her lips.

'I'm your Ma and your Ma loves you more than anyone ever loved anything.'

Then, she pulled both ends of the bootlace with all her strength.

At that moment, someone cried out. But it was not the child. Cora was suddenly blinded by a hard wall of light as the cupboard door opened. In the brightness, a woman's dark silhouette spoke with a West Country voice.

'Oh, my sweet Jesus!'

Cora blinked up, numbed. But the woman was already on her knees, flinging away the bootlace and scooping up both the child and his meaty skinless twin into a white sheet. Deftly, she wrapped them tight. The smeared yellow head of the tiny boy poked out. His eyes were fixed shut. Then, with the darkly leaking bundle in her arms, the woman gave Cora a swift blank look and started to run. Feet pounded the corridor. A door slammed. And, apart from the gurgling of the hot water pipes, Cora could hear only silence. Her child was gone. Gone forever. And she'd never even called him by a name.

She should do it now; knot both bootlaces around her neck and tie them somehow to something. If only she had the strength. But what did it matter? She could finish herself off any time. For now, she felt capable of nothing but sleep. She managed to raise herself on to her bare feet and limp along the corridor leaving a trail of bloody footprints on the grey linoleum. As she opened the bedroom door, a shriek from inside echoed down the corridor. Jane's stricken face was as good as a mirror. Cora said something about her courses being bad this month, and then fell on the mattress into a stupor.

It can't have been for long. Hands were on her arm, shaking her, shouting things at her. Through the veil of her eyelids she saw a mouth moving inside a grey beard. And behind that, a domed black helmet. She tried to ask for a drink but her lips were too dry to speak. Then Dr Grainger's words became loud enough to make sense and a deep black pit opened.

'Wake, girl. Wake up. You are to be taken to the Bridewell.'

TWENTY-SEVEN
December 1885

imaginem

The moon killed any chance of sleep. From Cora's low bed, the kitchen seemed drained of colour but brighter than it had been by day. Sharp silver light picked out the edges of every funnel and ladle hanging from the dresser. But when Cora closed her eyes, she saw only Mr Bowyer's dismal face sneering at the idea that little Cora might have had a companion.

She clamped her eyelids tighter into darkness. How could Alice Salt not exist? It was true that Cora had no exact recollection of Alice's arrival at the Union house. Alice had slipped in, somehow, when Cora had been standing at the front the school room and Mr Bowyer had rapped his cane on the blackboard. That's not how any other child was ever admitted. And no one seemed to notice her except Cora. It had been odd too, that Alice was never given her own tasks in the work room, she always just helped Cora. Even the Bolger girls never goaded Alice directly. Cora alone had been the object of their torments.

Cora pulled the dense grey blanket over her head. She seemed to have learnt so much from Alice; about the japanning workshop, the dressing of little brothers, the killing of small animals. Where had all that knowledge come from if not from her workhouse sister? Perhaps Cora had simply overheard the conversations of the other girls as she wandered, friendless, around the schoolyard or lay silent in the night-time dormitory. The other girls in the Union house came and went as their families' fortunes changed but all of them, old-hands and new-girls alike, seemed instinctively to think that Cora was odd. Even those other orphans and foundlings who knew only the workhouse as home shunned her. Cora was too solitary, too clever, too unpredictable.

Whipping the grey blanket away, Cora leapt off the bed. She pressed her bare feet on to the icy tiles and breathed a shuddering lungful of braised air. Her own thoughts must have brought Alice Salt to life, but when faced with the stark reality of a small dead boy, imaginary Alice had evaporated.

The half-medal shifted on Cora's chest. She dragged the twine over her head and padded to the window. The moon hung silver-white behind a tangle of naked branches and beamed its harsh light across the engraved metal: *IMAGINEM SALT...* And so, it seemed, Cora had. Was it just a coincidence that the name she'd given to a made-up sister was the same word that appeared here, on a token that she did not see until years after Alice had gone? Perhaps she'd been shown, at some blanked-out point in her childhood, the strange token that was her only possession. From where she used to stand at the blackboard, she'd certainly seen the stamp of Salt & Co on Mr Bowyer's japanned inkwell. But now she'd no doubt, that her own half-medal had been made, like its close relatives upstairs in the medallion collection, in the factory of *W Tonks and Sons*.

Cora brought the half-medal closer to her face and angled it into the moonlight. At the edge of the word *SALT*, the moon's glassy brightness revealed a small notch that might be the corner of another capital letter. An *E* probably. Perhaps *SALT* had been formed simply by a random cut through the centre of the medallion. At any rate, it had nothing to do with Alice, because she'd only ever lived in Cora's imagination.

Coolness trickled down Cora's back. What was this thing in her hand? Where had it come from? She'd used it for so long to conjure up false memories of a girl who never existed. Yet someone had left the half-medal for her. Someone real.

Cora went to her mattress and pulled up the grey blanket to wrap around her shoulders. The kitchener was still blood-warm as she sank into the Windsor chair and pulled her feet underneath her. From here she could look the white moon in the eye. The blank round face did not seem to care that she had murdered one child and tried to do the same to another. It shone as fiercely on her as it did on everyone. Cora saw that the pattern of her existence had been determined by her birth and by all of the circumstances that had surrounded her since. So she understood now that if she was ever to have a life better than the one she had so far endured, she must make herself into someone else.

closed carriage

The outdoor pump ran sluggish with water about to freeze. Cora cupped her hand and gulped a searing mouthful of it, then patted her cheeks and brow with cold wetness. She was still awake, still alive. No one had noticed any change in her despite what she now knew about herself. Only Cook had raised an eyebrow and asked that morning if she was feeling peaky. But Cora had shaken her head and let Cook explain how to sort broken laboratory glass and other gainful rubbish into piles for the rag-and-bone man, and how what he paid would go toward the servants' Christmas dinner. Perhaps Cook would not have been surprised to hear that Cora was a murderess.

Smashed glass and tin cans were now sorted into neat piles by the yard. Grey mist coiled though bare trees as Cora threw a last shard on to the heap. Crows shrieked and rasped. Then, out of sight, fast hooves pounded on the carriage drive. The sound was too impressive to be the totter's cart, and he was not expected until tomorrow. The wagon, if that's what it was, seemed to pull into the turning circle at the front door and the hooves came to a stamping halt.

As Cora went indoors, cold air gusted through the passage from the front door. There were voices in the main hall but she went to the scullery without glancing their way. The sink brimmed with pots and plates, gravy stagnating into white spots of fat. She struck a Vesta and lit the burner, staring at yellow tongues of flame that pushed a skin of dull moisture over the copper. She knew what a good person should be; someone like Cook perhaps; not always friendly, but calm and kind and honest. Although a person like that living inside Cora's skin would have been trod into the dirt long ago.

The scullery door rattled and Cora sensed a commotion somewhere in the house. Then with a crack of air, the door burst open and Mrs Dix filled the doorway, crow-black apart from the pallor of her face.

'Bring a bucket of water and rags to the hallway. Directly, if you please.'

Cora nodded and reached for the leather bucket below the sink and some floor cloths. Something must have spilled badly.

She followed the housekeeper towards the hallway and into a wintery draught that carried a nasty, familiar stench. As they approached the bottom of the main stairs, Cora saw that the front door was wide open. Outside, a driver stood between two harnessed carriage horses, struggling to keep a grip on their bridles. The entrance hall was full of people; a burly fellow in blue calico fatigues, a taller, younger man with a dark beard; and, slumped on the bottom stair and covered in pale reeking vomit, the missus.

Mrs Dix stood back to let Cora pass. 'Come, Cora. Wipe her clothes down first. The carpet can wait.'

Cora took a gulp of air before she stepped forward. Trying not to tread in the sour lumpy puddle around the newel post, she pulled a cloth from her apron and doused it in cold water. Bending down, she began to wipe at the mess on the mistress's skirt. The sick was slimy and wiped easily from the dense wool but it left a dark stain curdled with a pungent alky smell. Cora shot a look at the man in blue standing with one hand on his hip and the other on the banister. Her heart skipped faster as she put the smell of the back wards together with the asylum blue. And as her damp rag moved up from the skirt, Cora saw that Mrs Jerwood's arms were strapped into a canvas straitcoat.

Vomit was pasted into the buckles and folds of the restraint coat and spattered through the mistress's wiry hair. Cora did her best to wipe and scoop it away, rinsing the rag as she went. She could not help catching the lifeless stare of the missus's dull eye.

Cora slopped the rag back into the bucket. The tall bearded man was frowning at her so intently that his eyebrows had fused almost into one. Cora coughed. The water might as well be sick.

'Shall I empty the bucket, ma'am?'

Mrs Dix leaned her head against the closed door of the morning room.

'All right. But take it outside this way. And use the outdoor pump.'

Cora nodded and held her breath until she was over the threshold. Outside, the air was threaded through with wood smoke and frost. The carriage horses, heads lowered and flanks steaming, were harnessed to a windowless van entered at the rear by a set of fixed steps.

Cora breathed deeper as she strode across the gravel, and felt herself lighten. She might have been a workhouse pauper and a felon but she was not, thank God, a lunatic. Her occasional queer turn didn't really count. The life she'd lived would have tested the strongest of minds. And if what she'd been through had not already sent her completely mad, nothing ever would. So she'd be spared, at least, the tortures that the missus was about to endure: the straitcoat, the padded room and the mind-deadening chloral. Any life was better than that.

At the paddock fence, Cora swung back the leather bucket and sprayed its foul contents across the yellow grass. The alky smell was overpowered by earth and smoke. Behind her on the drive, heavy footsteps crunched and she turned to see the tall bearded man coming her way. He seemed to smile as he caught her eye but an uncertain frown remained uppermost in his expression.

Cora walked on but he caught up and fell into step beside her.

'I beg your pardon, miss. Please, excuse me while I take the air for a few moments. I must travel back on the inside of the closed carriage and need to fortify my constitution if I am not to suffer the same misfortune as our patient.'

His voice had a friendly lilt to it, Scottish perhaps, but his features still looked perplexed. Cora wasn't sure if she was meant to reply. But the man continued to speak.

'Forgive me, but I overheard the housekeeper call you Cora, did she not?'

'Yes, sir.'

'Cora Burns, is it?'

Her heart missed a beat, and then another. She stopped to face him.

'Who wants to know?'

'Oh, I do apologise. I should have introduced myself. My name is Dr Farley. I am the assistant medical officer at Birmingham Asylum. Would I be right in thinking that you were employed in a situation there some... time back?'

Heat pulsed through Cora's neck. 'I don't remember you.'

She turned and walked on past the back door as Ellen pulled her head away from the scullery window. Dr Farley cleared his throat as he hurried to keep up.

'Oh no, that's right. My employment there is relatively recent. So, you are Cora Burns?'

A tickle of irritation wormed through her gut. 'Do you want something of me?'

'There is a patient of mine to whom you may have a connection. And having now met you, I feel sure of it.'

They were at the pump. Cora held the leather bucket and began to crank the handle. Dr Farley stood awkwardly to one side, watching. Water sloshed and spat as it swirled around the bucket. She would have happily tossed the swill over the doctor's soft tweed jacket and loosely knotted tie.

'I'm not an educated person, sir. So I haven't the foggiest what you're on about.'

'I'm sorry. Here. This will explain.'

He reached into the jacket and pulled out a white envelope. She felt her eye twitch as she glanced down. *Miss Cora Burns.* So he really had known who she was before he came here. Cora hung the bucket's handle over the spout, metal screeching as she pumped. The envelope quivered like a funeral lily in the doctor's hand. His brow furrowed deeper.

'Oh, I do beg your pardon if you are not able to…'

Cora let go of the pump and snatched the stiffened paper from his hand.

'I can read.'

'Yes, of course. I hope I did not insult you.'

'I must get on.'

She reached forward and lifted the bucket from the pump, water sloshing on to his unpolished shoes.

'Oh, of course. Good day, Miss Burns.'

He bowed his head slightly and turned, walking with long uneven strides into the deepening darkness.

coals

21ˢᵗ Dec 1885

BIRMINGHAM ASYLUM,
WINSON GREEN, WARKS.

Dear Miss Burns,

Do forgive my forwardness in addressing you directly, but I am hopeful that you may be the person who might provide great assistance to a patient of mine and perhaps learn something to your own advantage. If you are not the Cora Burns who was born to Mary Burns in the early part of 1865 in Birmingham Gaol, then destroy this letter forthwith. If you are that person, please read on.

Your mother, Mary Burns, was admitted to Birmingham Asylum from the gaol in June 1865 and has remained here ever since. Do not be alarmed; she is a most pleasant lady and much recovered from the time of her first admission. Her most obvious remaining symptom is an inability to speak. Her only known utterances have come during sleep or under hypnotic trance. At these times she has been heard to mention, most affectingly, her lost 'babe'. It is this child whom I take to be you.

If you have no interest in meeting your mother, I cannot apportion the slightest censure. A reunion would undoubtedly stir up strong emotion for all concerned. I am, however, very hopeful that this emotion on Mary's part could be powerful enough to reignite conscious speech. Should you be kind enough to agree to my proposal, you may find that the encounter produces perhaps unforeseen satisfactions.

I would be more than happy to reimburse any expenses (travel etc) which you may incur. I also understand that the asylum may not be the happiest location for a reunion and you may prefer to join Mary and myself on an outing. I would suggest the terrace of hothouses at the Botanical Gardens as a pleasant spot at this time of year.

Should you feel able to accede to my suggestion, kindly reply using the enclosed stamped and directed envelope suggesting a date and a time at your convenience.

Yours most sincerely,
David Farley MD
Assistant Medical Officer

Cora read the letter again, more slowly, but her heart raced faster. It could not be so. How could her own mother have been living mere yards away during all of the time that Cora had worked at the asylum? It was too far-fetched to believe. Yet she felt, despite herself, a tightening in her throat and a warm gathering in her chest like the beginnings of a sob.

She gave a start at the sudden clatter of the stool that she had wedged against the scullery door falling to the floor.

'Cora?'

Ellen's eyes had a cold glimmer as she pushed into the room. Cora stuffed the envelope into her skirt and picked up the stool.

'Am I wanted for something?'

'Aye. A box of coals. For the master's bedroom.'

'Before he retires?'

'He already has. And says he doesn't want any vittles at all. Just some coal bringing up.'

'Right.'

Ellen glanced sideways at Cora's skirt where a stiff corner of paper stuck out of the pocket.

'Who was that gentleman with you on the drive?'

'The doctor that took the missus away.'

'Where has she gone?'

Cora snorted and folded her arms. 'Where d'you think? To the lunatic asylum.'

'Oh my! What did the doctor want with you?'

'Only to thank me for clearing the mess she made on the stairs. Anyways, I'll go for the coal.'

Cora reached for her shawl from the doorpeg and Ellen jumped back to let her by.

The glow from the kitchen was dulled by a squall of hard rain. A thin line of white light picked out the brick path from the blackness around it. Gusts whipped around Cora's head as she opened the coal-house door and reached inside for the shovel. Lumps of coal punched into the box. She tried to picture how her mother's face would be if they met. Might it crumple satisfyingly with tears of guilt as Mary Burns, shocked into speaking, begged Cora's forgiveness? Cora would take her time weighing up how to reply: *I forgive you* or *I don't*.

But, in truth, it was just as likely that Mary Burns' face would yawn and gurn before breaking into the high-pitched cackle of an imbecile. Or then again, if Mary was anything like her daughter, the muteness might be just a clever ruse. Everyone knew that the grub was better in the asylum than the workhouse.

Cora hauled the laden coal box into the house and pressed her weight against the back door until it clicked shut. At the top of the back stairs, she stopped to wipe her face with a clean corner of her apron. The cotton came away from her skin damp with rain and coal dust and still smelling faintly of lunatic's vomit. Cora held her breath, and realised that someone nearby was crying.

Mrs Dix's door was nearest. Perhaps she was heartbroken that she could no longer spend all day watching a mad-woman sleep. But the whimpering was too thin and distant to be the housekeeper. Cora went softly along the landing to the door between the master's and the mistress's bedrooms, and put her hand on the doorknob. The crying had become no more than a shudder of breath.

Violet's bedroom must once have been only a cupboard. There was no fireplace and the window was as high and meagre as a prison cell's. On the miniature bed, Violet looked as big as a grown-up.

Cora placed the coal box gently by the door and went to kneel at the bed. She put a hand to Violet's hair. The girl's face did not rise and she mumbled fitfully into the pillow.

'Is it Cora?'

'Yes.'

'Where did they take her? Do you know?'

'To the asylum.'

'What is it like there?'

'Clean and bright and warm.'

'But scary? Full of lunatics?'

'Don't fret. She will be looked after and made better.'

'It is not right, though. This is her home.'

'I didn't know you were fond of her.'

'When I was little, I used to call her mamma even though she said my own mamma would not like it. That was when she was well sometimes.'

'Perhaps when she returns from the asylum she will be well again.'

Violet rolled over. Her face was creased and scarlet; her eyes pooled with tears. She put a finger to her lips and signalled for Cora to lean closer. The high window made a bang in the wind and the mantle flared. Gas fizzed through Violet's whisper.

'Do you think he will send me to the asylum too?'

'Why do you think such a thing?'

'Because he says the experiments are at an end. There is nothing more for me to do.'

'But he'll look after you, I am sure.'

'Like he has looked after her?'

Cora could not think how to answer. There were indeed asylum stories of 'inconvenient' people being abandoned in the private wards. And if they stayed there long enough, they would become mad anyway.

'Can you take me to my real mother, Cora?'

Cora sighed. 'I don't know…'

'I long to see her, and my sister, more than anything.'

'Let me think on it.'

Very solemnly, Violet took hold of Cora's hand and planted on it a hot kiss.

'Thank you, dear Cora.'

Cora felt her own throat tighten as she tip-toed back to the coal box and closed Violet's door gently behind her.

There was no answer to her knock at the master's bedroom so, as quietly as she could, she let herself in. A hissing wall-light, turned down low, threw a dim glow across the cluttered room. The tapestry bed curtains were half-pulled and a shape lay unmoving beneath the damask coverlet. Cora picked her way between the piles of papers and books towards the fireplace. A medicinal scent of camphor cloaked a deeper odour of bodily staleness.

In the corner of the room, something moved and Cora's stomach gave a jolt as she saw a woman's face. But it was only her own reflection looking back at her from the cheval mirror. Her heart was still beating too fast as she bent to the grate. Orange veins riddled between the dark embers. Carefully, she lifted the coal-box lid and used the tongs to select a few dusty pebbles of coal, placing them beside the brightest spots in the fire.

'Who is it?'

She froze. 'Cora, sir.'

'Oh yes. Cora Burns. It had to be you.'

His voice was slurred. Perhaps he had been drinking.

'I've come with coals, sir. To keep your fire alive.'

An unpleasant snorting came from the bed. She placed a final coal in the grate and carefully poked in some air, then replaced the tongs on the fire stand.

As she stood up, she could not help but look at the bed. The master had propped himself up on one elbow, a grey fog of hair around his pallid face, his eyes piercing into her. But then his body, beneath the covers, began to shake. The shaking grew to a heave. Cora tried to look away but couldn't. Was he laughing at her? Or doing something unspeakable? The snuffling and racking from the bed continued and Cora darted for the door. But as she slipped out, she realised that she'd heard such a sound before, many times in fact, at the asylum, where it was far from uncommon to hear a man weep.

TWENTY-EIGHT

THE
WYVERN
QUARTERLY

SPRING
1886

PRINTED BY
CORNISH BROS,
37 NEW ST, BIRMINGHAM

An Essay on Nature, Nurture and Negative

How may human paternity be established beyond doubt? It is a question which has perplexed the male of the species down the generations. For, whilst motherhood is an undeniable fact, fatherhood can be regarded as a relationship that is always under suspicion.

Take, by example, the experience of a most august scientific friend of mine who has generously agreed to the retelling (with complete anonymity) of his own sorry attempt to discover consanguinity with a person who was otherwise a stranger. The circumstances of his salutary tale had begun more than twenty years earlier when my friend, most unhappy in his marriage and frustrated by repeated failures in academia, found some solace in an anthropological study within his own household. The subject of this study was his kitchen maid; a lively, willing girl who was always pleased to engage in his investigations. The more world-worn readers amongst you will have no surprise in learning how this unsuitable association progressed, or that it ended with the girl falling into a shameful condition that consumed my scientific friend with regret.

Happily for my friend, the kitchen maid departed the household of her own accord before her condition was entirely apparent. Enquiries were made thereafter into her whereabouts but she had disappeared so completely that my friend could only conclude that she had returned to her north-country home, or had adopted a new name. There the matter seemed to end until, many years later and quite by chance, my friend found himself again confronted by the kitchen maid. He found her in the very lowest situation of society imaginable, yet the girl had not apparently aged nor changed in any way he could divine, except for the colour of her eyes. The reader may jeer. What sort of man of science is he, you might ask, to ignore the obvious? This girl was clearly related to the kitchen maid; perhaps even her daughter and so, quite possibly, his own. Yet I must sympathise with my friend's initial disorientation. The very striking resemblance of the two females threw him back into the stew of youthful emotions that had infused his sweet but doomed liaison with the kitchen maid.

The daughter's name gave no clue to her parentage but sensing the accuracy of his intuition and the possibility for a prodigious advance of his anthropological studies, my friend invited the girl to take up a place in his household. At this point, knowing my own interest in heredity, he asked me for advice regarding the best way to establish his new servant's paternity without her having any awareness of his investigations. The two methods which I recommended, namely: the *composite photographic likeness,* and the *numerically quantifiable moral test,* have both been described in contributions of mine to earlier issues of this journal (viz. **Character, Crime and Composite Photography** *WQ* Summer 1885, **Experiments in Human Nature** *WQ* Autumn 1885) and I shall not bore the loyal reader by repeating my commentary on these techniques. Suffice it to say that a correlation of physiognomy and character is the best measure for determining paternal kinship that we currently possess.

I will not embarrass my scientific friend with an account of the subterfuge he embarked upon in order to obtain the data – photographic and otherwise – for his comparisons. He was nevertheless successful in producing a composite likeness of himself and the girl, as well as several well-observed moral test scores. The results of these investigations, however, were not conclusive. Although some of my friend's facial measurements were replicated in the girl, her maternal resemblance was overwhelmingly dominant. Measures of intelligence and character may have pointed to features in common with my friend's highly developed rational mind, but these were counteracted by the girl's illogical urges. These must stem, he assumed, from the same excess of passion that had been displayed by her kitchen maid mother. In the end, my friend began to feel that the girl he had found was, indeed, his own offspring but sadly, no test yet invented could prove it.

I was most disheartened by my inability to assist but this episode at least allowed me to revise my theory of human development which has been so long in germination. My photographic endeavours have also provided a simile which, I hope, illustrates my conclusions. In my analogy, the production of a man is likened to the manufacture of a photographic print. The flash of creation (by which I mean *conception* in the case of the human and a timed *exposure* of light in the case of the photograph) determines the influence of *Nature*. It is then *Nurture* (upbringing in the case of the human, or the developing process in the case of the negative plate) which provides the detail, the finesse and the fulfilment of the final outcome. Any photographer, amateur or otherwise, will tell you the many ways in which inadequate skills in the developing room can alter or indeed ruin a perfectly good image. Excessive or inadequate application of chemicals, an accidental ingress of light, clumsiness, or a fault in the timings can all result in a final print which is too light or too dark, or which is lacking in definition and detail or which, indeed, is fatally smudged. I do not need to spell out how accidents and errors in the upbringing of a child can have parallel effects.

So I must ultimately conclude that *nature* and *nurture* have separate but complementary effects on the 'negative' that is each human being. One force cannot be said to have pre-eminence over the other; both are working together to fashion the final product. Although it may have taken me many years to arrive at this theoretical position, I now feel the truth of it with vital conviction. I must therefore declare that my long study into the workings of heredity and human development is at an end. Although I feel sympathy for the pain and anguish expended by my scientific friend in his quest for proof about his natural child, I must also confess that I cannot help but be glad of his travails. Without them, I should not have reached my final conclusion which, I have no doubt, will stand firm against the buffeting of newer theories and more sophisticated research for many years to come.

Thomas Jerwood Esq.
Spark Hill, Warks.

TWENTY-NINE

December 1885

the hot-house

Cora had visited the Botanical Gardens once before, although on that occasion she did not actually go in. It had been a summer Sunday and she had been persuaded by the asylum kitchen maids to join them on a jaunt. They had taken the horse-drawn tram to Edgbaston but once they'd got to the Gardens' wrought-iron entrance gate none of them wanted to pay two bob for a ticket.

Instead they'd walked up and down the leafy road outside, peering through gateways and over the top of a high wall at the oddly coloured trees and glass-house roofs. Cora had larked about and got rowdy. Soon, they were all bent double, laughing hysterically and drawing frowns from boater-clad passers-by. Those same respectable onlookers, now on a fur-collared Boxing Day stroll, might have recognised Cora from her previous visit, but she could not quite connect herself with that careless shrieking girl.

Today, there was no bother about the entrance fee. She gave her name at the turnstile and was handed a ticket left for her there by Dr Farley. The rotating iron cage screeched as she pushed through into the gardens. There was little to see; the bare trees were unremarkable and the beds dug over and brown. She was glad she had not wasted her own money. The doctor had even said that he'd pay for the trams.

And Cora had nothing better to do with her day of Christmas leisure. She might as well see his mad-woman for herself and then tell the doctor to his face that he was wrong. How could Cora have lived for two years in the same building as her own mother and not known? But if by some queer twist Dr Farley was right, then she'd acquaint Mary Burns with a few opinions that would keep the woman dumbstruck even if she'd a mind to start talking.

At the end of the gravel path, a metal arrow pointed to the glass-house door. Inside, Cora gasped into fetid air that was as warm as a July heatwave. Giant ferns, impossibly green and glossy, surrounded a stone pond where orange fish rippled the brown shallows. Water trickled and dripped. Somewhere nearby, voices whispered. The stench of stale water gave Cora a sense of being inside a glass vase of week-old cut flowers and she felt suddenly suffocated by the humid air.

Then a cool draught crackled through a fan of stiff pointed leaves. 'Miss Burns?'

The doctor's softly checked trousers and tweed jacket were almost hidden by the tangle of foliage.

'Would you come this way? The air is more agreeable.'

He was holding open a glazed door, his eyebrows frowning despite the smile on his mouth. Cora passed through into fresher air and breathed in a whiff of lavender and lemon. Winter sunlight beat through a wall of glass.

Dr Farley nodded to the left. 'I told Mary to wait here in the Arid House. She is a little agitated, but mostly on account of the excursion. I am not sure when she last left the asylum.'

Cora had already seen the woman wearing inmate-brown. She was sitting on a park bench at the far end of the long glass terrace and surrounded by dead-looking plants with needled columns and spiny pads. The woman's head was tilted up at the glass roof with an expression as empty as the sky. In that instant, Cora knew who she was.

Dr Farley indicated for Cora also to sit while he remained standing on the terracotta path. His voice became loud and deliberate.

'Mary, this young lady here is Cora. We have talked about a person of that name several times.'

The woman glanced at Cora but there was no flicker of recognition. She stared down at her hands folding and re-folding them on her knees. Dr Farley's voice became softer.

'You remember, don't you, Mary, that when you had a child, you called her Cora?' Dr Farley nodded to Cora. 'Perhaps it might help if you were to address Mary directly.'

Cora, still standing, wetted her lips. There were several questions she had fashioned over the years in preparation for this moment. *Did it give you satisfaction to abandon your child to the workhouse? Did you never consider what damage your neglect might do?* But the pitiable appearance and strange familiarity of the woman in brown robbed Cora of her conviction. The woman's gaunt, agitated bearing supplied answers to those particular questions that were more forceful than words.

Cora took a breath and sat down beside the woman. 'I'm Cora.' The woman's hands quickened their folding. 'And I'm glad to meet you, Mary.'

The woman twitched and her hands clenched into a grip that whitened the tips of her fingernails. Then her lips moved and a groan burbled in her throat. Dr Farley leant down, eyebrows flexing.

'What was that, Mary? Did you say something?'

A slight mumbling whispered from her lips. The woman's dull hair, pulled into a plain knot, was streaked with grey; her china-blue eyes ringed with redness.

'Not...'

Cora came closer. 'Yes, Mary?'

'Not Mary.'

Dr Farley hovered on bent knees. 'What did she say?'

Cora turned her head away. She did not want him to see her face and somehow fathom her thoughts. Cold layers of certainty seemed to shed from her like the shrivelled leaves of desert plants.

She put her mouth by the woman's ear. 'I know, Annie, I know.'

Then, without a thought for the doctor standing close by, or for the over-dressed couple pretending to contemplate a prickly green ball, Cora unfastened the top three buttons of her jacket and fished inside for the twine around her neck, then laid the half-medal on her palm. Dr Farley stooped down but Cora cupped her hand above the woman's lap so that only she could see the engraving.

'Did you give this to your babe?'

The woman blinked and slowly nodded.

'That means you gave it to me.'

For a second, they looked at one another straight. The woman's eyes glowed with a brief glint of light, then her lids flickered and she looked back at her hands.

Cora's heartbeat filled her ears. 'Where did you get it, Annie?'

Dr Farley fidgeted above them. '*Annie?*'

He swallowed and seemed about to say more but Cora would not let him break the thread she had spun.

'Did it come from the house where you had a situation?' The nod might have been mistaken for an intake of breath. 'The house of Thomas Jerwood?'

The woman's eyes closed.

Dr Farley stiffened. 'Um, Miss Burns, if I might just...'

'Did you take it, Annie, from Mr Jerwood's collection?'

Then the woman's eyes opened wide and her head convulsed, her mouth working back and forth as if chewing on a lump of meat. Dr Farley leaned over her, determined not to miss the smallest utterance. But Cora raised her own voice with a forced indignation that she no longer felt.

'Did you steal the medallion, Annie? Is that why you went to gaol?'

The woman shook her head, tears pooling in her reddened eyes. And then, with a north-country voice as gentle as the glide of stream-water under a crust of ice, she spoke.

'I did not steal it. Master gave it me.'

maiden

Light beamed from the kitchen but the rest of the house looked dead as an empty grate. Cora stood outside and felt the darkening air reach to the bottom of her lungs. It seemed as if, until today, she had been holding her breath for a very long time. Maybe even now everything would still go on as before. But she did not quite see how it could.

Inside the kitchen, Cook had pulled the Windsor chair to the table and was holding an illustrated newspaper under the light. She looked up as Cora came in.

'There's tea in the pot if you want some.'

Cora nodded as she folded her shawl. 'Is anyone else back yet?'

Cook shook her head. 'Still out spending their Christmas boxes.'

'Have you not been anywhere, Cook?'

'I'd rather stay here and put my feet up in the warm.'

'Is there no one you wish to visit?'

'No.'

Cora poured the tea into a cup and took it to the table. Cook sat back leaving the illustrated newspaper spread open. Beneath a heading *Gaol for 'Maiden Tribute' Procurer*, black and white etchings showed a heavily bearded man resting his hand on the shoulder of a small, terrified girl who wore nothing but a gauzy shift. Then, in the next illustration, the same man stood defiant in the dock before an angry-looking judge. Finally the same man, in prison stripes, sat forlorn behind his cell door.

'How long have you worked here, Cook?'

'Too long, I'd say.'

'Longer than Mrs Dix?'

'Longer than any of them.'

'Was there ever a girl worked here called Annie?'

'We've had lots of girls come and go.'

'But did you hear of one who left quick? Because of something to do with the master?'

Cook's face clouded. 'You should keep your voice down. Or better still say nothing about it.'

'There was, then.'

'It was before I came. In fact, I took her job as kitchen maid. Annie Bright they called her.'

'What was said about her?'

Cook shrugged. 'That she left one night without a word. Everyone thought it was because she was in the family way. She was never heard from again.'

'But it had something to do with…'

Cora raised her eyebrows towards the ceiling.

'It was servants' gossip. Nothing more. I've managed to stay so long in one place because I don't set store by such things or repeat them. What makes you so interested?'

'You heard the missus. How she called me Annie as if she really thought that's who I was. I've been thinking it must have been another servant here that caused her confusion.'

'Perhaps you look like Annie Bright.'

'Yes. I must do.'

Cora lifted the cup to her mouth but found that her hand was shaking. The teacup rattled against the saucer and a dribble of brown tea slopped on to her skirt.

'Are you planning to leave here, Cora?'

'Why do you say that?'

Cook sighed. 'I'd rather you didn't.'

'I hadn't given it a thought.'

But Cora saw with a crystal flash of certainty that she could not stay. It didn't matter any more that she had no money and nowhere to go. She saw also what she must do before she left.

She stood up. 'Does anything want doing upstairs? Shall I take up some coals or hot water?'

'No, no. Don't trouble yourself. It's still your Boxing Day.'

'I'd rather be occupied.'

Cook shrugged. 'You could take Mrs Dix some pork pie. Help yourself from the larder if you want some too.'

'Thank you. I will.'

The odours of uncut bacon and over-ripe cheese that swilled from the open larder door almost made Cora slam it shut. But she put the oil lamp on a slate shelf and leaned her head against the basket hanging on the back of the door. Everything in the windowless room seemed tonight to have a longer shadow and a stronger smell. She had not eaten since morning but her appetite had evaporated.

She might have inherited her mother's face, but Cora could no longer blame the bad she had done on Annie Bright. The boy in the workhouse would have been suffocated, and Samuel scarred, and a bootlace wrapped around her own babe's neck regardless of the blood running through Cora's veins. Those crimes had come about because of the circumstances she had found herself in. Her feelings and provocations on each occasion had been entirely different, as had the aftertaste of the shame left by each outburst. Neither could she, in fairness, blame her faults on any inheritance from her father.

Taking the lamp, Cora climbed the back stairs, her boot soles tapping in the silence. Along the landing, she put her hand to the brass doorknob and gently twisted, but the library was locked.

'Cora.'

She jumped, but already knew that the voice was Violet's. The girl was in her nightdress, her coppery hair loose around her shoulders and her feet bare. Cora licked her lips as she tried to think of an excuse for trying the door, but Violet had already understood. She reached up to whisper in Cora's ear.

'I'll say my needlework is in there and I'll ask Mrs Dix for the key.'

years

Warily, Cora set the oil lamp on the tapestry footstool and glanced at the bookshelves as she mouthed a silent question: *is he behind there?* Violet, perched on the edge of the armchair, hardly bothered to lower her voice as she answered.

'He hasn't moved from his bed all day.'

Cora nodded and bent down. A black silhouette bulged across the library curtains but the shadow was thrown by a small Staffordshire jug with a cheerful glazed face.

'What are you doing, Cora?'

'Looking for something.'

'Something to do with Alice? Did your teacher tell you where she is?'

Cora breathed in and felt a pain under her ribs. 'Alice is nowhere. Except inside me.'

'Oh.' Violet's chin trembled. She looked down at her lap and began to bunch the nightdress into her fingers. 'What about the dolly? Did you sell it?'

'No, I threw it away.'

'Why?'

'I was stupid.'

Violet looked up aghast and Cora shrugged, but bit her lip as she turned away.

The medallion box was heavier than it looked. Cora heaved it from the cabinet shelf with both hands and carried it to the stool. Inlaid doves cooed silently to one another on the lid.

'What are you after, Cora? A medallion?'

'Only half of one.' Cora kneeled beside the footstool and pulled at the twine inside her collar. 'The other part of this.'

The half-medal revolved darkly inside the dazzle from the lamp.

Violet blinked. 'Is it yours, Cora? May I see?'

Cora laid the token on the footstool and then lifted the lid of the velvet-lined box beside it.

The medallions' engravings looked sharper in the lamplight; the rabbit more furry, the boat more densely rigged with sails. Cora pressed gently on a velvet corner and the tray of coins tilted upwards. As she had suspected, there was another layer beneath.

These medallions were also bordered by capital letters; a circle of words with a Roman number at the base, and each had its own picture: a hot air balloon, a desert pyramid, a measuring device. Both trays held twelve coins, but in the lower layer, one of the velvet roundels was empty.

'Can you help me, Violet? Tell me what any of the words mean and the years?'

Violet frowned. 'I don't know Latin.'

'But you know the numbers.'

She nodded, beaming, and came to Cora's side to lean over the medallions. The tip of her tongue slid along her lip as her finger moved along the row.

'1884, 1883, 1882, 1881…'

'They are in order?'

'Yes. 1880, 1879, 1878…'

'What about this empty hole? Which year is missing?'

'1863 has the microscope, then there's the hole, then 1865 with the beehive. I always wondered what happened to 1864.'

'Do you think that mine might be it?

Holding the dirty twine away from the velvet, Violet fitted the half-medal snugly into one half of the vacant recess. Its bronze was more worn than the others but the coin was, without doubt, part of the same family.

Violet's face contorted. 'Perhaps it used to say *1864* but the *V* got chopped off.' She giggled. 'I shouldn't like my *V* to go missing. Then I'd be *Iolet.*'

Cora saw then, punched into the corner of the box, the end of another name: '…onks & Sons'. It had been truncated by the lower layer of coins, which must also be removable.

Her fingertips slithered around the velvet trying to get a grip but the tray was wedged into the box and her nails too short to find any purchase.

'I need something to prise this out.'

Violet jumped up. 'A paper knife?'

'Yes. Is there one?'

Padding to the desk, Violet eased open the drawer then handed Cora a flat-bladed silver opener with a bone handle. Cora pushed the knife's rounded end into the tight fissure between the box and the tray. Her heart gave a leap as the layer of coins, with the half-medal still in place, began to move. Gently, she levered out the tray. But the bottom of the inlaid box, apart from a lining of deeper blacker velvet, was bare.

Cora banged her fist on the footstool and yanked out the half-medal in irritation.

Violet stood up and backed towards the desk. 'What's wrong, Cora?'

'I was sure it would be in here, the other half.'

'Will the lining not lift up?'

Cora pulled at the velvet but it was stuck down. She sighed and tucked the half-medal away, rubbing the back of her neck above the twine. 'It's not here.'

'Let's keep looking, shall we, Cora?'

'I wouldn't know where to start.'

'The chest of drawers? Or the ethnological shelves?'

Violet came cautiously forward then, clutching to her chest the japanned photograph frame. She lowered the woman's likeness into the lamplight.

'Perhaps, Cora, there's time for you to have a look at this for me first. I mean a really good look, and tell me if you see any resemblance to my real mother. Maybe when she was younger?'

The monochrome woman gazed primly from the frame. Over-sized buttons ran up her billowing satin dress from skirt hem to throat. 'Does she at all resemble the lady you met in Birmingham?'

Cora thought of Mrs Flynn's sallow face framed by a tattered shawl and almost laughed. But she brought the likeness closer to the light. She had not realised until now how young the woman in the likeness appeared. The sitter's finger marked her place in the closed book on her lap, the toe of her shoe was just visible on the low stool.

'She looks more like the mistress to me.'

'Well, Mrs Jerwood is my mother's cousin,' confusion rippled across the girl's face, 'at least that's what I was told.'

'Have you ever looked inside the frame? There may be something written on the reverse of the print.'

Two spots of colour had risen on Violet's cheeks. She glanced at Cora, then placed the frame, likeness-side down on the footstool. Pressing her fingertips on to the pasteboard cover, she slid it, along with the cabinet-portrait beneath, out of the metal runners. Two likenesses, almost identical, fell side by side on to the stool. Violet looked from one to the other and back again.

Cora bent closer. 'Are they the same?'

In both photographs, a woman sat in the same button-adorned crinoline dress, with one foot on a low stool and a closed book on her lap. But in the hidden print, her finger did not mark a page, and the whole of her slipper, as well as a bare ankle were displayed underneath the raised skirt.

Violet picked up the first familiar image and turned it over.

'*FMJ 1861.*'

Cora's pulse quickened. 'Mrs Jerwood?'

Violet nodded.

'And the other?'

Violet's fingers hesitated over the new photograph. Shielded from the light, it had retained more sharpness of detail and tone. This might have explained why the other woman's eyes appeared livelier and her hair a different colour, except that in truth, nothing about the two faces was the same. Their features were entirely unrelated.

Violet glanced at Cora wide-eyed, then she turned the print over and read from the back in her deliberate childish voice.

'*AB 1864.*'

But Cora had already known what she would say.

THIRTY

1884

cell

Thinking of it afterwards, Cora wondered if it was the whiteness of her cell that had pushed her into the frenzy. The walls and ceiling were lime-washed to such a dazzle that her eyes were hurt even by weak winter sunlight through the dirty window. At night, the caged gaslight burnt dimly but without rest. When she closed her eyes, the red glow behind her lids sometimes seemed even brighter than the mantle. Once or twice, at first, when she couldn't sleep, she'd let herself imagine the clean darkness of the linen cupboard and the sweet-cheese scent of her babe's lardy head. In those instants, he had become almost real. She'd swear she could feel his heaviness on her forearm and the dear tug of his little mouth on her teat. But she knew that she must not let herself drift into those thoughts. A soft hole at the centre of her mind beckoned her to fall into it.

When she'd been brought, dripping with milk, from the Bridewell and stripped of her liberty clothes, they'd given her a breast flannel to wear inside the prison stays. They had made no comment. Her condition must be common enough on the female wing. She'd rinsed and wrung out the sodden flannel each night. But as the days went by, the cloth became drier until there was nothing to wash away. After her third change of linen, the breast flannel was not returned to her. She had cried out in anguish at the loss. The babe was receding into her past. Soon, his slippery weight and special smell became only vague memories. Even months into her sentence, she would touch her breasts hoping for a blue-white drop that would keep the fact of his existence alive. Their dryness made her want to beat herself to a bruise.

At first, the gaol had not seemed like much of an adversity. The hard certainty of each day had a familiar air: the rolling of the bedding into a tight bundle so that it could not be sat upon; the straightening of the tin cup and plate, and of the prayer book and Bible into the prescribed prison pattern; the pointless sweeping of the scrubbed boards. Cleanliness, as the squinty-eyed wardress liked to say, was the prisoner's only luxury. As long, Cora thought, as you could put up with the pong of the lidded bucket.

Sensations of the workhouse came back to her through the rough itch of the prison bonnet, or a gristly mouthful of boiled bacon, but most especially in the tar-sweat odour of the oakum shed. The winking and leering of toothless women as they unpicked coir ropes into hairy piles would always make Cora grateful for the empty confines of her cell.

Even though prisoners weren't supposed to speak to each other at all, the females always found a way to satisfy their nosiness. There was plenty of hoarse, underhand chatter in the exercise grounds. It was always: *what you in for?* And: *how long?* The wardresses would scowl and point from the perimeter, but they could rarely be bothered to walk over. Cora would sometimes reply: *drunk and riotous – six weeks with labour*, or *larceny of a cheese – three months*. Most of the other prisoners came and went so quick they didn't cotton on. But a few, who were in as long or longer than Cora, would glower and put it about that she was a habitual liar. Which was saying something in such company.

It was after the truth had got out, she later realised, that things went bad. Squinty-Eye had brought along a new wardress to show her how to check that the cell was in order. The woman, who seemed too tall and respectable for the job, tried to strike up conversation.

'So, F.2.10, will you be in here long?'

Cora had no idea what to say. 'Yes, ma'm.'

Squinty-Eye squinted even harder but the new wardress pressed on.

'What I mean is, how long shall you serve?'

'Nineteen months, ma'm.'

The woman's eyebrows arched and she licked her lips with a salacious tongue. 'Goodness! For what offence?'

Cora opened her mouth but found that she could not speak.

'Attempted murder,' Squinty-Eye squeaked. 'Tried to do away with her babby so he wouldn't grow up bad as her. But the little imp must have been too quick.'

Her face wrinkled into a snicker and the new wardress's eyebrows brushed her crimped fringe. The cackling voice was loud enough to carry right along the perforated iron galleries and all ears on the female wing would be pressed to the doors. Everyone would now know. The new wardress's eyebrows sank into a frown as she slammed the cell door and clanked the key in the lock.

It was that same night when Cora took the frenzy. The gaslight fizzed and the red light behind her eyelids began to burn. She pushed herself face down into the plank bed, but could not shut out the light or sleep, or even lie still. The wardresses always knew there would be trouble if anyone started pacing about at night but Cora could not stop herself. There was a nagging ache at the base of her gut where her babe had been. And once she had let the thought of him in, the ache became a stab.

She took up her prison skirt from the narrow bench and rolled it into a tight bundle that fitted into the crook of her arm. But it was too small and too weightless. The blanket stripped from the plank bed and wrapped around the Bible was better. Cora folded one end of the coarse felt to give the semblance of a head. The bundle had a weight and a jointed feel that allowed her mind, if she closed her eyes, to bring him to life.

As she paced, she let herself rock the bundle, trying to think of a song that babies liked but she doubted she'd ever known one. Even so, a nasty tuneless hum came from her mouth and grew louder. Her eyes would not stay closed; a bash against the bench made them flip open. Then she saw the grey lump in her arms with a too-big head folded into a grimace, and could think only of the thing that had slid out of her after the babe in a mess of meaty gore.

Her shriek echoed as the blanket bundle ripped open and the Bible punched the gaslight cage. Cora's hands slammed against plaster until red smears decorated the white walls. Then a key rammed into the lock and the cell door sprang open. Cora clenched her bloody fists and the new wardress, still on duty, cowered behind Squinty-Eye.

'What you been doing?'

Cora heard herself screech. 'Killing what came out of me.'

The wardresses edged closer leaving the cell door wide open. Behind them, the gallery seemed to murmur with concentration.

The new wardress had a softer tone. 'Do you mean your baby?'

She moved towards Cora warily but there was a determined look in her eye.

Cora felt herself begin to shake. 'Not my babe! The nasty raw carcass of his twin.'

Both wardresses were in front of her now, hemming her into the corner. In the half-light, Squinty-Eye's gnarled face still had a look of concern.

'And was it joined to your nice babby with a twisty cord?'

Cora began to nod, heavy tears dripping from her chin. Then she took hold of her nightdress collar and gave it a hard downward tug with her bloody hands. The sweat-drenched cotton ripped, opening her breasts to the air. But in that instant, both wardresses pounced. Each grabbed an arm and wrenched it behind Cora's back.

Cora lashed out with her feet but Squinty-Eye deftly avoided the kicks. The new wardress was so fired up that she did not notice the blows. Between them, they pinioned Cora to the plank bed, roping her arms and legs to each corner. Squinty-Eye stood back panting, hands on her hips and sniggered down at Cora.

'You silly mare! There was no "twin".' She gave a howl of laughter. 'It was the afterbirth that was all, what the child feeds on in the belly. Without it they'd die.'

The new wardress, glowing with triumph, wiped her hands on her skirts and asked if they should put a blanket on Cora, at least over her bare top parts. But Squinty-Eye said no, leave her to cool down and work up an appetite for gruel. She'll be on nothing else for the next month.

Cora held her breath until the door locked. She was glad of the cold. Shivering would keep her awake for the whole night so that she might regard the warm fold of madness inside her brain and decide whether or not to fall into it. She understood now why lunatics succumbed to that tiny private world that no one else might enter. Losing her reason seemed like such an easy path.

And it was a path that she should, by rights, have already taken. Why did they not lock her in a padded back ward as soon as the little workhouse lad was killed? Only, perhaps, because she was not really to blame. It might have been Alice Salt alone who'd covered the boy's face until he was still. Cora could never understand herself without knowing what had really happened in the schoolyard privies. And for that, she must keep her wits long enough to find Alice.

Cora resolved, then, to stop herself thinking of the small body that had come out of hers. If the babe was to visit, he must do it, along with that other little boy, only in dreams. That way, she'd be sane enough on her release to look for her workhouse sister. Icy draughts skated over Cora's clammy nakedness but her trembling had stopped. The point of her existence was now clear. She breathed the fetid prison air and smiled.

THIRTY-ONE

December 1885

procurer

Cora's knuckles rapped on mahogany then she held her breath and listened. The master, without doubt, was in there. Earlier that morning, as she was carrying away the untouched breakfast tray, she had seen him shuffling down the main stairs in his brocade dressing gown and then heard the thwack of the study door.

The half-medal was sticky in her hand. She knocked again.

'Yes?'

His voice was bad-tempered but weak. As she went in, he glowered up, his pen hovering above a page dense with handwriting and crossings-out. A litter of similar pages covered the carpet around his feet. He seemed unsurprised to see her.

'So? What is it?'

'I have something to show you.'

'You have, have you?'

Cora stretched out her palm, the dirty twine dangling. She could not tell whether he even looked at the half-medal but he gave a sharp sniff as if at some brown sloppiness on the sole of his shoe.

'It is one of yours, sir.'

'Is that a question or a statement?'

Cora hesitated. Wrong-footed by his calmness, she could not think how to reply.

A smile ghosted across Mr Jerwood's lips. 'Come, girl. Do not underestimate me.'

The accusations that had swilled around Cora's head since seeing Annie Bright began to slip away. Perhaps the master was so fenced about by his cleverness and high standing that nothing Cora could reveal or threaten would leave any dent. Of all the questions that had come to her, she could remember just one.

'Did she steal it?'

Mr Jerwood sighed. 'She may have later become a convict but she was certainly not a thief.'

Sudden coldness ran through Cora. There had not even been mention of a name yet the master understood exactly. Everything she'd imagined must be true. Her hand closed over the half-medal and dropped to her side. She had not realised how terrible it would feel to be right.

The steel nib tapped on the inkwell.

'Is that all?'

For the first time, Cora recognised something familiar in the crease of Mr Jerwood's mouth. She saw too how his coldness and cleverness might, in a gentleman, be counted virtues. Her fist tightened on the half-medal.

'No. I have a proposition.'

He snorted. 'You think that I would any longer be interested...'

'In what I have to say, yes, you will.' Cora took a step closer. 'But first, I want to know how you were able to find me.'

'Find you? No, no. I did not look for you, nor even know of your existence. I simply came upon you by chance and then noted a lineal resemblance.' He smiled faintly and red thumbprints seemed pressed on to his cheekbones. 'Your token, there, confirms definitively my intuition.'

Cora felt the ice at her core melt into rage. This man was more criminal than her or her mother, yet he would never be locked up. She surged forward, looming above the shrunken figure in the chair. The sharp point of the half-medal spiked her knuckles. How easy it would be to punch the coin into his eye. Blood and ink would spatter his handwritten papers. The wound would be savage enough to revenge even Annie Bright's miserable life. But Cora let the half-medal bite only into her own hand.

'I think the time has come, sir, for you to pay your dues.'

'What?' The master's laugh was hard and hollow. 'You think that anyone would believe your unlikely tale? Who's to say that your father is not some canal-side ruffian? For I daresay that sort would have been very much to her taste.'

White heat seared but Cora lowered her face slowly and steadily towards the master, her physical strength pulsing over him. There was a satisfying up and down movement in his throat.

'Ah no, sir. You mistake me. It is not my own story, nor even Annie Bright's, that people will find most shocking.'

He blinked and for the first time Cora saw a flutter of uncertainty behind his eyes.

'Whose then?'

'Come, sir, you cannot be ignorant of the criminal trial that has been in all the newspapers these past months.'

'I do not see how...'

'The guilty gentleman had taken a young girl for his own purposes from her impoverished family by means of cash. And for that, this gentleman was convicted of procurement and abduction and he now finds himself residing in a gaol cell. Newspapers throughout the land denounce him as a procurer.'

Mr Jerwood stared at the writing on his desk. His face did not flicker but his skin, already pallid, seemed to whiten.

'And so, by this, you seek to extort something from me?'

Cora took a long breath and made sure to remember the words she had prepared.

'For myself, I seek only the wages owed to me. And my underthings and boots for decency's sake.'

His eyebrows raised. 'Nothing more?'

'Not for me. But there is most certainly more due to Violet and her family.'

A noise that was both cough and laugh ripped the stuffy air. 'Ah yes.'

Cora straightened and did not bother to lower her voice. 'You have done wrong by them all and now you must put things right.'

'And why do you imagine that I would?' He turned to face Cora, his gaze re-lit. 'All you think you know is nothing more than servants' tittle-tattle.'

'It certainly is not. None of them have said a word.'

'So on what basis do you make any allegations?'

The half-medal pushed from Cora's balled fist like a chisel. Again, she stilled the itch to punch.

'They are not allegations, they are facts which I learned from a talk with Mrs Flynn on my visit to her home in Coventry Street.'

Dullness drew across the master's eyes like a gauze curtain and Cora knew that she had won. But she would leave him in no doubt.

'So I think it only fair that you should compensate Violet for all of the years that you have made use of her. And you can do this by giving her a proper education and sufficient provision until she can make her own living as a teacher.'

'You have it all worked out.'

'Her family must be provided for too and Letty, if she wishes it, be placed in the same school as Violet.'

'*Must*?'

'Do not underestimate me either, sir. I know that when Violet was not much more than a babe-in-arms you bought her, like a laboratory animal, to be measured and examined throughout her life as a specimen in your collection. This tale is a sensation which would be of great interest, I'm sure, to the *Birmingham Gazette*. And perhaps, even, to the police.'

He tried to smile but his mouth quavered. 'Oh bravo. Very clever. Except for your surprising failure, whilst you have me in such a fix, not to seek more for yourself than a pair of boots.'

'You agree then, to my proposition?'

'As long as, once you leave this room, I never set eyes on you again.' He picked up the pen with a sarcastic flourish. 'And so, Miss *Burns* will that be all?'

'Excepting to ask, for Cook's sake, that I may stay here and finish my work for today.'

Cora waited for his frosty nod of assent before turning her back on Thomas Jerwood. As she let her hand loosen from the half-medal, its jagged edge seemed suddenly blunt. Cora could now see that whatever parts of her nature had come from her father or her mother, the fierceness of the grit inside her was all her own.

farewell

Next morning, as if it were a Sunday, Cora dressed in her Melton jacket and linsey skirt but she left the print dress that she had worn through the past months folded on the scullery counter.

Cook was sitting in the kitchen with an elbow on the table and a hand on her brow. She looked up as Cora came in and sighed.

'You're definitely going then.'

Cora went to the dresser for her belongings. 'Yes.'

'What did you do to offend him?'

'He just didn't like my face.'

Cook shook her head. 'There's only two weeks until Ellen goes.

I shall never fill both posts at this time of year. No one will brave the mud.'

Cora picked up her clean underthings and pocket. She knew that if she could stay, she'd likely be able to take Ellen's position and then, in time, work herself up to be a kitchen maid. But her path lay elsewhere and she knew not to look back. She wrapped her things inside the nightdress.

'I've done everything in the scullery. Potatoes, boots, pans, knives. That should help get you by.'

'It grieves me to lose you, Cora.'

'Me? Why?'

'You are a rare worker. And honest.'

Cora laughed. She shook her head as she stuffed the old muslins she used as handkerchiefs into the pocket. Cook tapped the corner of a blank white envelope against the scrubbed tabletop then angled towards Cora.

'He's left this for you.'

'My wages?'

'I suppose. Although it doesn't feel like there's any coin. Apart from one perhaps. You should open it and make sure he's not diddling you.'

'It'll be right.'

She pressed the thick envelope carefully inside her pocket. Then Cook held out a sheet of yellow paper folded twice and addressed: *To Whom It May Concern.*

'Here is your character.'

Cora nodded and pushed it into the pocket then she told Cook that she was going to the privy. But as the kitchen door closed behind her, she slipped towards the main house, tip-toeing over the parquet floor past the study towards the morning room where she knew that Violet would be.

At first it seemed that the room was empty. Then she saw the girl on the window seat, her knees tucked up beneath her and her green dress almost hidden by the folds of the curtain. Violet's heavy lids flickered. Her face was shiny with perspiration and the unnatural redness of her lips was puckered and cracked.

Cora crouched into the milk-sourness of the child's breath. 'I must say farewell, Violet.'

'Don't go. I'm poorly.'

'I have no choice.'

'Because of the photograph?'

'In a way.'

'Was that you in it?'

Cora shook her head.

'But she looked just like you.'

'It was my mother.'

Violet's brow wrinkled with confusion and a tear ran down her cheek.

'I wish you were my mother, Cora.'

Cora took hold of Violet's hands and folded them into hers. The girl's skin was paper-white and despite her hotness she was shivering. How fragile she seemed. It was so easy for any child to disappear; in a shudder of nameless fever, as much as in a press of petticoats. Cora's own son, she knew, was as likely dead as alive. Nature may have already passed a verdict on her deeds.

Violet's limp fingers suddenly gripped. 'What is to become of me, Cora?'

'Don't fear, Violet. Mr Jerwood will look after you. He has promised.'

'But what if he doesn't? Who else will help me?'

'I will.'

'How can you? Where will I find you?'

'You can write to me.'

'Where?'

'Care of Thripp & Son, Corporation Street. Can you remember that?'

Violet nodded solemnly and wiped at the salty trail on her face. Cora prised her fingers from the girl's and stood up.

'I will go and tell Cook that you are not well and must have some toast water in your room.'

Violet gave a bleary smile as Cora, with a lurch of her heart, closed the door.

In the privy, once she had tied on the pocket, Cora opened out the sheet of ruled yellow foolscap written in Cook's neat childlike hand.

To Whom It May Concern

CORA BURNS

I have known this person for some months since she came to work for Mrs Jerwood as 'Between Maid'. Mrs Jerwood is indisposed and I have authority to deal with servant matters in the kitchen and scullery. Cora is a hard worker and a quick learner who is decent, respectable and reliable at all times. She is fit and strong and has done a grand job with – knives, pans, crockery and glassware. She is unafraid of dirty work – coal boxes, skirtings, windows and the like. She keeps herself neat and clean. Her appetite is modest. She has slept without complaint in the kitchen and her constitution is tough. The reason for her leaving is entirely the result of her employer's circumstances and not the girl's conduct. It saddens me greatly to have to say goodbye to Cora. I would recommend her for scullery, maid-of-all-work or even housemaid positions in any respectable establishment.

Signed: Mrs Flora Shirley, Cook
The Larches, Spark Hill, Warks.

Cora read the character twice over but still she could not take her eyes from it, nor hardly breathe; her heart was too full. No one had ever had such good to say about her. The odd thank you or gratefully raised eyebrow was as close as anyone at the workhouse or asylum had ever come to showing appreciation.

Cora read again the pretty name on the foolscap: *Mrs Flora Shirley.* No one in Cora's hearing had ever called her anything but 'Cook'. She certainly wore no ring, and had made no mention of any life except her years at The Larches. So a husband seemed unlikely. Cora guessed, although she would never know for sure, that she and Cook shared a heartache in common.

Cora returned to the kitchen intending to make clear her gratitude, but once there she could not find the right words. Cook stood at the table flicking through a small pile of envelopes.

'The postman wouldn't come in for his Christmas drink. He said he had no time. I suspect the sherry at Tyseley Farm may be more plentiful than ours.' She held an envelope out to Cora. 'Here's one for you. Just in time.'

'For me?'

Cora flinched at the extraordinary sight of her name on a stamped and franked envelope. *Miss C Burns, c/o The Larches, Spark Hill, Warks.* was written in an elongated hand. Could it be Mr Bowyer's? Perhaps he had thought of more unpleasant details to unburden upon her. So perhaps it was for the best that she was about to move on and leave almost no trace.

Taking up her shawl and her bundle, Cora breathed a last lungful of the kitchen's gravy-infused air. Then Cook offered her a hand to shake. The skin felt unexpectedly soft and the grip firm.

'Goodbye then, Cora. Where will you go?'

'There is a shop that once offered me a situation. I will try there first.'

'If you have no luck, ask at Taylor's registry. Tell them I sent you.'

'Thank you, Cook.'

Cora had no illusion that Alfred Thripp's offer may well have had some other motive but his true feelings would show themselves soon enough. If there was any funny business, she could move again; Cook's warm words on her character gave her the sudden freedom to look for a situation whenever she chose.

'And write to me, please, to let me know how you fare.'

'I will.'

Cook's cough seemed to cover a tremble in her voice. 'The other thing I must say to you, although I'm sure you already know it better than most, is that once a child is grown, he will have very little need for a mother.' She held Cora's gaze for a long moment and then looked away. 'You'd best get off now, if you are to catch the quarter past tram.'

coin

Dense white steam billowed as the whistle piped for any final passengers. The few that had already come aboard huddled on the tram's bottom deck, but despite the dank air Cora climbed past them to the open benches above. She wedged herself behind the glass half-panes under the canvas roof where no one might see what she was about to read.

Once the engine wagon had chugged the tram car to the top of the hill, Cora pulled the envelopes from her pocket. She put the worrying mailed correspondence on her lap and felt the thicker envelope from Thomas Jerwood. She had hoped there would be more weight to it. Three months, near enough, she'd worked in his house. So if he'd been generous there should be at least two whole sovereigns inside. Her heart sank at the shape of only one.

The tram clattered along, picking up speed, its walls knocking against Cora's knees. Cold gusts blew in from the bare meadows. She eased open the gummed flap and began to pull from the envelope a folded wad of apparently blank white paper. But as the sheets emerged, Cora saw that although one side of each was indeed plain, the others were covered in fancy black print. Her hand froze. There was no mistaking the first printed word she could decipher: '£Five'. A five pound note. Heart thumping, she checked through the sheaf, counting. Ten of them. Fifty pounds. She had never imagined ever in her life to see so much money in one place.

Cora blinked up at the houses coming into view. The first gable end was painted entirely with an advertisement for Bird's Custard Powder. Yellow and red letters swam through the mist. *Custard without eggs! A Daily Luxury.* Cora felt suddenly weightless, as if both she and the envelope full of five pound notes might at any moment fly up from the seat and float together on to a slippery rooftop. She put a hand on the edge of the bench and gripped it tight. Many unpleasant consequences could be imagined from this strange windfall. She could not shift the feeling, so long ingrained in her mind, that good fortune must sooner or later be twinned with bad.

Cora pushed the notes back into the envelope and remembered the coin still inside. She reached in, expecting it to be a sovereign but as soon as her fingers touched the half-moon shape and familiar metal bumps, she knew that it was not money. She looked around to check that she was still alone on the top deck then, on her rocking palm, she laid together both halves of Thomas Jerwood's annual medallion for 1864.

The Roman date, with the missing *V*, was now complete, and there was no mistaking the bronze profile of the striking Grecian goddess on the coin. Youthful and beautiful, Annie Bright's legs and bosom bloomed through the drapery of her scanty robe. One of her bare arms stretched out across the plain background that Cora knew so well; the other rested on a tripod-mounted camera as her hand adjusted the lens.

But the words around the border, which Cora had always imagined would release a message once both halves were reunited, only became more unintelligible.

IMAGINEM SALTEM EST INDICIUM INGENIUM.

Their meaning no longer mattered, though, because Cora knew the message could have nothing to do with *Salt*. Her belly churned with revulsion for the tawdry fantasy portrayed in bronze. If it had belonged to her, she'd have chucked the whole medal over the side of the steam tram. Instead, she stuffed both halves inside the blank envelope with her money.

The tram rattled on through a close pack of red streets and smoking rooftops. In the road ahead, parallel iron rails gashed the asphalt before disappearing into mist now thickened by coal smoke. Cora pulled her shawl tighter. It wasn't far to the next stop and if she didn't want her face speckled with smuts, she should move downstairs. But there was time to open the posted envelope and at least see who it was from.

Gum crackled as it opened. Again, inside the envelope, there was paper that had the look of money. But it was the printed black type at the head of the bond that brought Cora a heave of relief.

6ᵗʰ December 1885   *BIRMINGHAM ASYLUM,*
                                 WINSON GREEN, WARKS.

Dear Miss Burns,
I must thank you, most sincerely, for taking the trouble to meet my patient today. Mary seemed most heartened by your visit, although she has not yet said anything. I herewith enclose a Postal Order for ten shillings to cover your expenses.

I also have a message for you from Matron Abbott who has been assisting with my private research and, under strictest confidences, has become familiar with this case. Matron says that you may remember her from when she first came to the asylum as senior attendant on the female wards. She has not revealed to me the purpose of her message which is simply: 'John Burns, Marston Green

Cottage Homes, Marston Green, Warks.' except to say that this person may be a relative of yours.

Perhaps, at some point in the future, you may feel inclined to visit Mary here at the asylum. If so, please do not hesitate to write to me first.

With kind regards,
Dr D Farley

The tram was squealing towards a huddle of black figures at the roadside tramstop and Cora realised dimly that in order to make sure of a place on the lower deck she should start to get up, to gather her things safely and to ease her way down the rickety staircase. But she could not move.

Even though it was morning, lights still burned in some of the terraced houses across the street. The creamy glow of parlours fringed by velvet and lace would not long ago have seemed as remote from Cora Burns as a gentleman's country estate. But no longer. And a conviction now burned in her as fierce as a photographer's lamp, that she would, quite soon, arrive at the place she had been heading to all along.

THIRTY-TWO

Research Journal of

David Farley MD
Assistant Medical Officer
Birmingham asylum
January 1886

Sat 2nd

My first entry of the New Year allows me to record how much I should be thankful for despite my recent professional disappointments. I foresee heartening progress for Mankind during the coming year. In England's industrial towns, a workers' breakthrough seems imminent and I (along with several new Comrades) intend to play a guiding part in the coming revolution by establishing a Birmingham Branch of the Socialist League.

My research into the uses of hypnosis in the treatment of the insane has made a significant start, despite the difficulties, and in the course of this work, I have formed an invaluable bond with Matron Abbott. She has provided me with practical assistance, wise insight and a degree of moral guidance without which I fear my research would already have floundered.

The fact of the matter is, however, that hypnosis has had no discernible benefit on the condition of Mary B. It is true that she can say a few simple words but these are only 'yes, sir' and 'no, sir', phrases which seem to have been ingrained into her by habits of servitude. Even the meeting with her long-lost daughter which I took such pains to arrange, seemed without advantage.

Matron Abbott has, however, prevented me from being too downhearted about the lack of immediate success with my experiments. She emphasises the importance, in any healing process, of the passage of time. Mary's vocal chords may gradually loosen. Miriam also encourages a further search through the asylum record cabinets in the hope of unearthing another clue about the root of Mary B's condition.

Sun 3rd

After chapel, Matron and I spent this morning amongst the dusty casebooks and admission files in the administration office cupboard where, as I suspected, Miriam's shrewdness and tenacity paid off. Whilst trawling through a box of loose papers marked 'Correspondence', she came upon a letter dated June 23rd 1865 from a Dr Marsh at Birmingham Gaol to my long-gone predecessor here at the asylum. The letter requested the admission of an unmanageable prisoner, one Mary B–. I shall transcribe the said letter which eloquently relates her circumstances.

Sir,

I write to you personally about a most extreme medical case with which I am now seeking your assistance. It concerns Prisoner F.2.11 and these are the sad facts:

F.2.11 was admitted to the gaol on 22ⁿᵈ March for a sentence of six months' duration on a charge of attempted suicide. She had been pulled by a boatman, several weeks previously, from the Birmingham and Fazeley canal. Once her pregnant state became obvious, the constable was called and he duly placed her in custody for her own safety. The prisoner offered up nothing about her circumstances. She refused to tell either the boatman who had saved her or the policeman any name or directions. The name she later gave in Court (Mary B–) may be regarded as dubious.

I daresay that the judge who meted out the said sentence did so with the interests of the child uppermost in his mind. The prisoner appeared unstable upon admission, in particular becoming tearful when the requirement for silence on the wing was enforced. She co-operated in general, however, and duly gave birth on the gaol's female wing to a healthy girl on 3ʳᵈ April. Thereafter, her state deteriorated. Although she succeeded in feeding the child, her tears were copious and her pacing of the cell whilst rocking the poor infant, became almost ceaseless. When her final breakdown arrived, it was only due to the vigilance of one of our newest wardresses that the life of the child was preserved. The said wardress, hearing a commotion inside F.2.11, flung open the door to find the prisoner stripped to the waist and violently shaking the babe against her breasts. The prisoner was screaming at the top of her lungs that, as the child would not feed, it must be dead. Needless to say, the poor mite was making almost as much noise as her mother, but the prisoner was unable to recognise her babe's thrashing movements nor hear her lusty cries. The prisoner began to beat savagely at her teats and was rescued by the brave wardress who, in the ensuing melee, received a severe injury to her eye.

It was decided, for the good of both, that mother and child must be separated and the babe is now lodged under the care of the Birmingham Poor Law Union. The mother's condition, as you may imagine, has deteriorated further since her daughter's removal and she has been under almost perpetual restraint in her cell.

Given that I see no likelihood of this prisoner's improvement in her current habitat, I am requesting a Certificate of Committal for her immediate admission to the Borough Lunatic Asylum. Once I am in receipt of your assent, I shall have her brought to the front entrance under close escort.

I remain, Yours etc
Jeremy Marsh MD

I can add little comment to this tragic tale except to say that in a more humane and equal society, one free from poverty and prejudice, I have no doubt that Mary B would have preserved her sanity.

<u>*Thurs 7th*</u>
*I have received today, by the third post, a most curious postscript to the case of Mary B. This is a note from her daughter, thanking me for the postal order and passing New Year wishes to her mother. Also included in the envelope from Miss B–, although not referred to in her note, was an item which I take to be a gift for her mother. The item is a commemorative bronze medallion cut in half. When placed together, the two halves show a clear image of the young Mary B wearing Grecian dress and operating photographic apparatus. The date shown in Roman numerals is 1864 and the Latin inscription around the edge reads 'IMAGINEM SALTEM EST INDICIUM INGENIUM.' I have translated this (perhaps badly) to mean: '**A likeness is an indication, at least, of true nature**.' Of course, 'ingenium' can mean 'character', or 'genius' as well as 'nature'.*

I went immediately to show Miriam the medallion and to ask her what she made of it. Her eyes widened at Mary B's elegant image. Miriam noticed, which I had not, that the way the medallion is cut makes 'SALT' into a separate word. Could this be a reference, she wondered, to Mary B's home village? I suspect, however, that it was simply a coincidence. Mary B must have acted at one time as an artist's model but for whom is perhaps best left, like the other delicate details of her history, swathed in the fog of the past.

Miriam and I agreed that it would not be wise to show the medallion to Mary B, at any rate, not now. The patient seems to have recovered some of the equilibrium that deserted her before Christmas and she is back at work, although not in the kitchens. The sorting room of the laundry seems challenging enough for her at present. Miriam took the medallion and said she will see that it is safely placed in the inmates' store cupboards. Should Mary B ever become fit to leave the asylum, she will be welcome to take the medallion with her.

Fri 8th

Matron Abbott kindly took a moment from her normal duties to visit, with me, another patient whom I have identified as a possible subject for hypnotic therapy. This lady is a private patient who has been incapacitated for many years (though kept mainly at home) by hysteria and monomania. The focus of her fear appears to be the short drop between the surface of her mattress and the floor. This overarching terror of a fall from the bed has kept her largely captive upon the said item of furniture for more than ten years. What occasioned her initial reluctance to rise, no one knows. I am, however, hopeful that hypnosis may be the key that will unlock this patient, whom I shall call Frances J, from her bed-ridden prison.

I have decided not to advise Miriam, at least for now, about the connection between the story of Mary B and that of Frances J. There is a whiff of scandal about their connection which is somewhat improper. Instead, as we left the private ward and went into the main corridor, I told Miriam about my hopes for the Birmingham Branch of the Socialist League. Having read the Manifesto, she is a little sceptical, especially with regard to Mr Morris's disdain for 'bourgeois property-marriage'. What exactly, she asked (with a mischievous smile on her lips), did he have in mind for the 'kindly relations between the sexes' that would replace marriage? She broke into a giggle at my blushing attempts to reply but nevertheless she agreed, most readily, to accompany me to the inaugural branch meeting on Saturday evening next.

THIRTY-THREE

3rd April 1886

birthday

Cora had told Alfred that it was to be her twenty-first birthday that Sunday so that he would not think it odd when she asked for the loan of the cashmere walking-dress. He had agreed immediately and asked only, in the event of a sitter wishing to borrow it on Saturday evening, that she should come to the shop on Sunday morning to put it on.

A few months before, this intimate invitation might have worried her but Cora had got the measure of Alfred now and knew that she could trust him. Perhaps he'd seen enough of his father's sly way with women to remain entirely straightforward himself. If old Mr Thripp had still been living above the shop she might not have accepted the situation there. But Alfred assured her that his father had gone to live more or less permanently with a sister in Weston-Super-Mare having the intention, once the warm weather came, to buy a photographer's van and a donkey.

Alfred had seemed genuinely delighted when Cora returned to the shop on a late December afternoon and asked him if he still had need of a model. He had stroked his sandy beard and said that there was in fact another opportunity that she might consider. He had been thinking of taking on a maid-of-all-work but could not really justify more than a few hours of charring to service his cramped rooms above the shop. What he really needed was a photographer's assistant, but again he couldn't support a full-time position. If, however, he could find someone who would be capable to do both, a live-in position might be possible. Cora had thrust the foolscap character into his hands and said that she'd sleep in the studio if need be. Alfred had laughed at that, but the upstairs cubby hole which had housed Cora's makeshift bed was not much better. She sat on it now, to take off her grey wool shop-dress and put on the cashmere stripes. The grey dress was ingrained with the faint chemical smell of the developing room which Cora liked to savour each time she took it off.

After a couple of months of living in, Alfred had agreed more readily than she'd expected when she suggested moving out to her own digs. She promised that it would be close by and she'd still have the stove on before he was up each morning. He'd been entirely decent with her whilst they were living and working all day together in the same close space but both had felt the unspoken strain on the boundaries of respectability. Rumours of anything untoward between them would be bad for business.

Cora slipped the ruched skirt of the walking dress over her undergarments. Recently, she'd bought a modest bustle and had been getting used to it in the narrow confines of the shop and practicing how to sit very upright on the edge of a chair. But the new shape made all the difference to the fit of the walking-dress. It flowed smoothly over her small waist to a froth of soft fabric behind. She'd also bought a simple dark bonnet with wide silk ribbons, cut well back from her brow, as well as cheap but well-fitting kid gloves.

Once she had put them all on, she eased herself down the narrow stairs into the shop. Alfred was waiting at the bottom with his arms folded and when he saw her his face flushed red into his beard.

'By Jove! You look magnificent.'

Cora could not quite meet his eye. 'Please don't.'

'It's true. I always knew you could look extraordinary.'

'Well, thank you, and also for the loan of the dress.'

'If you have the time, I could take a souvenir likeness, for your birthday.'

'Thank you, Alfred, but I should be getting off.'

'Very well.' He turned to the counter and picked up a small package then came back towards her offering it out in his hands. 'Please accept this instead.'

Her smile held a twinge of apprehension. She hoped that he would not embarrass her with something too extravagant. But as she pulled open the tissue paper, her smile broadened. Inside was a set of three lawn handkerchiefs bordered with fine lace.

'How kind of you, Alfred. They are exactly what I would wish for.'

She did not like to admit that she could now make the old pudding muslins into dusters, or to tell him that this was the only birthday present she had ever received.

Her skirts swished as she went to the counter and opened the strings of the velvet reticule on her wrist. The old sacking pocket, as well as the Melton jacket and linsey skirt had gone on to the totter's cart early in January. As soon as she'd had a chance, she'd taken a crisp five pound note along Corporation Street to Lewis's and bought the shop-dress and a proper coat.

Cora put the handkerchiefs into the reticule beside an assortment of silver coins and a folded brown envelope then she pulled the strings tight. Alfred unlocked the shop door.

'So, where are you off to for your birthday jaunt?'

'Into the countryside.'

'To Cannon Hill Park?'

It was a place they had visited several times recently, taking with them the dry-plate camera and a Rover Safety Bicycle. On the last occasion, Cora had finally got the hang of riding unaided. Alfred had been overjoyed with the photographs.

'No, further than that. By train. I've never travelled on the railway before.'

'Never?' He looked aghast. 'My goodness. Well then, that will be a proper treat. Please keep the dress for the whole day. You can return it in the morning if you like.'

He really was good to her. Perhaps in the future, when they might be on a more equal footing than now, and he understood a little more of her past... but she could imagine him only being horrified at her story. And she'd soon tire of his kindness. Once he knew where she was really going today her time at this shop might swiftly come to an end but by then, she hoped, she'd have learnt from him as much as she needed to know.

journey

Cora did not flinch when the clerk in the ticket office barked that there'd be no second-class carriages on the Coventry train today, so was it first or third she'd be wanting? *First* she said without missing a breath, or being sure that she had enough shillings in her reticule to cover the cost.

But the price of both tickets – a return for herself, along with a single half-fare back – was only three shillings and ninepence. The first-class carriage did not seem especially luxurious, although it was clean and the seats appeared newly upholstered. She sat slightly sideways to accommodate the bustle and breathed out with relief that she had the carriage to herself.

Then the partition slid back and a large middle-aged woman entered in a heavy cloud of purple taffeta. Cora looked up, her jaw set firm, expecting a scowl of disapproval. But the woman's face broke into a friendly smile. Cora must seem, at least on first glance, like someone genteel enough to be in the first-class carriage.

'Good morning to you.'

Cora nodded, unsure how to reply. With luck, conversation would be quelled by the huffing of engines under the great glass roof, and the shouts outside the carriage window from the porters and guards on the platform. But the woman sat down directly opposite Cora and as the locomotive eased itself into the sunlight, she smiled once again.

'What a fine morning it is! I feel that spring is here at last. Do you have far to go on your journey?'

'To Marston Green.'

'For recreation?'

'Not exactly. I'm visiting a relative.'

There was a slight stiffening in the woman's features. Did the mismatch between Cora's apparel and her way of speaking give off a vulgar whiff? Cora's senses prickled. Although not exactly coarse, the woman's own voice had a definite lilt of the town.

'Is your family home in that village?'

Amid the clatter of iron wheels, Cora began to pull off her left glove. 'No, madam. I am visiting my mother-in-law.'

'Without your husband? Oh, that is good of you.'

'I am a widow, you see.'

Cora's hand lay exposed on her lap revealing, on her ring finger, the plain band that she had got for a few bob from a pawn shop.

'Many condolences, my dear. Was it a sudden loss?'

'Very sudden, yes. My husband was an engineer and taken in a gas explosion. One day he was there, the next he was gone. In a puff of smoke.'

'How tragic! And do you have no little ones to comfort you?'

'Oh yes. A little boy, John. He is almost three now and has been staying with my mother-in-law.'

'I see.' The woman flung another glance at the ring, and perhaps also at the roughened redness of Cora's hands against the fine cashmere stripes. Her voice jumped into an oddly high tone. 'But you manage to live alone in town?'

'Not any longer. John will be returning with me to my new lodgings. A delightful villa in Pitsford Street.'

In fact, Cora had found a room with a widow-woman, Mrs Barker, on Allison Street which was not all that far from the Flynns, but on a sunny corner by the new brolly works. There was weekly washed lace at the parlour window and a private yard with a flushing lav. Mrs Barker had said she'd be glad of a kiddie about the place. It would be six shillings a week extra to look after him during the day.

The large woman's taffeta ruffles murmured with the swaying of the carriage. Her smile hardened. 'How marvellous that you have found some way to support yourselves.'

'Indeed. I recently used my compensation from the Corporation to purchase the lease of a small shop in Nechells.'

The last part, at least, was almost true. She had seen an advertisement for the lease and might even visit the shop.

'And what will you sell there? Haberdashery perhaps?'

'Oh no, likenesses.'

What remained of Mr Jerwood's fifty pounds would be more than enough to purchase a full set of commercial photographic equipment.

The woman's shocked expression was swallowed in a grinding of wheels and the screech of a steam whistle. At the window, the colours had gone from grey and grimy to the brightest of greens. The trees, just coming into leaf, were drenched with dappled light and the first pink blossom budded in the gardens of red-brick cottages.

It was not long until, in a blur of steam, the engine jolted to a halt and a voice outside boomed: *Marston Green, Marston Green*. As Cora stood up, resplendent in the bustled walking-dress, she felt a shiver of satisfaction that she could still lie so well.

daffodils

The 'Cottage Homes' were not cottages at all but large, detached villas with fancy chimneys and gauzy curtains at the sash windows. Two rows of them stretched along the daffodil-lined driveway beside a chapel and a school. New brickwork glowed orange in the afternoon sun and yellow-headed birds, bold as budgerigars, darted in and out of the hedgerows. Cora had never heard birdsong so deafening.

She stood in shadow at the front door of the porter's lodge and wiped her face with one of the new handkerchiefs from her reticule. Sweat ran from her bonnet into her eyes but her mouth was entirely dry. This wasn't the sort of place she had been expecting. Not in the least. What child would choose to leave here for the soot of Allison Street?

Her hand hovered at the bell-pull as she wondered whether to turn away. Then, inside, footsteps clipped on a hard floor and the door opened.

'Mrs Burns, is it?'

The woman wore pale lilac cotton with a collar starched white in the manner of a nurse. Her fair hair was piled into a lace cap. She was not much older than Cora but a wrap of brisk confidence made her seem matronly. Cora nodded and stepped inside the hallway.

'And do you have the discharging letter?'

Cora took the brown envelope from her reticule and the woman smiled.

'I'm Miss Mooney, Johnnie's house-mother. He's such a dear little thing. He hasn't been with us very long but is already something of a favourite. So clever. And such sweet sayings he comes out with.'

There was an Irish twist to her voice and a natural friendliness in her round, open face. How the children must love her.

'Would you care to wait here, Mrs Burns, whilst I fetch him?'

She indicated a row of wooden chairs alongside the bottom of the stairs and Cora eased her skirts on to what looked to be the largest seat. Then Miss Mooney disappeared behind a varnished door.

Encaustic tiles, spotless as new, made a pattern of brown and blue stars that repeated neatly around the staircase. A lace curtain flapped at an open window and through the gap came the faint trickle of children's voices, singing. Cora could remember all of the words: ...*The balm of life, the cure of woe, the measure and the pledge of love*... But she had never heard the hymn sung so eagerly.

Cora took a sharp breath and let it slowly out. She had thought to pluck the boy away from the sort of bare grey rooms she had known as a child. That thought had given her confidence that however lacking she might be as a mother, her love would always outdo the indifferent stare of a workhouse attendant. But this place was perhaps better than any home she could ever provide. If the boy wished to stay, she would not force him away.

The varnished door burst open. Miss Mooney led the way, bending down to the small figure at her side. Cora sat frozen as they walked together over the brown and blue stars. The boy wore a pale calico jacket with short breeches and black stockings pulled up over his knees. His head was hidden in the folds of Miss Mooney's skirts.

Miss Mooney kept hold of the boy's chubby hand as she nudged his shoulder with her elbow.

'Come now, Johnnie, say hello nicely to your mother like we practised.'

The lilac cotton flapped as John shook his head.

Miss Mooney smiled at Cora. 'Don't you worry, Mrs Burns. 'Tis usually like this on a first meeting. Perhaps if you were to take off your bonnet and gloves? The effect can be a little overwhelming to a wee one.'

'If he would prefer to stay here...'

'Oh fie, no! Every child wants their ma. Even if they don't know it yet.'

Cora untied the silk ribbons and laid the bonnet with her gloves on the chair. Her heart was thudding so hard she was sure that it might, at any moment, stop. Above the folds of lilac cotton she could see a mop of dark hair that had been wetted and combed to one side. She directed her gaze toward the small hidden face and took the deepest of breaths.

'What a pleasant day it is for a walk along the lane. If I had someone small to help me pick the pretty flowers, I could take a nice yellow bunch of them home with me.' A rosy cheek appeared at the edge of the lilac skirts. 'And if he'd like a ride on the choo-choo train, I have a spare ticket.'

Miss Mooney winked at Cora then held out to her a small bundle wrapped in a navy blue handkerchief. As she stood to take it, a softly furrowed brow emerged from the shadow of the skirts. And then, in a rush of hotness which seemed to swallow Cora's heart, a pair of large and serious stone-grey eyes blinked into the light.

THIRTY-FOUR
October 1886

made

The girls were holding on to each other and giggling so hysterically that both of them thought they might be sick. No one else in the huddle of stiff Bluecoat pinafores thought that anything was funny but the two new girls, who were twin sisters, were absorbed in their private bubble.

'Are we sure it's her?' Letty whispered.

Violet nodded sagely in reply then collapsed again into peals of hiccupping laughter. Letty told her sister to buck up or Miss Arnold, not knowing which girl was which, would chastise them both. But the sight of Violet trying to arrange her face into seriousness caused Letty to fall back into hilarity.

'Ada! Stop that nonsense.'

Miss Arnold had noticed the silliness and, for once, she had got the right name. Letty was still startled by it. At home she'd been called Letty ever since Violet was taken away, which was before she could remember anything very much. Ma had seemed to decide that in transferring Violet's name to the remaining twin, she had made her matching daughters into one. Even though they were now reunited, both girls thought it magical to share a name as well as a face.

When it was time for the class to straighten themselves into neat rows, Miss Arnold directed those at the front to sit and others to stand at the back on a low wooden bench. She did not quite have the energy to separate the Flynn twins so they were left standing together in the middle of the group, secretly, or so they thought, holding each other's hand. Miss Arnold instructed everyone to put on a straight face and so keep the likeness from blurring. But the twins simply could not stop themselves beaming at the camera. And behind the lens, the lady photographer could not help but smile back.

Anyone examining the school photograph, even years into the future, might marvel at the alikeness of the grinning twins. But a close search would also reveal the slight differences between them:

Violet's taller stature and her meek, somewhat lop-sided smile; Letty's pock-marked skin and the enlarged pupil that made her right eye appear black. Closer scrutiny still would disclose, amongst the girl-scholars' dark sleeves and spotless aprons, two furtive hands holding on to each other tightly. And although the photograph caught no more than a few frozen seconds of an October afternoon, the sisters' fingers would remain forever entwined.

Acknowledgements

This novel was begun in 2013 on the Writing a Novel course at Faber Academy. Thank you to the tutor Richard Skinner and to the other students for putting me on the right track. I'm grateful to all of the dedicated writers, published and unpublished, who continue to share wisdom and fiction-focused conversation with me.

Some exceptional professional readers and editors have helped me to raise my game as a novelist. Massive thanks to: Jacqui Lofthouse, Sarah Savitt, Sam Copeland, Imogen Roberston and Lorna Gentry. I'm also hugely grateful to the judges and administrators of the following competitions for unpublished writers: The Bridport Prize, Mslexia Novel Competition, DGA First Novel Prize and thebluepencilagency Novel Competition. Recognition from these fantastic organisations kept me writing when I might otherwise have given up.

The Conviction of Cora Burns would, however, still be hidden inside a ten year-old laptop if it wasn't for the faith shown in the story by David Haviland and Andrew Lownie at the Andrew Lownie Literary Agency, and then by Ion Mills and Clare Quinlivan at No Exit Press. Thanks also to Katherine Sunderland and Claire Watts for making the book and the campaign around it so fabulous and to Elsa Mathern for a genius design.

Many friends and relatives read this book at various stages and provided feedback that was always useful. Thanks to you all, especially: Caroline Fox, Trish Tazuk, Eileen Milner, Sally Kirby, Lynne Thoms, Pete Thoms, Polly Milner and Emily Milner. Dave Milner spent a few of his last days reading the manuscript with a characteristically sharp eye for typos. I'm so glad that he saw my work.

I'd like to thank Berkshire Record Office and the marvellous staff and volunteers at Woodcote Library. Artangel facilitated the public opening of Reading Prison for a short period in 2016 and I made at least four visits there to sit in a cell with the door closed. Gaynor

Arnold, whose novel *After Such Kindness* helped inspire this one, very kindly showed me around central Birmingham.

I couldn't have written this story without my two wonderful daughters whose different personalities sparked my interest in theories about 'nature versus nurture.' Thank you also to my parents for a lifetime of love.

The person who really made everything possible, and whose opinion matters to me more than any other, hasn't yet read this book. This is because I didn't think that any of the drafts before this one were good enough for him to see. But you can read it now, love.

For information about the historical background to *The Conviction of Cora Burns*, please go to: carolynkirby.com

The Conviction of Cora Burns
Reader's Questions

1. How do Cora's reactions to others change through the course of the novel? What influences have the most impact on her changing behaviour?

2. How much sympathy do you feel for Mrs Flynn? What would you have done in her position when faced with Thomas Jerwood's offer for her daughter?

3. What do you think happens to Cora and her son after the story ends?

4. 'Cora had been made wrong from the start... cursed by her place of birth and her mother's blood' Can we ever separate the influences of 'nature' and 'nurture'? Can you 'turn bad into good'?

5. 'Traps, as it were, can be laid.' Do Thomas Jerwood's lofty intentions for his research projects justify the methods he uses?

6. If Thomas Jerwood was alive today, what kind of research might he be interested in or studying?

7. How would a child who kills be treated today? What do you think is the right approach for society to take in such cases?

8. 'House burglars are marked out by the prominence of their jaws.' Is it possible to tell if someone is a criminal?

9. In mid-Victorian Birmingham, the prison, lunatic asylum and workhouse were built side-by-side at the edge of a growing town. What does this show us about attitudes to the poor, the mentally ill and the criminals in Victorian Britain? How have attitudes changed?

10. The original title for this book was 'Half of You'. What other titles do you think might work for this novel?

11. Which parts of the book stood out for you? What do you think was added to the story by the extracts from 'The Wyvern Quarterly' and Dr Farley's journal?

12. What does the book say about life and conditions of domestic servants in the late 1800's?

NO EXIT PRESS
UNCOVERING THE BEST CRIME

'A very smart, independent publisher delivering the finest literary crime fiction' – *Big Issue*

MEET NO EXIT PRESS, the independent publisher bringing you the best in crime and noir fiction. From classic detective novels, to page-turning spy thrillers and singular writing that just grabs the attention. Our books are carefully crafted by some of the world's finest writers and delivered to you by a small, but mighty, team.

In our 30 years of business, we have published award-winning fiction and non-fiction including the work of a Pulitzer Prize winner, the British Crime Book of the Year, numerous CWA Dagger Awards, a British million copy bestselling author, the winner of the Canadian Governor General's Award for Fiction and the Scotiabank Giller Prize, to name but a few. We are the home of many crime and noir legends from the USA whose work includes iconic film adaptations and TV sensations. We pride ourselves in uncovering the most exciting new or undiscovered talents. New and not so new – you know who you are!!

We are a proactive team committed to delivering the very best, both for our authors and our readers.

Want to join the conversation and find out more about what we do?

Catch us on social media or sign up to our newsletter for all the latest news from No Exit Press HQ.

f fb.me/noexitpress **𝕏** @noexitpress
noexit.co.uk/newsletter